Last Man

Planet

Croften Grebe

Table of Contents

To Claude-S, Craig-W, Frank-T, and Mick-C for shedding some light on my darker days.

Acknowledgments

A big thanks to Solomon Elias, Natalia Adler, Jordyn Anderson, Portia Jones, James Horn, Alexander Caldwell, and Norman Mathews for bringing this project to fruition.

About the Author

This is book number 1, and if you send a nice pleasant
email, you will get a nice pleasant e-mail in return
croftengrebe@gmail.com.

Chapter One

It was another bleak morning, bastarding freezing and pissing down as usual. As far as he was concerned, Friday was just as bleak, if not bleaker, than the rest. The storm warning had been issued late last night by the Met Office, and for once, they had actually been bang on the button. Murray had been miraculously transported back into the realm of the living less than a minute ago by the sound of hungry lions in the great African Savanna. Linda had thought that because she had read the declaration, this was the new way to wake up and face the day.

As opposed to his normal morning routine of barely functioning on automatic pilot mode, the lion or lioness gently whispered in his ear, instantly energising his persona. Murray had leaped out of bed and adapted into what he felt was a defensive stance for a microsecond, prior to his brain remembering the interest shown to a pretentious alarm clock advertised in the equally pretentious Sunday magazine. He has a piss, showers, and puts on his work rags. The socks don't match, but socks are socks. Just as long as there is no indecent exposure involving the toes, they are good enough to wear. Feeling slightly more human, he boils water, and after several, instantly reviving cups of tea, he smokes, pondering the day ahead. Murray has now fully surrendered, and all the resistance to the idea has dissipated. A smoke ring slowly glides across the table as it swirls and fades, dissipating into obscurity. He gives into the fact that he has to earn money, puts on his going-to-work head, and is now heading off to another episode of toil.

Murray thought that the best part of residing in one of the outlying areas of the county was that there were no street lamps to thoroughly depress the streets and houses, like in the town where the sodium-infused light casts an ethereal haze on everything, creating an undeserved image of utter desolation.

The streets were empty apart from the odd discarded pieces of rubbish that, for some reason, had developed an automatic dispensation to being deposited into the conveniently placed receptacles. Murray drives past the resident town drunk, who was sheltered in his preferred doorway, having another extremely animated conversation with his imaginary aggressive companions. In an ultra-protective stance, one arm righteously pointing and stabbing the air around him, the other desperately clutching the cheapest bottle of fortified wine that money can buy.

At a distance, it looked as if he was resplendent in some new spangled trend, the brightly coloured speckled jacket, with one matching speckled trouser leg and shoe. Still, on closer inspection, his fashionista attire was an identical match to the pavement pizza that was fermenting nicely in steaming lumpy puddles surrounding his feet.

Murray no longer drives the works van, which in his humble opinion, is a worthless piece of shit. It starts, stops, and goes from A to B. The firm's owner thinks of it as a perk. He had simply told him that he would not under any circumstances use his own car on company business, '*a perk my arse.*' It spends most of the time recharging or being repaired. The last time it broke down en route to a remote hydro station. Murray smiled, remembering, threatening to torch the vehicle on the spot. The owner, appalled at the idea of being viewed by the electro-media as non-eco-friendly, had offered a wage increment to resolve the issue. The final deal agreed upon included exemption from anything to do with the electro vehicle and a reasonable personal fuel allowance in view of transportation to and from work.

He knows that his boss will religiously quadrupole check every hour that is claimed and will take great satisfaction in skinning him for a tenner here and there. Murray had worked that out a while back and pretended not to notice. He, on the other hand, stole nothing. He was not even a member of the inadvertently-forgot-to-return-the-borrowed-works-tools-and-equipment-club.

The sound machine is blasting away hypnotic percussive sounds, concerted by slightly out-of-tune electric guitars, intertwining, performing the call and response, almost as good as oral sex as the singer oozes out what she just has to say. Her obscure eastern European accented English, delivered with all of her heart and soul, was electrifying and got Murray every time it was played.

Oh honey, please leave me alone.

All you've done here is moan.

Please, please leave me alone.

Just leave everything you don't own.

Then get to fuck, right out my home.

Please, please, please leave me alone.

Please, please, please leave me alone.

Please, please, please leave me alone.

Screeching to a halt for the cameras, perched like vultures on the works gates. Murray depresses the horn for longer than necessary, sticks his paw outside the rolled window, and gives the reverse victory sign to the old reprobate on duty. The Major, as he liked to be called, had treated him to a relentless campaign of intimidation at the start of his apprenticeship. Over the years, Murray had gradually worked his way up, and now that he was in charge, there was no way he was going to be nice and courteous at the entry and exit stops, where the Majors' security cameras were positioned. He knew that he was not going to report him. Murray purposely refused point blank to take part in pressing the intercom and swiping activities associated with the electronic tracking systems.

Once, he had to endure the misfortune of meeting the Major outside with his hag of a wife, witnessing in real time the incessant complaints that omitted from her gob. As much as he was within his rights to dislike this man, one could not help but feel his pain. Murray had even had a drunken confession, informing Linda that if she ever grew old to be a horrendous old hag like her, he would become an avid believer and pray to God for hours on end every day that she would conveniently drown, quietly in the bath.

Fridays at work start with a meeting with the owner. He is the guy in charge of the money. He does not do anything; well, that is not quite true. He moans lots about stupid things, and Murray sometimes had got to phone senior on the hotline and inform him. Yet, again that young Wrightson is being a god-dam twat. Old Mr Wrightson does not mind him complaining about his sole offspring, but senior is highly offended and objects strongly to Murray bringing the big guy into the conversation. Mr Wrightson had a great idea of converting him years ago, but that did not go down too well with his fellow happy clappers when one of them complained bitterly that he found Murray's boxers in his daughter's bedroom lying next to her pants that had shown more than conclusive evidence of deflowering. It was a big deal for Murray, and she actually was a nice girl, hell, he and Linda even ran away and got married, and even now, he refuses to go to her parents' house. He doesn't care what the reason is; it is just eternally null and void on the conversation list.

Murray makes his way up to the moneyman's office. The old crickety stairs creak and moan with every point of contact. Craig Wrightson would have been quite normal, except this was all he knew. He had never done anything, he had never been anywhere, and this was the sum total of his sole existence. As per the stupid rules, Murray knocks twice and shakes his head while waiting for the light to come on. Entering the drab office, which was just as drab when it was originally decorated over a hundred years ago. They exchange the normal pleasantries, neither of them meaning one single syllable of it.

"Well, Murray, I see you have purchased the two quid washers rather than the fifty pence ones that I empathetically instructed you to purchase."

The monotonous drone went on for fucking ages. Murray wishes his phone would beep. Maybe someone had kidnapped his kids. Perhaps the house was on fire. Maybe his wife's vibe had broken.

Please, god, just anything, to make him shut the fuck up. He just had to give in: it was almost like being a dog, being held firmly on the shiny table at the veterinarian surgeon's, just about to be put down, and no matter what happened, you knew that your eyes were going to close forever. He is about to give Murray the memorised speech and demonstrate how he is at the elevated position of director, the head of the company, and Murray is a mere paid-by-the-hour employee who has no say in how, why, where, or when the finances are allocated.

Murray, on the other hand, thinks he is a tight-fisted reprobate who would have no hesitation in removing the plug connecting the life support system of a sick, near-to-death relative and replacing it with his phone charger just to save twenty pence.

*Thank you, God. T*he phone bleeps into life, and it is his wife. The high-pitched remonstrations bleach out from the speaker. Murray can't help but feel sorry for him, he had never been able to get into the "Yes dear, I believe you are correct." He was more of a 'you are fucking shitting me' type of guy, not wanting to hear any of the private tales of woe and having enough of junior for today, he got up, gave the guy some space, and got out of the office.

Murray got to the end of the corridor and sparked up a cigarette. Instantly he was greeted with a "You are not allowed to smoke in here" as they pointed at a sign in stereo. Murray stared at the sign, stared at the couple, ripped the sign off the wall, shredded it into pieces, delivered it like non-virgin confetti, and told them to fuck right off.

Consulting his smartphone, he started a message to the dad about his son's winging non-stop about the shitty washers and whither he was truly aware of the total false economy of this direction. Adding that you only get what you pay for and changing our current suppliers to some cheap shit from overseas does not really cut the mustard.

To keep the peace, he sheepishly heads out to the smoking area and lights another cigarette from the remains of the first one. No smoking inside the building. They work with loads of dangerous things that not only just kill you but also leave chemical particles that last in your dead and rotting carcass forever, but it is against the health and safety regulations to have a cigarette whilst you are merrily toiling away.

He has just calmed down from DEFCON 1 and observes that they are missing a few people; He notices Fat-Boy. He is the shop supervisor who is, in theory, meant to help run things when he is dealing with penny pincher Wrightson and other pish. Imitating a magician's post-trick abracadabra pose, 'Where are all the bodies that are missing?' Thinking that it is very unusual for people to be off on a Friday, Monday is the most popular day to pull a sickie. Even his dog hates Mondays. Fat-Boy informs him, in-between coughing in his hands and over Murray, that they have phoned in sick or someone has phoned in on their behalf. Murray looks at Fat-Boy, and he does not look too good; he tells him to sod off and get himself home and stopping the proverbial question before it is asked. He nods, letting him know that the clock card will be taken care of. This is just to stop Fat-Boy from crying about the hire purchase quagmire his mother has gotten immersed in. Murray remembers having to send him home when he was an apprentice with a broken leg, 'please, Mr Black, don't send me home. My mam will kill me.' He would have been sent to prison for keeping Fat-Boy at work. At that time, Murray had gone and explained to tighter than two coats of paint Wrightson that his mother was a God-fearing woman and it would probably be a better idea if he took Fat-Boy home in his nice car rather than him in the shitty works van that they expected him to drive. Fat-Boy gets in an executive-style car, gives Murray the finger, and with a toot of the horn, is taxied off home. Don't you just love Fridays?

He has promised Linda, Murray has sworn on more than his soul that he will be a responsible human being. This very day, straight after work, he has vowed to come straight home and not end up like the usual drunken bag of bone and water that usually falls in the door in the early hours. If he is lucky, sometimes it is possible to make it to the settee, but sometimes it is not too successful. Linda knows this is one of his drunken moves and stealthily reconfigures the furniture arrangement before going to self-isolate in the spare bedroom.

Murray was in a habit in his drunken states of switching on the music player and being a considerate soul. He would put on the headphones before singing his heart out. As

Murray had an eclectic taste, he would have all sorts of genres to select from, classical, various guitar bands from the dawn of time, and some jazz, but he thinks it must have been the soul rendition that really pissed her off. He awoke that morning with the headphone cable cut, sliced neatly with the carving knife, which had been used again and impaled singers' picture to the wall above his head. Linda told him a few weeks later when she decided that the war of silence was over that it did not make any difference to his attempt at singing, 'your eyes were tightly closed concentrating on belting the chorus and you were that drunk that you did not even notice the quick swift slash of the blade on the cable nor the impaling of R&B princesses picture above his head.

Murray has promised to be good; Murray has promised to be a saint, as expected; there has been no promise of anything in return. Linda's brief statement had been straight to the point, "Just come in from work on a Friday just like fucking normal people do. Is that really too much to fucking ask for?"

It is getting near stopping time. No visitors today, and more to the point, no accidents. Sure, every once in a while, somebody cuts a finger, or somebody spills a cup of coffee over themselves or the unfortunate person sitting next to them. Mrs Petra Primrose from reception, affectionally known as man-hungry number 2, is going around the shop floors in high heels, pencil skirt, fishnets, and tight jacket

10

collecting the lottery money, and as her husband is going to his astronomy club, she is winking at the guys and terrorising any of the young apprentices who are unfortunate enough to caught, snared in her radar.

Barry looks about as if he is either going to piss or shit himself. "C'mon Barry. You know my George is going to play with his telescope. Come over to mine, and we can share a sausage supper!" This routine has been going on for years, Murray has even had to tell her to keep out the gents' toilets, but she can't help it. Barry just does not know what to do. He has to go down and interfere. "Petra, get to fuck back to your office and keep to fuck out the shop. If we win a small sum on the lottery, I am sure the guys would all donate and buy you an updated electric toy. Now go on sod off."

Barry comes and thanks him once she has vanished; Murray tells him it was nothing. The older guys on the shop floor disappear out of his sight as they know it pisses him off big time when they could have easily stepped in and stopped the young guy's predicament, but no, they would rather have the ammunition for the verbal entertainment at the clocking out station.

He calls Barry on his mobile and tells him to disappear an hour before stopping time and leave his card as he will clock him out. Barry starts to thank him, but Murray stops him in mid-sentence and tells him to have a great time at the weekend and reminds him yet again that he has to start sticking up for himself. Barry starts to thank him again, and Murray kills the call before he completes the sentence.

The time is unrelentingly marching on, so if he gets stuck in, he should be able to sign all the timesheets, material requests, and all the other bits of paper with X marks the spot that requires his signature for Monday morning. Big Ann, the van is normally here to collect and take all the forms over to Wrightson's office, but she is not in today. She really is one of the nicest, warmest people he has ever met and always puts aside one of her excellent home-baked cakes and pastries for days like these.

Murray had just about finished signing all the debris and knew it was just about time to go because he could hear the guffaws and cheering from the clocking-out station. Primrose must be at it again, sashaying up and down the clocking-out queue, entertaining the troops, poor George, her husband, must be guaranteed a place in heaven for putting up with this.

Mr. Black is going to the pub just for the one swift beer, and then it is straight home for a nice weekend. No work for the next couple of days; hell, seeing as he is going to be an angel, he may even be rewarded with some unscheduled passion as it has been a while since they have been away, just been that busy at work for so long it will do them the world of good just to escape for a few days.

It's only three o'clock, and the pub is already getting busy. He heads in through the double doors homing in towards the bar entrance. Murray nods to a few faces he knows and ignores the ones he does not know and does not want to know. Again, there is an odd bout of coughing going on. The giant TV is bolted to the wall, covered in a protective screen, and is generally worshiped when the football is on. It is now showing one of the news channels but in silent mode, and nobody glances at it unless the Russian weather girl with the sprayed-on clothes makes an appearance. None of the regular clientele understood the Russian language, and he doubts the majority of them had no inkling where the actual country was located, but legend had a tale that there was a mass brawl one night in the bar and the fight was something like what you would witness in the Wild West; until someone shouted the weather girl is on.

Murray meanders his way through the dregs of society, the ones who have gambled their whole week's wages and lost the lot and are just drinking the last of the dregs to develop the courage to go home and confess to their battle-axe of a wife. The ones who have never worked but manage to be in here every day always have cigarettes and money to spend on the booze and the bookies. Their kids are in rags, but to them, that does not matter.

He makes his way to the quiet corner avoiding at all costs of the pool table area. The young team are embedded in there, and guaranteed someone will get a thumping, whither it be this afternoon or tonight, either way, it is Friday and a guaranteed certainty. His pint arrives, and he doesn't need to order it. The barmaid knows what he drinks; Murray never gives her any grief he is just a quiet drunk, not like some of the regulars. A few of the guys have banged her, but he is married, and it is well-known that he does not play with fire. Murray settles into the corner and has his first sip, mmmm this is wonderful. He had not had one of these in ages, okay, about a week.

Murray does not read the papers, watch the news or have any interest in international politics nor current affairs, but he does like a crossword puzzle. He knows for a fact that he will never be able to pass the famous broadsheet test in twelve minutes, but that does not mean he is not allowed to like words. He has the paper out and just attacking fourteen down. It has a six followed by a nine-letter word; straight away, Murray thinks that Wanker Wrightson will fit in nicely. He is really tempted, but that has nothing to do with the clue, so he won't bother.

The pint glass is at fifty percent capacity, and Murray is just about to guzzle it down when another one appears. He does not want this! He has made a solemn promise. Murray looks at the barmaid, and she nods over to the snug. It's some of the guys he used to hang with at school, they had continued to hang about together after that for a few years;

but jobs, girlfriends, girlfriends & wives, her majesty's prisons & immigration to hot countries tend to separate everyone. You bump into one another every once in a while, and most of the time, it is just a *hi, how are you doing? Oh, did you hear about so and so he's dead,* or *did you hear that he got married again and the oh, he is in prison in South America and can say, ouch, that really fucking hurts, fluently* in the various indigenous dialects.

In the snug, there were five of the old classmates all meeting up. It was great to see them. He had not seen them together since Dave Woods's funeral ages ago. They had only been out of school, not for even four years. Dave had acquired a car, some souped-up purple thing, and was getting a blowjob while driving on the big dual carriageway outside town. Amyl Nitrate is not a good idea at any time. When their bodies were eventually cut from the wreckage, Dave was headless, and his girlfriend had multiple fractures and broken bones, but the rescue doctor reckoned she might have survived had she not had Dave's pecker lodged in her throat, completely restricting her airway. They had several toasts that night to the lost and disappeared, but most were addressed to Dave hung like a donkey woods. Not only were the toasts getting more outrageous, but the rounds and the prices were also. Murray thinks that he had spent and drank a little on the excessive side.

Everybody goes through the *remember when you did this* or *when you got caught doing that*. When it was Murray's turn, it was remembering when they all got the measles in primary school, and you were the only one in class not to get it. Yes, he remembered all right, "You bastards started calling me the mutant, and it was not until your parents came to my mum and dad asking them to tell me to stop battering you that the abuse stopped." Someone added, "You bastard! You knocked out my front teeth, and all you said was sorry honest Mr Smith, the bat just slipped out my hands!"

The alcohol is flowing non-stop; Murray guesses that his willpower has evaporated, just like his chances of a romantic liaison at the weekend. One of the guys asks him, "Murray, are you still working for God fearing and God seeing?" He nods, not even wanting to think about work. He might as well make the most of this. It is going to cost him dearly with the bride at home for yet another broken promise.

The coughing is still in the background. When Murray goes to the bar for his round, Breda informs him that he is in serious shit for not going home on time, and it will cost a lot more than a measly ten-quid bunch of flowers to escape the very possible premeditated castration for his failure to arrive on time. She and Linda go back a long time, and he is sure they share more than many secrets. Breda serves him and then appears with the mop and bucket. Somebody just had a coughing fit and spewed all over the toilet walls. She thinks that there is some bug going around as several people have gone home saying that they are not feeling too good.

Murray is now pretty drunk; he can speak but is uncertain as to what language it is but its sure sounds okay to himself. The time is around eleven o'clock, and he says his farewells, a couple more tequilas, he thinks it was a couple, a few never to be followed up drunken promises to keep in touch, and it is time for the off. He is drunk enough but not stupid enough to even think about driving; Breda always comes over once he has had more than one to confiscate the keys and has saved many a customer's driving licenses over the years in avoiding them being stupid in even attempting to drive.

The hunger has arrived. He has not had anything to eat and makes an attempt to order a Chinese takeaway in Sun Yat-Sens Eternal Garden. Unfortunately, they are unable to interpret his unregistered alien dialect and produce a special sign from under the counter saying fuck off in block capitals letters. Dumbfounded and defeated but still hungry, Murray staggers out of the establishment and sidesteps along with a combination of backward and forward steps towards the taxi rank. It seems like ages before he gets there. Murray cannot find any taxis but manages to locate a seat on the bench just outside the office. There are very few people around and still no transportation for hire. Deep in his drunken stupor, it takes him forever to find his cigarettes, even longer to find his lighter, and longer yet still to spark it up. Sinking deeper into the variable drunken wavelength that presently encapsulates his less-than-feeble existence, Murray has a few more cigarettes, but still, no taxis have appeared. The hunger has dissipated, and he now feels like shit.

As he sits swaying on the bench, the homing beacon inside his head has just flipped into active mode, Murray just wants to go home and crawl into his bed. He decides that maybe if he starts walking, he might be lucky enough and be able to stop a taxi, or somebody who actually likes him will take pity on his soul and give him a lift home. He starts to move his torso in the correct direction. Occasionally he has to stop and cough. Even though he smokes, he is still fairly fit, but this cough is not pleasant at all. The majority of us smokers bring something up from time to time, and as long as it is not bright red or shit, we are generally quite unworried this stuff is bright green and tasted worse than shit.

Chapter Two

The coughing is getting worse, the bouts are increasing in length, and the more he coughs, the less energy Murray has to keep moving. He cannot phone Linda to come and get him; she has warned him umpteen times before, *"even if the planet is on fire and you are the last hope for the salvation of humanity, don't even think that I am your rescue."*

He possibly stumbles and sways about ten baby steps, then his body tightens up, and he sprays some more of the green stuff out his nose and mouth. The time in between the bouts is getting closer. Through the moving, see-through curtain of rain that moves in time with the breeze, his vision senses a small-corrugated workman's hut somewhere in front of him. Slowly and with avid determination, he pitifully continues his advance. It has now started raining in earnest.

The time is not going anywhere. Murray thinks that he has been on the same spot for hours on end, and he does not have the energy to walk but manages to crawl the final leg of the journey and then finally drag himself into the hut. There is an old piece of plastic tarpaulin, and he deposits himself on top of it, rolls about in slow-motion wrestling and eventually tucks in the edges, inventing some sort of makeshift protection.

It is still pitch-black outside; Murray is awake and thinks he could still be alive. He has a look at himself and has observed smarter-attired dead bodies in murder documentaries. Glancing at his watch, or where the watch should have been, all he has is a series of bruises, cuts and a filth-encrusted arm. The rest of his body and clothes are not in much better shape. He is not exactly full of energy, and it takes a massive effort and an even more considerable amount of time to extract himself from the foetal position and force himself in between the moans and groans into a contorted seating arrangement.

From his new vantage point, he can see the outskirts of the town, not a light on in the place, no sign of traffic. Rummaging through his pockets, the ones still connected to his clothes. Murray searches for his mobile. Maybe it's time for the grovelling phone call, where he intends to plead guilty to everything and anything just as long as Linda comes and retrieves him. Murray will be a saint for as long as it takes to attain forgiveness. The work phone is nowhere to be found, but he finds his lighter and, several light years later, the cigarettes.

At last, Murray is able to stand up and very gently checks himself out; no broken bones, lots of bruises, missing pieces of skin, gravel rashes, a few rips and tears on his trousers and the jacket has only one sleeve. He sparks the cigarette up, and it tastes more like shit than normal. The cough is just his

20

normal smoking cough, nothing like the belly buster he had sometime earlier.

The sky is beginning to change. In the distance, the darkness is starting to disperse, replaced by a faint ribbon of light that slowly permeates the horizon. The odd bird song is sticking a stiletto into the silence. The birdsong is not that loud, and accessing the data in his surprisingly retained memory bank, Murray has no recollection of the dawn chorus being this quiet before. His internal calculation completes the cycle and predicts that if he gets off his fat arse and starts walking, he could be home before the neighbours start rising and detect the resident down and out, participating in the walk of shame, whilst trying to sneak into number five, undetected. It will be bad enough to put up with Linda's incessant complaining for however long, but for the neighbours to witness his transgression would be a bloody nightmare.

Just as he starts walking, a light drizzle starts, and this, at least, he hopes should be able to remove some of the accumulated grime that has attached itself to his skin and clothes. The pace is hard, Murray is still sore and not feeling one hundred per cent, but at least he is making an effort to return home. We are almost halfway there after he tentatively negotiates the section with the hill in situ. Murray takes a seat and slowly smokes his last cigarette before making the last half-mile stretch to base camp Alpha.

At this part of the journey, Murray moves as quickly as possible. Sure, he trips and stumbles in the missing and cracked sections of the road, but he just about manages to maintain his balance. As Murray passes the houses, he detects no sign of the curtain twitchers, and luckily for him, he has not been spotted and identified by an early morning motorist.

Quietly approaching the house, he looks in the pocket for the keys; this pocket is one of the missing ones, and Murray automatically opts for plan B. Tipping over the third flowerpot to the left-hand side of the door with his foot furnishes him with the spare set. He is expecting to be set about with the mad woman armed with a marble rolling pin, and due to current circumstances, he will only be able to furnish himself with the briefest of excuses to defend himself until the melee subsides. Hesitantly he makes his way into the house.

Murray breathes a massive sigh of relief. It is quiet; he grabs the DIY clothes from the shelf in the utility room and slithers into the shower. Now in a confined space, he realises that he smells more than fairly unpleasant and to be straight to the point, he thinks he is fucking stinking. Murray opens the window and as he removes the offending clothing, dispensing with them out the window. Hopefully, he will be able to bin, bury or incinerate them undetected later. The water is not scalding hot but warm enough to get a decent wash and shave. He feels more human now, and he realises that it is time to grow a pair, as it is now time to face the music.

Coming out of the bathroom, confidently walking as if everything is normal and just a regular morning, Murray heads towards the kitchen. He will rustle up Linda a nice pleasant breakfast and for the hopefully added extra brownie points, he will conjure up one of those special coffee things that she likes, and when the torrent of verbal abuse is unleashed, Murray will just have to plead guilty to any and all crimes she has managed to concoct during his unscheduled absenteeism.

He finds the phone in the kitchen and checks it. There is no signal and an unread message from three days ago. The message just says one word 'ASSHOLE'. Murray is dead. He has been gone for fuck knows how long; he has no clue where he had been. Murray does not bother with the surprise breakfast; he will just go and face her now.

Linda is still in bed; Murray had checked their bedroom but found her in the spare room. The room is a little untidy, a pile of empty over-the-counter medicine bottles are discarded on the floor, and the blue bucket for depositing puke in when one is a little under the weather is upended and has shared the contents with the carpet. Linda is not moving. The closer he approaches, he notices that Linda is not breathing. Linda is gone. Murray examines her a little closer and notices that she has that green puke stuff congealed on every visible orifice. Murray dashes to the kitchen, fuck! The mobile phone is not working. He tries the landline, not even a dead tone or any static interference. Linda is cold and stiff, and nobody will be able to resuscitate her, but he has to try at least and call it in.

He tries the next-door neighbour's house, a family of five; the front door is not locked. Entering, he shouts a warning that it is Murray and tries several times and gets no response from any of the inhabitants. Murray checks all the bedrooms and finds them all dead -the same scenario as Linda. To be sure, he goes and double-checks Linda and all the phones. Murray also checks the TV and radio, but to no avail. Buggerall is working.

The car keys are hanging up by the telephone table. Grabbing them on the way out the door, thinking that if he heads towards the police station. At least they will be able to help him and explain what the fuck is going on. Murray pulls over at a few of the neighbour's houses, and apart from a mad barking, snarling canine, he finds no signs of life.

There is no radio reception in the car and no signs of any other traffic or life on the journey into town. The police station has a big guy behind the desk. Murray hopes he is sleeping and has his fingers crossed that he just does not turn into Mr Grumpy when he wakes up. There is no need to wake him as Murray closes the distance, the green slime syndrome encrusted eyeballs, and nostrils are visible, and he is displaying the full Monty of the symptoms. Going to the non-joe public side of the front desk, he reads over the notes to see if there is any useful information on who to contact and where you go to get help. He thoroughly searches the station, and all he manages to locate are more dead bodies.

Murray detours through the town on the way home, choosing the long way back. He zig-zags throughout the housing scheme, honking the horn continuously to alert people to his presence with all the noise, but no reaction. A few stray dogs look at him and turn away, totally uninterested. He needs a cigarette. Murray has none on him, but Linda sometimes has a spare packet in the glove box. No luck here, only an unopened packet of mild ones, some packets of cigarette papers, and wait a second... He finds a joint and sparks it up. What are the police going to do if they pull him over? "Excuse me, Sir. We have reason to believe that you have been partaking in smoking illegal substances, and with the evidence we have uncovered in search of this vehicle. We have no choice but to arrest you and take you into custody, even though you are the only living person we have found so far?"

The car is now stopped on the deserted high street, no lights, no people, no sound and no nothing. Murray goes into memory mode, rewinds the grey matter and sees if he can remember any clues as to what has happened. Insufficient information is recovered from his available files. Murray quickly realises that he has no recollection of any warning or remote idea of what has occurred. He turns the ignition key and heads home, if he leaves Linda in bed, she will start to decompose, and Murray thinks if the circumstances were reversed, she would never leave him like that.

Entering the kitchen, he puts some sticks into the multi-fuel burning cooker, fills a pan with water and waits for it to boil. His stomach sounds like it is on a hunger strike, but he doesn't want to eat. He reckons that he has not eaten for at least a couple of days and eventually forces a few chocolate biscuits down his throat. No hot water yet, so Murray goes for the can of fizzy option. He thinks he can hear his phone beeping, but again, like the house phone ringing and Linda's siren tone, it is just nothing but his overactive imagination.

Linda still looks as if she is having a peaceful sleep. Still, deep down in the remnants of his tattered soul, Murray is fully aware and comprehends the full implications that she has departed from this plane of existence. Once she is washed and dressed, she looks at peace with this world. Looking out the bedroom window, Murray sees the vibrant abundance of her favourite flowers in full bloom. This is Linda's special time of the year. Together they had done lots of work to the garden over the years. He goes to the shed and gathers up the big blue roll of tarpaulin, the same one they used to line the rockery. Murray carries it through to the bedroom, places it on the bed and gently wraps up Linda with the entire roll. To seal the overlapping material and keep the package tight, he uses an assortment of wood glue, duct tape, masking tape, string and anything that he can find that will hold the package firmly together.

Murray was not particularly close to any of the neighbours and never attended any barbeques or social get-togethers, but he cannot leave them to rot. The family of five are still in the same positions as he found them, the aroma of decay is a little sharper. Five minutes later, he returns with the petrol; gently walking through the house, he evenly distributes the contents of the can throughout the interior, starting at the top and working his way back to the front door. Several feet from the entrance, he discards the can in one of the intricately ornate rose beds and lights the old newspaper. With a whoosh, the petrol ignites, and the flames rapidly expand throughout the dwelling. There are seventeen houses in their little enclave. Some of them he knew by name, and some of them he did not even know what planet they came from, still, he had to do the honourable thing and at least try and dispose of their bodies. Murray would like to think that they would do this for him. The wild dog that runs at the patio door when he appears will have to be dealt with. At the next house he goes to, Murray looks to see if they have anything that he could possibly borrow. Straight away, he spots the keys for the black 4x4 truck outside in the drive, which he imagines will be more than handy.

Apart from the dead owners in the living room, this house is very smart and pristine. The kitchen has a huge collection of tinned food. He might as well take this, as Murray imagines it will be quite a while before the supermarkets reopen for business. Come late afternoon, he has done four houses and has had done enough pillaging from the deceased for the day. Murray drives the 4x4 around the corner to his house and unloads the purloined supplies into the front room. He has not been greedy and has only taken tinned goods and only the ones that he can read the labels, the foreign stuff that he could not pronounce nor recognise. He just left well alone.

Even the upmarket, unopened tin of luxury individually wrapped biscuits holds no appeal for his appetite. He goes for the easy option of a can of orange juice. This lasts halfway till it gets poured down the sink. To no avail, Murray tries the TV, laptop and phones, but there is no mains power supply, and even when the batteries are still retaining a charge, there is no signal. Murray goes back into the kitchen, makes some tea and has a couple of joints courtesy of Linda's secret supply in the car. Apart from the black 4x4, the only other item that he borrowed that is inedible was a side-by-side double barrel shotgun and a few boxes of cartridges to go with it. Placing the gun on the table, and as he has never used one of these things, he slowly tries and figures out how it works. Feeling confident with his newly acquired skillset, he proceeds to remove some empty cans from the recycle bin underneath the sink. Taking them outside and placing them on top of the fence and returns with the gun, inserting the first two cartridges in the holes at the top of the barrels, he closes and takes aim. A box of cartridges later and several holes in the fence, the cans are gone. Returning to the house, he checks all the doors are locked, seeing no point in unplugging all the electrical appliances. They are left as they are. He unrolls the sleeping bag and tries to steal some shuteye.

Sleep doesn't come easy. Murray thinks maybe he should have a little drink or three but thinking of the last time he got drunk and what he had awakened to, he has decided not to bother. Tea is a better solution. None of that horrible green stuff, the fruity flavoured stuff or that stuff that is meant to be therapeutic but only gave him the trots, breakfast tea will do the trick. Going through a mental list of all the remaining houses, including the rabid dog's house, there are seventeen in total. The dutiful neighbour has done the honourable thing with five, so he figures that leaves eleven to deal with. So far, he has no plan as to what to do next.

Murray rummages around the house till he finds some paper and a pen. The population in this area was around five hundred people, and as of yet, it was he and only him that he had seen in the last few days. The maths works that out to be less than a one per cent survival rate. As much as he loves Linda, she is starting to stink. That decomposing sweet smell that almost sticks to you is starting beginning to out smell the latest dousing in expensive perfume, which was liberated from the dressing room of the rather snotty neighbour who thought that she was something special and permanently looked down her nose at them. Their dressing room is the toilet. Sadly, Linda must be taken care of. Murray just does not have the balls to torch her. Sleep must have come eventually, as it is light outside. Murray has no idea what the time is, lately, he has never felt the inclination to check as there are now only two times that he is aware of, day-time and its brother, night-time.

He had maybe, what feels like a maximum of three hours of sleep, the stove gets gently persuaded to come to life, and he puts on a pan of water to heat. There are no eggs for breakfast, so he blindly selects a tin for his morning munch. Murray really wants toast and scrambled eggs. The last time he looked at the bread before it got tossed in the next-door garden, it was green and extremely furry. As there is no electricity, the fridge's contents have been emptied and thoroughly cleaned with disinfectant and is now known affectionately as tin cupboard number two.

Once he is washed and dressed in fresh work clothes, he examines the blind selection. In his random choice, he has picked a tin of chopped tomatoes. Putting it over to the side, he reopens the cupboard and selects a tin of processed meat. Carefully Murray extracts the meat from the tin without needing urgent medical treatment for his digits. It gets sort of chopped up and added to the tomatoes that are now simmering in the pot. No doubt, this is not the best meal he has ever had, but he must have been hungry as the plate is almost so clean it could be returned to the cupboard without washing.

During his brief sleep, Murray came to the conclusion that today Linda was going to be interned in the garden. She was always messing with the plants outside. Murray was the proud recipient of a lifetime ban as she more than often reminded him that every single plant he touched just seemed to wither, then die, and he is, without question, unable to identify the subtle differences between weeds and plants.

One of the neighbours is one of those guys who has every known gadget available on the planet. The gentleman in question might not be able to operate any of them to their full potential, but nevertheless, he has them. Several hours later, the mini-digging machine arrived in the back garden. If satellite maps were available, one would be able to see the trail of utter devastation leading there. Murray can't call dial-a-dig as the phones are dead, and he does not think there are any gas or electric mains. Gently he scrapes the flowerbed and places it to the side, then proceeds to excavate a hole deep enough for Linda to lie in. It does not take long to master the machine's array of foot pedals and a couple of levers.

Murray will now have to go shopping in the town. He thinks the black 4x4 is big enough for this task but lies in the storage area and pretends that he is dead just to get a feel of the available space. He takes a selection of ropes just in case. The coffin shop is near the centre of the town, not on the high street but is subtly located in one of the side streets so as not to keep people too far away from the other shops. Not a soul in sight, Murray does his usual Mr-mister-noisy routine, driving around the town incessantly peeping the horn. Still, as normal these days, there are no complaints from the local noise abatement society.

These places would normally be staffed with truly genuine people who would support families in their desperate hours of need when dealing with the loss of a loved one. As he suspected, no one was here today to assist him in his hour of need. They had never really discussed death and the whole mortality thing. Murray was a borderline non-believer, and now he has converted to a dedicated one hundred and fifty per cent non-believer. The display area is full of polished-grained woods; he wanders around and eventually selects the mahogany one with ornate brass handles and the plush red velvet interior. After securing the lid onto the body, he slowly manhandles it to the vertical position and moves it corner to corner style edging it out the open door, which he has jammed open with a big black bible which Murray had just booted under until the movement ceased.

On reaching the vehicle, the tailgate was already down, and he slid the newly acquired item onto the bed until it rested against the back of the cab, it was not an exact size, but the ropes secured it firmly in place. The drive home is uneventful, and the traffic today is surprisingly very light.

After donning the single-usage, white, all-in-one PVC suit, the respirator with the replaceable filter type used by painters and the yellow marigolds. He re-enters Linda's room. The smell is only bearable as Murray has also come in armed with half a dozen cans of assorted air fresheners and emptied the contents as he tentatively went in closer to the body. There was no way he would carry her all the way through the house. Love her or not, let's be honest, she was stinking. A little heavy-handed, he opened the curtains and, with the over-applied unnecessary force, had actually pulled the curtains and the rail from the wall. Opening the windows, Murray is immediately refreshed by the gentle breeze. Linda is as stiff as a board, and he gently lifts her over and pushes her out through the window. It's hard to tell which end is the feet and which end is the head, as Murray had used that much plastic sheeting on her she could actually pass as a rolled-up carpet. Balanced as best as he could possibly manage, Linda is wheelbarrowed to the grave.

Eventually, after all the stops and starts, with her falling off and then placing her back on, he manages to get her there and places her in the coffin he had already deposited in the back garden. Linda, resplendent in her newly fashioned PVC outfit, is just a little on the big size for the coffin lid to stay firmly on. The neighbour with all the gadgets solves that problem by kindly donating a few cargo straps; Murray connects them together and forces the lid into position with the ratchet mechanism. Gadget man also supplied the slings for attaching the coffin to the mini-digging machine. Lifting it up, the now full coffin is gently manoeuvred above the grave and slowly lowered until it embraces the exposed earth at the bottom.

In this country, it is an ancient tradition that when you attend a burial of a loved one or a close friend, you place something in the grave. Murray had gone back into the house and gathered lots of items, all Linda's jewellery, the fucking shoe collection and their wedding album. These items are gently placed into the grave. Before starting to return the earth and finally replacing the flowerbed on the top, Murray goes and changes; he had never been one for really nice clothes, but he did possess one good suit. Returning to the graveside, he looks as if he has been invited to a wedding. Murray has even put a flower in the lapel hole. He wishes that he could say something really nice and thank her for all the happy years and all the happy times that they had shared, but the words completely fail him and Murray sobs uncontrollably as he says goodbye to his trusted companion, his wife, his best friend that he had envisaged to spend his entire life with.

When it is complete, the suit, the shirt, the tie, the whole kit and caboodle are removed physically from his body. Nothing that he has on is ever going to be worn again, and he adds it to the pile of discarded clothes from his drunken Friday night and incinerates the lot. Later, when Murray starts to stop sobbing and starts shivering in the cool breeze, he realises that it is now dark and he must have been out here for a long time.

Murray cleans himself up in the lukewarm shower and dresses in his working clothes. Again, he has no appetite. He rattles together a joint and cracks open a bottle of vodka. The bottle has an unpronounceable Russian name and by the proceeding fumes emanating into the atmosphere that will eventually assist in the depletion of the ozone layer. He thinks it could be a suitable replacement for rocket fuel, never the less he starts drinking it anyway.

He knows that getting drunk will not resolve anything, and he will surely feel like shit in the morning. Murray drinks and smokes away through the small hours, wondering why he only survived, 'there must be others, there must be others.' He repeats this as he thinks of starting a search, picturing all the places in the surrounding area. The camping lamp starts to flicker. Murray unglues himself from the seat and lights a candle.

The bottle top flips off easily and eventually stops making a noise as it rolls and slides across the floor. He should go and pick it up but sees no point in doing so, as it is almost certain that he will be a repeat offender. The beers go down steadily. He smokes away, staring at nothing, thinking of nothing but Linda.

Murray sits there, the tears running down his face. He relives his life with Linda, where they met when they met and all the people who tried to put her off him for good. He thought that was rather unfair. Okay, he was a little rough around the edges. Sure, he had a different accent. The most galling aspect of these people was that none of them even knew him. None of them had actually had a conversation with him. In their eyes, he was just scum from a working-class family, a hey-jimmy bastard and a bead rattler to boot.

It amused him no end. These so-called people who had tried to blacken his name never had or had never attended church for a long time but still felt righteous enough to curtail his chances of gaining employment and his chance of a decent future just because they did not like the way he spoke or looked. He loved Linda with all his heart from the first day he had set eyes on her, and not one day went by without him telling her so.

Chapter Three

Murray is in some sort of van; his hands are handcuffed to a wooden type of bench, the well-worn wooden slats making it anything but comfortable. The cuffs act as an unnatural umbilical cord, keeping him in check as he sways backward, forwards, and side to side, perfectly synchronised with the vehicle's motion. They are not driving fast, and they are not driving slowly. The journey, as far as he can remember, has been steady but bumpy as fuck.

The meat wagon comes to a sudden halt. Seconds later, a single thud on the van's roof reverberates inside the vehicle, and momentarily everything goes quiet. No sooner than the silence had subsided, a barrage of projectiles had been launched. Murray was blind, the light did not penetrate the dark material that had been placed over his head, but he could still differentiate the sounds of the direct hits.

A voice appeared out of nowhere, "Okay, sunshine, it's showtime." Murray is roughly manhandled out of the van, firmly held, both on the right-hand and left-hand sides. He can hear the people and the Police shouting: "murdering bastard!", "Black should hang!", "shields up, advance," "bring back the death penalty!", "stand firm," "hope you rot in hell forever!" and all sorts of other niceties.

The hood has been removed, and Murray is being processed, then, in quick time, temporarily relocated in what is known as the holding cell. The passing policemen just glare at him. A passing prisoner tries to spit on Murray as she passes. One of the escorting policemen whispers, "Don't take it personally, creep. I think she really likes you." The dents on the walls look like they are the result from someone's head inadvertently colliding with the hard surface. Murray sits in absolute silence. Even his breathing would fail to register in anyone present, hearing range.

A while later, the cell door creaks open, and he is escorted up the stairs into the number one courtroom. Initially, there is a hushed silence as Murray enters the room, but that does not last long as the still moment is broken by a solitary shout of "Hang the bastard!" which in turn is followed by a collective verbal assault on his eardrums by the unruly gallery.

The judge bangs the gavel as hard as possible, demanding at the top of her voice, "Silence in the court! Silent in court! I will remove anyone who causes a disturbance," immediately signalling with her finger with the black nail polish for the court usher to remove the worst offenders, "Any more disturbances during these proceedings and the offenders will be taken to the cells, and I can resolutely guarantee to one and all that there will be a maximum mandatory custodial sentence to follow, do I make myself clear!"

Murray thinks that she must have watched some American TV shows as she points another finger from her other hand with the bright red nail polish to a big chap and utters, "Olla amigo comprendy!" There is more muttering from the gallery to his left, followed by a cry of "Black must die!", immediately the black nail finger is in action, the judge nods again to the court usher, and the offending person is removed from the court.

Once order has been fully restored, the prosecutor for the crown is invited up to speak, and the jury looks at him with all those sympathetic big doe eyes. They follow his version of the story, word for word; with their faces reacting with stretched open mouths and hands coming up to their faces in one of their *oh my god* gestures. The only reactions from the jury that are amiss are the ooh's, ahhs, and hissing.

Jonathan Redford Martin QC, is... to put it politely, is a big suave bastard. He was decked out in an expensive Italian handmade suit. At the current exchange rate, it would have most likely paid for the grocery bill of a growing family for a year and some. He has all the necessary accessories to compliment his expensive threads. The shirt was a one-off, made from some exotic material from the far east that was only available every five years.

He glances once too often at the *'I am a fucking rich bastard'* watch. The honourable Anouska Flemington looks at what is present in front of her. The Judge makes him wait for a full five minutes before she nods, granting permission to address the jury. Ms. Flemington wishes she could have given the ancient Roman death signal for the overdressed, jumped-up prick in front of her to be hung, drawn, and quartered.

The prosecuting lawyer thanks her Ladyship and performs like a seasoned thespian with all the hand gestures and facial expressions which any Hollywood director would have been more than delighted to capture. Jonathan had practised in front of a mirror for hours on end to get every nuance of his opening speech pitch perfect. The newspapers love him, Murray is not too sure, though, about the four ex-wives, but he hopes the dog bites frequently when JRM goes home.

Mr Prosecution, struts with a capital 'S' up and down the well, like a prized peacock in the pre-mating ritual. The only sound in the courtroom is his voice, which he deliberately varied in volume to accent certain phrases and alleged facts. His carefully chosen words were sometimes delivered slower to empathise his utter revulsion towards the heinous criminal acts that had allegedly taken place. The forensic reports stated that the condition of the bodies; the men, women, and children, were so badly deteriorated and unrecognisable that they had to cross-reference every single dental record to ascertain the identity of the corpses.

As the story unfolded, most of the jurors were crying. Murray was riveted by this performance and thought that Jonathan Redford Martin QC should be nominated for sainthood.

For some inexplicable reason, Murray has no defence lawyer to stand up for him and say anything on his behalf. This fundamental entitlement bestowed on nearly every human soul on the planet had somehow been inadvertently waivered. Murray is not even allowed to say anything. Several times he has been warned by the judge, and her painted fingernails to keep quiet.

The never-ending parade of witnesses comes and goes, and not one of them has anything nice to say about him. In their collective opinion, Murray is a murdering bastard, just bad to the core of his being, a problem child from a broken home, an ex-juvenile delinquent who just never wanted to be a law-abiding citizen and who always thought that he was well above the law. They even had the audacity to wheel in one of his old school teachers from the retirement home and, after a brief interlude, while the batteries were replaced in his hearing aid. He stated, for the record, that Murray was an unwanted extraneous influence who constantly displayed an extremely aggressive nature in any class he was trying to teach and that he just knew that even at that young age, it was his destiny to spend time in prison.

If Murray had a solicitor representing him, he would have asked them to object to his testimony on the grounds that a man with the non-deplume of Dirty Dougie is hardly an upstanding citizen and illuminating more than serious misgivings about his opinion leading more than doubt to his character and therefore his credibility as a witness for the crown. The judge thanked him for his testimony, and he was wheeled back to the residential care home, Murray hopefully wishing that he received some much-needed electric shock treatment while in the bath.

There is no recess for lunch. The jury is invited to go away and makes its deliberation. A short while later, in the minuscule of the elapsed time that it had taken, it was not even worth going into their room. It might as well have been orchestrated through a revolving door for all the seconds it had taken. The foreman holds the paper like it is the biggest winning lottery ticket ever and proudly hands it to the bailiff.

The court waits in absolute silence as the full-to-capacity crowd all sit still, with bated breath, for the judge to administer the verdict. "Murray Black, you have been found guilty of murdering all your neighbours," and putting on the dreaded black cap sentences him to thirty-one life sentences with no chance of parole. She addresses the courtroom that due to the horrendous crimes that Murray Black has committed against humanity, she would like to have him hung, drawn and quartered or burnt at stake, but due to the law being changed several hundred years ago, this was unfortunately not possible now in this modern civilised age.

Murray wakes up in a sweat, looks around, and relaxes as he instantly recognises the kitchen. The clothes were soaking wet and clinging to his body. This was the worst dream that he had ever experienced. The irony of it all was that he would not even hurt a fly. On several occasions, Linda had even threatened him with divorce if he brought any more stray animals home. Even so, Murray was well aware that he had been absent without leave for a few days and had a huge gap in his memory, but he could never have done any of this.

The remaining vodka glugs out from the top of the bottle as he pours the contents down the sink. Murray shivers and shakes for a while as he recovers from the sheer terror he had fully experienced during the dream and eventually drifts off to sleep.

Daylight comes as a welcome relief, the birds have returned this morning, and as he lies there and listens to them chirp, it makes him think he surely must not be the only one to have lived through all this. Surely there must be others out there. He will just have to look harder.

Murray is still recovering from his nightmare. Thankfully, he had stopped dreaming before he was incarcerated in one of her majesty's secure pleasure centres, but Murray is still visibly shaken. The ashtray is overflowing, but there is about half a joint. Without any hesitation, he relights it, and it does the trick. Another one, along with a couple of cups of tea, and he is up and running. The remaining stash of hard liquor all join the Russian vodka and glugs down the drain.

The remaining houses belonging to the now-deceased neighbours get a more intensive search prior to being set alight. His plundering of the tinned goods is more successful, and he even manages to get a couple of tins of powdered milk. The good news is that the rabid dog is dead, it wasn't rabid after all, and it had died of thirst. Murray did not burn the dog, feeling like an asshole for planning to kill it in the first place, and he supposes that due to the nightmare of the previous night, he felt duly obliged to bury the poor creature. After Murray had transferred and stored all his newly acquired provisions, he was heading back into town. Murray's estranged brother stayed at the other end of the town. His green stuff, sorry, Linda's green stuff, was almost gone, and frankly, Murray did not think he would get another night's sleep without it.

Mr Black had pretended for years that he did not know where she got it from, but the quality was, without fail, always top-notch. He knew his brother was the one. Where he stayed, the street is quite unusual. It is along a country lane, and the easiest manoeuvre is to drive right to the end and do a quick turn in the hotel car park. This would allow you to park at the passing place just outside his house, in pole position to escape with the hidden contraband. All through the town, Murray had peeped the horn constantly until his hands were tired and his ears were sore, and again, he had received no requests to keep the noise down. As Murray reached the car park, he was amazed at the spectacle unfolding before his eyes.

There was a woman on top of the old concrete lamp post, the type that had the light situated in the overhang position— dressed in a vibrant bright pair of yellow pyjamas with one slipper on and one slipper off, barking at a pack of stray dogs that were barking and growling back at her. Shifting the automatic transmission into neutral, old habits die hard, Murray gently slowed the car to a halt.

Luckily for her, Mr Black had brought the shotgun along. Before the window was opened, he checked that it was loaded. Holding the gun in his right hand, he leans over and opens the passenger window enough to squeeze the barrels out, just enough space to elevate the gun up or down. The dogs had stopped barking and were momentarily assessing his presence, not giving them time to think, Murray fired two shots. He missed completely with the first one and whacked another one in the backside with the second shot. This was enough to scatter the pack, he quickly reloaded, and before Murray had the time to signal her to come down, she was sprinting across the car park now with no slippers on, and before he knew it, she was in the car.

She spoke rapidly for a few minutes and, seemingly not stopping for a breath, continued to talk non-stop. Mr Black was beginning to wonder if she could perhaps breathe through her ears. Murray did not have a clue what she was saying. He did not recognise the language but thinks it may have been from somewhere in or round about some region in southeast Asia. She pointed to the gun, looked at Murray, mimed the shooting of the dog's scene, and also that his *bang, bang* was no good. She said no good about fourteen times. Murray thought this was maybe her name at first, but then he slowly realised that she did not speak any English.

Heading out of the car park, Murray stopped at his brother's house, she looked at him, Mr Black was not even going to attempt to try and explain what he was going in for, but as he was going to take the gun along with him, she said 'no good.' She played charades again in the car, and this time it dawned on Murray that she at one time had been in the army and she could shoot. Contemplating that if he gave her the gun, she could just shoot him and steal the car. Murray put caution to the wind and handed it over. She looked at him again with those big brown eyes that were big enough to capture souls for all eternity, and this time pointed her fingers to the barrels, indicating the cartridges. Murray was getting good at this. It only took a few seconds, and he handed over the bag containing the remaining cartridges. Murray's first attempt to open the door to get out of the car was rejected by a 'Uhhuh!'; she then proceeded to open the breach, remove the cartridges and look down both barrels. The only comment he received before she reloaded was 'no good, no good!'

Pointing to the dashboard clock, Murray counted out the ten minutes he intended to be in the house. She let him open the door this time. Her feet were a worry to him, but walking around over the uneven gravel path did not bother her in the slightest. She insisted on going to the front and scanning all around; she, with a nod of the head, indicated that it was okay for him to proceed. Baby brother's house was a mess, it was always untidy, but this was much worse. They found him in bed with his two dead concubines. How his brother managed it, Murray never figured it out, but one was never enough for him. After a five-minute scrummage throughout the house, he found a box or two and a couple of large black refuse sacks containing what he had come for. Murray did not bother looking for any food, as his brother had always been a dedicated takeaway fanatic. Prior to leaving, Murray said his goodbyes to his brother and his concubines and then started a fire that would hopefully spread rapidly throughout the house.

'No name' was still only dressed in the pyjamas and would require some additional attire. At the town's retail park there are some clothing stores. Indicating left, they take a slight detour on the way back. After the required game of charades, Murray eventually persuaded her that some clothes would be a really good idea. She was a quick shopper and even let him hold the gun while she changed, quickly filling a shopping trolley with a selection of clothes. She held her hands out for the gun, and Murray was instantly demoted back to the position of trainee trolley chauffeur. It did not take long to load the car; he started to drive them home, but just as they approached the exit, she shouted, 'no good, no good!'. Murray stopped the car, and before he knew it, she was off heading towards the sporting goods store. Reversing the car to her shop of choice, Murray exited the vehicle, took a brave pill, and followed behind her. He found her in the gun department.

Already she was behind the counter and looking at the rifles. She never even picked a selection to try the weight or feel. She just instinctively knew the ones that she wanted. Four rifles later, she had moved to the telescopic scope section, taking one out of the box and discarding it with a 'no good, no good!' after several minutes, she selected four suitable ones. Next, she tried the bolt action and, making sure it was not loaded, pulled the trigger straight away. Murray knew what she was on about. The rifles on display automatically before they were put on show by strict shop policy had their firing pins removed.

Luckily for her and Murray, one of his relations worked here for years. They had managed to assist him in gaining his first adventure into gaining employment. On leaving school, Murray was working here during the summer before his apprenticeship started, so he instinctively knew where the firing pins were kept. He indicated to her via charades that he knew where they were located and led her to the cabinet. Again, her gunmanship was amazing. She quickly found some tools and stripped the guns down, exposing the section in which the crucial part was missing. Ten minutes later, they were heading out of the shop. It actually took two trips carting the guns and all the ammunition.

They were now in his house; after unloading the car and storing most of the stuff in the living room. Murray gave '*no good-no good*' a quick-guided tour around the house. Bathroom, shower, he even showed her that you had to fill the cistern or else it would not flush. Making their way back to the kitchen, Murray asked her if she was hungry, and exhausted by the frequency of the charades, he just opened one of the tin cupboards and pointed to his stomach. She devoured three tins of sockeye salmon and promptly fell asleep on top of the makeshift bed he had set up in the kitchen. Murray went and got her a blanket and gently covered her. She muttered something in her sleep, and he was sure it was '*no good, no good.*'

Murray stayed awake long enough to have a tin of beans with some added form of constituted sausages added from another tin, several cups of tea with that disgusting powdered milk, and to get to sleep, he had a couple of bedtime joints. Mr Black set up another makeshift bed in the corner of the kitchen, stocked up the stove with some sticks, and added some dross just to keep it going overnight. Murray sat on his bed, and before he knew it, he was sound asleep, and this time thankfully, no dreams.

When he awoke in the morning, 'no good, no good' or whatever the fuck her name was, is now wide awake, and by the wet hair and the smell of freshly brewed coffee, she had been up and about for quite a while. She had some more tinned salmon, and he had some more beans this time without the added tasteless sausage thingamay-majiggeries. In his pre-sleep state, he had thought about rerunning his calculation on the survival percentage, but as it would not even generate them towards a single digit to the left of the decimal point, he figured it was a waste of paper, pen, and thought.

Once breakfast was over and done with 'no good,' went through to the living room and selected one of the rifles. She then proceeded to strip it down completely, clean it thoroughly and reassemble it with the firing pin. Murray watched intently, but there was no way she was going to allow him to join in, so he went outside, had a smoke, and spoke to Linda for a while. Murray had been out in the garden smoking weed and generally just listening to the sounds of the wind breezing through the trees and the occasional bird song when 'No Good' came out of the kitchen with a can of fizzy juice for Murray and a can of diet something for herself, immediately she pointed at the half smoked item in the ashtray and shook her head, this time she did not say no good.

They sat there for a little while, saying nothing. She had a cigarette, and he finished the remainder of what was in the ashtray and eventually retreated back into the kitchen. Producing a couple of blank books of paper and pens, he handed one set to her, and with the other one, Murray wrote his name in block capital letters, pointing at his name and then himself. He said his name slowly: Murray Black. She attempted to say this for quite a long time, and the nearest recitation they got to this was *Money Back*. Inside Murray's head, his brain waves drifted off for a second, "Ladies and gentlemen, tonight we are proud to present the finest rock 'n' roll band in the land! Please give it up with feeling for No Good and Money Back!"

Now it was No-Good's turn. Her writing looked like broken matchsticks stuck together in strange configurations. It was absolutely beautiful, and in a mere flourish of her hand, she had created this masterpiece. The only problem was that Murray did not have a clue what it all was supposed to mean. An unregistered alien script would have been much easier to translate. He kindly asked her to remind him that they should pay a visit to the library the next time they had to go to town, and she just smiled.

They sat in silence for a few minutes, and she went through the shooting at the dog's scenario, miming the dogs and Mr Black's actions, making it clear that his shooting skills were, at best, not very good. No Good selected a few tins from the cupboard, looking at the pictures and if the contents did not appeal to her, Murray was sure he had heard her say 'yuck,' and after she had half a dozen tins, she handed Murray a rifle, grabbed one for herself and they then proceeded outside.

No Good in front, and they causally walked down to about the halfway point in the street, looking around she spotted a garden bench that Murray had not incinerated during his 'burning the neighbour's extravaganza' and persuaded him to help her put it in the middle of the road. The cans were placed on the bench, and they then proceeded to walk back.

No Good took the rifle from him and fired several shots adjusting the scope a couple of times and after firing a few confirmation shots. Seeming pleased with herself, she handed Murray back the rifle. She indicated that he was to start at the left and work his way across. Murray was made to lie on the ground, making himself as comfortable as possible, holding the rifle as steady as he could. Murray pulled the trigger, but nothing happened. He looked at No Good, arms folded across her chest. She shook her head, reached down, and switched the safety off. This time Murray did manage to shoot and hit nothing. "Back no good! Back no good!"

Most of the day was spent on this. Eventually, she had taught Murray how to synchronise his breathing, which enabled him to shoot a little better, the part where Murray was taught to squeeze the trigger rather than just pull it was almost sensual. A few more adjustments were made to the scope to allow for his slight pull to the left. Mr Black would not be qualifying for the sniper of the year competition anytime in the near future, but he could sometimes get as good as four out of five shots. On the other hand, she would get a one hundred percent accuracy every single time.

The afternoon was almost spent, and they headed back to the house. Murray went for a cold shower, and she started cleaning her rifle. Once he had returned, she taught him how to clean. They spoke no words. It was more a conversation of noises which included grunts, various squeaks produced out of squeezed lips, and animated facial gestures. As of yet, they had not, at this point in time, developed a mutually understandable sign language.

Murray made dinner; he did not think it was one of her favourite meals because, after the first mouthful, she spat it in the sink, which reminded him that he must remember to add tinned fish to the shopping list. They spent the rest of the evening drinking tea and communicating on paper, little drawings and words you could just make up. So far, they had almost filled up the two books with lots of sketches, even more, scored out sketches, and lots of question marks.

In conclusion, they had gathered that she was from South Korea and had spent several years in the army but did not give any details. The matchstick name Murray was unable to decipher, so she was still being called No Good, and much to her efforts, he was still being called 'Money Back,' now shortened to 'Back.'

Murray, in turn, gave her the sordid details of his life so far, explained where he had worked, the mini digger in the back garden, and the newly filled-in hole beside it. For the explanation for all the burnt-out houses, Murray had to go and find more paper, and for this, he had embellished his sketches with various highlighter pens, various colours representing the fires, and the rabid dog was done in red. No Good nodded as if understanding the actions,

Mr Black had taken this and assumed this was a sign of approval, thinking that this was exactly what she would have done. The only exception was the dog. No Good indicated that she would have just shot the dog when interrogated by the next set of sketches. Murray had a drawing loosely indicating a dog being killed, skinned, cooked, and eaten. She just looked at him and said, "Yuck!"

Time was getting on—pretty dark outside, but no breeze or rain. Murray put the water on to boil, and No Good went into the ex-living room, which was now basically a big storeroom. During their pen-and-paper conversations, she had indicated that eating tinned food every day was really not a good idea. In asking that would the animals not be infected, she, when understanding the question, burst out laughing and, through a mime, of lying on her back with her feet and arms in the air imitating a dying animal in the process of stealing its last breath. Then promptly followed by a big performance of where are all the dead animals' question, and come to think of it, he had not seen any, not even any road kill.

No Good had purloined the biggest torch Murray had ever seen. This must have come from the gun shop. She diligently dismantled and cleaned all the components. He watched, fascinated at the care and dexterity of her delft hand movements as she reconfigured the device back to its original shape and function. Mr Black awarded No Good ten out of ten for having no spare parts left abandoned on the table.

After tea and the obligatory smoke that went along with it, they got dressed to go outside. This was her idea. No Good advised him what to wear. He had no clue as to what they were about to do.

Chapter Four

The area where the house was situated is surrounded by lots of open countrysides in all directions with the obvious exception of the town's location. They had walked for about half an hour. Standing beside him, she removed the rifle from her shoulder. He was about to do the same when she gently shook her head and gave Murray the big torch. He was instructed to stay at her side and shine the beam of light across the fields, and if an animal was spotted, he was to stand as still as possible until she had taken the shot.

The torch worked, and he slowly weaved the beam left to right. They would stop every ten to fifth-teen steps, and then if nothing was spotted, they would repeat the process. By the end of their nocturnal hunting expedition, they had both fired five shots. No good's total was three rabbits, a pheasant, and a duck. Murray had a grand total of three holes in the ground, a branch out of a tree, and a splash in a pond.

They headed home; by candlelight, Murray cleaned the rifles this time, and she checked and pointed out his mistakes, No Good went for a shower, and he gutted and skinned the rabbits and de-feathered the birds, dumping the bits that they could not eat in a neighbour's bin a few houses away, just far enough away as not to smell the stink when they started to decompose. The water was freezing by the time it was his turn. No point in complaining; next time, he would go first. When he finished, No Good sat at the kitchen table engrossed in composing a list. Murray had a peak at it, but it still looked like fucking matchsticks.

By the time he had awakened in the morning, she had been busy. Not only was there a pot of tea on the go, but amazingly the truck was all ready for their journey into town. Halfway through his tea, she presented Murray with a little present; the shotgun now was in a compact abbreviated form compared to its original, the barrels and stock had been shortened. It would fit snugly in the door recess of the truck door and his rucksack nicely. No Good played with the radio all the way into town, the lights would come on, and you could change stations with the selection buttons. You could even search for stations, but they did not even receive static. Murray tried explaining that it was a complete waste of time, but she was determined to try and try.

They arrived at the supermarket. There were several in town, and this one had the smallest meat section. Murray thought that this would be the least smelly. He dutifully grabbed a trolley and followed her in. They wandered around for some time before they found what she was looking for, lots of cans with strange writing on the labels that he would not even look at. The stuff he did recognise was the rice, curry powder, some but not all of the spices, and sanitary towels. No Good spent a considerable amount of time in the electrical department. It took her so long going through all the adapters, plugs, and cables that Murray managed to rattle together a joint and smoke it while she deliberated the available choices and combinations.

Murray had just finished smoking when she completed the last selection. On the way out of the car park, she indicated that she wanted to go back to the hotel. She never bothered trying to describe this verbally. For this, she had prepared a rather neat little drawing showing her atop of the lamppost with the snarling dogs below her. There is no other way to put this. The hotel was stinking of rotten corpses. They had a few boxes of fume masks that had been liberated from a painter's van. Helping and checking that each other's face gear was correctly attached, she went in front, and Murray followed like a dedicated puppy.

It had turned out that she had survived on bottled water and crisps for two weeks, cheese and onion had been her preferred choice, but when they were depleted, she moved on to other flavours and going by the pile of empty packets outside her room the bright green and yellow, pickled onion must have come in at a close second favourite position. Her room was very tidy compared to the rest of the hotel; she grabbed some clothes, her phone, and her laptop. On the way out, she took Murray through to the conference centre. She had been here for an industrial demonstration and was part of the delegation.

The photographs on the big whiteboard showed her with a group of people representing some engineering outfit, with a big exhibition on CNC machinery for nearly every known application thinkable. All of the pictures of the demonstration experts had nametags on them except hers. Murray took one of the brochures and started to thumb through it. No Good removed it gently from his hands and casually dropped it on the floor.

Now that Murray knew what she had done for a living in the old world, he took her down to God-fearing and God-hearing. The place was dead. Not a living or dead soul was on site. He took her through the workshop and showed her all the machines. She was not impressed. Most of these machines were at least forty years old, some of them they had to make spare parts for, and much to her disappointment, there was not even one CNC-controlled machine on the premises. Murray even took her on a tour of the offices, the procurement, wages, and Human Resources department. The Human Recourses was always questionable as they were forever changing the goalposts and tended to get extremely upset if the guys from the shop floor requested a meeting for clarification on the changes, especially on the proverbial overtime and pension issues. Just as they were about to leave, Murray noticed the big boss's door was slightly ajar.

He had not brought his rifle in, but removing the sawn-off shotgun from his rucksack, Murray motioned No Good to be quiet and pointed to the door. Her rifle at the ready, Mr Black proceeded forward and gently edged the door further open with his foot.

Mr Wrightson was sat at his desk, shirt and tie, immaculately clean and irrefutably dead. There was some froth around his lips, and it was not green. Murray's Friday morning nemesis had survived and ended up being here for his final moments. No Good was staring at Murray. He thought he had suddenly lost all the colour from his face; he had to get out of the room and get out fast. Murray handed her the sawn-off shotgun and headed out the door. She said something to him. He had no idea what the fuck it was. Murray just held up one of his hands, as in give me some space here. Whatever she thought it meant, he never asked her. Mr Black headed towards the bathroom and got there just in time to spew all the contents of his stomach all over the bathroom wall, never quite reaching the great white telephone or the sink. Murray returned to the office, No Good looked at him and gave him a handwritten note; it was penned in Craig's semi-calligraphic style of writing.

I have unfortunately survived this pestilence that has removed all my family and friends from this now woefully dreadful plain of existence. Everyone I have known, friends and foes alike, are all now gone. I spent several days going around the whole area searching for anyone else who may have survived, but it was useless, I first checked all the houses of all the people I knew, and after that, I went around knocking on strangers' homes. This is a punishment that I cannot bare; I also cannot think why God would curse me with this penance to live in a world devoid of love and companionship and therefore have come to the conclusion that this is a thing made by and delivered by man himself. For all my departed friends and colleagues, I wish them god's entire everlasting blessing, and may God forgive me for committing the ultimate sin.

Murray was gutted; this was the guy who would harass him for overspending the briefest sum of pennies, and here is the same guy spending his last days looking for people, to comfort them, just because of his unbreakable faith in humanity. Murray wished that he was half the man Mr Wrightson was.

She looked at him and said, "no-good, no good" Murray did not think she was referring to the dead Mr Wrightson but more to the fact that he was as white as a fucking sheet. Murray needed some fresh air. He left the office and ended up sitting in the rest area. This was a designated non-smoking area, and although he did not think the rules were applicable now, he had several cigarettes, one after the other.

There was no way Murray could leave him here like this. He is not religious, nor did he feel any sort of moral obligation, but taking him home and burying him just felt like the right thing to do. Murray is pretty sure that if it were the other way about, Wrightson would have done exactly the same thing.

Murray's head was stuck somewhere up his arse, and he was in no condition to drive, traffic or no traffic. Murray was still in no fit state, motioning to No Good the steering wheel, he got in the passenger's side. She switched on the ignition whacked the transmission into reverse, and took off at full throttle; Murray reacted immediately, knocking the transmission into neutral and turning the wheel anti-clockwise to avoid a collision with the stationary forklifts.

The truck came to a halt. Murray looked at her and said, "Fucking no good! Fucking no good!" Taking back over the driving duties, they arrived at the coffin shop. It was not as clean as his last visit, but they managed to get a coffin, and, on the way out, he kicked the Bible out from under the door, allowing it to close. The Bible he picked up and chucked in the back of the cab.

Getting Mr Wrightson into the coffin was easy; well, once Murray broke his legs with a sledgehammer, it was. Rigour Mortis had set in, and he was firmly froze in the sitting position, and there were no more "L" shaped coffins available. Wrightson stayed in the posh part of the town. Murray had rarely been up to this part; in fact, he distinctly remembered the only time he was here was when he had a

63

summer party for all the employees and their families. It was made clear that Murray had to attend, and he also had to be on his best behaviour. Murray had stayed the obligatory couple of hours and fucked off discretely when no one was looking.

Arriving at the house, there was no need to go in. The fresh graves were on the front lawn. It was only fair to lay him to rest with the family. They rummaged around and found a shovel Murray started digging his grave, No Good offered to give him a hand, but he politely refused. She went off, a little miffed, to do something in the truck. When the grave was deep enough, Murray went and got her to help lower the coffin into the ground, it was not a perfectly smooth operation, but they managed to get him interred without breaking the coffin. The earth slowly returned to the hole. Murray felt it would be disrespectful, dead or not to even smoke at this time, so he did not bother, but he did remember the Bible in the back of the cab. Murray retrieved it from the truck and placed the Bible in the grave. He had no coins in his pocket, but strangely enough, he had five of the two quid washers in his back pocket, and Murray put them gently into the grave, not thinking badly of the guy at all. He thinks this man was one of the good guys in this world, but just sometimes a twat to work for.

The grave was finished. Murray nodded his farewell to Craig, went over to the truck, and drove away. He thinks that due to the episode of No Goods' driving experiment that they should wear their seat belts. They don't have any available A&E department or doctor surgeries to go to get treated anymore. They only have themselves. She was not too cooperative on this request, but the infamous Black stare swayed the argument.

They have not communicated on the way home. The plunder from the electronics department in the supermarket consists of plugs and cables to connect her mobile and laptop to the USB input located on the dashboard. Murray thinks a wireless connection is available but keeps his mouth shut on this option. After all, according to the brochure that he had picked up at the hotel, she is the resident fucking expert. They arrive home, and by this time, she has the dead phone connected to the USB, Murray could piss her off the way she has pissed off him and switch off the engine, but she is that determined that she would only keep her mobile connected and completely drain the batteries. The keys were left in, and the engine kept running. Murray completely ignores the goods in the back of the van, and No Good concentrates her efforts on finding a suitable adapter to accommodate the laptop; maybe he should go and check that the pushbikes in the garage have air in their tyres.

Today so far has been quite a day. Murray stokes the embers and loads up the stove with bits of sticks and a little coal. At present, he is most definitely not in the mood for tea.

He grabs his stash and walks out the back. Oblivion does not come easily. Murray tries really hard, loading up the joints, he gets a little head-on, but he is still a bit cut up with an unexpected find today. If he had checked the motorcycle, he would have taken it out and blasted it open along all these now empty roads, no traffic police, no problem, but after the seat belt debate, that would be not only pretty irresponsible but completely hypocritical, but it would be truly wonderful. Linda frequently tried to persuade him to sell his pride and joy; it was on the assumption that they would raise a family, but Murray thinks the real reason was that she was sick of never-ending engine oil stains on her bras and pants.

He has been out here for ages, just immersed in deep contemplation about where they are, their situation, and if he could have done anything to save Mr Wrightson. Murray had never even heard No Good approach. She looked at him with those big brown eyes and, with her hands, motioned that he should wash his hands and come in the house to have some food.

The kitchen is bright. There are about a dozen candles spread around the place; there is a mellow smell of jasmine, lavender and the incandescent shadows bounce on the walls, and the ceiling, dancing to the soft music coming from her now charged mobile phone now connected to a small pair of cylindrical battery-operated speakers. Murray was expecting her to try and try calling, texting and emailing home. She really is quite an expert. He would never have thought of this. Murray was so far inside himself, reliving deep distant memories, that he did not even notice the light change.

Murray does think that he will never cook again. The meal she has made is as good as, if not better than, any restaurant food he has ever remembered tasting. The duck, rabbit and pheasant curry just inundates his taste buds with a combination of delicate flavours and succulent meats. They have some yellow rice; No Good has excelled herself as they even have some sort of flat bread. Murray would have been over the moon with this alone, but with the combination of this spread, the way it is presented on the table, he has just orbited Pluto. There are some rather expensive unopened champers on the table.

No Good offers Murray a big carving knife and points to the bottles inviting him to open one. This is the method you see in romantic movies where the head wine waiter, usually with the greased back hair, chops the top of the bottle with one slash of the knife and da na! The cork jumps out, and he pours without spilling a teardrop of honey-coloured liquid. Murray's luck would be that he would probably chop off one or two of his fingers, smash the bottle in the process, and the champers would be everywhere. Murray declines the knife and does it the old-fashioned way. The fizzy stuff makes him fart like a backfire from a tractor, but he really does not have to tell her this.

The champers make her giggle as school girls do, she even burps, but it is not rude. They both burst out laughing. There is no five-star dining etiquette in this house. They have eaten like royalty tonight; there is still loads left on the table, but it will not go to waste. No Good gets up and starts to tidy up the table. Murray puts his hands up and takes over the required task. It is the least that he can do. She must have been cooking for ages. Murray has just about finished tidying up, the dishes are washed and stacked on the drying board, and the pots have been washed, dried and put away. The remaining food was put into the storage containers, and unfortunately, the remaining bread was scoffed while he was tidying up. The selected playlist has just finished, and he can now hear the tinkle of a little bell.

No Good was in the spare room. All the previous occupants on top of the dressing table had been removed and placed neatly in the corner. Several pictures, some monochrome with tints of yellow and some that look fairly modern, were on the edges leaning against the wall. An empty glass jar contained some incense sticks emitting some sweet fragrance. She was on her knees, quietly chanting some ritual rhythm, occasionally lifting up the small crystal bell and giving it a gentle chime.

This was private, and having no desire to be invasive. He about turned and headed back into the kitchen. The tractor backfire sounded a couple of times. Luckily, he was nowhere near the naked flames. Murray poured the last of the champers into his tumbler and opened the other one. When No Good returned, she found him sitting on the bench with a glass of champers in one hand and a joint in the other. She went and got her glass and lit a cigarette, and came to join him on the bench. The night sky was breathtaking. Murray didn't know how many stars were up there, nor any of the names of the constellations, but she seemed to know many pointing from left to right. He could have listened to her all night.

She was a little cold now, so they retreated back to the kitchen; Murray pointed to her phone and asked with fingers, grunts and groans if she wanted to put on some music. In reply, she looked at him and, with a smile, went out of the room and returned with his guitar. It had been a long while since Murray had even looked at this, never mind played it. He put it on his knee and strummed down the strings once. It took him a couple of minutes to retune it. He then gave her his best Elvis impersonation.

Woke up this morning, and I was feeling so blue.

Ain't anybody on this planet except for me and you?

I wanna hear you baby, wanna hear you say my name,

Money Back and Murray Black just ain't the same.

Maybe I could shorten your name and just call you Soo

Ain't nobody on this planet except for me and you,

Were on this lonely planet baby,

And I got the lonely planet blues.

Murray rattled out another couple of made-up verses. Maybe she had heard of Elvis, maybe not. Nevertheless, he got a standing ovation. She stood up and gave him some of that close hand clapping. Murray stood up, curled his lip and in his best Memphis accent, "Thank you, ya all Elvis has now left the building," with that, they put most of the candles out and fell asleep in our respective makeshift beds.

It is now morning, and again smarty-pants is first up. Murray grabs a cuppa, puts some of last night's food on a plate and joins her at the table and chairs outside. He finds her with a big glass of water, and he cannot help but notice the open packet of painkillers hanging half out of her pocket. Murray feels great. Champers never gives him a headache. She has placed a large-scale map of the region on the table and had drawn a circle in red pen. As he looks closer, it is the symbol of an airport. He gives her a glance and is tempted to ask her what time her check-in is and whether it would be better to check in online, but he bites his lip. Instead, Murray puts his arms out and makes plane noises, looks up at the clear blue sky and then changes his stance to his palms up in front of him, meaning ain't no planes today, baby.

Looking at him, then back at the map, and it's those big blue eyes again, "Okay, don't forget your passport, we'll go." Murray knows that it will be a waste of time. The normal travel time between here and the airport is about two hours, and at the least, the batteries will get a good charge. He thinks to be fair. It is his turn for the music. Murray exhumes his mobile from the pile of stuff in the living room. No Good goes and checks for a suitable connector in her personal bag of goodies, and he starts to pack the car.

They reconvene in the kitchen in about an hour later. She checks the guns and makes sure the sawn-off is loaded and on safety before handing it to him for safekeeping. She checks the contents of the car as it is going through an imaginary list and nods her head in approval. They get in the car and are just about to set off when she raises her hand and jumps back into the house, returning with a large bottle of water, the tablets in her top pocket and the map. Murray does not know why they need the map. He knows where the airport is located. Murray has been there a few times, it's dead easy to find, a big flat place with lots of planes, security men and expensive carparks.

As he drives, she connects up his mobile, and they drive in silence for a while. The town is desolate. They don't even spot a stray dog. They pass the occasional stationery vehicle; it varies from car to car, cars with attached caravans, HGVs and the oddest of the lot was a Mr Whippy ice cream van. They were either empty or had dead people with the green stuff, but the saddest of the lot was a minibus full of nuns.

They checked every single vehicle for signs of life, but they found no one.

They were now about halfway, and the road ahead was blocked on both sides of the carriageway. It looked like there was a huge jam up ahead at the approach to the roundabout, and it was just packed solid. They could attempt to clear one side, but it would take days, and they would have to go and get some heavy machinery to do the task. No Good had the map out in a jiffy, placing it on top of the bonnet. Murray pointed his finger to where he thought they were, and she retraced the road with her finger going off at the first turnoff. He pointed to the second one, which went straight through the big industrial town on our left. It would add some time onto their journey, but Murray is positive that they would keep the plane on the runway till they arrived.

The town had seen much better days; it once had been a major industrial force in the area. The main source of heavy engineering and its subsidiary industries providing employment to many people in the area. All the big manufacturers had either moved abroad or been put out of business by cheap imports. Their attitude was why should we even try and compete with the overseas manufacturers when we have to supply the workers here with everything, the red tape is legalised strangulation, and if we move abroad, we don't even have to supply them with safety boots never mind the regulatory comfy fit hard hats. Needless to say, the town had a huge unemployment problem, the local and regional officials tried very hard to revitalise the area, but you can only have so many call centres.

By this time, the mobile on charge had picked up enough juice to pump out some sounds, Murray was in the mood for some soul. He had just switched it on when grumpy chops looked at him, pointing at the empty pocket where painkillers used to be located. Murray switched it off and looked for the nearest supermarket. It was no big deal. He had not brought any fizzy juice. He can get some at the same time she gets the painkillers. After a few wrong turns, they eventually arrive at the supermarket. The carpark has a couple of hulks of burnt-out cars, no major crime scene. It was the local teenagers' Friday night entertainment. The competition went along the lines of stealing a car, the more expensive, the better, driving it to a pre-arranged destination and then torching it. They had even used the carpark beside the police station. It was a street credibility thing with the local yobs.

Chapter Five

The thoroughfare outside the main door was strewn with an array of litter. He sees a pram with several boxes of whiskey in place of a baby lying on its side, the rest just looked as if it was a looting-in-action job. There was not a soul about, they quietly rolled up to the main door and waited a few minutes. Murray thinks that No Good's head must have been at bursting point, with a herd of dancing elephants wearing steel toe-capped boots, she nodded and jumped out of the truck. He followed suit, stopping for a moment to light a joint, but he could not find the lighter. Murray removed the bag from his shoulder and put his hand in for a rummage, retrieving a green one he sparked up just as she was walking in through the now glassless double doors.

The shopping isles were laid out in the multiple four-in-a-line configuration with enough space for stereo trolleys to weave in and out. Murray thought that maybe grumpy chops would like a bag of cheese and onion. Maybe he should chuck in a couple of packets of pickled onion just to keep her happy. He was only getting passed the first aisle, and he had to tread carefully. There was broken glass, food cans and all sorts of debris decorating the floor, some shelves had been broken, and their contents spilled onto the shelves below, and the overspill had cascaded, adding to the accumulated mess on the floor.

Murray watched as No Name was turning the corner two sections up and was just reading the display sign for the buy three get two for free offers on the cheap industrial gut rot vodka mixers impregnated with the even cheaper industrial fruit juices when he caught a whiff of rancid body odour. Murray never even got the opportunity to turn around. The impact to the back of the head sent him head first straight into the pyramid-shaped display of the cheap mixed tropical-flavoured alcohol. Several of the bottles must have smashed as his back was getting wet. Murray rolled about with the glass bottles, some had fallen on top of him, and others were spinning and rolling in multiple directions. He pivoted on his side just in time to see the big guy swing the baseball bat for a second helping at his head, Murray arched his head back as far as he could, and the bat missed him by millimetres. As the bat passed, he rolled away from him and picked up a couple of the bottles on the floor on his way back up to the standing position. The drunk's movements were sluggish. He now stood in front of him, Murray chucked one of the bottles, and it sailed straight passed him. He grunted and took another step forward just as the other bottle smashed on his forehead.

This just gave Murray enough time to duck past him and retrieve the rucksack. Moving around the corner, he had one hand holding the bag the other was withdrawing the sawn-off. Murray discarded the bag and swivelled around just in time to see the bat getting pulled back over his head for what would have been the killing blow when he pulled both triggers and blew the top of his head off. Murray saw no sign of No Name and headed to the last point where he had seen her. He ejected the spent cartridges and reloaded from the just-in-case ones sleeping in his pocket.

The ongoing commotion sounded as if it was coming from the adjacent aisle. He thought that they had come this way, going by the trail of destruction in front of him. Murray rounded the corner, and No Name was standing with her shirt and T-shirt ripped open, exposing her perfectly formed petite breasts. The way the guys are whooping and hollering, Murray does not think that they have never seen a pair of tits before.

No Name is cornered in the back-to-school department. The first guy pulls a knife from the back of his jeans and takes a step forward, brandishing the knife from side to side. No Name does not move a muscle. She stands perfectly still, focusing on the guy's movements. He gets close enough to take a stab at her, as he lunges forward and shoves the knife hand towards her stomach, No Name takes one small step back with one foot and changes her position by ninety degrees allowing the knife to sail past her, in the moment she grabs the knife arm with one hand and crashes her elbow at full force into the region of his solar plexus, he goes down and does not get back up. The other two heroes are

76

momentarily making a decision about whither to run or stay. Too late, No Name has picked up the dropped knife and threw it at the one nearest to her. The blade catches him in the chest, he looks at it unbelievably, his brain not convinced that it is actually there. When his heart stops beating, his brain no longer requires convincing, and he topples dead on the floor.

The other guy with the long straggly hair has had the decision made for him; he is off and running. He is in so much of a panic he does not notice Murray until he introduces him to the double barrels. One shot catches him on the shoulder, and the other crashes into his heart, and that range it is instantly disintegrated.

No Names breasts are still out on display; they look for the clothing section to find some replacements. She finds a pink tee shirt, and it is then that Murray notices the snarling white tiger tattooed on the top of her arm with the number: 707 in bold lettering underneath. She raised her eyes; sitting on a conveniently placed pallet of crates of beer, she lit a cigarette and slowly exhaled the smoke:

"Well, Mr Murray Black, I suspect that you are, shall we say, surprised by what you have witnessed. My name is Bong Cha, and it roughly translates to ultimate girl. For every delegation we send overseas, my government always provide a couple of special forces personnel too to watch over them. My cover was that of a CNC expert.

I was a serving second lieutenant in the white tigers 707 division. It is nearly the equivalent of your special forces. I say equivalent because we are better. My country is not contactable, and as far as I am aware, this is global, not just in your area. When you finish your cigarette perhaps, we should go and find a chemist's shop, and if you allow it, I could put some stitches in the back of your head, thank you very much for being my knight in shining armour, but I can assure you it was very unnecessary. However, it was very gallant. As you can appreciate, in our part of the world, we have many enemies our neighbours are not as considerate as you. You checked to make sure that your neighbours were dead before you set them alight ours would have no hesitation burning us alive, so please understand why we are a cautious people. Mr Black, you have many admirable qualities, but how do I say this? You sound fuck all like Elvis, so shall we go. And by the way, my friends call me Cha."

What is he meant to say to this? One minute she is up a lamp post clinging for dear life, evading a ferocious pack of staring dogs the next, she is a trained assassin? His back is still wet. He puts his hand up and wipes at the dampness. Cha informs him again that they will have to find a chemist's shop where she can stitch him up. They head back out of the shop; Murray picks up the rucksack stuffing a few bags of crisps into it as they leave the shop.

Cha is driving, and Murray rolls another joint. She has firmly advised him to put on another jacket as when the adrenaline stops, he will get cold. Murray asks about the driving at God fearing and God hearing she says that it was to test his reflexes and also tosses in do you know dogs just love cheese and onion crisps? That's why they were barking. This last part was said with a big smile on her face.

By the time they find a chemist's shop, he is on his third joint, the atmosphere between them is not exactly relaxed, but he must admit she is quite a girl, Cha indeed. Taking one of the battery-operated camping lamps with them into the chemists and in the back of the shop, he is instructed to sit in the chair and just relax "You can do anything you want, but please don't sing." He knows she is just teasing him, and she knows he knows too. Cha rummages about in the drawers behind the counter. "Murray, I cannot find any anaesthetic, but I advise you to be very still and not struggle. I promise to be quick!" She is not teasing him now. She is winding him up.

Second Lieutenant Cha reappears from behind the counter, looking the part of a surgeon general. The lab coat is pristine white, Murray knows she is smiling like a Cheshire cat behind the procedure mask, and as she stretches and relaxes the sterile gloves, he can almost hear her giggle. She has a white plastic box stencilled with the words procedure kit, which she places in his hands and tells him

79

not to drop it as it is the only one in the shop. After putting on the gloves, she shines a torch around his wound, assessing the damage. Murray asks her if he will have to sign any consent forms and does she need to know the contact details of his next of kin. She does snigger at this and tells him this is only a formality, and she has already filled in the forms in Korean, and if he really wants to, he can read all the details before he signs. This is going on while she is shaving around the wound area. The shaving complete, she then rechecks the open wound looking for any foreign matter that has embedded itself inside. She hands Murray the form and a pen from the counter, "Please sign, Mr Black" as he looks at the form, she pours some sterile liquid into the wound it does sting a little, but staring at the form keeps his mind momentarily away from the pain

"I notice that there is no writing on this form. Why do I have to sign?' Cha inserts the threaded curved needle approximately two millimetres away from the edge of the wound. As he tries not to move, she tells him that the form is filled in with invisible ink and just to trust her and sign. Murray thinks she is liking this game, as he signs, she pushes the needle through to the other side of the wound, gently wrapping the material several times around the needle driver, then a little tug and twist, she then cuts the first stitch, "One down another thirty-nine! To go."

"Am I allowed to ask a question?"

"Okay, but only if you must," she replies.

"What type of material are you sewing into my head?"

"Well, let's see, we had a choice of the following, polyester, polypropylene, polystyrene, catgut, nylon and silk. I guessed that if you had the choice of what I had to work with, you would have picked silk." Okay, soldier boy, the stitches are all done. Come back and see me in ten days and if you are in any pain, please come and see me immediately. She removes the gloves and mask and reaches into the coat pocket. She hands him a little container of painkillers. "Take a couple of these every four hours to numb the pain."

The vehicle is still there, and they have not received a parking ticket for abandoning the vehicle on the high street. Cha assumes the driving position, and Murray changes his shirt in the street before jumping into the passenger's side. He is handed a bottle of water, *oh yeah, the tablets.* He takes a couple and swigs them down with a couple of gulps of the water.

When he awakens, they are just about there. While Murray was napping, Cha had to drive around a few diversions. He notices that there are a couple of large boxes in the back. Cha notices him looking and informs him that she passed a couple of big army trucks and just had to have a look.

The entry barriers leading to the drop-off zone are down, but Cha just detours onto the gently sloping grass verge and avoids them all together. The 4x4 cruises to a stop opposite the terminal entrance. Cha reaches over behind her seat and hands him a bandoleer containing a multi-coloured selection of long curved magazines, and then reaches over again and pulls out a utility belt and one evil looking Machine-gun, all courtesy of her non-scheduled stop at the army trucks. Murray desperately needs to pee, so he goes to the rear of the 4x4 and pees over the back tire. His urine is stinking, "that's the adrenaline coming out of your system" When he is finished, he is handed a camouflage jacket. Mr Black looks at the sergeant's chevrons on the sleeve. The name tag reads Copeland 506368. Murray asks if he had been promoted. Cha stands to attention and salutes. "Well, Sir, not really, but enemy snipers are trained to take out the leaders first, so perhaps we should get a move on, sarge!"

Prior to entering the building, they agree to be cautious, especially after the last foraging adventure, which resulted in a small disagreement with the newly installed management of the supermarket. They ignore the car park. It is a short-term stay; it only contains about half a dozen vehicles sporadically parked across the enclosed tarmac. Surprisingly the revolving door still operates; Murray looks slightly perplexed until he sees the solar panels reflecting the last of the rays from the big yellow thing in the sky. The interior of the building is not in total darkness. This is due to the amount of special glass used in the construction.

They take their time, and following Cha's lead, they search everywhere, and there is no one to be found dead or alive. The duty-free section has had the metal shutters pulled down, and all that is visible are the shop names. Murray has a look at the display board and checks the key plan; all the shop names are listed as per their numerical order, and apart from maybe one of them fancy watches that you can purchase for the price of a modest family home, he does not think there is any merchandise that would take his fancy.

The airport must have been closed early. The terminal is empty, the trolley stand is neat and tidy, there are no dead bodies lying around, and this place is absolutely spotless. They hear a noise coming over from their left, ducking down behind some partitions in the nearest seating area. The noise they hear is getting closer. It's an old lady with a walking stick.

They stand up and make their way over to meet her, waving so as not to startle her. She must be about eighty years old. They say hello and introduce themselves; her name is Roberta Stevens, and she informs them that she is sixty years old. They ask her if she has seen anyone else. She informs them that she has not seen anyone for ages and then asks them if that is the shuttle from London has at last arrived. She has been trying the desk helpline, but the phone, just like the toilets, seems to be out of order.

Neither of them has the heart to tell her the truth that there will be no more shuttles from London today or any other day soon. She tells the pair of them that she is here to meet her son and family who are returning from Australia because it is too hot and has too many poisonous little beasties, "Can't even hang your bloody washing out, Margret is bloody petrified of being assaulted by one of the poisonous mountain frogs. You know the café is not even open. I have helped myself a few times to some of the food. If you see that manager guy, you make sure and tell him that I am no tealeaf and I have left some money on the counter and tell the bugger I want my change." They have some spare bottled water and snacks in the bag. They give her a selection for free and inform her that they will have a look about and see if they can get an update about her son's plane.

When they are out of earshot, Murray looks at Cha, who was staring at him in disbelieve when he was talking to the old lady, "What did you want me to tell her, sorry Roberta, Johnny Boy and his family are all dead, somewhere, and there are not going to be any planes for the foreseeable future, I just could not be that cold-hearted." One thing is for sure Roberta is the only one here, they search everywhere, and there is no one else to be found. The airport must have been notified and closed early.

"Okay, Sargent, let's go and check out the control tower." Murray can see it in the distance. It's about half a mile away. They walk and have some small talk; Cha's acquired a pair of military binoculars. They are in use, and she stops periodically and scans the surrounding area. Still, nothing was moving except a small flock of crows, gently moving with the breeze, sometimes moving their wings to change altitude or direction, other times just drifting aimlessly in and around the air currents. The tower is empty; again, no one has been in here for a while. He had never been in one of these buildings before, and the number of screens for something this size was quite formidable.

Murray thinks Cha has been in one of these buildings before, maybe not this one but something very similar. She is intently scanning the room, looking for something. He is playing with the control panels, flicking switches, turning dials and opening drawers. She is now opening cabinets and shifting things about. Murray moves around the room drifting from one operator's station to the next. The station he is at just now has got larger drawers and double sets; there is a stash of red and yellow crisps in the first one he opens, along with various notebooks and pens. He commandeers the food and puts them in the rucksack. The next one has an enormous pair of binoculars. The same sort of thing you see in old World War two movies where the guy with the white jumper is atop the sail on the submarine scanning the horizon for enemy ships and aircraft only to be straffed by machine gun fire from the plane attacking from the direction of the sun.

Mr Black was so busy with his burrowing into the desks that he did not hear Cha going out to the external viewing platform. He grabs his recent acquisition and goes out to join her. She is oblivious to his presence, intently scanning the runway. Standing beside her, he puts the extra-large size of binoculars to his eyes and joins her. "You really get an amazing view from here." She looks at him, directs his vision to the far left and asks him what he can see. Four smallish white aeroplanes, one red with the royal mail insignia and a truck with 'danger inflammable' emblazoned on the side.

The sun is starting to sink as they make their way back to the main terminal. The crows have gone now, and it is only them that are moving. They decide to stay the night here rather than travel home in the dark. Arriving back at the terminal, they unload the 4x4 and head in through the revolving door. Roberta is in the same place as they had left her, only this time, she is sound asleep, with a well-dog-eared copy of the monthly periodical lying open in her lap at the page displaying the title, dangerous frogs of South America.

Their kit is laid near her but not too close to startling her when she wakes up. Murray puts his sleeping bag over her to give her a little more warmth. Cha has set the map out on a table; using a couple of battery-operated camping lamps, she is intently looking at the map, calculating distances and measuring roughly with her fingers.

In the meantime, Murray has put a pan of water on the potable stove and searched for an extra cup for Roberta. He returns in perfect time; Roberta has just woken from her late afternoon nap.

"Tea or coffee, what is your poison?"

"I'll have tea, please, and do you have any of them chocolate biscuits with them birds that like to go fishing? My Johnny Boy loves these and tells me it is almost impossible to get them over there. I think that's why he is coming back, that and the poisonous frogs."

Murray makes the tea and helps her over to the table where Cha is calculating now on the white Formica table. When she is settled in, he goes and searches for some chocolate biscuits. If he brings her back the type she had asked for, she will stash them in her bag, keeping them for Johnny Boy.

The mini supermarket at the other end of the terminal has no doors, well none that are locked and the best thing about it is that there is no meat or fresh vegetable sections, shopping here is actually quite pleasant. They have a varible selection of chocolate biscuits on display. To be on the safe side, Murray takes a packet of each. When he arrives back, the girls chat like they have known each other for years. Roberta is in charge of the conversation. The biscuits are placed on the table. Roberta puts down her knitting, no doubt something for Johnny Boy and tells him that she does not like chocolate biscuits. She sips her tea, "So Cha, tell me about your eight brothers?' Murray looks at Cha behind Roberta's back, holding up eight fingers and holding them palm wards up. It's only when Roberta stops for a breath that Cha has the chance to hold her index finger to her head and rotates it horizontally to indicate that she thinks Johnny Boys' mum is fucking nuts. All this has put Murray off eating, and he escapes outside for a smoke and some fucking peace and quiet. Roberta can breathe through her arse, and Johnny Boy is probably unaware that she has escaped from the locked ward in a secure mental health facility. For the record, Murray would have walked to Australia if she was his mother.

When he thinks that enough time has elapsed and Roberta has fallen asleep, Murray goes back to the table. He looks at Cha and asks her why she did not tell him about her eight brothers. She looks Murray straight in the eye and tells him about the additional five sisters. They smile at this. Roberta is wrapped up in a sleeping bag, has another one rolled up like a pillow and is fast asleep.

Cha then starts to tell Murray about the plan for tomorrow, pointing at the map, "We are going to look for more people in the morning, and it is just not possible that this is all that's left. On full tanks, that plane can fly for at least four hours and point at the map, which means we can cover this area."

He leaves Cha pondering over the map and goes and does some duty-free shopping; if they are going to calculate any time, then they will need watches. The shutters are easy to open, and Murray returns with a selection of top-quality watches. There is even a spare one for Johnny Boy. He has acquired a selection of expensive cashmere overcoats, the type that you see people wearing indoors and never out in the rain. As Roberta had their sleeping bags, they had to sleep on something.

At breakfast, they manage to persuade Roberta to come with them and even to promise wholeheartedly to keep an eye out for the shuttle arriving from London. She would be very disappointed if she were not here when it arrived. He gave Cha her watch; it was a green expensive one, the exact same as his. Hell, he even got the same type for Roberta, but she told him it did not suit her.

They take their vehicle around to the area where they keep the small planes; it turns out to be the local flying club. The area is checked, and apart from one mangy cat, there is not a soul here. Cha has a walk about the planes trying to find one with a full tank, finally settling on one with twin propellers. The battery is dead, and the deal is that Murray

89

spins the prop, and she depresses all the buttons and levers. She is taking the piss once again, and he thinks that this is entertainment for her and Miss Stevens.

Murray connects the plane's battery terminals to the jump leads. Several attempts later, a belch of thick black smoke and the engines bursts into life. He opens the passenger door and directs Roberta up the boarding stairs. Cha comes out of the pilot's seat and helps settle her in with her knitting and the dog-eared monthly periodical. Cha has even managed to rig up a set of headphones so she can hear what they are saying, but the headphone set that she has been issued Roberta with the microphone mysteriously does not work.

The take-off is perfectly smooth, and the plane levels at about a thousand feet. In the co-pilot seat, Murray raises the binoculars that were borrowed from the air traffic controllers' desk, and anytime he thinks he sees something, Murray does his duty and informs the pilot. Roberta had cottoned on to this and has prodded Cha on the back of her head with a number four knitting needle every time she spots something that she thinks may hold their interest, so far it has been four scarecrows, a caravan park and mummy and daddy swan with their cygnets on a river. They have been flying in a grid section, searching the surrounding area like an owl quartering a field for its next unsuspecting victim, and they have seen no signs of life down below. One of his jobs is to mark the map in yellow highlighter every time they exhaust one area and move on to the next.

Roberta is now awake and terribly disappointed that there is no trolley service available and, therefore, no snacks or drinks. Cha receives another prod on the neck, and as they look in the direction that Roberta is pointing, they see a huge help sign with an arrow pointing to their right. The plane banks to the right and drops down to five hundred feet and circles for a closer inspection. On reaching the help sign, they look for signs of life. The first sweep reveals nothing. They are tempted to give up and go back to the airport but reconsider and go for a second pass. This time they see a guy on a roof waiving what looks like a couple of white pillowcases to try and attract their attention. Cha dips the wings to indicate that they have seen him. Murray marks the location on the map as the plane banks to the left, and they head back to the airport.

Cha touched his leg and pointed to the fuel gauge. It was time to go, banking to the left and increasing their altitude. They are headed back to the airport. It did not take long to find their bearings, and very shortly, the runway was in sight. Cha pulled a lever, initiating the humming of the hydraulic operation of the landing gear, followed by the clumping sounds of the wheel struts locking in position. Roberta clapped enthusiastically as the plane landed perfectly. The aircraft slowed, coming to a gentle stop at the terminal doors.

After disembarking, they headed back towards the tabled area. Daylight was slowly disappearing; they had decided to stay here tonight and would continue with the exploring at first light.

Cha and Murray set up the camping stoves and the required ingredients, making sure that Roberta approved the selection. Mr Black made his apologies to the ladies and was heading to the gents. Roberta wanted to go also, so Murray did his expected duty and gave her his arm and acted as her chaperone, escorting her to the toilet area. By the time they had reappeared, the dinner was ready, Murray had no idea what it was, but it tasted great. Roberta must have been starving as she ate it vigorously; adding a slice of bread and butter would have been nice to clear the plate. The girls were chatting away like two old friends over a cup of coffee, and Murray headed outside to smoke. When he returned pleasantly stoned, Roberta was fast asleep and snoring in the chair. They moved over to another part of the tabled area so as not to disturb her with the plans for tomorrow.

They made love that night. It was gentle and passionate, all that happened was an accidental brush of the hands, and that was it. They disappeared around the corner into one car hire kiosk not to disturb Roberta.

When he awoke in the morning, Cha was busy boiling water, and Roberta instructed her how to make the perfect cup of tea. Murray set about gathering all the gear that would be loaded into the 4x4. They informed Roberta that they were going to look for other survivors and invited her to come along, assuring her that if they saw the shuttle arriving, they would turn back immediately. She agreed, adding that due to her travel sickness that she would have to go in the front. After a quick breakfast, Murray started to load the vehicle, Cha must have been out here earlier as the storage area had been rearranged, no big deal.

Chapter Six

They headed towards the vehicle, Cha was walking tentatively with Roberta, who was clinging on to her as if they were negotiating a small perilous mountain track. Murray walked in front and smoked a cigarette while waiting for them.

He had nominated himself for the driving duties, and Cha sat in the back. They drove through the winding roads, only slowing down when required to negotiate around the abandoned vehicles. They had been in the car for about an hour when Roberta pulled a snub nose 38 from her bag, "Pull over, you hey jimmy bastard or I will put one in you right now," adding, "That, slanty-eyed bitch in the back should stay perfectly still and any sudden movement will result in your brains decorating the car." Murray slowed and pulled the car over; Roberta pulled a radio out of the bag. "Mama bear to Baby bear, I have two packages to collect. Proceed to collection point."

"Baby bear to Mama bear messaged received, and we are on our way."

The now prisoners were told to get out of the car; the gun never wavered and was pointed directly at Murray's head. Cha did not seem to be bothered in the slightest about this. Murray, on the other hand, thought that he should have worn the brown corduroy trousers. Cha stared at Roberta opening her clenched fist, releasing the bullets that were until recently residing in the revolver, and kicking her legs away. "I should have told you last night that while you were escorting Grandma-ma here, I had a look in her bag and found these." Roberta was actually quite a foul-mouthed monster, threatening them with all sorts of retribution, invoking promises of death and or dismemberment and, if they were really unlucky, possibly both, once her son appeared. This was reduced to an inaudible drone once the duct tape was applied firmly to her cesspit of a mouth.

Murray was instructed to tape her hands and legs. They bundled her into the car and reversed a hundred yards back up the road. This would give them a vantage point where they could see any oncoming vehicles. Cha went to the back of the car, opened the boot and reappeared with a jet-black sniper rifle, this one had a tripod arrangement at the front, and the bore looked like it was big enough to kill armoured-plated elephants. Putting the gun down, she looked Murray straight in the eye, putting her arms around and preceded to give him a passionate kiss. "Don't worry, Elvis, it will be okay," they had a cigarette while Cha gave Murray the plan as to what was going to happen.

The radio squawked into life; Cha motioned just to ignore it. Ten minutes later, they heard the sound of engines. A police all-terrain vehicle and what looked like a school minibus were approaching. As per his instructions, Murray hauled the evil Grandma-ma out of the 4x4 and, grabbing her by the over-dyed peroxide hair, forced her to her knees and placed the reloaded 38 to her head. Cha worked the bolt action and chambered a 50-cal. round. The radio squawked again, demanding that the prisoner be released immediately and that if they surrendered now, they would be treated fairly.

Murray pressed the transmission button on the radio and informed beloved Johnny Boy on the receiving end that unless they stopped their vehicles and got out with raised hands, that mama bear was getting it. The vehicles stopped about fifty yards away. They were six of them, the big one dressed in tweeds and a driver in one, three guys and a woman in the other. All were carrying weapons except the big guy. The big guy in the tweeds announced over the radio that his name was Mr Macdonald, and he was the sheriff, and they had to surrender immediately. On his cue, two of his guys started to move towards them. Cha adjusted the telescopic sight, which was almost the size of a television set and let loose a single shot. The guy in front's head exploded on contact with the bullet, all that remained of his head was an unrecognisable stump. The other members of the troupe, on seeing this, dropped their weapons and started to run away. Macdonald was red in the face and started jumping up and down, screaming at them to return.

"Last chance Macdonald, surrender, or Granny gets one in the head," realising that the game was up, he sunk to his knees and raised his hands. Murray approached, leaving plenty of room for Cha to shoot him should he try anything. On reaching him, Murray kicked him in the side of the head and cuffed him. The cuffs were procured from the contents of granny's handbag. Now that they had them safe and secure, Cha started asking questions. Question number one was not answered. The scope zeroed in on the departing troupe of escapees about half a mile into the field. The bullet decapitated the one in front. Question number two, no answer, another dead runner. This continued until all the escapees were no longer on this plane of existence. Murray stepped forward and pressed the .38 to the evil granny's head, "Start talking, big boy." Macdonald pleaded with them not to harm his mother and spilled the beans on his set-up.

Being a fully paid-up member of the head firmly stuck up the arse fraternity, Macdonald honestly believed that he was better than everyone around him. When the sickness appeared, he thought that it was his destiny that he should be in charge. He and mama bear had rounded up all the survivors they could find and convinced them that they would be better off under his rule. The ones that refused were forced to work.

Initially, Mr Macdonald was a little hesitant to reveal the location of their base. Cha poured water over mama and told him that his mother was going to burn if he did not comply. He confessed, informing them that the prisoners were locked in cells in the town's police station and armed guards patrolling it. Macdonald was cuffed and secured in the front passenger's seat, and mama bear was chucked on the floor in the back. It took twenty minutes to reach the town. They parked out of hearing range of the police station and quietly observed the situation through the binoculars.

They took turns to watch. It was two cups of tea and an hour later before they saw any movement. A no-smoking policy must have been in place, as the two guards had come outside for a cigarette break. They were perfectly relaxed and leaning against the wall; one produced a packet of cigarettes and offered them to the other. The bullet killed one before he managed to exhale the first drag of the cigarette; on this, the other one stood frozen in abject terror before the second bullet swiftly sent him to accompany his companion in the afterlife.

Driving to the police station, Macdonald was escorted through the door, revolver at his head. Cha took the lead in searching for the prisoners. Cautiously they enter the building, going slowly from room to room, checking that Macdonald has no hidden surprises awaiting their arrival. Once all the rooms were cleared in this corridor, they opened the double doors and came to a junction. Large red arrows point left and right, indicating holding cells and recreation facilities. Macdonald has gone quiet and is visibly shaken. They head straight towards the cells; their guest is dragging his feet, and it takes a few slaps to get him motivated enough to continue.

The door leading to the cells is locked, and the famous Black glare and their guest tells them where to locate the keys. Murray thinks that Macdonald has just shit himself, and a damp patch is slowly spreading on his tweeds. They unlock the main door to be greeted by a snarling almost albino Retriever, the dog is not interested in them, but by the snarling, she looks like she would really like to sink her teeth into Macdonald. Cha wants to shoot the dog, but Murray does not agree and tells her the dog will be fine. He asks Macdonald which key and number four comes out in a stuttering whimper. Murray goes closer to the gate, and the dog calms down, comes over, sniffs, and licks his hand. Animals have always liked him; it is just people that he had problems with. Murray has a left-over snack in his pocket, he offers it to the dog, and Murray thinks that he has just gained a new friend for life.

The first cell they come to is empty. Murray looks at the lock, then looks at Macdonald, who is whimpering in the corner, being outstared by his dog. He barely hears the number eight. Murray motions the dog over by tapping the side of his leg; she must have been well-trained and comes over straight away, rubbing her head on his leg. Cha shoves

Macdonald into the cell and locks the door. Cha looks at Murray and sees his glassy eyes talking to the dog, "No animal movies for you." Murray smiles and invites her over to introduce her to their new friend. By this time, they can hear subdued voices, and what they see shocks them to the core. There are four women in one cell, and ten guys cramped into another opposite at the far end of the corridor. Murray shouts out that they are here to save them and asks if anyone is sick and needs medical attention.

A lippy woman shouts out that they all need psychiatric treatment, but in the meantime, a cigarette would be greatly appreciated. Everyone bursts out laughing. Even the dog seems to relax. Murray has only a few remaining in his packet, which he gladly shares. He tells Cha that he is going out to the vehicle for a carton of cigarettes. She says no problem and starts trying the keys to open the cells. Murray returns with the evil granny, who is chucked into the cell that the women were secured in. She is still taped up and lies, moaning on the floor. He is just about to close the door when the dog squeezes in past and pees on her; Murray guesses that she just does not like the Macdonald's.

Every prisoner has a shaven head; the women look tired and worried and are still reluctant to say too much. The guys looked beaten, bruised and confused. They usher everyone into the canteen, and Murray and Cha take their time and assure them that they are not here to take over, emphasising that they are only doing the decent thing and informing them that they are all free to go. As it gets dark, they decide that they will leave in the morning. The stores are plundered, and everyone has a beer. Gradually, the ex-prisoners open up and tell their stories. They listen to them all. Suddenly the lippy one pipes up, "Anyone seen Leanne?"

She is located in the guard's recreation room, spread-eagled, naked and tied to a table. The lippy one informs them that as she was a non-breeder, Leanne had been selected for the guards' Friday night entertainment. Murray wants to go and castrate Macdonald; Cha tells him that she agrees whole heartily but now is not the right time. Leanne is released from her bonds; Murray leaves the room and lets the women take care of her. The other prisoners have removed the tatty overalls, showered and recovered their normal clothes from the storage room.

They are all starving and explain that they were never fed enough; Janet, the lippy one, takes over and sets about organising the evening meal. She has a cigarette permanently stuck in her lips and looks to be enjoying every drag. Murray asks her if the cigarettes are okay. She is about twenty-five years old, reunited with her normal clothes, which consist of skin-tight leather trousers, bright pink hi-tie boots, and a faux snow leopard skin jacket. She informs him that, at this present time, a joint would go down a treat. He just laughs and walks away. This neither puts her up nor down.

The meal is ready, Leanne is sleeping in the corner, and everyone is concerned about her. The bastards have been raping her at every opportunity. They assure everyone that they are no longer any guards left and they have nothing to fear. Eventually, the conversation arrives at the Macdonald's. Murray explains that even though he wants to go and kill the both of them, he has to empathise that the decision on their fate belongs to them and Cha, and he are not entitled to a say in this.

There is a bit of murmuring all around till Janet taps the teaspoon on the side of her glass, and everyone shuts up.

"The way I see it is that we should have a vote on this, no long debate with additional amendments, no secret ballet, just a straight yes or no."

Lots of nods move in unison, and an elderly guy asks, "What are your recommendations, Janet?" which receives, "Ah, for fuck's sake, you make me sound like the first minister." Janet takes a final drag and, after exhaling a long plume of smoke and suggests, "Perhaps it would be a good idea to ask Leanne as she has suffered the most."

"C'mon, guys. I am not in charge, Barry, you were a shop steward once. Organise the vote for tomorrow, and we will do it properly. Everyone is entitled to a say." The dog barks and, with a big smile, "Yes, even the dog is entitled to a vote," with this, everyone bursts out laughing.

"I don't know about everyone else, but I need a drink" more cheers erupted from the assembled throng of the ex-prisoners.

Murray and Cha had every intention of slipping quietly out the main doors and sneaking away unobserved, but when the recent captives got wind of this, they pleaded with them to stay the night and leave in the morning, reluctantly they agreed, and Cha, the dog and Murray slept in Macdonald's room. He was intent on going straight to sleep, but Cha had other plans. Sliding on top of him, she put her fingers to his lips, indicating that he was not in a position to refuse. The dog is lying by the locked door with her paws covering her eyes.

Morning arrives, and again he wakes up alone. Cha and the dog have vanished, reaching over to her side of the makeshift bed. It is still warm; there is no sign of any disturbance in the room, therefore no need to panic. Murray pulls himself together, and after all the necessary functions, he heads outside for some fresh air. The dog that is happily involved in playing fetch with Cha; spots him. Murray is not sure who is enjoying it the most. One is barking, and one is laughing. "No animal movies for you either." Propeller tail runs over and drops the newly acquired ball at his feet. Murray happily joins in the game. He tosses the ball over in

Cha's direction, and the dog playfully barks twice as she goes to retrieve it.

Cha's smile is infectious; it was not that long ago he had nothing to live for. Murray struggled for a while, fighting his inner demons, constantly asking himself, why me? Why am I still living when everyone he knew was gone? It was tearing him apart, and then Cha put a spark of life into him. Murray already owes this wonderful woman so much, and he would do anything for her. Murray reaches out and puts his arms around her, kissing her gently on the lips. Today she looks different. There is only a subtle difference, she has her hair tied back, and that's not what he is detecting. It is not a bad change. He is feeling something is just different, anyway, she looks fantastic, and Murray is over the moon that she actually likes him.

Cha tells Murray that as they are keeping the dog, they have not discussed this. It is just a foregone conclusion, as everywhere they go, the dog follows.

"The dog needs a name. I have been calling her Charlie, and she likes it" Murray hunches down and ruffles the dog's forehead, gently stroking the space between her ears.

"Well, Charlie, what do you think?"

The propeller tail syndrome answers his question. Murray looks at the T-shirt. Cha looked at him and said, "Janet gave me this as a present. She told me that it was her prized possession. It reads Hector the Reflector and the

Invincible Shortbread Giraffes world tour Govan 20. the last two digits are missing, but it's the thought that counts." Murray tells Cha that it suits her.

They return to the station and start to pack up all their stuff back into the vehicle. Heading to the canteen, they walk in in the debate in full swing.

"Why is she," the guy points at Leanne, "Even entitled to a vote, she is not one of us!"

This raised a fair bit of shouting from both sides of the camp. Janet and her pink doc boots walked over to in the blue and white football shirt and squared up to him. You had to give her full points for her bravado. The football supporter was about a foot taller and at least a hundred and twenty pounds heavier.

"Now you listen here. The old world is gone. There is no more green team, no more blue team, no church of this and no more church of that. There is only us, and who cares if Leanne is a Muslim? She has been through more than any of us, she is entitled to her say, and if you don't agree with this, you can fuck right off, right fucking now."

Number Eight backed down, visibly shaken. Janet was still in his face "have you forgotten to say something?" Eight says sorry to Leanne, and the mood of the room relaxes a little.

Leanne tells her story of how she ended up here and all the humiliation that she had endured. It was brutal, to say the least. "That bastard stole my virginity. Then his mother deemed me unfit to breed just because of the colour of my skin and then provided me as entertainment for the guards." Granny had worked a points system. The crueller the guard, the more points allocated, and whoever got the most points got to rape her first. Every orifice on her body has been violated.

The big guy in the football top approached Leanne, tears running down his face. "I am really, really sorry. I hope you can forgive me. I cannot apologise enough. What would you like done with the rats in the cells?" There was not a dry eye in the house. Leanne said only one word: "Death."

The approval was unanimous, and it was pointless having a vote. The Macdonalds were pushed, dragged and kicked out of their cells and led out to the front of the building. Granny's tape was removed, and the venomous words that came from her mouth would have embarrassed a sailor. Cha had enough and delivered a perfectly executed three-fingered clenched tiger claw jab to her throat. Grandma now lay still on the ground.

Mr Macdonald started to speak, "As you are all are aware, I am the last standing relation to the royal family, and I am destined by the hand of God to be in charge. By the authority invested in me, I demand that you release me

106

immediately and let me take my rightful place. I…" was the end of the speech, someone had chucked a rock, and it hit him straight in the mouth. That was it. The assembled crowd moved in on him and started to kick, punch him and beat him continuously with anything available: Murray saw an old piece of metal fence post being repeatedly jammed into his bleeding head. By the time they were finished, he was an unrecognisable heap of human garbage awaiting the flies and dogs to disassemble his carcass. Someone produced a meat cleaver and, assisted by another, removed grandma's head which was now being kicked around like a football.

They were ready to go now and started to say their goodbyes, give them their very best regards, and wish them all luck. They bump into the guy who no longer has the blue football top on. It had been replaced by a T-shirt advertising some Italian resort for the rich and famous. You could not help but feel a little sorry for him. His parents had named him after the full 1971-72 European cup winners' team. What abuse he must have received growing up. He was called Sandy for short and was engrossed in attending to Leanne's immediate needs. He informed them that her real name was Mia, and she was pregnant, and he would do everything possible to take care of her and ensure to his last breath that the baby was born in a safe non-bigoted environment. Murray asks Mia if she is okay, and she says, "Yes." Adding, "I hope Mr Macdonald and his mother are in hell sucking dead dogs' cocks where they belong." There was not really a lot that they could say to this. Cha and Murray wished all the best and bade them farewell.

There was one last job to do. It took them about half an hour to track Janet down. She was sitting in MacDonald's office, perfectly relaxed, stretched out in his big swivel chair stretched out with her boots on his desk. Cigarette in one hand and a small bottle of beer in the other. The door was open, but Murray knocked anyway. "Sorry to disturb you, but I have a parting gift for you." He hands her the matchbox and a couple of packets of skins. By the look on her face, you would think she had just been handed the keys to heaven. Janet rattled a number together quickly, sparking it up, exhaling with the clicking of her jawbone, producing several perfectly formed smoke rings, poking the joint through dissipating rings. She had a few drags and offered it to Murray. He accepted. "Hmm, that was nice; not had anything that nice for ages. All of us can't thank you enough for what you have done."

Murray was thinking that he was going to be offered a T-shirt, but it never appeared. He was going to ask about the band's name emblazoned on the shirt she had given Cha, but he thought better of it and left it alone. They tell her that they are off and wish her all the best for the future. She informs them that most of the ex-prisoners were going to hang about for a couple of days and when they were fully used to being free, they would probably go their separate ways.

They were back on the road again; Charlie was in the back. When they were several miles away, Cha asked Murray to stop. The vehicle slowly came to a halt. He had activated the lever to indicate that they were pulling over. She looked at Murray as if he was nuts, "Sorry old habits," Raising his hands up in surrender; She just smiled. Getting out of the 4X4, she jumped in the back seat with Charlie and removed the heavily studded collar. Charlie approved with a single bark, a wag of the tail and a lick; the now redundant collar was chucked in the adjacent field, another bark of approval.

***

The nightmares are long gone and just about totally erased from his memory bank. Murray sees Linda in his dreams; they are full of colour and so realistic that he absorbs every frame, picture by picture. Linda was his sun and moon, Murray had never ever imagined what it would be like without her: sure, they had their moments, but the great times significantly outweighed the bad times. They had never passed the buying little surprise presents for each other stage, and every day before he went to work, Murray would look at her sleeping and think she was wonderful and cursed no one in particular for having to go to work in the first place.

The room his universe had died in had been gutted, cleaned, cleaned and cleaned again, but Murray could not summon enough courage to go near the door, never mind cross the threshold. He always was under the impression that she was resting; Murray knew that she was dead, but sometimes, no disrespect intended, he had been seriously thinking of sealing the place off, just bricking up the whole lot, not out of badness, just the right thing to do. The dreams used to have voices and background noises: the works, but recently the volume is submerging into a tide of sounds transforming into a barely inaudible hum.

There is a change happening to him. He really does not know what it is but a change never the less. This thing with Cha is not just a sex thing, sure! The sex is great. It's a connection, not a positive/negative chalk/cheese balance but more like equals. Now that he remembers, a while back, they were discussing what they should and should not be doing. Murray explained the local weather seasons. They had two: damp and cold and damp. They were several months away from entering the latter. Cha produced the pens and paper, and they both jotted down all the things that should be prioritised. The lists, apart from Murrays grammatical mistakes, were identical. The quantities listed, even the sequential order of the materials required. Murray thought, at the time, she had been cheating and had somehow managed to get a quick swatch at his scribbles. This was not too far-fetched considering her previous vocation.

The clever bastards with the Theoretical Digital Brain logistical department or whatever the fuck it is called would write an epic paper on theoretical microbiological theoretical protein DNA strand micro-reassembled plasmatised proteins, and the multiple entered, multiple lettered unfucking pronounceable words that they were really just guessing at in the first place.

Murray thought it could be the smoke, but as of late, he has not really been too bothered about it. He still has the odd one, but even that is turning into a rare event. The sensation is ceaseless, not an uncomfortable incessant continuation but more like A, B and C. You just know the next one. Normally he is pretty deep and not very good at showing anything, including emotion. Murray struggled with the fake "Pleased to meet you," shaking lots of hands and sycophantic smiles! And avoided compulsory after-hours work events for years, eventually getting a doctor's certificate recommending a dispensation stating he had a serious hand infection. Murray just can't fake it. He just can't, and pretending is off the menu.

They have been driving a while; Charlie has developed a fondness for sticking her nose as far out the slightly open window as possible. Cha has been dozing and now is just starting to stir. The journey back is almost complete, and to be honest, he could do with a good wash. She asks if he has stopped for a break, and Murray tells her, "No, I thought I'd just let you sleep."

"Hmmm, that was nice."

The rucksack at her feet was rifled for eatables, and she scoffed two packets of cheese and onion crisps. Charlie was pretty miffed at not being invited to the tasting session and turned her head away, pretending to sulk. If it had not been for the fallen tree, they would have arrived home before dark. Murray stopped the engine, and they checked the house for any signs of uninvited guests. Charlie was more than happy to perform the sniff and piss routine. The bare minimum was unpacked, and they set about bringing the house back to life. Once resuscitated, Murray volunteered to cook but was firmly rebuffed with a "You wash, I cook." He is human again and has even managed to shave without leaving the impression that he had used a grinder; he was really shit at shaving. Cha had told him ages ago, "Hey, Elastoplast face. Try shaving with your eyes closed." Murray had finally given in and tried it. No more red streaks on the towels.

The meal, he thinks, was fish, potatoes and some other things that were a mixture of animal, mineral or vegetable. His plate had one refill. Hers had two. Beer supplies were low. He was going to mention it, but the food list on the recently installed whiteboard had already been updated, the addition for the beer marked out in capital letters in bold red. They discussed the oncoming changes in the seasons and agreed they should find somewhere else to stay. As much as Murray loved this place, he fully understood the dangerous implications involved if they did not. They had about eight weeks to restock and search. Cha had fallen asleep mid-conversation. Murray covered her up with a blanket and tidied up. Rather than disturbing her, he just curled up in the chair opposite.

As usual, the smart-ass had gotten up before him. It must have been long ago as she was washed and changed. Her skin shone like porcelain.

"Hi, baby. Sorry, I just zonked out. I'll make up for it tonight," winking, she put the breakfast on the table. Cha informs him that she no longer wants to sleep alone and that they should start looking for a new dwelling today. Their maps are fairly limited, so they do it grid by grid. Some days turn out to be just another fruitless search, returning with a little reward for their efforts. Charlie loves these adventures, and as soon as her door is opened, she's off, never venturing too far out in front but sniffing at every opportunity. The hackles have been displayed a few times recently, and to their relief, it was a cat, a dead paper bag and a discarded tyre.

Chapter Seven

Their journeys are always via the largest supermarket in the area, and they concentrate the pillaging in the main warehouses so as not to advertise their presence: but they realise that they can't live on cans alone and have to supplement their diet with the odd bit of hunting. When it comes to shooting, Murray is the active shooter Cha works as the spotter and informs him every once in a while, that he is improving, adding that before he asks, that he is nowhere near ready to try the .50 cal. Murray gets most of what he attempts to shoot with the shotgun; his rifle skills still require some adjustments luckily his tutor is very patient and when Murray misses, Charlie looks at Cha with one ear up, the other one down with her head slightly tilted to the side.

The cleaning and the inspection of the weapons are down to Cha, Murray has never had his rifle pass her inspection; there is always something that requires correction. The 50 cal. is a monster and he watches as she breaks it down, click, turn, click, twist, and turn. Each item is cleaned with that cloth, gently rubbed with this oil, and "When you are looking at this part you must look out for the following signs" by the time, she had finished reassembling the weapon Murray had been told everything, the speed of the projectile, the curvature of the Earth, what the various coloured tips were used for, the range, etc. Without really thinking he asks how much this would cost in old money: "The price of three detached family homes and some change should cover it."

They try their hand at fishing. Murray thinks that he is much better at shaving. The traditional rod and reel method is not proving very successful, they achieve much better results by just leaving baited hooks overnight and returning in the morning to check the lines. Since they had started sleeping in the same bed, Murray has not dreamed of Linda. Charlie sleeps at the top of the stairs, occasionally disturbing the still of the night with her tail going ten to the dozen chasing rabbits in her sleep.

The search has been on going now for about a month and bingo, Murray thinks that they have found the place; unbelievably it is an old watermill. The location is well off the beaten track. The grade two listed building has undergone some restoration work, sadly the work is incomplete and daylight is visible through some of the lower and upper floor ceilings. It is repairable but it will take time. Cha agrees that it is perfect, although there was not a chance of completing repairs before winter and all they can do is survey the complete house. Charlie likes it here: running up and down the stairs barking at anything and everything. Eight bedrooms, two dining rooms, a large reception room, a coal Shute to the basement, and a large kitchen. The biggest job is the roof everything else will be manageable after that.

The outbuildings are mostly full of rusting old junk and all will need to be cleared. They come to the outside entrance to what was to be the waterwheel-driven generator. The majority of the original workings had been replaced, the inverter and the generator had been stripped and it would need to be completely rewired. Murray used to make some of these units at work so he is confident that they could be battery-free in the future.

Charlie has decided that she is going to settle down on the first landing, grabbing her blanket she swings it this way and that way until she times it down to the last millisecond with a partial release it is transformed into tonight's makeshift wraparound nest. The reception room has an open ceiling extending up through to the rafters. In the corner, a small fire emanates the sound of the sticks reaching full flame. They are too tired to cook and share what is left in the snack bag, Cha has been munching non-stop lately. Murray gets the last remaining chocolate bar; she has the nuts, the energy bars, and most of the water.

The jazz band are blasting it out big time; the tune used by strippers all over the planet is loud and clear, his eardrums are shocked into submission as the alarm clock slowly increases in volume and refuses to stop until Murray depresses the self-destruct button. He is being prodded gently and as he is not responding quickly enough, he receives a more pronounced poke in the ribs, "Come on honey, wakey-wakey!' It's Linda and she playfully pushes him out of the bed. Murray switches on the light, walks over, and terminates the strip-tease tune which is now playing at maximum volume.

Linda is sitting up, "Wow honey, you look like you have just seen a ghost, you're not a having a whitey? are you?' Murray is several shades lighter than Peely Wally and goes over and touches Linda's hands and face, she is real, this is real, her hands are now holding Murray's face and she is looking into his eyes. "You sure look like shit, just take the day off, once in your working life will not do you any harm!"

Murray mumbles something incoherently and heads for a bathroom; his eyes are closed firmly as he shaves in the shower, the temperature he automatically turned up to be as warm as possible. Once Murray is fully convinced this is real, he has a quick blast of cold. Opening the bathroom door, he asks "What day is this?"

"It's Friday, numbnuts, and don't you be forgetting that you promised that you will not come back pished tonight and for just this fucking once, I mean how many times have you made that same promise and staggered through the door, maybe just once, we could be a normal couple and have a normal Friday night." Murray was now sorry that he had asked but the dream is still whizzing through his head and he replies, "I have changed my mind and I am not going, I want to spend it with you, you are right in what you say." At this

Linda is now out the bed and standing naked in front of him, Murray is mesmerised by her breasts they are perfect, and her arms are folded over them deliberately blocking his view. "Are you shitting me?" "Straight up, no." Murray explains that he had thought about it for a while and asks her what she would like to do tonight and makes a point of asking her how she is feeling.

Linda looks at him, "Are you on something?" Murray assures her that he is not and has just decided that it is time to grow up a little and that he promises to do better. "Murray the flattery is great but you better get to work or you are going to be late." He takes her in his arms and kisses her on his way out the door.

The drunk is still in the doorway, he presses the buzzer, surrenders his ID to the scanner, and faces the camera, "Good Morning, Murray Black 892178" static fills the line only to be replaced with "Fuck off," as the barrier is released.

The growing mountain of paperwork is ignored and he switches on the T.V. Pointing the remote like a phaser as he bleeps through the current news programmes, feeling like a total twat. *"And here is Morag with today's regional and national weather forecast..."*

The premises are starting to come alive: Wrightson's & Sons, Mechanical & Engineering Works limited which has been in operation since 1924. The shop floor is yet another non-smoking area but he lights up one all the same. An apprentice approaches; coerced into this by some of the older guys, "Is it okay if we smoke also?" Murray surrenders his packet of cigarettes and walks out the door.

The phone conversation with Linda was quick, Murray faked the 'was I meant to bring something home tonight?' question but he was just performing a reality check, reassuring himself that she was well. His brain was not in overdrive, he thinks it was in hyperdrive. Murray checks the news channels again, and the correspondent on American news reports that due to the collapse of the various digital currencies the USA has tabled a motion to offer the dollar as a viable worldwide currency, the offer includes guaranteed annual growth over a... The camera goes back to the local news presenter, "We are sorry, presently we are having a technical issue with the previous report and hand you over to the sports news with Morag." "Today the management of the two main football clubs from Glasgow issued a rare joint statement supporting FIFA's complaints and subsequent fine against the SFA. The remote control is now set on kill..." he switches off the TV.

Wrightson is on the phone; on the receiving end of another batch of incessant complaining, the high-pitched yelp is clearly audible even at this distance. He slowly puts the phone down, before he can say a word. Murray apologises for not knocking before he entered. "I was thinking that it was time I got more involved in the client stuff, I know I have been there before, Linda and I had a good talk last night and I think it is time I manned up." Murray coerced him into agreeing that going home would be a fantastic idea and he would go in his place to the Future Engineering Presentation. Murray assured him, that he would check that the place was all locked up. Not taking no for an answer Murray purloined Wrightson's invitation as he escorted him out of the office to his car.

They were ambushed by Mrs Petra Primrose from reception, Murray fobbed her off, not interested in the piffle that was going to emanate from her gob. "Please give me two minutes and I will give you my undivided attention," Instantly regretting his choice of words, with her hands on the hips, adopting a stance like she was the most important person in the universe, Primrose exhaled a slow measured breath. Wrightson was gone he found Mrs Primrose and instructed her to gather all the supervisors. Murray did not make any excuses nor give any explanations, "Wrightson's away for the day, everyone can go at lunchtime, don't clock out and leave the keys on my desk."

The hotel car park was adorned with various billboards advertising Futures wares and shares. Murray was a little early and headed for the bar. The rancid-sounding upmarket coffee cost him a tenner, he sat outside smoking, the drink arrived and was ignored. With the thank you all for attending, the sycophantic applauding, and smiley welcome speeches over, Murray watched the guests from the various companies being introduced to the latest technological advances that can exponentially increase profits.

He leaves the bar and presents the invitation that he had purloined from Wrightson's desk. Murray explained the Managing Director had been called away on an unforeseen family emergency and proffered apologies. He explained that as the Engineering Manager, he is more than interested in the advertised technological advances. Searching through one of the Future Engineering brochures, surprisingly Bong Cha is not listed in the directory of available experts. Pretending to be engrossed in the brochure Murray wanders from stall to stall. Asking technical questions and getting in turn facts and figures based on manufacturing capacity, cross-referenced with investment parameters. A quick projection was composed, and the highlighted figures compared showed all the mostly positive advantages. It outlined the minimum investment and all the services included. Additional services were outlined for further investment and with that a custom-built factory was available and the government was offering substantial funding grants for projects involved in the urgently needed reinvestment in the country's endangered engineering industry. Business cards are exchanged and Mr Black was informed to expect a revised copy of the projected figures to share with the board of directors.

There is a demonstration-taking place describing the new CNC machine code that is about to revolutionise the manufacturing industry. The tag on the jacket is ignored as is the large digital display is showing all applicable areas of the enhanced programmes. Graphs and charts are being cross-referenced to and compared, but not that long ago, that voice.

Hovering around, joining the post conversations. Murray manages to bump into her, apologising for being so clumsy. He relates to her facts and figures quoting her script word for word. The props are great, a big dark-framed pair of glasses, the hair flattened, parted to the side, the little demure walk, all the pens, badges and he has to admit she looks the part. Murray does not know who she is meant to be, but she barley looks like Cha. They walk over to the wall-mounted displays, he is handed a card: Ms Sun Yak Lee Chang: Senior Mechanical and Electrical innovation Officer: a phone number, several mobile numbers, and an email address. On the flip side the same only in the lingo he takes as to being her indigenous language.

She is standing close to him; she uses the clasped glasses as a pointer. "Yes, Mr Black we have an undeniable connection and as of last night my homeland has been uncontactable." Opening pages, the glasses are back on; momentarily in Murray's head, she is sitting reassembling the fifty cal.

122

"There is nothing here for you, you should go home." The reference manual is closed and the Innovation officer is intending to head towards the next potential client wanting a customised projection and the bottom line is how many employees could he permanently dispense with. The references manual is opened and closed again and the innovation officer tells him, empathically that he should go home, with a curt nod she walks away.

His mobile is now showing a low power warning with a full bar and is now fluctuating with an on-and-off signal. He calls home and it rings and dies; "We are experiencing some technical difficulties with the network in some areas, please try again later." The car is abandoned in the drive, Linda is up and about. The TV is on and she is playing with the remote, all that is up on most channels is we are experiencing network problems blah, blah, blah, and the national broadcasting company has a big blue screen, declaring that normal operations will resume as soon as possible.

Linda is a big daytime TV fan and is so disappointed that she will miss her favourite show and it's the disgust of the programme makers and the leading participants that truly revolt her. These people have trawled humanity and coerced these poor souls into portraying people that they are not at all like and the really sad, sad reality of it is that some people actually believe it all is true and with the phone, "our helpline" they have been generously donating to the company coffers at £2.50 a minute, "Please hold you, are number twenty-seven in the cue and an operator will be with you as soon as possible, thank you for holding."

"Are you feeling, okay?" Linda looks at him.

"Yeah I am fine, no problem"

Murray volunteers to go and stick the kettle on. Polka dots are the theme of this kitchen and they have the polka dot tea-cozy; which covers the polka dot teapot, which is a perfect match for the polka dot mugs. While the brew is masking, he goes outside for a cigarette. The resident Robin looks a little worse for wear and tear. A soon-to-regret challenger to the throne has been, chased, pecked even shit on by the resident little monster and he still has the audacity to sing a full volume, no doubt celebrating retaining his territory, especially after another victorious assault on the young pretender.

He delivers the tea, "It's okay Murray if you want to go to that get-together with your mates, I honestly don't mind, I was a bit harsh and you can go, it's okay." He explains to her –*okay* he lies to her that he had phoned the guys up and already has confirmed that he was unable to attend, adding that there is no place he would rather be than with her, right here, right now.

"Stop Murray," smiling and shaking her head. "I think if you don't stop this, I'm going to be sick" Murray surrenders and pretends that he is once again engrossed in the crossword. The big black screen on the wall was still showing we will get back to you as soon as possible messages when, Linda emerged from the bathroom, blowing the air out from a slightly protruded bottom lip to try and remove the hair partially covering her face. Murray reaches over and gently assists with his finger. Linda puts her hand to her mouth to stifle a small cough. "Don't start it is nothing!" it is not a full-blown snarl but he backs off and gives her some space. The PC has fired up but all he has displayed is the news page that won't open and a jumbled explanation that is unable to connect with the server. The landline has just the continuous engaged tone no matter how many times he presses the kill button and redials.

Murray finds her in the room, she looks like shit but still manages "Okay smartass, I am feeling a wee bit off today, please just get me the sick bucket and I will tell you if I need anything else, Thanks, baby." Returning with the bucket, complying with her wishes and he only returns, periodically to empty the green puke. After what seems like forever, she has stopped retching, he bathes her face and gently dries it. Murray hears a faint, "You should still go out tonight, I will be okay." He tells her that she is his sun and moon and without her, there is nothing and all the other nice things that he should have told her over the years but never did. She mouths the word, "wanker!" and falls asleep. Murray has a violent coughing fit and just about manages to make it through the bedroom door, clutching his stomach, writhing in pain vomiting on his feet, and the walls and he is fully aware of starting to black out and heading for an imminent crash landing on the floor.

Murray is awake; well, he thinks that he is awake. His eyes are open and he is working out where he is located. His toes are slowly regaining some feeling and when he is able to operate all his stiff limbs and aching muscles as gently as possible, Murray carefully unglues his head from the carpet. Sitting up, Linda is dead and Murray is still as gutted as the last time. Every visible orifice on Linda is now enveloped in the green slime which has congealed and hardened. Sobbing like a five-year-old, Murray wallows in self-pity, banging his head off the wall. Eventually, he starts to calm down and makes moves to tidy himself up. First, he wants to smoke, the soiled clothes he had on were discarded, and a trail leads to the kitchen, Murray grabs a couple of items from the work clothes pile and all that he has on now are the once-famous rock band faded tee shirt that was been washed so frequently that the emblazoned logo has faded into obscurity and equally dull indiscernible boxer shorts. He manages to spark up, exhaling, thinking nothing about anything, just smoking.

The shower is lukewarm going on to turning cold when he emerges, clean shaved and all signs of the puke removed, it was everywhere. A couple of patches of missing hair, plus some additions of colourful carpet fibre, and feeling almost human. He gets dressed, smokes, and smokes some more. The 750 twin motorcycle is outside the driveway at the junction ready to join the main single-track yet-to-be-named road, having been completely checked, a spare petrol tank secured on the back of the seat. The other petrol tank in view is empty just like the others and has been splashed throughout the house; all the windows and doors have been deliberately left open. Whoosh! The house goes up in flames. He closes the gate, and Murray and the motorcycle high tail it out of there not looking back. The roads are empty and surprisingly he does not ride like a madman; it is a steady ride with no surprises. Craig Wrightson is located just where he had expected to find him, Ignoring the note. Lifting the side stand, he noticed yet another leak, as Murray kicked her back into life.

There is no immediate sign of Ms Sun Yak Lee Chang: Senior Mechanical and Electrical innovation Officer or whatever the fuck she was going to call herself today, but he has to look. The hotel is devoid of all signs of life; everything is as he remembers it, everything that is, except Cha. Lots of Future Engineering glossy brochures and a few in-your-face advertisement boards. Murray checks her room and it has been left tidy. Even the empty crisp packets have been folded into little neat triangles before being placed in the bin. A message with bright red lipstick has been finely scripted on the bathroom mirror, Watermill Cha.

The crash helmet is now attached firmly back onto his head. Murray tries to kick the bike into life, she gives in on the second attempt and he takes off, for a few seconds he slows, pulling in the clutch, selecting neutral, and applying a little of the brakes, as he reaches his brother's house, but changes his mind at the last minute, revs up, drops the gears and leaves. As soon as he can, Murray opens her up again, they do a close 95 never quite consummating the courting couple relationship.

The road to the grade 2 listed building is just exactly as how he remembered it, Murray has just slowed down and skidded to a halt at the main entrance. Killing the engine, persuading down the kickstand, and in the process of removing his helmet, Cha comes out to meet him.

Murray is struggling big time with what he is supposed to be saying, doing, and feeling, and Cha sensing Murray's profound initial confusion puts her arms around him and playfully bites his lips. He is no better off at this, but the swiftly delivered kick to his block and tackle hits the spot and Murray folds instantly to the ground. "What the fuck did you do that for?!" He barely managed to sputter out the words while clutching his family planning unit. "We are not going to have you wallowing about in a state of perpetual, pitiful self-loathing and you are one way or another, going to snap out of this multigenerational, encompassing traditional Scottish trait and get back with the fucking programme! I know you have many questions, as do I: but really what the fuck do you really want me to tell you, I know as much as you do and I'm sorry about your balls." Murray was sorry that he had asked the question in the first place.

The apology is accepted and Cha helps him up. She hands him a lit cigarette as he takes a seat. Looking at his hair she tells Murray that she likes what he has done with it, he nods indicating the same about the house, not quite fully recovered enough yet to speak normally. Leaving him to recuperate, she returns with tea, beer, and a can of that expensive last man on the planet with added ingredients that allegedly can help you cheat an international medical test. He drinks all three. She tells Murray her side of the story and she also confesses that she had the same dream, real, as it was a dream, only a dream. "We could discuss this for days on end never achieving a conclusion and unmasking the hows and whys to all our questions. What is important is that we are here."

Realising that she, as always, is correct. Murray settles and relaxes a little. Taking his hand, she says, "Come on white boy, let me show you what I have done with the place," slapping his arse to move it. Some of the fires had been set, the ones that were still burning were drying the place out, and the other dampened remnants indicated that the chimney needed to be swept.

A new sleeping area had been set out, undressing and then rolling on top of him, she told Murray that they can talk about it later. "Morning handsome!" was his wake-up call, as she quickly dressed. Following her to the kitchen Murray caught the cigarette packet with one hand and the pair of denims with the other. Naked as the day he would die, his block and tackle are partially energised, Murray had just plain forgotten to get dressed. He pulls on the trousers and pulls on a cigarette.

After the search and rescue mission for his remaining clothes, Murray finds her at the table, breakfast is ready. He still has not got the foggiest idea of what he is eating but he has two plates full. She has one. Before anything is said between them Murray declares, "I am okay" reaches for his tea, and reaffirms, "We are good, no problems."

Mr. Craig Wrightson the second has been removed unceremoniously from the building. His legs were broken the quick way, wrapped in an old tarpaulin, and treated like he was precious cargo; secured firmly on the bed of the roads department truck along with the digger and the generators. Murray had thought about the coffin but did not want to disturb him from his plasticised slumbers. The digger scraped the ground and Wrightson is now resting near his loved ones. Murray had his goodbye note in his pocket, £2.58, and no washers. He handed Cha the one-pound coins to chuck in and he wrapped the note with the change and dumped it. The grave was covered, Murray said a few brief words of condolence and they left.

It takes a fair amount of time for them to unload the small temporary generators. They are placed in positions around the house where they think that they will be most appreciated. The industrial hire types are left till the morning. One of the small generators is hooked up and it is so fucking noisy that it has to be switched off. The battery lamps are fine for now. Murray's offer to cook is treated with contempt and utterly ignored and he is handed a .22 rifle to clean. Gathering all the kits required. Cha ignores him totally as he cleans with this cloth. Always, check this piece closely looking for signs of… Thinking nothing of it he places it in the corner.

Dinner is ready, some tin of meat, rice, and a sauce. Murray has his usual double helping and she has one. He is allowed to help tidy up; they have tea and she wants to inspect the rifle. Murray hands it over and the small magnifying torch is shone here and the strobe light is operated there. The rifle is handed back with congratulations.

Returning from walking and talking outside they plan for tomorrow. "I was serious I do not want to sleep on my own," as she gently pushes him to the bedroom. Murray is not allowed to sleep; he is not allowed to refuse. He remembers to put his clothes on before arriving for breakfast. Midafternoon they have unloaded everything, and the industrial units have been positioned where they will be required. They are now out hunting, Murray is the active shooter and she is the spotter, today he misses nothing. They have acquired enough hot water for a bath and Murray gets sloppy seconds. No complaints. This place is perfect, the newly reconfigured water supply is in operation and now they have good, clean running water. The heating system requires a major overhaul but gradually the house is becoming more habitable every day. The local building merchant yards have been visited and they have slowly worked their way around and have stocked up on the building essentials required for the repair list that is growing arms and legs on a daily basis. This next yard is located near the supermarket that introduced them to the baseball fan and his mates. They decide to be cautious, and arrive after the small detour via the abandoned army trucks; this time Murray gives Cha a hand to transfer the containers into their vehicle.

Chapter Eight

Unseen they arrive at the supermarket, taking position behind one of the burnt-out cars, Cha blends into the background. The one with the long straggly hair appears from the badly vandalised doorway and straggles along walking, the feet splayed out at the ten to two position the shoulders swinging at half speed, walking as if he owns the planet. His legs give way beneath him as the black blade slits his throat while her other hand clamps his mouth to curtail his attempted screaming. The remaining three amigos are located in the newly converted, drink, sleeping, garbage room and three bursts from the suppressed semi-automatic machine gun laid them to rest.

The yard they had located was massive it had all the poles, boards, and fittings that they would ever need. Everything is loaded to the maximum and even though they used one of the yard's trucks it still takes several trips more than envisioned to accumulate all the required items. Time was disappearing quickly, the days rolled into weeks before they decided to visit the airport. Murray was allowed to cook that night, he does not know what it was called as the labels were missing. Murray ate most of it and Cha had half a plate full, but at least she never spat it into the sink. She, however, did say something in Korean it could have been *"that was delicious honey"* but most likely when translated it would be something similar to *"she would rather kill herself, by jumping off the tallest building she could find, rather than eat that dross again."*

Their vehicle was stashed in some overgrown scrubland. From the vantage point, they were surveying the airport. Grandma-ma, oh how sweet Grandma-ma was dropped off about eight o'clock in the morning and uplifted by two of the thugs any time after three. On further observations at various locations, it was duly noted that there were: nine bad guys, four women, and ten guys being held captive. It's ten the next morning when they arrive at the airport and meet a lovely old lady who informs them, that she is waiting on the shuttle with Johnny Boy and his family arriving home from Australia, where you get all them poisonous mountain frogs. They patiently go through the various acts of her performance; they don't think the grand finale was going to end catching her red-handed going through their stuff and calling them in on the previously exposed hand-held radio.

At first, she vehemently denied any skulduggery and tries to sell the idea that they would like it, they would be taken care of. That was until they had heard quite enough of her spiel and her bag was unceremoniously emptied revealing the .38 and the foul-mouthed Granny that they had dearly missed instantly reappeared.

"You slanty-eyed two-faced disease-ridden bitch and you are nothing but a fucking bead rattling hey jimmy immigrant bastard." The duct tape was applied quickly and all other noises she made were only understood by her and her alone.

The play went as scheduled, Mr .50 cal. was assisted by his multi-coloured little helpers and as expected they stole the show. thump! One guy: headless, thump! Another guy in the field separated from his head and arms, Thump! Thump! Thump! Johnny Boy Macdonald and Mummy Dearest were wrapped up nice and secure and dumped in the borrowed school bus. Murray had the dubious pleasure of driving it to the area that they had reconnoitred. Murray had been banned for life from cooking, but he was proudly still the Numero Uno at making tea. Today's selection was a traditional Scottish mix that you can drink anytime you want, they take turns to watch for movement at the police station. During her break in delft movements, Cha gave Mr .50 cal. a pedicure, during Murray's break he had a joint. He had eventually wiped-out Linda's secret stash and took their much unknown and positively uncertain future into consideration. Murray had done his duty and returned to his brother's house, retrieving all the available supplies and biding his baby brother a final farewell Murray silently went through several happy childhood memories before setting the house on fire.

They were on their third cup of tea; someone had scoffed all the biscuits out of the stash. All Murray can locate is the resealed type of nutritional energy bars that are almost impossible to open never mind eat, so he starves. At this, he hears the bullet being chambered and Thump! the first guy is decapitated a small section of him trying to escape through the rough hole in the wall. Thump! the last guy was too shocked to move and was rigid with fear, wetting his pants when the last bullet removed his leg.

The state-of-the-art, American-made sniper rifle was partially dismantled and sent to sleep in the custom-made case. Cha handed Murray a semi-automatic to take with him on the bus. "Tap, tap, click, slip, pull" She nodded. Parking at the police station they ignore the pile of flesh and head straight for the cells. Charlie was immediately released from her chain and studded collar. She crawls as low as she possibly can and whimpers with her ears fully back at Cha, Murray gets a bark, a sniff, and a big wag of her tail. The gobby one that's wishing she was wearing her Hector the Reflector and the Invincible Shortbread Giraffe tee shirt is startled to be handed a goodie bag. Her cell door is unlocked. Leaving the keys in it, Charlie leads the way and they escape.

Janet surveys the contents, a carton of cigarettes, several packets of skins, and one zip-locked plastic bag containing several ounces of top-quality weed. "Right, you lot let's get these doors opened I have it on good authority that the MacDonalds are patiently awaiting your presence outside." She let them get on with it, rolled a big one, and was exhaling a single smoke ring when the screams of the MacDonalds being ritually decapitated reached her, her thoughts were a fitting end to a truly despicable family.

As they were not going to make it home before dark. Cha pulled a short cut and they settled in the old chemist's shop for the night. Charlie slept by the door, paws over her eyes. Early the next morning they arrived back, Charlie immediately whizzed about the gardens, and the surrounding area, every path, and track belonged to her and she wanted everyone who could listen to know that she was home.

Murray finds Cha sniggering in the kitchen; all she has on is the nurse's jacket, taking her by the hand Murray leads her to the bedroom. They just potter about for the rest of the day, not getting upset about anything.

The lighting project has come on leaps and bounds both of the girls are highly impressed with the results. The current flow from the hydro-generated electrical current is at present just about nearly enough to power a single string of miniature LED tree lights. This job only gets worked when adverse weather prevents the advancement of roof repairs. Most of their time has been spent with the scaffolding there is so much of it the house looks like a fucking castle. There was no other safe way up to the roof. This alone has taken a while longer than anticipated and the roof repairs including the refurbishment of the chimneys are nowhere near complete. All the rooms are now soot free and drying out slowly.

They make a great team, it could be shooting, and stealing anything but as far as the cooking is concerned, Murray is presently not even permitted to spell it. Every once in a while they take some time out and spend some needed together time. Murray has been learning to paint, his teacher is very patient. Her watercolours are like pictures you see on nice pottery whereas his resemble a ventriloquist's dummy covered in greenish-yellow slime. Murray's are presently on display near the main fireplace where they are set alight and sent up the chimney taking the chill off the stack before ignition.

Charlie is lying on her back trying to catch the afternoon rays on her belly. Murray is halfway through a joint when Cha shouts "Tea's up." As of late, he is serving a total ban in the kitchen. It works out that he is just too messy, Murray pleads for a not proven verdict, but an objection is raised on the grounds of premeditated waffle, piffle, and balderdash. The judge grants in her favour and no appeal now equates to a lifetime ban. He can go in and eat and drink what he wants, but no cooking still means no cooking. Chas' cooking is, without a doubt first class and as far as Murray is concerned, he could be eating at a five-star restaurant with every single meal.

Murray still has not completed the repairs, the length of heavy-duty copper wire that they were attaching will prevent the roof from developing into resembling one of his

138

watercolours. All the new cowls are somewhere here but as he never labelled the boxes it will be an extensive search and rescue mission to locate them. The scaffolding resembles a medieval siege tower, albeit the stretched plastic sheeting now deflects wind and weather not burning sulphur and great big fucking boulders, however in a certain light. Some days Murray requires an extra set of hands and as expected she owns everything mechanical. When he gets it wrong, one hand covers her eyes and the other simulates a wanking motion, sometimes her thumb and index finger join with her nose indicating that "Something is stinking" and then she smiles and points the red nail at him.

Charlie's favourite part of the day was the walk. If Cha's head was buried arse deep in a book or piles of books with yellow stickers here and green stickers there are stickers every fucking where. If he would ask her something, the reply would be "Yes baby I believe that was Tuesday-ish last week." It would sure make a lot of sense to her but did not mean a whole lot to Charlie and Murray.

At this he would grab his jacket and a gun, even though they had seen nobody in weeks it is still a necessary precaution to be armed at all times, they would then sneak off, By Charlie's directions and she would charge at full speed across the edge of the pond, through the swamp and meet Murray over the other side. He takes the slightly drier route and she is always located at the same spot. The main roads are over in this direction and in all the time here all that has produced hackles and from Charlie lately are as follows: An overgrown tire, two escaped plastic bags, and an old abandoned fridge. They still love it up here Charlie sits surveying her kingdom and Murray smokes. Charlie somehow always ends up dirtier on the way back and only after a big splash in the pond and a good shake will they let her in.

Several weeks later Murray has completed the outside, apart from announcing that the siege is over and the invaders will be withdrawing. The elusive cowlings had finally appeared and the last one securely fitted. Damper, colder, and damper were slowly being replaced by darker, even colder, and damper. Herding up the assortment of bits and pieces of the excess construction materials and the tools used to whack them together. Murray was now in the process of removing them, "Tea in ten!" Thumbs up, he signals the message is understood. He was about an hour late. No big deal, but now that is done, hopefully, he does not need to go back up there for a while.

Cha greets him in the kitchen, all the books, books with stickers, big fat books, small slim books most of them have been tidied up and stored away and all that remains on the table are three. Sitting back feet stretched on the table, she blows a long steady plume and flicks the unwanted remains into the fireplace. A quick stretch, a couple of steps, a quick embrace, half a dance move, Murray will never learn. She has him pinned to the chair; the mischievous look is there, "Uh-oh, here we go." He does know who is beaming the most. Reaching over: book number one was a manual for the large green machine in the kitchen, the title was long gone but he could make out 1924. Murray goes to say something and the finger with the black nail is touching his lip. "I thought if you repaired or changed it for a different model..." book number one is withdrawn and replaced by book number two which has the partially destroyed cover, volume 682 resplendent in stickered pages indicating long forgotten delicacies, that he has, maybe? mentioned in the past and she is fully aware of the fact, that Murray would quite willingly part with his soul for anyone of them.

"I could make you some of these" sadly this is then replaced by a stained blueprint of a revised plumbing and heating schematic, "When you get some spare time!"

At this she was off, giggling. Charlie had found yet another bright yellow ball. They head upstream for a change, walking hand in hand Charlie whizzes in front of them, disappears, runs through them and they laugh. Most of the time is spent in the big room. Almost everything is in here, the ham radio gear, which is now an abandoned pile of neatly-labelled wire, lies on top of the radio journal's last entry...

What had once been a compulsory twice hourly, daily, nightly, petering out to weekly and now they just don't. Murray would watch and listen to the multi-channel, multiple-band, multi-lingual sweeps the geographical nuances eventually breaking down to reveal her native tongue. Her linguistic coverage was impressive but her natural tones were breathtaking. This was the only time that he had ever heard Italian spoken without every breath sounding like a lie.

Now that the evil twins are sleeping. Splayed on the chair, a rather large happy cigarette and the second can of the last man on the planet is on its last swallow when he is confronted with the girls, one's getting jacketed up and the other is already in take-off mode. This was a setup, "The gear was on the table Gov." Hands up, Murray asks "Where are you two going?" the blank stare and the ear is replaced by a smile and a bark with the autocorrected reply of "Just putting my jackets on now!"

It has been a long time since they have spent time like this, either he had had to fix this or invent something to repair that, not to mention the odd "Strange how that does not fit, it looked okay the last time." Murray is on a guided tour; Charlie is in the advanced position sometimes she is there to greet them, pretending to be lying in wait to deliver the fatal ambush, sometimes sprawled out on the once upon–a-time perfect lawn and sometimes she has gotten bored waiting, is now actively involved in digging various exploration holes.

The growing calendar has been produced inclusive of all the planting dates and charts with the allocated tasks. Vegetable plots have been marked out, some of them even partially prepared for the next step, and Murray is shown around what she had been up to. He is not expected to get involved straight away. Cha's favourite place which fills her with pride and joy is the Orangery she pronounces this in a French accent which, to be honest, makes the hair on the back of his neck stand up.

The place is tucked out of the way, not sure if it is part of the house or part of the building but, it has no windows on the north side and big huge mostly dirty windows out in front. Murray is thinking that he could grow some decent weed, and Cha is thinking more of "tomatoes, peppers, asparagus, avocados. Some shelves over here, the stove could be routed there, maybe some hot water could be diverted? instead of a conventional ground heating system is it possible, here? We have some seeds but I have started a wanted list!" Abruptly ending with a "what do you think?" and then she was off again "cross-pollination, cross-plant infestation separation, root germination, and we could have a small greenhouse added here and maybe another over there and you would need a tool shed, There is an orchard not far from here as you can see by the pots, twigs one, two and three are on their last legs and are in desperate need of some intensive care."

"I'm all in" and tells her that "I will do half a week on the plants as the other on the heating; you can pick the days and tasks." Before he has even finished trying to speak, she had delivered yet another speech this time with more descriptions, diagrams, and locations adding "I have been thinking about this for quite a while, let's be honest Mur? we can't live on tins for fucking ever!" Finally managing to get her attention Murray tells her that Charlie and he are all in, we can go through the details tonight and it can be the last run before winter.

In the late afternoon, it could be the green stuff, it could be her, screen-by-screen they are mentally wandering through her descriptions of what is to be, colours, sounds; Murray can even hear and see birds in there, alas it will not all be tomorrow but sure they can start. At dinner he is informed is going to be a surprise and in a roundabout way, he is told that if he really wanted to, there was enough time to get freshened up. Murray takes the hint, reappearing with another tee shirft displaying another dead musician. The jeans and socks are a pre and post-identical set.

There are more lights on than normal, candles are placed high out of the way of the demolition tail, battery lights in all shapes and sizes are scattered high & low, the big brass holder with the seven candles and the Santa candles can't help but make one smile. Dinner is fantastic, the steak is out of this world, albeit Murray is not too sure about the addition of the pear crumble, but he eats the lot.

These late-night conversations have covered everything; over the weeks they have covered most topics from the unadulterated silly to the downright outrageous. One of these was how many cocktails you can make. Murray's total had amused her for months; it was two medium tins of last man on the planet, a bottle of sparkly wine, one small glug of vodka the one that the label looks like a radiation warning and one of them condensed concentrated fruit juices to hide all traces of the original ingredients. The jug was on the table, and Cha had remembered, "of course, I will have more crumble" In between gulps, sips, and burps not only worked their way through the shopping list but also the jug. "Don't worry I made two" and she goes to retrieve the refill. Murray should offer to help or even start to tidy up but as far as he is aware a lifetime ban in the kitchen is still forever.

Murray rolls and sparks up; Cha joins him a second later. Sitting in his lap, stealing a puff or three. She tells him that she thought that she would have to charm him in all sorts of ways to get his cooperation, brandishing the fur coat and dangling the ushanka in her other, "My employer is delighted Mr Black that we do not require this time to torture you." It was delivered in her finest Moscow accent between burps. This is better than the TV, and he wants more details, but she is not playing, but God bless her, she had wired up some sounds. He does not know what it is but they dance, she dances on her own, until the jury-rigged power supply dies. It may have been playing like this for ages as the slow dance seemed to last forever. The clock on the mantelpiece says three o'clock but it always says three o'clock.

This is the drunkest that they have been in a long time and she always tortures him over his country's linguistic history, how many names for this, "I think there is at last official count about seventy." This was delivered in the underwater dialect, and unless you felt as if your head was underwater would not understand a fucking word of it.

The special part of his native tongue was renowned for a large collection of words that when fired off at record-breaking speeds without any spaces with and not excluding long spaces where fuck all is said followed by intermittent and almost certainly non-related exclamations of oh fuck, followed by full flowing conversation that is somehow related to the last untranslatable noise. There is not an automatic recording formula for this and many a Scotsmen has been arrested in a foreign land and later released, free from all impending charges as nobody could understand what the fuck they're saying.

She is going through the basics, trolleyed, melted, buckled, steamboats, oot ma face, oot ma tree. It works out that her favourite and after much internal deliberation she informs him is 'steamin' She says the translation makes her gag and want to immediately contact the international agency for disease control.

Cha disappears for a while; Murray is invited up to dance again, even though there is no music playing, the woman with the fur hat on top of the headscarf, and half on half-off fur coat informs him, "Baby dance or the Lubyanka." Murray is now the best dancer in the house. He is now imprisoned on the chair, the woman from the KGB is now gone, and looking through the one eye that is not seeing in triplicate, she is saying something, the volume gradually panning in "I made you a present, it took me forever." When it is ignited it looks more like a death machine from an early episode of a once-famous sci-fi show.

The headscarf is gone, and the gypsy woman from northern Spain complete with the curls and one huge hooped earring is telling him "That she is alone and he has to protect her" something muttered about a rare herb. They have fallen asleep in front of the fire; A solitary Santa candle sheds the only light. The other candles have just transformed into lumps of wax. The battery ones are either broken or the batteries need replacing. Murray has a vague recollection of throwing some at the bins. Charlie is patiently waiting at the door wanting to go and do what dogs want to do. Murray wishes that he could open the door with mind control and suffice to say he is but a mere mortal and gets up and lets Charlie out.

Cha has the fur on and says "Hi baby," and hands him the jeans. All he has on is the headscarf, which is now being worn as a bandana. Rather than wait for the imminent arrival of the hangover Murray sips at a can of the last man on the planet and puffs steadily at one he had made earlier. Mr Black's brain tries to collate enough information to figure out if he is an animal, mineral, or vegetable when he is transferred back to reality with "Breakfast."

The woman who is now only wearing an ushanka announces that "It is fish, fruit, and some water" before Murray can say anything the beaming smile in front of him tells him that it is good for Bobby, she kisses him and goes back to sleep. Murray really no longer cares what the world has got in store for him; as long as it starts with that smile anything is possible.

It will be a truck each for this expedition. Murray has started on the vehicle that Cha will be driving, he is making sure that all is in good working order. The minor adjustments are complete and the cab is all wiped down. Just to blow the cobwebs out of her he takes it for a little spin. It should take much less time to prepare and check his vehicle as he has never really liked driving and sees it as more of a chore. As long as it all works, he is good. He is at the stage of having it running checking out the various electrical readings before taking it for a spin.

The mean machine is dropped off at the big house; Cha is back to her supermodel self, what she sees in him, he will never know. After lunch her test drives over, she is fuelled and provisioned for the journey. Murray's vehicle is now finally ready, the detected leaks and the loose and nearly broken items are all now repaired.

The routine is standard, and by the numbers, they make their journey. They figured that it is going to take about three days, their tracks will be covered there and back and that is what takes up the time. When they go shopping, they always try and enter the premises through the back or side doors and never crash in through the front. So far, they have seen no signs of anyone, nothing has moved, and nothing has changed since the last time. The time before that or at any time, the spare fuel dumps, the secret places. All is the same the only noticeable difference is how quickly the vegetation grows when it is unchecked. A minor deviation here and there but as of yet, no roads are blocked. Their first stop is only an overnight stay; this has been used previously and has not been touched since the last time they were here. It has that damp spell about it and he persuades Cha to sleep in the cab. They don't hang about in the morning as soon as the sun is up, they are off.

Batteries exchanged, fluid levels checked and vented, the telehandler sparks into life, a bit of smoke but that will dissipate shortly. Murray gets to be the operator and her hand signals are outrageous, at one stage he gets out of the cab to complain but the fur jacket being opened to reveal the most perfect breasts in the world out manoeuvres him. "Yes, Mr Black you want to say something?" for once he is speechless. Loading continues, without any more distractions or unexpected exposures. Early afternoon they call a halt for a breather, the munch is good, it is not fish and Bobby does not complain. They walk with Charlie; she had just been let out of the cab and was off sniffing and peeing on things. The list is checked and adjusted; it means that by the time they have wrapped up things here, it is way too late to move.

Chapter Nine

The good news is, if they are lucky by tomorrow, they could quite possibly make it out of Dodge before sunup. The odd couple had done this loads of times, they always take their time. Drive stop, look about, listen, always the same. Their routes are covered over and where necessary they even leave false trails.

In about an hour the retail parks security fence is opened and Murray informs nobody in particular that they are here for wholesale today, Cha is on for the telehandler here and luckily for her Murray cannot find a fur coat. In no time at all, the selection is complete, all bagged, tagged, and then secured.

Charlie and Murray play; Cha quarters the garden centre selecting everything on her shopping list when all the pallets are full and all loose items boxed. The selection of material is considerably larger than what was envisaged and will require some careful packing. It is the early hours when it is complete and they are full. They get about three hours of sleep before dawn. Charlie is not happy sharing the back seat with a flock of fruit trees; Murray shares the front with a selection of seed trays and assorted garden implements.

Daylight is fading; they are all delighted to be back and strangely enough, they are all bursting for a pee. A quick check and their house has remained just as secure as they had left it. The items that need to be returned to the house are ejected in the hallway, all except Mr .50 cal. and his custom case. He is immediately dismantled, cleaned, and goes back to sleep in his cubbyhole, along with the assortment of brightly coloured shells and other accessories.

Charlie and Murray disappear out the door; giving her the much-accustomed bribe they drive the monster around to the garage. Charlie leaps about catching up on re-smelling old friends. Both Mr .50 cal. and Cha are sound asleep. They go for a walk, Charlie savouring every scent, feeling rather proud of herself as she pees everywhere she can. Fetch is not an option she is way too busy.

It is old, the intricate iron and stonework is everywhere, sometimes right in your face others partially hidden out of view, and totally different from elevation to elevation, the main wall at the north carries massive stairs, and others subtler and more hidden decorate the once very ornate gardens. Murray had left the doors open and it looks as if they now have a resident robin, he chirps about as if approving of the pending conversion. Screen-by-screen he is still wandering through her description. The old braziers had been filled with debris that will burn and Charlie is off chasing shadows.

Murray's lifetime ban is still active and it has been made clear to him on many occasions that the kitchen is just a no-fucking-go-zone. He has launched various appeals but the last one was eventually agreed to be translated and it worked out along the lines of 'you are a dirty messy bastard,' sort of put a sudden end to any future culinary dreams and aspirations in the kitchen department. The just-in-case box comes in handy. From the selection, he has borrowed two chocolate bars, a .28 with a 42A on the side. From his vantage point, Charlie sniffs and rolls about. Murray sees water gently flowing this way, gently curving back under, "Woof!" the chocolate bar is now dropping to the ground Charlie's food sensors have come into play automatically calculating the treat or no treat distance. The chocolate bar is dead and gone, someone is sitting waiting, thinking that this was an award-winning performance and could possibly warrant another treat. Someone else was thinking that was the last one. She makes bigger shadows thinking that she is a lion.

Murray finishes his break and heads down; Cha is waiting in the shadows, Charlie now at her side. "Hey" followed by a "hey" and a touch. "I saw the light and just came up to see what I was missing." He tells her that Charlie and he had gone for a little stroll and ended up here. "Anyway, thought you could do with the rest." She looks about, Murray motions tap, tap click, slip and pull, nodding in the general direction where he has left it. Sometimes he forgets to take the thing and "baby" is followed by a shake of the head at his forgetfulness.

"Anyway, I could have sworn that I detected a sign of water from up there, a pond over there working its way over here under there." They are in the process of heading back, Cha wants more details about the water, especially the plants. A bunch of magpies are jumping and squawking about, Charlie ignores them, she is presently stalking a pile of leaves wondering if it will ever stop moving long enough for a surgical strike. As much as Murray would love to play, he is ignoring her and sorting out the wood. Bobby and he had had fish this morning and they can do anything. Cha was going to join in later, the last time he had seen her she was melting Santa's legs in the wax pile making enough to pour into the moulds with the wicks hanging like small mammal tails. Murray has stocked upstairs, and now making space at the side for more piles. The wood was all cut and split ages ago. Cha checked his fingers every day just in case he was missing one of his pork sausages.

Charlie and Murray were on their way to the garage, this is where he keeps all the bits and bobs required for making, fixing, and inventing things all stored away. It is not pristine laboratory clean or even documentation tidy, Murrays filing system is ahead of its time and has not fully caught on yet. He knows where most things are hiding; Charlie knows where he keeps the spare Charlie snacks. Charlie has been paid the standard tariff and is waiting patiently in the cab; all they have to do is shift some wood. A couple of hours later

She has been paid in full. They can't have her running about machinery and don't really like locking her up, Charlie has proposed a standing order on snacks paid in advance.

Cha meets up with them in the Orangery; Charlie is admiring twigs one, two, and three which are still in need of intensive care and the dog is wondering if she will get to play with them. The newly acquired plants are brought up here sorted and wrapped up nicely and snugly so that they will not require any intensive care. They stroll down in the evening like lost teenagers, looking for a place to hide, usually from Charlie. The four-seater is gradually getting closer to the hearth. Lately, they have ended up here, sprawled sleeping in front after more late-night chatting.

Entering the big house, great the fire is blazing away, "I nearly forgot," and she hands him some candles all that is left of Santa, his beloved is an intermittent black streak on a few of the purple-coloured candlesticks. Murray loads up the spares and sparks them up. "And I have this as well," the book was opened on the table and the picture was of the Orangery with the flowing water. All the writing has disappeared but it does look like something similar.

"Morning Baby," Bobby's telling him just eat this don't grumble, Murray slowly starts to materialise. "Hi Baby" the finger with the black nail polish stops the next words… Cha is dressed, well she has on a fur coat and a pair of wellies. "I will make breakfast in a bit, bye baby." By Charlie's directions, it's full speed across the edge of the pond, through the swamp and he meets her over the other side. With the changing temperatures the mixture of the pond water and swamp muck has produced Charlie the swamp monster, she is delighted and stinks to high heaven. Crossing by a drier route, the trail of broken swamp monster parts, leads to Charlie at her favourite spot, just sitting, just watching.

Meanwhile, Murrays dressed and... After last night's conversation on the Orangery, the pond, flicking through the pages, being careful not to spill any ash on it. He sees lots of pictures; lots of people painting most of the words are missing, and parts of the pages have been ripped out.

Murray leaves a note; "Cha I will be at the garage." No doubt this will translate to, smoking weed, with his feet up, really missing his fucking headphones, and should have something ready. Hammer, tape one, tape two, masks, snacks for Charlie, Murray is just getting to the item of snacks for himself and the girls are there. Murray thinks they have been watching him for a little while, A packet of a snack bar in hand, Charlie had grassed, pinkie promise, it was not the last one, Murray has one straight away and put the rest in with the tools.

She has on more than the fur coat, "Sorry Charlie was wanting to explore and it took longer to get warmer when I got back."

"No problem." He shows her the assorted bag of tools, adding, "Something told me that you liked the water idea."

They talk about this lots as they walk over, Charlie the swamp monster is slowly retransforming into Charlie the dog. A Robin is jumping about flapping its tail and rapping out a warble. Some seeds are placed on a broken-up table, the actual top now slopping down slightly due to the damaged and broken legs. "I brought these as well, sit down and I will pour."

A grubby flask is produced the once green outer shell looking like it had received more than its fair share of knocks, drops and plane crashes by the number of dents it, was opened, Murray got the flask lid come cup and a small china cup and a saucer was produced from the bag along with the find of the year: A carton of long-life milk that allegedly lasts forever. This is better than anything, Murray can't remember the last time he had a proper cup, and he knows the milk is not real but they can pretend. The first sip is absolute salvation. The ripped-up book is here, Murray shows her where he was standing and how they used the different elevations; they try and trace what is in the pictures. It is agreed Murray is going up the stairs and directing, "Over a bit, yip a bit more no too much, yip just about there, yip spot on." The paint is presented, in three colours and she can decide which one for which. Detailed descriptions are not required at this point just a brief outline of what he is seeing.

Every once in a while, they stop and cross-check. The brief outlines in red, yellow, and green depict imaginary settings. The robin is still warbling away.

Murray needs more tea; Cha takes notes and sketches a rough outline. As always, she is radiant, seriously she could have been a supermodel; Murray on the other hand looks like a truck has dragged him through the fields backwards and sideways, a scarecrow would be a suitable description and the scarecrow would probably be more admirably attired.

Charlie goes to where she likes to watch, and they eventually catch up with her, looking like two teenagers who are returning from science class and still excited about the last lecture, imaginary pens and terraforming equipment changes the picture in front of them. One of the big whistles that the fingers go in the mouth for producing instant volume is let loose and Charlie barges in the door ahead of them.

Cha goes to the place that Murray is not allowed to enter, the fire is coaxed back into life and Murray Blackface goes to freshen up. A very quick cold shower and an even quicker change of clothes, it is the same design on the shirt, another dead rock star, it could be a different size; the jeans are identical to the previous pair only cleaner.

The tea is ready, for once it is in a pot and an opened packet of biscuits, 'sorry I could not wait' as she munched on a slice. "Thought you could do with a wee treat found these a while back but, well it's the thought that counts."

"Out fucking standing." Murray eats most of the biscuits, another pot of tea is on the go and they smoke as, the notes from the rough sketch are transferred to the master document.

The requests from Cha are never outrageous, if something is not possible, Murray always tries to provide an alternative, if that does not work, she will disappear into her easel and come back to him on that with another drawing depicting a different view and he will always try to work around it. They mark up all the notes and modifications, he will need a hand on certain sections but can structure the workload to incorporate most if not all of her ideas, let's face it she has never really asked him to do anything, it is the least that Murray can do, after all, that smile alone.

Mistakenly Murray had asked "What would you like first?" instantly regretting it, even before the response" "All of it!" Pretending to be a lady closing her eyes and turning her nose up at him, trying really hard not to smile, "I would like the wall over there, the small bridge over here with that bit extended here, here and here, the greenhouses were an X marks the spot, the sheds were anywhere over that side is good." Murray gets to work, it is slow and steady for him and his friend, the Monday hammer, they hope that they are making a good impression. Murray must have been at it for weeks; all the old stuff had to be taken down and dug out. He did not do it all at once, a bit here a bit there, and gradually it was taking shape. All the plants at present were in various places, Murray could identify four types the rest were all mysteries. Including the ones that he had dug up from an orchard about a mile away. Everything is well wrapped up in sacks even the containers of seeds are insulated against the dampness and cold.

Murray has even managed the boxes, containing the trays, tools, and other gardening things. He has set these out and hidden them under a blue plastic cover. In this pile he added the little bells, chimes, and things that he knows she likes, Charlie and Murray were not playing they were also collecting the little bits and pieces. Murray will not mention it and Charlie has assured him that her lips are sealed, with pinkie promising the works.

It looks like a mess but the pile of wood and all the bits are set out in the assembly sequence, additional wood, adhesive, and everything that was required was laid out. Murray was not showing off this was the way he was taught to do it from an early age and that was it. Many guys turned into animals, almost like one of their ancestors on the hunt for the last beast of the season, and his tribe is doomed unless he can find the packets of screws that he is now searching the trash for, whereas sequential order wins the prize.

The 28 and 42A have evaporated and he is on a double refill, but they have been busy. The large doors have finally given in and graciously allowed Murray and miss digger machine to enter. At last, they have just finished hauling in the last bag of sand and it is stacked over at the open space now formally occupied by all the building materials. The door is open and they have battery life to spare, the sound is just about perfect. He is in the guitarists garage pulling off a heavily muted solo in A with a equally deformed upstrokes, the most underrated love song ever, Murray is fucking miles away. Cha lets Murray get to the guitar solo before she starts clapping and hooting. His face is kind of red, but he just could not help it every once in a while, you hear some piece of music and it just kind of takes you over, most of the time Murray manages to keep this disease in check, but sometimes, just sometimes...

Cha puts her arms around him, "It's okay baby, no singing... Okay? We all do it, I dance when I think no one is watching." Murray lets the track die out, and switches it off, she surveys the area, "Sorry, I just sort of fell asleep," yawning she mumbles something about dinner and he can't quite make out the rest. She tells Murray that it looks great and that she loves what he has done with the place before the 'N' in dinner Charlie is off. They follow behind like two lost tourists, Murray is being told that she is so, so knocked out with what he has achieved, it is nothing, she is everything. Murray vaguely remembers muttering something like he looked like a scarecrow, sure he stinks and he could do with a shave and he remembers hearing something like,

"Monique is our finest and we will have her here tomorrow evening sir." The fire is on and the four-seater hungrily welcomes him into her open arms.

"Wakey, wakey Hmmm!" Murray is greeted by the "Don't argue Bobby likes it," mini-speech and kiss, a cuddle, and a smile. In his robotic state and with one and a half eyes open Murray dutifully obeys. He swallows whatever it is and gets rid of the taste with the water. Murray is nearly fully laced up and just about recharged when; woof! Charlie decides that it is time. The whole place still looks like a building site, he has even extended to the area outside, where they have a pile to burn and a pile to dump.

It is well after lunchtime, and Murray is getting peckish. The contents of the goody bag will need to do. Although, "Tea would be nicer," he mutters to no one in particular. He horses on, the new foundations are down, the cement mixer washed out, and he is contemplating what to do next while at the same time he is looking for his lighter. The traitor appears, Murray tries to stop her but Charlie runs straight through her tip, toe, jump, and skid. Clearly a full indication to the jury that this girl is guilty. With a bark she is off again, it must be getting late and her coming to get in would have been one of the secret deals that go on between female members of all families and their pets. At that Cha appears and tip, toes through a spot beside the already setting forensic evidence. Murray thinks it is great and has no intention of smoothing it over, the girls have disappeared. Got to be a sign that it is enough for the day. The concrete is protected and there is not really much else he can do until it sets.

There is some more frost and some snow on the ground this morning and Charlie is fascinated by the ice until she realises that she does like cold water. They have the fire on and Murray has started to play with the heating system. He has managed to locate, more by accident, Murray had come across the old drawings, they were ancient and compiled in linen. He could not understand them and thought he was way out and as he could not get a complete one hundred percent match until he realised that the holes were cigarette burns and they were just drawn around them, no expansion loops required, looking fuck all like that in reality. It was all done in heavy wall copper pipe; this must have been way, way before his time, the brass valves were many and belonged to a Sheffield address and thankfully not Italian.

Murray has been guilty of the following this morning, lots of swearing and cursing, he tries hard to be calm, but when the spanner slips and you nearly chop a finger off at the same time a little swearing is perfectly understandable. Murray has been chasing an airlock for hours on end. There are noises, and gurgling and he is still unable to eliminate that fucking banging.

"Tea baby," breaks the silence.

He squeezes out of the crawl space, a quick dust down. "No biscuits?"

"I could not help but notice you were having a bad day." A quick flash of her veranda and the smile, it does not even get dark here with that smile.

"How could I ever have a bad day with you?"

Cha is talking about going up to check over the Orangery and feed the Robin. Charlie has decided already and is lying at the door pretending that she has been waiting that long that she has died of boredom, she is lying on her back, her head tilted to one side and she had also slid her tongue out and rolled it to one side, that's enough for Murray, "Hold up I'm coming too." The snow is still falling and small patches are forming. Charlie is investigating where the leaves are hiding, that is until her nose gets cold. They walk arm in arm, with you know whom darting in-between them, then she bursts into fast drive and chases down some new scent.

So, the question on the table is, if you could get one thing, anything, what would it be, Murray has opted for a piping hot shower. Admitting that he thinks that he stinks and a power washer or a full washdown by a HAZMAT team would serve a better purpose. A hand goes over her nose, and then wafting away the imaginary dissipating stink 'room service' Murray objects, that was one item and she can't have it. Cha rejects his comment, with the panache of a sixth avenue attorney performing in front of a senate committee

"French style scrambled eggs, fresh wild forest mushrooms cooked gently in garlic butter, lightly toasted fresh bread," Murray can taste it and surrenders with, "Have you ordered for two?"

The warbling in the corner gives away the robin's position and only stops singing when the seeds and nuts are replenished in the feeder. Everything is checked over and the only visible problem is twigs one, two, and three are still in need of intensive care; there is a patch of dampness spreading over, and when they were getting relocated Charlie is in stalking mode.

Murray is going to go back via the garage; The AWD is the safest vehicle they have for this weather and he hopes with a quick change of battery that it will start. On the last cough it starts, they need this electricity supply sorted. Bad enough it was the last cough it was the second last battery. He switches off what he can and drives it about the yard telling her that he loves her profusely and would never dream of driving anything else. Confident that she will idle without protesting, he loads a few spare batteries in the back and takes her for a spin. Half an hour later, he parked out the front. The snow has stopped but now a thin covering has finally established itself everywhere. Cha likes driving, but Murray only sees it as another task. They are only going out for an hour just enough for juice, nothing too steep, and no rally driving. He should not have mentioned it, every gear was crunched through as quickly, as often as possible the AWD was activated and all the various available options were checked on the way down the hill and rechecked on the return. Stopping at the house Cha chucks him the keys "Don't forget the screen wash."

The four-seater looks even closer to the fire, and it has his name written all over it. He wakes up with Cha rolling on top of him, "Morning handsome." Murray says good morning back mumbling something about her being a supermodel and him a fucking scarecrow, but she does make out clearly that he thinks she is beautiful and he would not want to wake up in a world without her. Bobby has activated the incoming fish early warning system and he is mentally preparing the chemical division currently situated in his stomach to go on standby. Murray gets rid of the taste with tea, water, and more tea. The second pot has nearly been demolished, Cha has been out with Charlie, and Murray is having a 'peace with the world moment,' but that comes to a crashing end when the ghosts arrive. The flames are revived and he chucks some logs on the fire. Helping Cha out her wet coat they dodge and try to evade the spray that Charlie blasts out like an erratic lawn sprinkler. Wait till you see it, there are no longer patches of white and it is all white, the decision was made, and Murray is staying in for the day.

Cha has volunteered to give him a hand, he can't remember what she asked for nor what he had agreed to do in return, not that it would matter she knows he would do anything for her. So, the plan was Murray will shout a number and Cha will tell him stories. Murray's location will be in the loft and she will operate the now-numbered valves in the crawl spaces. They have done the guided tour, started upstairs, and then worked their way around the stations. "It should sound like a water dispenser recharging with a bit of reverse reverb."

She is in his face, "Does that sound like glug, glug?" and an impersonation of a drowning man.

"Perfect," he tells her.

All the fires have been lit and even in the room where Mr 50 cal and his friends sleep. Murray is not sure what to try if this does not work, the only option could be to chop sections out but it would not be easy and as it is that old, replacement parts would have to be made. Smartass has appeared with a T-shirt with 'plumbers do it better' emblazoned on her chest. She is standing there in front of him, hair pulled tight, beret on slightly to the left. Chest puffed out, high heels, and nothing else. Murray is too scared to ask about the letters on her makeshift tool bag, SP Ltd.

Murray has to join in or she will have him, she has been dying to rip the piss for ages. "Plumbers to position, Ground floor Valve number one to open, opened!" Murray heads towards the first floor and listens to the pipes. The same number is dead. Sequential elimination is the only way he can do it. Exiting from one crawl space to enter another. Cha is waiting for additional instructions, but with a comfy seat curled up inside some book. At last. It is number five, he takes a deep breath, "Plumbers to position, Ground floor Valve number two to open,"

"Can you wait till the end of the chapter?" slight delay followed by "Open baby, I'll try number six, it's a failure. Number three is the one."

In the loft the main valve is fully opened, his ear is firmly pressed against a pipe, the look on Murray's face, betraying his search for reverse reverb, both are located and vented. The process is repeated; the replies and the accents he received are varied.

"Seriously do I really have to?"

"I dunno Mr, being the weekend and excuse my French a fucking bank holiday we are looking at quadruple bubble before any of them will answer the phone, and sorry I am in the bathroom."

On the way downstairs, Murray is thinking that Cha has disappeared for ages, ah well maybe she is doing something special, perhaps steak with or without the crumble. He is not fussy. Something smells nice, Murray is tempted to have a quick swatch at the pots but the ban is still active. The lights are different some of the broken ones have been repaired, and the blinking ones have stopped blinking Murray hears a click behind him, "Just sit down Mr Black, my name is

Monique and I have been reliably informed that you are an urgent case." Her accent has a trace of danger and the perfume smells like heaven; He is just about to say something when a jug of the Last French Couple on the planet is produced along with two glasses, "Now drink Mr Black we need you to relax." Murray is informed that he is allowed to smoke, the one he had made earlier is burning, and it is removed from his hand.

Chapter Ten

Murray is persuaded to go up the stairs. There is a door opened along the corridor. More gentle prodding, and the bathroom is all lit up with candles. This must have taken her all day. He is instructed to get undressed; a hand reaches out for his glass. Monique gets in the bath with him, he motions to speak, and a finger is pressed to his lips, "No speaking allowed" is whispered in his ear. The refilled glass and the still-burning 24A are returned, and his hair is washed and cut when they have been depleted. Another finger to his lips, "Stay perfectly still and do not move," he had never been shaved by anyone before, and Murray could get quite used to this. He has always been pretty uncomfortable with the touchy-feely stuff, but this is nice. When he has dried and dressed, Cha is back in a kimono with the exquisite embroidered dragons, "How long does it take you to clean up? C'mon, dinner is ready."

Bobby and Murray are pleased that it is not fish. This is a meat type of dish, the rice is bright with some almost sweet currants or raisins speckled through it, and they both have refills. She has been drawing again; the pile of sketches is situated near the heat source; Murray pushes them away from the candles. The paper is starting to curl at the corners and has been reused from a previous shopping list. It is not a deliberate recycling attempt. It just happened to be the only paper about it. Murray asks to see them, another jug and a volley of 24A's, and he is writing colours in the margin or adding notes down the bottom. He has to read these out, and if it makes any sense at all, she agrees, they initial. They have been on drawing number three for ages, and as we get nowhere, the kimono is off, and a finger touches lips, followed by a "Baby, come to bed."

For once, no one is up before the other one, "Baby! I think I am blind!" Murray removes the kimono from her head. "Thanks, baby." Charlie is scratching at the door. His clothes are hiding, and still naked, he opens the door and Charlie bounds out, peeing before stopping midstream and chasing a flock of sparrows. Murray has found a jacket, and after some wrestling, it finally gives in. He manages to get it on the right way round; the zips and buttons remain a mystery and he has one hand holding it closed. The other alternates between holding the smoke, his juice, as he leans on the post outside, and he wishes it would stop the world from spinning.

Charlie has been promised a planetary constellation's worth of treats if she returns. Murray goes back in to hear a little voice pleading, "I am still blind!" reaching her hiding place. Murray crouches down and tells her that it is okay. "You are under the covers,"

"Oh," and a head pops out, and he receives a small wave and a huge smile, and she is gone, straight back under the covers and fast asleep in seconds. Every time that smile just wipes him out.

Charlie is still outside. In a last-ditch attempt, he shouts, "Okay, you were adopted, and I found you in the bushes, but I truly love you like a daughter." Charlie is now at the door and barely looks at him before pretending to be dead in front of the fire. Murray's brain has just about given up; he thinks that there is a slight possibility that he could be dead. Drinking more tea, he recalculates, stretches, scratches and lights up, exhaling, "Hmmm, I am human after all," to no one in particular.

Cha has not stirred. The fire is still going. He has to make his way around this hairy obstacle at the front. The arrival of the log basket gets Murray receiving the I was in the middle of a dream look. "Do you really expect me to move?" The warning klaxon goes off, broadcasting, Danger! Danger! Imminent collision! Charlie stretches, gets up, stretches again and walks off at the slowest speed possible. The log basket stretches his patience, and his muscles land safely on the now vacant hearth; Murray reloads the stack when he sees a hand coming out.

He reaches over and shakes it firmly, "Please to meet you," and is very tempted to add in, "Whats your name again?" Something is said. It sounded like nothing he had heard before. Some grunts and a foot begins to emerge and tries to make an attempt to come out. It feels slowly for the floor. Her toes tentatively acting as remote sensors trying to locate the discarded footwear. Murray shifts over one of the shoes, nudging it to enable the blind docking endeavour to take place. Nothing happens, several minutes go by, but then we get movement, the bulk of the entity sits up, and another set of sensors appears. These are faster at docking.

Sitting up, the residential four-seater monster is now fully erect. A head, like a newly emerging flower from a bud, emerges from the wrapped-up cover. There is a stocking still wrapped around her head. The mascara is heavy around the left eye, with a streak or two heading towards the ear. "Morning baby, love the look!" She looks at Murray, puzzled, and confiscates his best friend, inserting two fingers into his nostrils. She persuades Murray to stand up, and they slowly shuffle over to the mirror. He has similar looks, the finger with the red nail polish is at his lips, and the infamous Cha stare is in his face, "You really don't remember the tribal wedding ceremony?" and "I was so looking forward to calling you hubby!"

His best friends are not returned, but he does get a pot of tea as a consolation prize. He has surrendered the stocking, washed and dressed. Looking at himself in the mirror, he is shocked. "Morning, Mrs B," the woman with the pineapple hair, drinking a glass of life support, looks at him. Looks at her wedding ring finger and then just stares at him. "I am just going to pop to the office, it won't be long," adding,

"Remember to cancel that dinner invitation, and could you check what excuse we used the last time? I think we have to go with the car crash this time." Murray gets no words in reply. Cha is standing now; the spread has fallen, leaving her with just the high-heeled fluffy slippers and the stocking holding up her hair. She waves her hands in front of her eyes and covers her ears. Then he gets the pouted lips and the offhand dismissal wave. Ending with her looking at him, then looking at her wedding finger, then just glaring at him.

Murray does not even ask Charlie whose side she is on. They are in a frozen state; he switches on everything but the heated seats. Going back into the house just now is a no-win situation. Unable to achieve warp drive, he smokes while waiting for the compressed energy crystals to thaw the windows. Halfway down, Murray gets out and scrapes the remaining ice sliding the residue with a deft wrist flick. Beaming back to being himself again, he drives to the garage. Murray leaves the engine running to cancel the almost cryogenic temperatures.

The emergency supply box is raided, and his best friends, 28 and 42a, are in safe hands as he walks over to the motorcycle. The can of Last man on the planet is finished in one long gulp. The can is crushed and volleyed into the bin. This could bring back many memories, but these and so many others are now banished forever behind impenetrable walls, and access is firmly denied to everyone, especially himself.

Untying the cover at the front, it is pulled back all the way to the brake light. Murray removes the key and opens up the seat. Old habits die hard, and the contents of the secret compartment are stealthily put into his plectrum pocket. He drives back, taking the long way around. The roads have some snow but not undriveable conditions yet. One wag of the tail and a single friendly woof greets him when he enters. A note on the table declares Cha's undying love, and she is in the bath.

The once expensive red-soled heels lie abandoned in the corner, with all the clothes that the stylist had discarded. Murray can't help but smile at this, and to be honest, this will make him smile for weeks. He knows that she notices. Murray goes closer to the bath; her head resurfaces, blowing out a stream of water, followed by the hand that wants the ring. Murray had been rehearsing all the things that he wanted to say but just removed the ring from his pocket and placed it on the correct finger. It is a custom-made skull ring; it has been in the family for a while, and as he always suspected, that baby brother had sort of purloined this. He told him a long time ago that he had got it as part payment in one of his deals. Murray was informed that it was very old and the metal was very rare. His brother made him promise to take care of it, and one day he may require it back. It has remained hidden all these years; until today. The eyes are bright, ruby red; Cha informs me that it is perfect, her favourite metal and her favourite stone, adding that this wedding is forever and there is nothing that is going to alter this. No matter where they end up. No matter what dangerous situations they encounter, they are paired forever.

"Hmmm, think it fits better on the middle finger" she is out the bath in a second; "I knew you had a ring." Heading to the nearest non-foggy mirror to pose.

They keep themselves busy. They play board games. Cha is a terrible cheat and has pulled a stocking over her head and robbed him twice at gunpoint, once he had to hand over all his clothes. His objections were dismissed, quoting that the rules were simply out of date and a copy of the Russian Federation rules was available for a cross reference online. "If required!"

Occasionally he has offered to make dinner, more than several times, only to receive a counter offer of a duel. "Swords, pistols, or broken bottles at any time you wish." Murray still wakes up every morning thinking that he would not want to spend the next five seconds on this plain of existence without her. Not too sure about the fish, though. Winter is nearly over; Charlie will miss it the most when she is unable to get sliding on the iced-over pond. Murray thinks she is smart enough to figure out the ice is slowly melting and will not find out the hard way.

176

They have been trying to improve the hydro-powered electrical system between the indoor garden and house repair tasks. They have come to the conclusion that the water flow is the problem, possibly the feed pond. This will entail lots of work, which is currently impossible to fix. The water is just too cold to go in just yet, and to be honest, even though Mrs B is a qualified diver. What exactly is she certified to do underwater? Murray can only guess and really does not want to know, but nothing would surprise him.

It has been jointly agreed that to eliminate the dangers, the water must be temporarily drained off. They are having a day off from doing any chores or work, and so far, most of the morning has been spent in bed. That's is apart from the feeding of the fires and Charlie's necessary outings to do doggy things. The hot water is gurgling away, and Mrs B decides she would like a bath. This is announced from under the covers. Murray takes this as a hint that he is to run it for her and quietly slides out of the bedroom and turns on the taps. Seeing as it is a lazy day, Murray selects one of those smelly bath things and deposits it in the flowing water like a depth charge. Its colours and perfume slowly dissolve into the current. Murray will get a sloppy second dip unless invited in, but as of yet, no invitation has been issued. He has a quick shower and gets dressed.

Murray goes downstairs. Charlie is pretending she is dead in front of the fire; she has been in this position for ages and has fallen asleep. He notices her ears move to his footfalls, but she is relaxed that she does not open her eyes. Murray leaves her be and goes outside to check the weather. Finishing his smoke, he goes and checks the progress of the perfumed waters.

It is ready, he goes into the bedroom, and she has not moved from under the covers, but he knows that she is awake. Murray tells her that the bath is ready and as quick as a flash, she has bounded out of bed, a quick pose in front of him, and she is in the bath already. She never fails to amaze him, that smile just knocks him out every time, and she is never grumpy in the morning just wakes up and is full of life, ready for anything. Murray is granted permission and allowed to make tea while she submerges herself in the one little luxury they have.

Murray takes the tea up and hands her the cup. Mrs B's cup is ornately painted with brightly coloured flowers and vines whereas Murrays has a skull and crossbones on it with Danger Toxic in bold stencilled letters. They chat about what they are going to do. There is still no serious work today, maybe some shooting practice, except this time, they are going to take Charlie if they can prise her away from the fire. Sooner or later, she will hear an up-close firearm being discharged, and it is a good course of action that they get her used to it.

Murray gets suited and booted, takes some empty tins, and walks to their makeshift firing range. Charlie has decided to come along. Murray thinks she is just noisy and wants to know what he is doing. Everything is set up, and they go via the big indoor garden with the French-sounding name. Opening the doors, Charlie rushes in and barks to let the robin and anyone else know they are there; the robin just ignores her and twitters quietly on one of the favoured perches. The winter has left no damage, and everything looks pretty healthy, just a little on the cold side.

They play fetch heading back to the house; Charlie likes this game as much as Murray does. There is food and tea on the table when they arrive home. Murray gets a bollocking for not taking a gun with him, 'It only takes one mistake, and what if I am not there to help you, baby? This has to stop. We cannot always be lucky." Murray agrees and that he has to do better. The food is great as always, he does not know what it is, but he scoffs a double helping.

They head out with the rifles, Charlie is instructed to sit and stay, and Murray takes the first shot. He hits the target; Charlie is not upset by the noise and stays in position as instructed. The next shots are fired first, two shots together, and then multiple shots from both guns. Charlie passes the test with flying colours and is given a little treat as a well-done gift. As they were outside, they decided to survey the river feeding the mill to find an alternative solution to the rather dangerous prospect of going underwater. They walk upstream and along the way discuss the prospect of creating a temporary dam and diverting the flow away from the wheel, and this would enable them to check the feed pond output without going underwater.

Their thoughts are interrupted by the sound of some wood pigeons in the area in front of them, another test for Charlie. The homemade silencers are fitted. Murray never made them. Cha produced these one night after dinner, telling him they were not exactly military grade but would suffice.

Charlie was instructed to stay and lay on the ground. With various hand signals, they edged forward and decided who was shooting what. Murray opted for the ones higher up the tree; Cha had the lower and ground-feeding birds. Several pops later and six dead birds. Charlie was invited to fetch them, but she was not interested as they were not yellow and bouncy. The birds were put in the bag for later.

They continued their walk and pretty soon found a spot where the river narrowed, making it an ideal spot to create the temporary dam. It is a huge job and will require mechanical machines, trucks, tracked excavators, building materials, cement and rocks, and rubble, not to mention an alternative track to connect the blocked water flow overspill to the river further downstream, and hopefully, it will reveal the problem with the feed pond. All this talk is making them hungry, and they eat al fresco. Murray prepares the fire and Cha prepares the birds. Charlie watches with an avid interest hoping that she, at the very least, will get a little taste.

The book is out, and Cha is frantically taking notes, compiling a list as they speak. Murray occasionally turns the pair of birds when required. He is informed that they will need explosives to break the dam after the wheel and the supply area are inspected and repaired. Murray is asked if there is a quarry in the area. Cha thinks that industrial-type explosives and detonators may be available there, but Murray is unaware of any place in the immediate area. She tells him that it is okay if they do not find them anywhere and that she can probably make them with the stuff they have available. He had never tasted pigeon cooked on an open fire, it was fantastic, and Murray swears that he caught a glimpse of Charlie licking her lips. The chat continues until the light starts to fade. The fire is extinguished, and they cover up the evidence before leaving.

On the way back, they agree that the job is huge and it can only be done once the season has changed, but they also agree that if they want a decent electricity supply, this is the only way forward. They are now home; Murray cleans the guns. Cha makes tea and gets the paper and pens out. He restocks the fire and comes to the table to join her. The talk continues about the project. Murray smokes a joint and joins her in making the game plan list; the required machinery is listed, and if he knows where they can acquire the said piece of equipment, he mentions the place and area, and it is added in brackets. When they complete the list, it is extensive and covers everything they envisage that will have to be done to achieve the required results.

This has made them hungry; the remaining four birds are prepared, and Murray clears away the paperwork away and sets the table. They have a sweet curry with rice and wash it with the last of the bottled beer, which has been stored outside the open-air refrigerator. Cha has excelled in her cooking skills yet again; this meal is more than outstanding. He will have to add this to his expanding favourite meal list. They move over to the fire with the last beer and smoke while chatting. One accidental touch, and before they know it, they are naked and making love in front of the fire. Murray thinks that he will need to add this to the list, also.

"Morning, Mrs B," Cha has been up for ages. The debris has all been tidied up, and Murray is greeted with a huge cuddle and a passionate kiss. He could get quite used to this. Murray just can't help it, but Bobby is growing in his pants 'easy tiger.' The breakfast is on the table. They eat with grins like Cheshire cats. You would think that they were teenagers the way they go at it, it is never planned. It just happens, and they are not complaining.

Charlie interrupts their teenage antics, and Murray gets up and lets her out. She has had her breakfast and will not be out for long as she is always hopeful of a little titbit from the plates. It is wishful thinking on her behalf, as Murray's plate is always clean 99.9% of the time. Cha gets up from the table and has no clothes on except the T-shirt, "I hope you and Bobby are thinking what I am thinking?" they have a quickie before Charlie returns, life is just wonderful.

Murray tidy's up; okay, he places the plates and cups in the sink. Cha goes and freshens up and gets dressed. She returns a little while later and finds Murray outside with a can of last man on the planet and a smoke. She reaches out, and he shares the smoke with her. She forgets on purpose to hand it back. Murray is not bothered about this and has a ready-rolled supply in his top pocket; he removes one and sparks it up.

Charlie appears, looking guilty for some strange reason. They have no idea what their near-perfect dog could have done, but she will be instantly forgiven, whatever her imaginary or non-imaginary sin is. They intend to spend the day up in the Orangery; He likes the way Cha pronounces it in that French accent, and Bobby and Murray nearly passed out the first time they heard her say it. He takes the bag from her, putting it on the opposite shoulder of his rifle. Murray hopes the bag contains lunch as they have a busy day planned. Planting is still a little early, but they can prepare bits and pieces in advance. Murray thinks this is Cha's favourite place; his favourite place is anywhere as long as she is by his side. Charlie is the pathfinder and charges the way in front of them, not going that far ahead, and if she thinks we are taking too long in catching up, she backtracks and greets us with a bark and a wag of the tail to indicate hurry up. Occasionally she catches them having a quick embrace. It just happens, and being caught just makes them laugh.

They are greeted by the robins today. They are two of them, another Mr & Mrs. As he is not chasing out the newly arrived addition, they have to assume that it is okay and permission to stay has been granted. The birds have slowly been returning to the area, and it is only a matter of time before more residents are here. They are both excited about this prospect. The cast iron braziers are ignited to help thaw the Orangery out; it will at least take two weeks to remove the chill from the place. Cha disappears into one of the greenhouses. Murray thinks that he can hear her singing. It sounds like a cat in pain, but he would never admit to this, even under the pain of death. As long as she is happy, he is also happy.

In the meantime, he inspects the now-dried cement, sets about breaking up the previously positioned piles of gravel, and proceeds to load the wheelbarrow and move them to the allocated positions. Starting at the furthest away point, he starts on the right-hand side, slowly and methodically working his way down the course of the intended stream.

Ideally, the gravel should be rinsed to remove most of the dust and dirt, but they will take care of it by running the water through the course and the force of the current before introducing the fish will automatically clean it. Cha has not yet informed him of the fish, but he just knows that is what she is thinking. Murray is down to his T-shirt, the jacket has been removed, and the rifle is in the corner, but to save him from her wrath, he has an automatic stuffed down the back of his jeans just in case of any unexpected, uninvited eventualities.

The right-hand section has gravel laid out all the way down the line, and he has stated on the left section Murray has only just started and has dumped four wheelbarrow loads. The next one is being loaded when he hears lunch is ready, and he is fucking starving. Murray has no idea where she found it, and he has no idea how she got it in here, but the table is set, and lunch is on the table. Some sort of vegetables and rice in a sweet chilli sauce, with tea and juice. Murray eats the lot; some bread would have been nice, but we live in hope.

Cha has been busy preparing the seed trays with enriched pre-fertilised soil, reckoning that this will produce healthier plants that will have a greater chance of survival. Murray listens and nods, not really having a clue about what she is talking about. He was never very good at the gardening thing. Through his many attempts in his previous life, he was thought to be a bigger danger to plants than weed killer. Murray just never had the magic green fingers.

Murray is informed that if he was to bring up the big spare generators, they could rig up some lights and heaters in the greenhouse. She could start germinating some seeds, adding, "I could start with the seeds that your brother provided!" She did not miss a trick. Murray has had these seeds for ages; in fact, he has had them since the day they met. Murray collected them the same day he collected the bin bags full of grass. He had never mentioned it. She just knew. Murray will bring up the generator, but for now, there is still lots to do. He is hoping that the gravel will be completed today. They smoke, and he puts his arms around her, kisses her, and then returns to work. Murray is concerned that he does not have enough time to finish what he wants to do today, so he drops a gear and gets stuck in. The gravel now fully surrounds the course, the gentle slope of the banks is discretely stepped to encourage the gravel to partially adhere to the sides, the big brush is utilised in pushing the gravel over the edges, and gravity helps with the rest. Eventually, it will settle, and the water plants they still have to source will aid this process.

It is dark now, and they have both been carried away with their tasks. The sweat is dripping off Murray, and Cha tells him that if he was in a wet T-shirt competition, she would vote for him, slapping his arse, "Let's get you home, big boy, and out of them wet clothes." Murray puts the jacket back on, and they walk back to the house. Charlie is delighted and does not turn back once; her tail is like a propeller. They had missed her feeding time, but she does not complain.

On entering the house, Murray does as he is told. He reinvigorates the fire, it is nearly dead, and kindling has to be used to resuscitate it back to life when this is sparking; he adds bigger sticks and some logs. Murray heads upstairs. The bath is already running, and he is helped out of his damp clothes, but first, Cha removes the automatic from his waistband, which is also damp with sweat. Maybe he has overdone it today, but sometimes you have to go above and beyond to get things done. Murray thinks that she is pleased with the results. Now in the bath, he stretches out and lets the water spread over his aching bones. Murray closes his eyes for a second or two, only to be interrupted with a "Hey white boy, budge up, there is room for two." Cha washes him down, and he relaxes and lets her do it all.

Murray is helped out of the water, and she dry's him down and presents him with a light tracksuit. He has never worn one of these before but puts it on anyway, Cha is still naked, and he is that tired he can barely raise a smile. Murray thinks that Bobby is tired, also. Cha goes to stick some clothes on, and Murray deposits his frame on the four-seater, and he is sound asleep before she returns downstairs.

Mr Black, sleeps soundly and wakes up early in the morning. By all things, the smell of breakfast, Cha has made the bread thing, and it smells that nice Murray thinks that it could raise the dead. A "Morning baby!" greets him, "How are you feeling?" followed by a welcome back hug and an even more welcome back to the land of the living bunch of kisses. Charlie is also pleased to see him and comes over and nuzzles in for a neck scratch, just one of her multitudes of soft spots. He gets up; the tracksuit has to be removed. Murray changes into his normal attire. Everything that is placed in front of him, he devours. He takes the tea outside and surveys the weather; it is dull and overcast.

Cha hands him a present. It is the automatic, all cleaned, and sleeping in a shoulder holster. "I knew we had some of these. It just took me a while to remember where I put it. This should stop it from getting drenched in your sweat." Murray puts it on, and for a second, it makes him feel like a secret agent or a bad guy, not sure which one he would prefer. It certainly is more comfortable than having it stuffed down the back of his pants.

Chapter Eleven

The flower beds will be set out today, the last of the heavy work. Cha has insisted on being his helper, which Murray knows will mean the opposite, but he will bite his tongue, and he is more than sure that it will be an entertaining day.

They grab the kit needed for the day and walk up; the water level in the river is slightly higher than normal, and the season is changing but not quickly enough. A day of uninterrupted sunshine would be nice, but the only sunshine he will have today is Cha's radiant, supermodel smile.

The robin greets them with his territorial chirp and struts his stuff for everyone to witness. Cha reloads the braziers and sets them alight. Together they trolley over the bricks to the allocated positions. As always, they chat about things. One of the main recurring conversations is what happens when they meet other people. They can't exactly sit them down and vet them. Please fill in the application form: noting that section eleven will have to be complete, or your application will be null and void. They agree upon a series of subtle signals, nothing outrageous, no overt hand signals, only little changes to facial expressions, which they practice frequently. When it is Murray's turn to perform, all Cha does is burst out laughing and convinces him that he could have never been an actor. Cha could have been anything. She finds these simulations very easy to perform and is an expert at reading body language. Murray is not so good at it; Cha thinks that Murray would just shoot everyone on sight and maybe ask some questions later.

Enough of the nonsense. They lay out the foundations one brick high, all level, and following the designated contour of the pattern. It takes all day, and the results are not perfect but adequate enough for what is required. Over the course of the following week, they complete the task. The job looks great. Cha is the expert at pointing, and Murray is the expert at cleaning the cement mixer.

Their supplies are needing replenished; Murray's priorities are cigarette papers, tins of last man on the planet, and bottled beer. The other priorities are food and anything else that still remains on the multiple and growing want lists. It is agreed they will go on a shopping spree; the first task is to check the surrounding roads within their vicinity. This will give the batteries a decent charge, and it is always a good idea to check for any signs of movement since their last adventure. They drive for a while and pull over, scanning the area with the binoculars for any signs of movement. They spot nothing out of the ordinary; the only changes that they notice are due to damage from the winter, a few large potholes, some collapsed roofs, no people signs.

The low loader is fully checked, and Murray is driving this. Cha and Charlie are in pole position in the AWD, they are still in careful drive mode, stop and check. It takes a while to get to the town, they would like to rummage freely, but they also have to be careful.

The food shopping is easy, and a couple of stops and the food list is wiped. The tracked excavator is another matter; the yard in which they are located is a mess. Wading through the muck, Murray is unable to start the first couple. Everything he tries is to no avail, and no amount of swearing and threatening the machine with violence does not work either. It is so frustrating, and it is not just a problem of finding out what the fault or multiple faults could be. Murray has to take into consideration the time period that it has been lying dormant and the preventative maintenance that was done during its working life. A machine is normally a her, but, in this instance, it is only an it.

The fourth machine, after a bit of prodding and pulling, sparks into life. Murray declares, "She is a beauty!" A huge plume of black smoke is emitted from the exhaust and seems to last forever before it starts to dissipate in the still sky. Unfortunately, she refuses to move, the tracks are solid, and the mechanism does not even utter a single squeak. Solenoid-controlled valves, blocked hoses, dud fuses, he does not know where to start. Thinking that it could be electrical, Murray scratched his head, having a thought while at the same time having a little cigarette break.

Cha notices his perplexed state, "Hi baby, she will start, but she does not want to play. I have offered her a new hairdo and a new pair of dancing shoes." Cha looks at Murray and hands him a manual, "I was rummaging in the building behind us and found this. It is a bit grubby, but I think it should reveal the information required to get her working. There is also a spares area, so I think that's how you are always lucky and fingers crossed." Charlie does not like it here, not one bit, her ears are up, and she is sniffing the air. The tail is not wagging but straight out behind her.

Murray thumbs through the manual, notebook in hand. He jots down a few numbers and names and asks Cha to rummage in the spares department and see if any of these items come up during her search. Meanwhile, Murray gets out the meter and twists and turns the dials in between inserting the probes to check the electrical system. He locates several defunct solenoids and will have to replace a few dud fuses.

Two white cars roll into the yard. Murray has not phoned the dial excavator helpline, so they must be here for something else. He looks for his rifle. Murray has left it over beside his toolboxes on the low loader, too far away to go for. He will have to wait this out. There are five of them, three from one car and two from the other. No uniforms and no insignias. It's the big one who does the talking. He is the only one that has no weapon on show.

There is no formal greeting, "You are trespassing on private property and attempting to steal one of our machines. I see no registration and, according to our records, no signed. Approved paperwork, so we can assume that this is an unauthorised entry with the intent to steal, and with the vehicle that is parked over there," at this, he points to the low loader. "I say you don't have a leg to stand on." Luckily Cha had parked the AWD out off-site, and he hoped she would stay out of their vision if the worst came to worst. Murray hopes that she and Charlie are okay. He does really care about himself. Murray thinks that whatever she is up to, she will need some time. Murray asks the guy where the no-entry signs are located, as he have not seen any, and adds if you have the forms with you. Would it be okay if he could fill them in just now?

He receives no reply, two of them come over, and before Murray knows it, he is thumped on the head and tied up, hooded, and chucked unceremoniously into the back of one of the cars. The big guy is giving orders. The two thugs search the area for any other trespassers before he gets into the car with the other two goons and drives off with Murray in the back. He thinks that they are amateurs, as they have not searched him yet.

Cha is awaiting her visitors; Charlie is in the back room and has been given the command to stay. The two thugs are slowly going from building to building. Given the state of the yard, it is only a matter of time before they find her mucky footprints on the once pristine white floor. The door slowly opens one motions to the other at the mucky footfalls on the floor; they both enter tentatively, taking a couple of steps forward. They look everywhere, up, down, left, and right but fail to look behind them.

Cha is barefooted and has silently moved into position, forcing the barrel of the submachine gun into the nearest thug. She tells them to drop their weapons and kick them away. Hands-on your head, there is no discussion. With a swift kick to the back of the leg's floors, one of them and a split second later, the other one is knocked unconscious with a full-force blow on the back of the head with the submachine gun. The unconscious one is left where he lies Cha's knee pins down his companion while she cuffs his hands together. The other guy is easier to cuff and does not move.

Murray is driving in silence for about, he thinks, twenty minutes. On arrival at the destination, he thinks that it must be their headquarters. He is manhandled out of the car, force-marched, dragged upstairs, pulled downstairs several times, and eventually led into a room. Murray thinks this is just a ruse, totally to disorientate him. As he really doesn't give a fuck it does not have any effect on him. Murray is just going to ignore them. Eventually, the journey stops, and he is seated on a chair; his hands are untied only to be reattached together with a chin being fed through a ring on the table. Murray is left alone in the room; the hood is still in place. He gets as comfy as possible and promptly falls asleep.

Cha has been busy. Both the bad guys are taped up and secured to wooden chairs, and the arms, legs, and necks are all duct taped up. She has even taped over their eyes and mouths.

Murray is awake, and still, nothing has happened. This place is very quiet, and there are no sounds of any movement. Murray gets bored and goes back to sleep. He and Cha had many discussions, and he remembered the one about being held against your will. Relax as much as possible, he had always thought this advice sounded totally absurd, but on reflection, he now knows exactly where she was coming from. Maybe he was meant to shout and plead for company, but Murray is still not interested. His only hope is that the girls are okay, Cha is a survivor, and Murray is thinking positive.

The tape is yanked and ripped off from the eyes. The one who had just seconds ago had a rather large bushy eyebrow winced the most. All sorts of squeaks and whimpers emanated from his taped-up mouth. The other one barely moved a muscle and just stared at Cha. Charlie had joined the company and just sat there, omitting a low growl, and lips quivering showed off her large teeth.

"Okay, guys! We are going to play a game. I ask questions, and you reply." the towel is removed from the tray revealing a selection of persuaders: bolt cutters, hammer, chisel, various nails, and a blow torch. At this, she rips the tape from their mouths and backs away from them, making noises that she has left the building.

The guy with the stare tells the one who now has the waxed unibrow, "Keep your mouth shut. Tell the bitch nothing. My brother will notice we are late and come looking." Cha slams the back door and walks straight past them, not saying a word. Charlie and her leave via the front door. The car keys are still in the ignition. Cha drives in into the middle of the yard and opens all the windows, and switches it off. A can of petrol is produced, and she sets it on fire. If they are patrolling, the smoke will be noticed. Finding a secluded hidey-hole that gives her an uninterrupted view, she and Charlie go up position and wait. The guns are loaded; she shares a snack with Charlie, smokes, and has tea while playing the waiting game. They should be here soon. If she has to kill, then she will, but as Mr B is AWOL, the more she keeps them alive, the greater her bargaining power.

The door is opened, and several people approach. One of them has on aftershave. Murray thinks it smells like cat pish. His hood is removed, and a fat bastard greets him in a shirt, tie, and blazer. The other one is just a bruiser who stands motionless, trying to look intimidating. What is it with big guys? Murray will never understand the reasons that they think they are invincible. As far as he can it, they are just bigger targets.

"Good afternoon, I am J P Walsh, and sorry about the delay in meeting you. Lots of meetings today, and I hope you have been treated well." The cat pish is almost as nauseating as his delusions of grandeur. He says nothing and just looks at him like he is something he would have to remove from the sole of his shoe.

A knock on the door, and the trolley lady enters with the tea; she is shaking out of fear and dread or just old age. Murray does not know, but he will not get involved, but he does thank her for the tea. This gets a raised eyebrow from the smelly across from him. "Shall I be a vicar?" Murray is going to say, "Why don't you go and take a flying fuck to yourself?" but Cha's advice is ringing in his head, and he keeps my mouth firmly closed. Murray thinks he is nuts for asking in the first place.

JPW pours and asks, "Sugar?"

"No thanks, and just frighten it with the milk," this produces a wry smile, and Murray is waiting for the questions to start. The bruiser in the corner is still motionless; this game has been played many times before. Murray is offered biscuits but politely refuses. An unopened packet of cigarettes and a lighter and laid on the table. Murray has not had one in ages and will have one or two

197

before they realise he is not playing. He sparks up, the tea is at the perfect temperature, and Murray closes his eyes and remembers what his granny had told him. Always savour that first sip and go somewhere nice in your head. There is no point in being down, no matter what.

Opening his eyes, JPW is displaying another wry smile on his face; Murray would love to kick him around the room just to wipe it from his face, but he is presently not in a position to do so. A briefcase is produced and placed on the table, and a folder is withdrawn, fucking unbelievable, and Murray thinks for a second that he is in here for a loan. JPW takes his time pretending to look through the pages of information, but all this is bullshit. For all Murray knows, there is fuck all on the sheets, and this is just a setup to let him know who is in charge.

The tea is finished; Murray is asked if he would like another cup, and he politely refuses, the bruiser on cue opens the door, and the tea lady reappears. Murray tells her that the tea was fantastic, she wants to say thanks, but he does not think she is allowed to speak, so she slowly shakes her way out of the room. They all hear the clatter as she drops the tray outside the room. JPW raises the other eyebrow and mutters something under his breath.

Murray is asked, "Name, age, date of birth?" He answers truthfully and asks if he would like him to fill in the form. The bruiser takes a couple of steps forward but is stopped by a raised hand from JPW, both eyebrows are raised, and Murray is informed that even though it would only be a pen, they have to be careful and just answer the questions as truthfully as possible.

This goes on for about ten minutes. The questions are familiar, almost just a pre-employment form. The drone goes on and on. "Religion?"

"I'm agnostic."

"mixed comprehensive School."

"Living family members?"

"Nil"

"Occupation?"

"Unemployed."

This one nearly kills him, "Any affiliations with the Knights of Saint Columba or the Freemasons?" Murray looks at him to check if he is for fucking real and wonders why he does not just ask what foot he kicks with. At this, the folder is closed, "We can do this the easy way or the hard way," this produces a wry smile and a flicker of excitement in the eyes of the bruiser.

"So, let's try again. How many people are in your community?' Murray tells him that it is only him and, until this day, you and your guys are the only living souls he has come across. "If it is only you, why were you so intent on removing an excavator from a restricted area?" Murray replies that as there were no signs visible, he was unaware that it was a restricted area, adding that as he has loads of time on his hands, he was going to try his hands at landscape gardening. All this was said in the friendliest manner without any malice.

Murray must have hit a raw nerve. JPW motioned to the bruiser, who put on his black leather gloves, stepped forward a few steps, and proceeded to slap Murray about. He ignored the pain and discomfort and thought of Cha and Charlie. Murray's bank loan interview is interrupted by a knock on the door. He could make out of the subdued voices. Peter has not returned, and smoke has been spotted from the demolition yard.

JPW stops the beating and asks if Murray knows anything about the report. Murray asks him how he could know as he has been here for ages and is sorry but honestly, does he really look like the resident clairvoyant? This angers him, and he tells Murray that if anything happens to his brother, he will be held solely responsible. JPW informs the bruiser to send out a double patrol, and both of them leave the room. Murray hears lots of commotion from outside, whistles, shouting, and several vehicles starting. The noises evaporate as they drive off.

Twenty minutes later, Cha, from her vantage point, hears the fast-driving vehicles approaching. From the noise omitted, she counts three of them. Not killing them is no longer a viable option. As good as she is, the numbers will not be in her favour, but not to worry, she has been in worse situations before, and for this one, she has had plenty of time to prepare a surprise party. The yard has only one way in and one way out, and the vehicles screech into the gate area. The big mistake was that the largest vehicle stopped dead centre at the entrance.

Cha is at the highest vantage point she could find, and even though the RPG is designed for urban warfare and the manufactures warranty states that there is no dangerous back blast, she has taken care to make sure the immediate space behind her is clear. Charlie has been put into a safer area. All the safeties had been removed, the sights were activated, she aimed, The red safety lever was pulled in, and the red firing button was pushed forward simultaneously. The occupants did not stand a chance as the 84mm projectile exploded on impact. The force was large enough to lift the vehicle in the air and turn it sideways, blocking all useless attempts at vacating the carnage. Those inside who were not killed outright by the shock wave were either killed by the shrapnel or the flames. There was some screaming, but they could scream all they wanted. They are dead. They just don't know it yet.

It was all too quick for the would-be attackers, for those who managed to get out of the other vehicles were not as lucky. Several tried to dart to the cover of the nearest building. These were cut down by the grenades activated by the various connected tripwires. The rest were mown down by a short burst of accurate fire from Cha's machine gun as she advanced forward, moving from position to position.

The survivors, who were still moaning, were silenced by a single shot to the head as she searched the yard for signs of life. The light is starting to fade, and there will be no more patrols tonight. Cha thinks it is time to take the fight to them. She enters the room, and unibrow and his boss are shocked to see her. They are untied one at a time and handcuffed and shackled together. Leading them outside, they are even more shocked at the carnage and the smell of death that lies before them.

Charlie joins them from her safe zone with a commanding whistle from Cha. The flames and heat have died down enough to squeeze out the front gate. The prisoners are led out and taken to the AWD. They are gagged and blindfolded by the last of the duct tape. Cha takes advantage of their predicament, unlocks her un-connectable phone, and presses a few buttons to initiate a fictitious connection. "Identification Charlie Bravo 00248076 requesting air strike at 0530 tomorrow morning, confirm availability," a short silence is followed by Cha holding her nose and putting on a different accent, "Identification verification code required," more silence followed by her normal voice, Mike Bravo 810910, this was Murray's initials and date of birth backwards, but the fools in the back would have no idea. More silence followed by the fake voice, "Verification code accepted; availability of airstrike affirmative target map reference required." Normal voice "Map reference will be supplied shortly, Charlie Bravo 00248076 over and out."

Cha drives for a little while; for some reason, she is heading out of town, and her instinct tells her this is the correct way to go. Five minutes out of town, and she pulls into a layby. Disconnecting mono-brow from his partner and pulling him out of the car, she unceremoniously removes the duct tape from his face, the unibrow is completely gone. All that is left is a red mark and sporadic patches above the other eye. Some eyelashes have also been removed. She thinks this is why the tears are running down his face. He has also peed himself and is shaking.

She lights a cigarette and whispers in his ear, "My dog has not eaten today, and if you do not tell me what I want to know, I am going to slice you up slowly, and you can watch my dog eat." She puts the cigarette on his lips and lets him have a drag. He coughs profusely, spitting out the cigarette.

"I don't smoke." Cha takes another one out of the packet and starts asking him questions. Whispering in his good ear, "Are we heading in the correct direction?" he is wetting himself again but manages to nod his head. "How far away?" in-between sobs and shakes, he says, "About half an hour."

this goes on for a few cigarettes, and she finds out that they were about a hundred of them. There are no roadblocks that he is aware of, the guy in the back is called Peter, and he is second in command, and his brother is in charge.

Illuminated under the torchlight, he indicates the area on the map and describes it as an old farmhouse with a few additional buildings. The main entry point is on the front. The back entrance is only used in the summer months due to the swamp area. He is forced to lie on the ground while Cha goes through the motions of calling in the coordinates. All she really wants to do is finish her smoke in peace.

He is bundled in the front and has to give directions and distances as they drive, leave at the next junction, drive for about five minutes and then take the second on the right. The straight road for the next ten miles, and the farmhouse is over the next hill. The lights are killed before they reach the hill; with the flashlight, Cha fakes a double-check of the location on the map and gives Brian his instructions. Peter is removed from the car and receives a blow to the head before he is secured to the nearest tree.

Brian is frogmarched along the road. He has confessed that there is no night vision apparatus at the base, so they have plenty of time to rehearse his speech when he arrives, and just in case in the event that they shoot him, she has written a little note and stuck it in his pocket. At the same time, he was preoccupied with peeing, shaking, and whimpering.

They can see the lights in the distance; no searchlights are in action. Brian is told that if he wants to stay alive, he has to do everything that she tells him, and even though he can't see her, she assures him that she has a sniper rifle with a night scope and can take him out at a two-mile distance even in the dark. His bonds are removed, and he is instructed to shout his name and wave the makeshift white flag. They are only about 400 yards from the main gate. Cha has disappeared into the undergrowth before the single searchlight answers his shouts for help.

"Help! Help! It's me, Brian. Please don't shoot. I am one of you. I am Peter's driver. Please don't shoot me."

A megaphone breaks the silence from the camp, "Do not move and keep perfectly still, or we will open fire." The abbot's entrance on the main gate is opened, and two armed figures run out to meet him. On reaching their target, one takes aim while the other searches for him and confirms his identity. Cha watches in silence from her hidden vantage point.

Brian is escorted and helped into the enclosure. He is taken straight away to see JPW. The bruiser has joined the procession and marches in front, exerting his assumed position of authority. When he is taken into JPW's private office, it is blatantly obvious that he is a mess. His face is swollen, and he has soiled himself. The trousers are damp at both the front and rear. JPW gets him to sit down and tells the bruiser to send someone to wake the medic. Brian is given a stiff brandy to calm him down, which he gulps down in one gulp. JPW tells him to relax. He is among friends and tries to assure him that we are all family here, and he has nothing to fear.

He gibbers about a trained assassin with a high-powered rifle that can see in the dark kill at three miles, the impending air strike, the burnt body parts, the legless bodies, the explosions, and the rockets. She looks like an assassin in a television series, but this one is not an actress. She is a trained killer. It flows out of his mouth in one joined-up sentence with no spaces between the words.

He is still visibly shaken. When the medic arrives, JPW tells him to get Brian straightened out. He does not care what he injects him with as long as he can speak and tell us what is going on. The medic remonstrates that he could have a heart attack; the bruiser interrupts the conversation and tells him to do as he is told.

The medic rummages in his bag and jags Brian up. Brian settles and is about to give a calmer version of the previously described events. JPW stops him in his tracks and asks if Peter was harmed. "She never even looked at him, and as far as I am aware, he is still alive, but she has told me if you pull a fast one, she will cut him in pieces and feed him to her dog."

Brian goes through the story, even describing the handheld micro radio she had contacted for a scheduled coordinated airstrike at the farmhouse base. The bruiser gives his opinion that this is just a bluff and that technology does not exist anymore. JPW tells him to shut the fuck up, and he wants his brother back. Brian relays the exchange instructions word for word, just like Cha dictated, before clutching his chest and falling off the chair. He was dead before he hit the ground. JPW tells the bruiser to get this piece of shit out of his office, and he needs the chair replaced. Release our prisoner and, once Peter has returned, get everyone ready as we will hunt him and her down.

Murray is really bored now and has resigned to his fate that they are going to kill him. Murray hopes it is quick, and if he is lucky, he will be given a cigarette as his last request. He can hear hurried footsteps coming along the corridor. The door opens, and it is the bruiser and a couple of his chums. Thinking that they are here to take him away to be shot, he can be cocky and asks, "What, no tea lady this time?" for this, he receives a full slap in the face. The key is inserted, and his shackles are removed. Murray asks if he can go for a pee, but his question is ignored, and he is forcibly removed from the room. Amazingly he only goes down one flight of stairs before coming to the front door. Murray is escorted to the gate, the hairs on the back of his neck are erect, and he turns around and catches JPW staring at him. He looked very angry.

Chapter Twelve

Murray is instructed to start walking and not to turn back. He needs to urinate; his bladder is at bursting point. Unzipping his fly, he releases a stream of liquid, "Boy, I really needed that," he says to no one. From her vantage point, Cha witnesses the gate opening and recognises Murray walking. She reckons that nobody walks like him. She monitors his progress and watches the gate for any sneaky moves, daylight is starting to break, and as he is progressing up the hill, he hears her voice, "Don"t stop, and whatever you do, don't talk and keep moving I will meet you over the brow, and I assure you that I am okay and have not been harmed"

His pace quickens. He had no idea what to expect as they had told him, sweet fuck all, just to get out and keep walking. He is now over the hill, and the farmhouse is no longer in view. Cha comes running out of the bushes to his left, and she must have shadowed his movements from halfway up the hill; she is crying. She hugs him and tells him that she had thought that she had lost him forever. Murray is crying also, as he had thought the same. She informs Murray that she has to keep to her word and Peter must be released.

She takes him to where he has been kept tied to the tree. Murray removes the tape from his face, he just stares, and the unveiled hatred is all that comes off him. His leg restraints are loosened slightly to allow him to hobble home. He requires help to get up, and Murray pulls him up by sticking his fingers up his nostrils just to persuade him that if he tries anything, he will remove his nose. He grunts and curses Murray threatening all sorts of revenge as soon as he is able.

Murray would really like to beat the crap out of him, but rules are rules, and he has to send him on his merry way unharmed. Murray is a little miffed at this but does as he is instructed. Peter is dragged onto the road and shoved to encourage him to get moving.

They are in the car; Charlie is howling at Murray's return, and this makes them both shed a tear. He is just so happy that they are both safe. Cha says they have to move it as she does not think JPW and Peter will let this go. She remembers the way to the outskirts of the town they had visited. Once we get there, Murray gives directions for an alternate way home. He only hopes that the roads are passable. They have plenty in the dual fuel tanks and have spare fuel in the back, where they can. The accelerator pedal is floored, as they need to get out of the area pronto.

In the farmhouse community, the alarm has been sounded, and all and sundry have been ordered to assemble in the meeting area. JPW is on centre stage; his now freshened-up brother and the leading henchmen flank him. The PA system has been set up; JPW has on a camouflage jacket and at his waist a double-pistoled holstered belt. His excess belly fat will impede the drawing of the pistols. He has no intention of getting involved in the fighting. That is for the menials below him. He taps the microphone for the attention of the milling crowd, and when complete silence has been achieved, he begins his broadcast.

"Our peaceful community has been violated by certain individuals' intent on causing us harm, and with great sadness, it is my duty to inform you that only yesterday, twenty-one of our members were ambushed and brutally murdered in cold blood carrying out their duties. The fundamental idea of this community was to set up a new world where we could have peaceful relations with our neighbours, relationships that would require no military conflict, to trade and exchange ideas for the mutual benefit of all."

"Yesterday was an unprovoked attack; we all know that the world changed with the sickness, and like you, I had sincerely thought that these days were far behind us, but coexisting is not part of these vile humans remit, they brought death and fear to us in this very peaceful place and I beseech you all to put a final nail in their coffins, I plead to your hearts, your souls for our future and our children's future that we hunt down these invertebrates and eradicate their existence to ensure our prosperous collective future."

"We have to set up search parties and scour these lands to flush them out from their hiding place, remove them from our lands, and most importantly to, permanently eradicate them from our future."

There have been sporadic cheers, and comments for hunting the culprits down, the closing part of the speech had the crowd on its feet, clapping and cheering, indicating that he had the full support to hunt them down. JPW raised both hands and thanked all of them for their undivided support. He left the stage for a huge round of applause. One of the henchmen, the bruiser approached the microphone and informed the crowd that all drivers were to report to the transport area for vehicle allocations and all able-bodied men and women from the age of fifteen were to report for firearms and ammunition. The henchmen had divided up the surrounding area into sections, and a full search was to be implemented. The villains would be apprehended and punished.

Cha, Charlie, and Murray continue on trying to put as much distance between them as humanly possible. They have only encountered a few minor roadblocks. If they can skirt around, then they would do so. Their tracks were covered as much as possible. The only one major blockage had to have a few cars dragged out to allow passage through. These were near impossible to cover up, and for these, Cha left a couple of surprises for their pursuers. It feels like they have been driving for days, but in reality, it has only been about twenty minutes maximum. They periodically check the mirror, but as of yet, there is no one on their tail. Cha is deep in thought. Murray offers to drive, but she tells him that it is okay and he should rest after his ordeal. They make it home without any more unintended diversions or setbacks. Charlie is delighted to be back, and as soon as the car door is opened, she is off barking at anything and everything.

Cha sticks on the water to boil; Murray quickly resets the fire and sparks it to life. She has a beer while waiting on the water to boil, and for the first time ever, she asks Murray to roll her one. He dually obliges and rolls one for himself also; she gets up and gets him a beer. This is highly unusual, and Murray is worried. Charlie is barking outside to get in. She tells Murray whatever it is he is worried about not to, saying that no matter what hardships they are going to encounter over the next few days, it will be okay. Cha gets up, turns the water off, and returns with an unopened six-pack of beer. The ready rolls are sparked up. Charlie has been fed and is more than happy running through the house.

They move over to the fire; it is not cold, but the open fire is comforting. "Before I met you again at the Engineering thing, I thought you were nuts. I had never met anyone like you; I thought you were wild, unkempt, rude, and extremely bad-mannered. You had the attitude of an old rocker belonging to a faraway time with different rules that just did not exist in my world." She breaks to polish off her remaining beer, opens a couple more, and relights her joint.

"My world was full of rules, and all the training I had received did not prepare me for the new world and most certainly did not prepare me for a world with you. You have enlightened me to things I was unaware existed, you have made me cry, and you make me laugh, but most of all, you are the reason I can't wait to get up in the morning because, more than anything, you make me happy and this just wants to make me smile all day long." Cha has another break, and the beer is drained and needs replaced; she cracks open another pair. Murray rolls another couple of joints, she has not asked for one, but it will not go to waste. "Every day with you is an adventure into the unknown. You will tackle anything I ask and never complain, and compared to my previous life, where there was just darkness and an ever-present prevailing doom, you have brought brightness and eternal rays of sunshine, and what I am trying to tell you is that I love you Murray Black and I would be totally lost without you." More beer is gulped down. Murray tries to keep up and has a good head-on, but he is absorbing every single word that she is saying. He has tried to speak a couple of times, but Mrs B's glare tells him to hold it.

"Yesterday, these people tried to take this away from me, and that is unforgivable, I killed lots of people yesterday, and it was all part of a day's work in my old world. I honestly thought those days were gone forever and what angered me the most was that they had taken you away forever, and for the first time in my life, I was scared. They had no right to do this, we had done nothing wrong and posed no threat to them or theirs, and for this, they must be punished and will be punished."

Murray goes to speak, but her eyes say it all. Another set of beers is opened; he still has some of the previous one left, but he does spark up, and she reaches over and sparks one up also, another gulp of her beer, and she begins again. "I have no intention of living what years we have left in tears, and tomorrow I am going to hunt them down and kill them all. I am not asking you to come and help me, this is what I am trained for, and they really have no idea of the monster that they have awakened."

Murray takes this opportunity to tell her that he will follow her to the ends of the earth without hesitation and that he is coming with her. If she likes it, that is fine; if she does not like that is fine also, but he will be at her side as he still wakes up every morning thinking that five seconds without you would be an eternity that he really does not want to experience. The both of them are crying and not crying out of sadness but out of true happiness, just the pure joy of being together, knowing that there is a tomorrow and it belongs to them, and no one is going to take that away from them.

They should really eat to allow their bodies to soak up the alcohol. Cha asks Murray if he would like to cook, and they both burst out laughing, knowing that when he is sober, the kitchen is the mess that he leaves behind that is an issue. Just imagine what that would be like in this state. Cha cooks and drinks, and Murray smokes and drinks as she tells him her version of the events. It takes quite a while for her to get the story of the fake micro radio call for the airstrike. The voices are hilarious, and when she tells him how she made up the call sign and authentication code with his name, date of birth, and an old bank account number, Murray is laughing so much he nearly wets himself.

They drink and laugh until the early hours. None of them wants this day to finish, but they end up falling asleep entwined in each other's arms as if they are about to face their next day like it is the last day on the planet. Cha has wakened before him, and Murray is now being nudged by Charlie's head. He opens his eyes, "Morning, baby." He says to Charlie, knowing full well that Cha can hear him. She just smiles, knowing that she is and will be the only one.

Cha has a purposeful stride to her this morning, and Murray gets this feeling that they are going to be busy. Breakfast is all laid out, and as usual, he doesn't know what it is. He doesn't ask what it is, but Bobby and Murray just eat it. "I hope you like cold fare, as that is all that we are going to be eating for the next few days, so make the most of the breakfast, baby" When she says baby, she is looking at the dog, her back is turned when she says this, but he knows, and she knows, he knows. "I will meet you up at the shed."

Murray scoffs until he is full and washes it down with a pot of tea; oh, how he misses the old tea lady that rattled as much as her trolley, collecting the last two tins of the last man on the planet, his guns. He jackets up and heads up to meet Cha.

Cha has been busy, an area of the floor has been covered with various tarpaulins, and on top of this, she has laid out what looks like every bag of fertiliser. The ones with the blue writing were laid out over in the corner. Murray guesses the ingredients were not suitable for her recipe. "I have left you a drawing on the table. Can you have a look at it and tell me what you can and can't do?" Murray has a look at the scrawl. He reads the margins as he walks about. He mentally is ticking what material is available and what possible alternative he could use.

The farmhouse regime is interviewing the patrol leaders and going over the reports. They are slowly marking up the maps and putting pins and elastic bands to indicate the areas that had been searched. Starting from outside the nearest town, the four active patrols are quartering the areas. Each is given a specific area, and if required, every factory, every building, and every house has to be searched, and any signs of human activity had to be reported. All the collated information as yet has been fruitless, and there have been no sightings of the quarry.

The patrols set out every morning at the same time, driving in a convoy until they reach their designated area, then they separate and start their searching. JPW is having breakfast. The table could easily seat twenty people, but this is his private time. The selection in front of him is his favourite part of the day, and he shares it with no one, not even Peter. In-between greedy mouthfuls, he goes through the latest reports, and all is good apart from the fuel consumption. Thinking that the patrols do not have to return every night. They would be more proactive if they could be out for twenty-four hours. Maybe one patrol out of the four could stay out, and putting it on a rotational basis, with some sort of added bonus, say a special cooked breakfast, would stop any moans. He will run it past Peter and his associates later, but he will finish eating and have a little snooze before presenting the idea. They are not going to object, and he will control the meeting, and they will leave, thinking that it is their idea.

The idea of him going on patrol does not appeal to him one little bit. If the weather was more pleasant, then maybe, and now that he thinks about it just before nodding off, he can't actually remember the last time he had ventured outside of his little kingdom. He dreams of being on safari in Africa, and the quarry is not big game. The hunted is the slanty-eyed bitch and the smart-mouthed boyfriend. His people are beating the area and sending in the dogs to chase them to their unavoidable date with destiny.

Murray meets Cha outside the shed as she rummages around the scrap pile. "Hey, Mr Fix it; what do you have for me today?" He shows Cha what he can and can't fabricate with the added alternative. She likes the oil drum that he has prepared. Some of the other items just get "Okay, that will do," and a couple gets "nope, sorry, that will not work," all of which is okay. Murray has no idea why she wants these, and he will modify everything and anything he can find to accommodate her envisaged plans.

They have lunch in the old office at the back, Cha has a map pinned to the wall and the top section of an old abandoned cane fishing rod acts as a pointer. In between mouthfuls of food, she points. Now they should be quartering the surrounding area of the base, and it should be about three days before they reach here. X marks the spot; she describes the area in detail, and Murray instantly knows what she is talking about. Cha proposes that they hit them big time at this place. It is perfect, and they can pin them in there for however long it takes. All they have to do is make mistakes, and as they have not been trained, it should be just a matter of time. "Once you have helped make the presents, we will need to go and observe and see if we can find them."

If they do not come to the area marked, we can find alternatives." Lunch is over, and he is about to spark up, Mrs B raises a hand, "Uh-uh! Once I spread the liquid over the modified chemical compound, you can't smoke anywhere near here, no naked flames, and it better if you smoke outside. Seriously and better still." She holds out her hand, and Murray hands over the lighters. He sometimes makes mistakes, and this one would be one that they could not walk away from in one piece.

Cha goes and starts to spread out the modified chemical compound until she is satisfied with the overall contour. She covers with newspapers, Murray's old paintings, and anything that will aid the process. She takes a note of the time and writes it on the wall.

Murray assembles in a large pile the nuts, bolts, nails, ball bearings, and washers all within the maximum and minimum size range. The modified detergent is slowly funnelled up to the pre-marked maximum line on the lemonade bottles. He has been given an amount of liquid that he has to pour into each. Once this is complete, Murray has to let them sit for the allotted time before he reseals the bottles. As instructed, he wrote the time down on the first available space.

The items that were the most difficult to find were the small electrical bulbs, which have come from various places, the motorbike, and the low loader. Murray thinks that they should be the winning contestants on the once popular tv show where the contestants had to make some outlandish device out of fuck all. The lengths of wire have been stripped to the required instructions and the ends soldered as per the requirements. Cha assembles the fuses, and he has guessed that the now-adapted lights are the detonators. The fuses are now inserted back into the various devices that he has fabricated and sealed on the inner and outer edges with molten wax. Murray is asked to assist in the packing of the devices, Cha pours some of the modified chemical compounds into the various holes and gently packs, and he goes in behind her adding in the scrap metal. The Barrels are loaded with the medium, and she carefully shares the lemonade bottles, which now just look like they are filled with bright blue slime. Added to this are layers of scrap and more layers of medium until they are solid. Murray carefully pop rivets the covers on using spark-free plastic-coated rivets.

Carefully they load everything onto the small truck and double-check that all is secure. Once satisfied, Cha and Murray pull the canvas cover over and tie it down, the daylight is just about done, and Murray thinks that they are finished for the day; nope, they are back in the small office. "Cold Thai curry and rice or Cold Thai curry." He opts for the first choice and washes it down with some fizzy juice. They are heading out and will set up the positions during the small hours. The journey is much longer than normal as they drive in the dark and only use the headlights when absolutely necessary, which means they only used them during the manoeuvres around their home base road, and it was pitch black all the way in from there.

Cha instructs Murray to where he has to park the lorry, and she helps him fully cover it with branches to help hide it from the road. The road at this section has a few abandoned cars. These are started by the jump leads connected to the AWD and are rearranged to their advantage. The access point from the North side is narrowed into single-file traffic, and the South end is now blocked completely. With this done and trip wire set, they head back up to their pre-selected vantage point and wait. Cha takes up the first watch, and Murray snoozes in the AWD, which is concealed from view in the bushes. He is woken several hours later, and Cha tells him it is her turn, and if he sees anything, he has to wake her immediately; otherwise, just wake her after three hours.

At the farmhouse headquarters, the patrols are starting to arrive. The reports are sent to the administration, where the pinned and elasticated indicators are moved on the map to represent the extent of the search coverage. The first night patrol is on duty and has sent back a report, "nothing unusual found an overnight camp located at map reference." This is marked with a single yellow pin, and in the morning, they will start searching the main road. Most of the closest outlying towns and villages have been searched, and as of yet, no signs have been found. It is JPW"'s intention to search the main road and establish an outpost at the first major bridge; from there, they can search back the way like a pincer movement.

A knock on the door, and the tea lady rattles in. JPW can't remember her name. He does not think he has asked her name, not that it will matter. Sooner or later, she will be going to the retirement home at the bottom of the cliff. Unfortunately, they just don't have a retirement facility to take care of the old and infirm, and why waste valuable resources?

What he does remember is that it is chicken Kiev tonight. It is Peter's favourite, JPW could keep some for him, but he will be out on patrol for several days, and it will not keep, so why waste it? The tea lady lays the salvers of food out on the table and leaves when JPW nods.

Murray wakes up Cha just before dawn breaks. She is annoyed that he has let her sleep longer than she intended, but she is tired, and nothing is happening here, so he does not see the harm. It is slightly warmer today, and the sun is trying to get out. It has not got its hat on hip, hip hooray, but at least it is not raining.

They shoot the shit and talk about anything and everything. They even manage a quick passionate love-making session. Other than that, they just watch the road and take turns going for little naps. They smoke and drink tins of juice. Cha mentions room service, and Murray promises that he will surprise her one day. At this, she is rolling about laughing, holding her stomach. He thinks at first that she is ill, but in between girly giggles, she explains that many wild mushrooms are deadly and unless he wants her to get sick, dead, or sick and psychotic that perhaps it would be a good idea to use some of them tinned button mushrooms. This amuses Cha for ages, and she tells him, among other things, that in her country, most women in prison are there for adding things in to their cheating husbands' food, and on the last report that she read, the lucky ones were the ones who died quickly, the ground glass was number one on the list followed a close second by the boiled and finely ground fruit stones. Murray tells her that he is allergic to fruit, and she laughs at his little white lie.

They hear the noise of the approaching mini convoy. Before they can see them, there are four vehicles. Cha scans with the glasses and does the running commentary. The lead car stops, and the guy in charge gets out. It is their favourite, Peter. He waves his hands in the air, and his core crew and camp followers vacate the cars. A chap in an army jumper advances forward, searching for whatever he is meant to be searching for. The rest stand around pretending to be tough guys ready for anything. The truth is they just look lost.

Cha is enjoying this, "nothing but a bunch of chancers." Murray asks if he can start killing them now, as he wants to go home and cook some mushrooms. She smiles and tells him to stop it, adding be patient little one. She is pretending to be the master monk addressing the impetuous student.

The guy with the army jumper ferrets about going from car to car. Stopping occasionally focusing on something that catches his interest. Finding nothing, he continues his search. He marches straight back to El Capo in waiting when he finds the trip wire.

Peter listens and waves his arms about again, and a couple of guys go back with jumper man. The rest look around the surrounding area, searching for the evil killers, not one pair of binoculars between them. Murray hears Cha muttering, "Unfucking belicvable." Jumper man crawls like a commando to the trip wire and more slowly traces it to the connected devices. He makes his way back to the two guys crouching behind him and issues some instructions. They go back to the group's parked vehicles and return with what looks like a ball of string. Jumper man unwinds several meters and hands the ball to one of his assistants, and again belly crawls to the trip wire. He manages to tie a loose loop around the fishing line using a couple of recently unattached wing mirrors as the balance point off and slowly works his way back. He removes the ball of string from his helper and trawls his way back to what he considers a safe distance.

He speaks to Peter, who instructs everyone to take cover, and the string is pulled. The trip wire has been activated, and nothing has happened. He gets up and walks forward with all the confidence he can muster and investigates. The devices are nothing more than two empty biscuit tins. Peter is fuming. All this has taken hours, and okay, no one has died, but what a waste of time. Peter issues instructions, and all the guys, except him and his driver, advance forward in their cars right up to the blocked road. They empty out of the cars and begin searching every single vehicle. Peter is fuming and scans the surrounding area; Murray is watching him through the high-powered binoculars and is sure that he is saying, bastards, where are you? He goes back to his car. He has had enough, and it is beef wellington tonight with duchess potatoes, one of his favourites, and if the driver puts his foot down, they will arrive before his greedy, selfish fat bastard of a brother has eaten the lot.

Chapter Thirteen

The seventeen guys that remain; search every vehicle, every bush at the side of the road. Pulling at every piece of litter, looking for anything that may be a potential danger. Murray and Cha hear a shout, and they guess that the whiskey has been located. The elite guard has stopped looking and set up camp. A fire is lit, and they cook and drink. Four guys are put on the lookout while the others party, the boss is away and will not be arriving back till mid-morning at the earliest, so what possible harm is there in having a wee drink or three?

Peter arrives back at HQ in time to personally deliver his report to JPW. "It was a diversion, nothing more than another tactic to waste our time, just like the imaginary airstrike." JPW raises an eyebrow at this. They proceed to the admin; the searched area is growing, and on closer scrutiny, the main road is the key. "I think we should head out there tomorrow on mass clear the road, if my crew has not already done it, then block off the bridge and search back the way and flush the bastards out." JPW agrees, and as dinner will be arriving shortly, they head back to his private office.

On entry into JPW's private sanctum, Peter tells his brother that it would be a good idea if he made an appearance. Good for morale; maybe he could deliver one of his inspirational speeches. They are interrupted by a knock on the door. The tea lady enters with the food, and both she and the trolley shake toward the table. Peter has the same family trait and raises an eyebrow at her slow progress. JPW notices and mouths, "soon" Peter is thinking one of the dollies in the main canteen could replace her, and hopefully, she will deliver more than food. The rest of the camp eats in the main canteen, and they will be having soup, followed by some form of meat, vegetables, and crude bread. Alcohol is only available on special occasions. JPW pours the once-expensive wine and selects the finest parts of the meal for himself, giving Peter second choice. Peter gulps his wine and tucks in, looking forward to corrupting the dolly once the shaky old bag has been pushed over the cliff and claimed by the sea.

Cha is awake and tells Murray the plan, the whiskey was laced, and all who drank will be sleeping. The remaining ones on patrol will be walking about, looking for things that are not there. Balaclavas on, the pair of them slowly make their way down to the area where the overnight guards have camped. The kit that Murray and Cha are carrying is heavy, and they are careful of every step in the dark. The heavy stuff is laid on the ground for now, just a little way off from where they are situated. She looks at Murray and tells him not to worry, reassuring him that everything is going to be fine.

The guards now have to be dealt with. Cha tells Murray to wait while she goes into ninja mode and slips silently into the darkness. Murray hears nothing, not a stifle of a moan and not one scuffle. As arranged, she sends the signal with the flashlight in two short flashes. Murray makes his way over to where she is. All the company is accounted for, and none are missing. The patrol members are all dead from knife wounds. The remainder is all in a drug and alcohol-induced stupor. They drag them all to the water"s edge. Removing their boots and trousers, Murray and Cha take the bodies out one at a time. The dead ones are launched into the current, never to be seen again. The unconscious ones are held under the water till they stop breathing then launched to join the rest of their crew presently surfing downstream.

They tidy up the area removing all traces of their presence except the transport, which is repositioned. The various pre-prepared party tricks are laid out and loaded, awaiting additional visitation from their pursuers. It has taken most of the night to set everything up, and they are really hoping for a full turnout in the morning. Anything other than that will be more than disappointing, and if that happens, Cha will come up with an emergency on-the-spot contingency plan.

After a final check of the kill zone, Cha and Murray return back to their observation point. All is clear everything is as they had left it. They take turns checking on Charlie.

She has been as good as gold, and they have promised to spoil her rotten when this is over. They were not that keen on feeding her tranquilizers but couldn't take the risk of letting her loose in the oncoming fire-fight. Together they go over the plan again and again, it is at the moment is all set moves. "Bad guys in position. Number one is set to go," Murray talks Cha nods. "Spotter mode on, unusual vehicle check, describe, count, people movements, and he adds that's "all I can remember." Cha bursts out laughing at this and tells him, look we have set up the best we can with what we had available. "I wish we had more kit, but this is all we have and we need to think positive, maybe tomorrow will be better."

At this, she disappears over somewhere behind the bushes, and after a few minutes, she shouts him over. She is lying on the ground with a blanket covering her. She confesses that she is naked and coyly enquires if Bobby is hungry. Murray does not need a second invitation and struggles to get his kit off without losing his balance. They make love several times, and he thinks they have gotten the extra energy out of worrying about what is going to happen in the oncoming hours, but presently all they have just now is each other.

Now fully dressed, daylight is starting to break in the distance, and Cha goes to get the food. She looks fatter when she returns. Cha chucks him a black waistcoat; it is a bulletproof vest, and unless the bad guys are shooting with high-velocity Teflon Eight A-coated bullets, then they should offer some form of protection.

Lying in wait, they ate the last of the curry and rice. Greedy chops ate the most, but Murray doesn't mind as Mr Chocolate provided a bar or two to keep him going. Cha produced an eight pack of last man on the planet. Murray has rolled a couple of bangers and is fully confident that the smoke is not, contrary to the last government statistics going to affect his abilities.

They are well secluded; the barrels of both Mr .50 cal. and Miss 7.62 are concealed with bits of bushes, leaves, and some hay and cannot be spotted from the road. Cha reassures Murray that it is highly unlikely that they have any thermographic imaging equipment, and even if they did, they would not be able to figure out how to use it. Murray is now lying on his back, just looking at the sky; Cha asks him, "Are you falling asleep on our first date?" He sniggers at this and crack open another tin, the half-smoked banger is relit while he rolls another. Mrs B gives him a gentle kick and advises, "No more till after playtime."

He replies, "Yip, no problem."

At the farmhouse, the fatty has assembled his crew, they even have some patriotic music playing in the background, and he even has the audacity to have on a khaki-coloured pith helmet. JPW tells the gathered ensemble that today is the day, and with gods help, after all, we are righteous; the crowd repeats, "We are the righteous," that the agitators will be purged once and for all from this land and they will live in peace forevermore. We are the righteous; the crowd chants the repeat incantation. At this point a priest appears it is Peter in some robes that were found in a storage room. The deal was hammered out during dinner was that the old tea lady that rattles was to be replaced by a dolly of his choosing as soon as they return. Peter wanted to take Mrs rattles a walk to the cliffs last night but after several bottles of vintage French wine and pissing himself on the three-seater JPW persuaded him that he could wait another few hours and gave him a solemn promise that it would be done as soon as they returned. The last word he added with raised eyebrows informing Peter that if she could not cook, she would be joining her ASAP.

Peter is on the stage resplendent in robes, with orange and purple sashes finiishing off the outfit with a mitre hat; He is a little grumpy as he has a hangover but delivers a sermon with the addition of, we are the righteous before saving amen and giving the sign of the cross. At this, JPW gets up from the chair and kisses the priest's outstretched hand, and announces in the microphone, "Gentlemen, your transport awaits you. God bless the righteous" it is repeated on mass as the gathered throng exit to the vehicles.

Murray and Cha don"t have to wait much longer; he is thinking that Bobby is getting kind of peckish when Cha looks at him. "Heads up, soldier, our fat friend, and his chums are nearly here."

The noise is overwhelming; through the binoculars, they have a scoff at JPW with his pith helmet leading the convoy. He is standing upright in a converted truck; the bruiser mans the added 50-calibre belt-fed machine gun. The convoy slows as it approaches the north-side gap, but it does not stop. JPW and his van go forward to a wider area allowing him to wave on the advancing force.

Murray counts twenty cars and assorted vans. They all pass JPW, and he salutes them as they drive to the southern hold; no one as of yet has noticed that the overnight crew is absent. The convoy stops, and they start to embark on a mission to clear the barrier. As the last vehicle passes the northern chokepoint, Murray announces, "Number one ready." Cha tells him, "Detonate!" the homemade explosive booms and creates a mini landslide blocking all access to the only escape route.

At the same time, one of JPW"s crew opens a door on one of the parked vehicles from the missing night patrol, and the multi-connected explosives containing the shrapnel and homemade napalm ignite simultaneously and create utter carnage. Those who are not shredded are running around on fire. The ones who are not wounded are shooting in all directions. Murray wants to shoot JPW but can"t locate him through the scope. He is about to shoot the bruiser working the 50-Cal machine gun, as he is just about to pull the trigger a round delivered from Cha and Mr 50 cal. beheads him. Murray empties his magazine on claimants to this position and shouts "Clear," and start replacing the now empty box magazine. He finds plenty of other targets to hit "clear,"

Cha has switched weapons and is also emptying magazines with her 7.62 weapon. Two of the remaining vehicles below are being redirected by Peter to attack their position. "Ready H1 and H2" releasing his weapon he activates and makes the circuits live. As the trucks start to traverse the gentle incline, Cha instructs Murray to duck, Peter is strafing their position with machine gun fire. "Detonate." The trucks are decimated by the exploding barrel bombs. One has been upturned and lifeless the other is rolling down the slope burning. Murray sees Peter trying to crawl away and puts five rounds in him before all signs of life are diminished.

Cha shouts, "Party pooper." Murray changes weapons and starts to shoot at the yellow car that is leaning over to the west. This has been loaded with petrol cans and has been set it up in the hope that the petrol will not ignite with the slower smaller velocity rounds and the petrol will seep out, hopefully run down the slope, ignite and burn all the remaining combatants. After firing about twenty rounds Cha tells Murray to "cease-fire."

They wait, both bathed in sweat. Some of JPW"s crew are still shooting and they are receiving sporadic fire from below but all the rounds are falling short. Murray notices movement to the upper left and catches a glimpse of JPW trying to sneak away but it is no avail the party pooper trick is starting to work. Through her scope Cha has noticed a trickle of liquid starting to spread down the hill. JPW has not got a snowballs chance in hell of escaping. Cha instructs Murray to wait and tells him that she can count about fifteen remaining weapons. The shots from below cease they are not surrendering but running about in flames trying to escape the fire. He changes weapons back to Miss 7.62 and together they stop the runners all except JPW, both of them are more than content to watch him burn.

JPW is now the only one that is left, and he waddles about trying to put out the flames, but it is no good. He must have gotten soaked and is now a human fireball. They should do the right thing and put a bullet in his skull, but he is a bastard, and why waste a good bullet on a pompous piece of shit like him.

There are no further shots from below, but they carefully scan and check the area for movement. Any sign of life is extinguished with a quick shot. The air is full of the reek of burning flesh. Murray is allowed a smoke break, and they take turns to smoke and drink a fizzy.

Murray and Cha have not fired a shot for about an hour and think that all the bad guys are dead. The flames are dying down, and the smoke has cleared sufficiently to get a better view of the carnage below them. Not one of their vehicles has been left drivable. Some of the occupants never even managed to get out. All that remains are several burnt husks; some have hands pressed at the windows others are just slumped in their seats.

Cha spots a legless burnt blob trying to move, and a swift shot and stops. Time to move, she takes up a covering position as Murray moves their gear. Charlie is starting to come awake, and he tells her sorry as he gently carries her to the AWD and puts her in the back seat. Two more trips and all their equipment is completely reloaded. Murray covers for Cha as she comes to join him. Murray drives, and they head over the adjoining field from higher up and make their way down to the north choke point. Charlie is still a little drowsy, and they leave her in the car.

At this point, both of them are very careful, and inch-by-inch, they make the way forward, and all are dead. Cha spots a couple of swimmers out in the water, and they take one each. The stench is unbearable, and it is everywhere; they check all the way down to the south choke point and start the collection. Murray has volunteered to do the dirty work. It was only fair, as Cha had done all the planning and all the dangerous jobs.

Murray unsheathes the machete and starts to remove the heads. He puts them in double black refuse bags, and when one bag is full. He moves on to another, several bags are full before Murray finds the prize exhibit, and he is grateful that JPW is still wearing the pith helmet, as this is the only way he can be identified. The bags are slowly transferred up the slope to the waiting transport. Murray loads them into the back. Charlie is now awake and barking. Cha drives for a little while before they stop and let her out. They are at a distance that they can no longer smell the overwhelming stench of death from the kill zone. Both of them still carry the smell, but that will be removed later.

Charlie runs about the field full of beans, and both of them feel like shit and are full of remorse for drugging her up, but she is back to normal and is running about like a puppy, barking at anything and everything. Murray and Cha have a can of the last man on the planet and smoke while they are waiting on Charlie doing her doggy things. They are en route to the farmhouse HQ, driving in silence. There are no incidents on the way there, and they are pleased that there is no traffic or obstacles hindering our progress.

Just prior to the last turn onto the hill before the HQ, they come to a halt, Cha heads out with a rifle, and as always, she is correct. They have constructed a checkpoint since our last visit. Two additional shots and two additional dead bodies. They do not even look at them as they drive past. Through the binoculars, Cha reports no movement in the guard tower, and Murray exits the car. Positioned about halfway down the hill, Murray starts to empty the bags and dumps the heads. Some roll down the slope, and some just stick to the tarmac. The one with the pith helmet rolls all the way to the gate. Most of the others just form an untidy pile. The gate opened, and a crowd started to form. One with a white flag starts to approach our position. They allow him to advance; when he is within hearing distance, Cha tells him their version of the events and informs him none of his friends are coming back, and if anyone from here ever tries to fuck them over again, they will return and unleash merciless vengeance and wipe them all out.

Cha gets back in the car, "Home, James." They drive off and do not look back. The drive home is uneventful, when they reach the blockage, a simple drive up the field and then go cross country until they find a suitable point to connect with the main road, it adds half an hour onto the journey. They reach home and check all is safe, there are no signs to indicate otherwise and Charlie is let out and runs about telling the trees and the pond that she has returned. The clothes are removed outside; they carry the smell of death and do not want to share it with their house. These are dumped on a piece of waste ground, and they burn them. It is the correct thing to do.

The pair of them enter the house as naked as the day they are born. "I don't know about you, but I could do with a bath," Murray asks if this is an invite. "Why not" she replies. He lights the fire and hopes it does not take too long before the water is ready. They are not hungry, but their bodies have been through much today, and hungry or not, they must eat. Cha rustles something up; neither Bobby nor Murray questions what it is and just eats naked.

The bath is what they need, and it slowly makes them human again. Murray washes Cha, and in return, she washes him. She gets out of the bath first and returns like the wild gypsy woman and informs Murray that he must shave. He is given a glass of Champaign to drink in-between strokes of the razor. When the shave is complete, she helps him out of the bath. He catches a glimpse of her stocking tops, and Bobby is on full alert. They only make it halfway down the stairs and make love for hours. The wild gipsy woman has been satisfied, and they are now at the table. Charlie is out for the count in front of the fire. They are far from being tired and are on the third bottle. Murray is rolling, and Cha is talking, "I think we should take a break and just stay at home for a while. I think it would be a good idea." She is drunk, and it takes her a while to get all the words out. He does not correct her. Murray attempts to speak, but the words she tells him sound like there are coming from the depths of the ocean.

They both laugh at this; Cha has persuaded him to have a stocking tied around his head, and she has applied some black makeup stuff to his face. Murray is not allowed to look in the mirror, and to be honest. He does think that he could walk to the mirror. Well, honestly, he could, but it would take a long time.

Cha thinks that it is time for a change, a new beginning, and wants them to shave their heads to symbolise a clean start, bearing their souls to the universe. Murray does not believe her and continues drinking and smoking, and yip she is not bullshitting. It takes her a while, but she manages to return to the table with a big bowl of hot water, scissors and some razors, and a couple of bottles of wine. On the wine, it does not matter if it is red or white, expensive or cheap. They will both taste like a cat's piss. Murray knows if he drinks it, he will regret it, but even though he is drunk, Murray still has no intention of letting her down. She wants to go first and requests that Murray cuts her hair. Part of him still thinks that she is bluffing and he refuses. It is only when she starts hacking it off that he stops her and grudgingly agrees to participate. He cuts it as short as he can and shaves her head as smoothly as possible. Murray leaves no cuts and no patches. Drunk as he is, she is still a super model.

It is now his turn, and when she finishes, he has several Elastoplasts, and for some strange reason, there is a small clump above his right ear. It looks as if she has shaved him with a hatchet. Cha takes a long time to say the words, but eventually, they come out in an understandable form, "Don't worry baby, it will grow back, and you look great?" She finds it difficult to look at him without bursting out laughing. Murray is still not allowed to look in the mirror.

The day's events are never mentioned, and it is firmly put behind them. Murray is awake first in the morning, and he is still drunk. He makes it safely down the stairs: balance and holding steady is a slight problem. A bottle of beer is opened; it tastes like shit, but it will keep the dreaded hangover at bay long enough for him to recuperate; self-medication indeed. Charlie is desperate to get out; he has no clothes on, and this does not register with him until he can feel the breeze of the wind on Bobby. The surface of the table and the surrounding area is a mess. Several ashtrays are overflowing, and there are more empty bottles than he remembers opening. Slowly his life support system perks up to near-normal levels. He selects a half-smoked from the ashtray and struggles to get his trousers on before he goes back outside. Murray is unable to do the standing up, the balance machine is still displaying error mode, and he has to surrender after several aborted attempts. The brain control department sends a text to try it sitting down. One leg in, two legs in, lift feet and pull up to knees. A little stand and crouch, and they have accomplished the mission. The room is a little unsteady, so he waits it out and gives it time to get itself back together.

He takes a deep breath, tells himself that he can do it, and drinks the beer in one go. He has to admit privately that it tastes fucking vile. It stays down but only just. The room is now out of focus, and the two of them go and let the dogs in. The dogs play while Murray steadies himself outside, and to stop the house from sliding, he leans against the wall to give it his full support. A lighter magically appears in his hand, and someone must have hypnotised him to perform the lighting ceremony. There is no round of applause and no fanfare, only a constant drone that is coming from somewhere inside his head. Murray hopes that if he ignores it and pretends that it is not there, then it will go away.

Murray thinks that he has been out here for ten minutes, and it's only when he starts to feel cold and needs a leak that he realises that he has been out here for fucking ever. Not the best hangover cure, but still better than taking head tablets or whatever the fuck they are called. Now Murray is functioning normally enough to tidy up. What can burn goes straight into the fire, which is also barely alive, he could play with it but lets the debris he has collected and piled on slowly heat up, and hopefully, it, like him, will burst into life.

The bottles are collected slowly, and after several trips outside, they have been deposited in the bottle; what do you call it? Murray manages to make it back in and has a wee rest before he attempts to wipe the table. The clock on the wall says it's 3 o'clock; that means nothing, as it is always the same time. Murray thinks if he has an hour—maybe three, he will feel fine, he does not think at this present he would pass a breathalyser or the dreaded employment medical, but he will be okay.

He coaxes the fire back into to life and completes tidying up the room. When Murray has finished, it looks almost habitable. Cha has not stirred, so he leaves her be. The shower fully energises him, and the VU meters attached to his internal censors are in the plus regions. Murray has even cleaned the guns. Mr .50 cal. is exempt and is left out, and grabbing a hunting rifle and a jacket, he whistles on Charlie, and they go for a walk. Murray takes Charlie's preferred route and lets her get as filthy as possible, and they play fetch with the once bright yellow ball. There is no one around, and the peace and quiet with the occasional birdsong are just about perfect. Charlie has had her fun, and they go and walk around everywhere, and all is as they had left it.

They finish their expedition off by checking the water flow; since the last time, the flow has subsided substantially, and he thinks it is possible that they could do it without machinery. It would take a considerable amount of hard labour, but as Wrightson had told him on a continual daily basis, an honest day's work is good for the soul. Time for a rest. Murray is sitting on a boulder, smoking, and Charlie is beside him. She has dropped the ball at his feet and hopes that he is going to chuck it for her. The ball is arced high in the air and crashes into the wooded area behind him. "Go fetch!" and she is off. Murray is just sitting, watching the water cascading down through the rocks and listening to the pleasant sound. Charlie brings Murray back to normality. She has dropped the ball at his feet and wants a repeat performance. He dually obliges and throws it with more force than the last time, and she is off again. Heading back to the house, she will catch up with him along the route. Cha has still not stirred and is still in the land of nod. Murray is restless and needs to be doing something. Charlie is hungry, which is not true; Charlie is always hungry. She is fed, and they head back out.

Murray grabs some stuff from the shed, and they walk back up to the water. When he was on his reconnaissance mission, it was observed that the most difficult task of diverting the flow of water would be at the section that was just a rocky area. If his memory serves correctly, this can be broken down with fire. The heat gradually weakens the structure and enables it to be smashed apart. The fire starts small, and he gradually increases it to cover the path that needs opened. He has dragged several dead trees and chopped them into suitable sizes. The heat removes the dampness, and soon they have a full-size blaze. Cha appears a while later. She is wearing some sort of woolly hat, the Scandinavian type, with ear flaps and big lengths of ties that look like ponytails. Her eyes remind him of a picture of Cleopatra in the school history books, the black and blue eyeliner extending out to a point. She greets Murray with a "Morning baldy!" and throws a similar woollen hat. This is fine as long as she is not going to try and introduce Bobby and him to raw fish. As always, she is stunning, you could dress her in a sack, and she would still be a supermodel. A flask is produced, and they have some soup. The end chunk from a loaf of bread would be a nice additional extra, but Murray thinks he can just about manage to keep the soup down.

He tells her the plan, and they spend the rest of the day just burning wood. She asks if he would like some explosives to do the job quicker, but Murray refuses to say that he would much prefer just to do it the hard way. Adding that he could do with the work. They sit, absorbing the tranquillity and enjoying the peace and quiet. For once, they have no beer and no smokes. Together they go into the woods, and they chop and drag more dead tree trunks out to build up the fire before they leave. Murray thinks that they will have to repeat the process for several days for it to work and if that fails, Cha can always blow it up. It is dark by the time they leave; they snuggle up on the couch, and they are not hungry and just lay in each other arms.

Chapter Fourteen

Murray gets up last; smarty-pants is up before him, "Hey you," as she puts her arms around him and kisses Murray good morning.

He replies, "Hey, you too," and responds, meaning every stroke, every touch, every single kiss. She tells him that she enjoyed yesterday. Murray jokingly asks if she means she enjoyed sleeping all day or being up by the river. She smiles and indicates with her hand that he is a dickhead. Breakfast over, they head out.

The fire is still going, and all they have to do is make sure it has plenty of fuel. They gather enough to keep it going for the day and start to dig. Starting at the top section and they slowly start the trench. This continued for about a week, and they progressed much more than they both expected. The ground was softer than anticipated, and she was just a devil with the pickaxe, shovel, and crowbar. More surprisingly is that the rock is starting to give way to the heat, and when they clear the ashes, the cracks are visible, and with a little persuasion from the toys, they manage to start the track. Work on this continues non-stop, and when they have removed all the soft rock, the fire relit to start the process all over again. It works out that they have to repeat the process several times before the desired results are achieved. The track is almost ready, some tweaking is required here and there, but most of the serious work is done. The job needs more fire to weaken the rock rather than sit about and watch it. The time is spent at the Orangery.

They fill the beds with more soil and rocks for drainage and to help the roots find something to cling onto. Cha is excited as she has a vision of how this will end up with all the colours, all the flowers, and all the scents. A family of bluetits has moved in, but as far as they are aware the Robin has no problems with them. The added birdsong brightens the place up.

Cha is the head gardener; Murray is the helper and digs where instructed. All the plants, trees, shrubs, and bulbs have been planted. The greenhouses are just about fully functional and are just requiring some heat. They had not been near any machinery for a while, not since the excavator adventure. They continue to potter about the Orangery for another couple of weeks. The rails are painted, as are the walls. Murray is not too sure about her choice of colour scheme, but it is hard to refuse her.

The hardest part about working here is the time factor, they have missed several meals and have often realised that it is the early hours of the morning and they are still there. They have even slept up here on occasion. There is always this gut feeling that the previous owners would approve of what they are doing. They are not available to ask, but somehow, Murray and Cha both know.

Murray has been invited to join Cha in the bath. It is not that often he gets the invitation, and they have been very busy for the last couple of months. It is agreed that they need some relaxing together time. Their hair is growing back; he has been told that he needs a haircut, only a trim this time, he hopes. Cha's hair is shorter but still more than suitable for the front cover of any glossy magazine. The bath is great; this is one of their favourite things. Murray knows that they usually have a fantastic love-making session at these events, but apart from that, it is one of those very special moments where it is just them. Murray has been promised a special massage and has been told that if he falls asleep, she will castrate him.

He is lying in bed, naked, face down, and she works on his shoulders. That is all he remembers. In the morning, Murray wakes up to a "Morning stallion!" She is taking the piss. It seems he lasted five minutes before zonking out into the land of dreams. It was the best sleep that he has had in what seemed like forever.

The run-off track is ready. The last batch of fire has allowed them to open up the rock to a suitable depth. The top end has been dug out where they are going to start the diversion. All they have to do now is block the channel to create the overflow. All rock that they have dug out has been moved to this area, and the small stones will be added to the pile of larger stones to seal any of the gaps in the temporary

249

dam. The larger rocks that are too heavy to lift are rolled over the edge. Sometimes, they land in the intended target area; sometimes, they are not so lucky. They spend several days at this, and so far, there has been no change to the flow of water.

Cha whispers in his ear that the woman from the KGB will be here tonight, and she is off to make dinner. This is her telling him not to be late. Bobby is nearly bursting out of his trousers when she opens the door dressed in her stockings, high heels, and nothing else. There is no dinner on the table. She is very demanding, and he and Bobby do their very best to satisfy her desires.

After breakfast curry, they head up to the overflow project. At the end of today, they start to see a small trickle work its way down the track. Murray volunteered to deepen the start of the channel. It is dirty work, and no change is visible in his efforts. The supply of rocks that they had stored for the job has been exhausted, and they have to resort to adding some of the derelict building materials that can be found in various parts of the property. Unfortunately, they will need means of transportation. The battery is dead, and a jump-start is required. Murray gets to push, Charlie barks, and Cha lets out the clutch. Shudder, shudder, and some smoke. Murray thinks it is going to die and pushes harder to try and help the momentum. Cha presses in the clutch, and they try again. This time the slope of the hill is more defined, and he hopes this works, as he has not got the energy to push the vehicle back up the hill.

A large plume of smoke and Cha revs the engine; they drive around for a while just to heat up the engine. In the real world, the vehicle should, in theory, be taken for a journey to charge the battery and put the engine and gears through its paces, but even now, all these months later, they still have no desire to leave their sanctuary. So, they continue to drive around the estate for an hour or two. Anything that is too heavy is not even attempted, and they only lift what is suitable. Having quite a selection gathered, they reverse into the nearest area. Getting as close as possible, the debris is transferred to a wheelbarrow, and Murray wheels it across for Cha to dump in the water. Eventually, they shifted several truckloads, and the overflow started to work. There is no visible change to the levels of the ponds below them, but the overflow is definitely in action. The feed pond must be the problem.

They decide to add more rocks and drive around collecting. Another wheelbarrow is added, and they try it in stereo. This makes a difference to the overflow; a break is called, and he smokes. The day is just about done, and they decide to call a halt to work and go off for a walk. The weather is nice, and they take the long way around. This is really the perfect end to the day; if anyone was watching, they were just a couple out on a romantic evening walk walking hand in hand. That is apart from the rifles hanging on their shoulders.

Cha spots the pheasants in the distance and lets go of his hand. They are too far away for his gun, and Cha's armament, even at this distance, would only blow them apart. Through the scope, they can see that they are oblivious to their presence. "What do you think, pheasant, tinned potatoes, and carrots?"

Cha replies, "Yuck." They edge back and take a slight detour through the bushes. This will take them out further up, closer to the prey. Murray fits the silencer on the way there, they are not going to be greedy, and one bird will be more than ample for the both of them. What Cha is going to make Murray has no idea, but he can taste it already. The flock has not moved from the area and is just milling about; they take their time and silently approach the large fallen oak tree that will hide them long enough to take the shot.

Murray kneels on the ground and steadies the rifle on the trunk as he takes aim. The bird is shot through the head and drops. The others do not scatter and only move away when they approach to pick up the prize. Cha plucks the bird on the way home, refusing to tell him what delicacy she is going to prepare. Murray pretends to beg her to tell him what she is going to make, but she does not reveal the identity of the dish. On entry to the house, Murray is barred from anywhere near the kitchen. He sets the table, lights some candles, and puts on a small fire.

He is sitting outside, relaxing and thinking how lucky they have been. Things could have been so different if he had not met Cha. Murray is wondering why the water is taking so long to drain off and is going through the possible scenarios to try and pinpoint the next course of action. His smoke is just about finished. He has the last drag and stubs it out, washing away the taste with a sip of water.

The shout comes from the kitchen, "Dinner, go and wash your hands." Murray jumps to it and runs in through the house. He is upstairs washing his paws and is at the table in a flash. They have honey-roasted pheasant stuffed with sweetened vegetables. There is a bottle of wine on the table, but Murray is still not a fan and does not partake. As the beer and fizzy juice have all been depleted, he sticks with water.

The old woman is decked out in a strange robe, and the symbols around the edges of the hood look more than a little familiar. He has no idea what they mean, but Murray has definitely, most definitely seen them all before.

She is directing them to the pond that is point blank refusing to empty. The area is cast in an ethereal light that moves with and around them. Cha stands beside him at the water's edge. The old woman takes her hand and momentarily looks at the ring, closes her eyes, and drifts away for a few moments; they are transported instantly, fighting for their lives, dressed in ancient clothes and throughout all the flashing imagery of the ensuing sword fight Murray distinctly sees Cha's ring. The one with the robe on takes them by the hand and leads them across the water. She is not menacing and is trying to soothe them in a gentle manner, telling them that there is no need to panic and all will be good, just to be patient. They stand still on the spot that she has chosen, and they look at their surroundings.

They are then looking at the old woman from various angles that act as a cross-reference to the designated spot. At no point did they feel threatened. Now they are standing facing each other, their hands are held upright, and they are touching. The old woman kneels before them and recites some long-forgotten incantation. They are encompassed in a glimmering light, making them feel like they are in the presence of someone that was way beyond good, somehow knowing that the old woman wearing the hooded cloak is here to guide and protect them.

Cha wakes Murray up in the morning. They are both still in bed. She is propped up on her elbows, looking at him to open his eyes. "Morning Mr B."

He replies, "Morning, baby." She is looking at Murray perplexed and asks him straight out if he had slept okay.

He is just about to reply, and she stops him, "By any chance, did you dream about a woman in a hooded cloak with strange symbols and a guided tour of the pond?" She goes through the dream from start to finish, missing nothing. Murray agrees with everything and adds nothing. It is exactly as he recollects it. "You did wash last night before you went to bed?"

He smiles at her, replying, "I was in the shower with you, and it wasn't just the water we shared!"

Going by their previous one and only shared dream experience, Murray tells her that it was only a dream. He will admit that it was pretty vivid, and yes, she was in his side of the dream, "But baby, it was just a dream, and if the old world existed, we could go and see a specialist, and he or she would have many possible explanations, but I am sure that there is nothing to worry about."

She is up out of bed and pulls the covers off, up from the bottom of the bed, to show him the dirty sheets. Pointing, adding, "How come your feet are still dirty?" They are up and sitting at the table, and the discussion continues. What about the symbols on the hood? They agree that they have seen them before, but both of them are dumbfounded as to where and when.

Cha has made a pot of tea. Powdered milk is quantifiably more than disgusting, but it is all that is available. The questions are flowing, but as of yet, they have no reasonable answers. Murray rattles a banger together; Cha claims it, and he makes another for himself. There is only one way to solve this. They get dressed and head up to the water. This is not a guaranteed way to solve the enigma, but at least they can relive the moment and follow as much as they can remember, step by step. On the way up, they both look worried. Charlie is just being Charlie.

On reaching the water, they notice that the level has actually dropped slightly in the main body of water to expose a previously unnoticed weir. The overflow is functioning properly, and the reduced flow of water has exposed the wall that was previously hidden underwater. This must contain the blocked water outlet. It is revealed to be about six feet wide and about twenty feet deep. How they had missed this was only down to the way the water had flowed over the uneven structure, creating an illusion of a stream. It was the only explanation that he could think of.

There is something that Charlie does not like about here, and she barks madly when they edge over the weir to examine it closer. Her hackles are up full, and she is now barking and growling and only stops when they return back to terra-firma. The water is manky, and centuries of silt and muck have made underwater examination impossible. Cha tells him that a shaped charge would be ideal, but presently they do not have any available in stock. Murray looks at her as if she is nuts and has no fucking idea what she is talking about. She looks at him and explains clearly how it can be done. That is great news, great news that she has a solution to the problem, but the not-so-good news is that they will have to go on a shopping trip.

They are both wary of adventuring over the bridge into uncharted territory, and that leaves them with the option of heading back into previously explored regions. None of them relish this prospect, but they don't have to overdo it, only the basic essentials, no extras. Cha calculates what will be required to blow an opening in the wall. The truck and the AWD, it has been decided, will both be required. This will cover any eventuality. They are still more than a little apprehensive. Sitting around talking about it is only going to make them worry more. Therefore, they are going now. No point in hanging about.

The jump leads to start the truck, and they drive out. A new route has been discovered, and if they drive through the farm tracks, it is possible to get to the area they have pencilled in to get all the items that are needed. It will take some additional time, but they have to bite the bullet, and now that they are back on the road, there is nothing that is going to stand in the way.

Arriving at the destination and although it is starting to get dark, they plod on regardless. Murray grabs one of the big flat pallet trollies, and Cha leads the way. Checking the percentages on the ingredient list, Cha goes from pile to pile until she has located the best combination. "This is the one."

Murray asks how many, 'all of them' it will be two trollies worth and two loads. Cha checks the bags for tears and discards the ones that she had decided are damaged. The first load is taken out and placed carefully on the truck. As quickly as possible, they repeat the process. It is now dark, and they are still fairly confident that no one is going to interrupt them, but they still intend to get it over with as quickly as possible. They drive to the second scheduled stop.

This place is a small fabrication shop that has produced a specialist service in exotic metal fabrication, and they are hoping to collect about half a dozen bottles of inert gas. The argon cage is full, and Murray pulls them out. He moves them over one at a time where Cha is standing, and he shows her the technique of inserting the bottled key and emptying the bottle into the atmosphere. Murray continues to collect the bottles, and soon they have all that is required. Murray asks Cha to get up on the truck, and he bodily lifts the empty bottles up, and at just past the point of balance Cha grabs hold and helps to steer them. Murray clambers up onto the bed and pushes and pulls them, sticking a wooden wedge in to stop them from rolling off. The loading is complete. They secure the load with several cargo straps and lock the ratchet to the closed position.

Their food supplies are getting low, and although they have in the past only used back entrances to supermarkets, tonight's time is of the essence, and as it is the closest, they revisit the supermarket where Cha had first shown him her tattoo. Apart from the skeletons, the place is devoid of any humanity. They select two of the largest trolleys that they can find and quickly help themselves to the essentials. Murray even manages to grab the few remaining packs of the last man on the planet on the way around. The presenter of a now long-forgotten TV show would have been proud of them. Cha goes back in and returns with another trolley loaded with house cleaning products.

They load up the AWD as quickly as possible, a quick hug and "See you when I get home," and they are off. The streets are empty, and they drive as quickly as they can to get the fuck out of the town.

The main road is reached, and the boot goes down. Murray maxes out at about 80, and this is kept up until the turn-off is reached. He applies the brakes and crunches through the lower gears selecting the suitable ones to take the hill leading to the farm tracks.

Once clear of the main road and out of sight, Murray works the indicator on the left and pulls over. He is bursting for a pee. Cha pulls to a stop, worried that there is a problem. In the torchlight, she catches Murray with his eyes closed, Bobby in his hand, watering some weeds at the side of the road. "Sorry baby, I just could not hold it in any longer."

She laughs at him, commenting that she can't take him anywhere, and scolds him like a mother speaking to her children, 'I told you to go before we left.' Murray ignores her and lights up a cigarette. She steals this and heads back to the AWD. He lights another and takes the hint, and jumps back into the cab. They should be home in about an hour.

Charlie is going nuts when they get back. This is the longest time that she has ever been left alone. They let her out of the house, and she runs in between and around them and then disappears to do what dogs do. They are waiting for her to return. The AWD has been switched off. Charlie returns and jumps up into the cab. Cha gets in beside her, and Murray enters from the other door. Even though everything is all wrapped up and secure, they are going to take the truck and store it overnight in the big shed. They drive around, and as the doors have been left open, drive straight in. The doors are closed, and they can relax now and walk home to the house. Charlie has still not settled and bounds away, then runs back, darting in between them. She is just delighted that they are all back together.

The shopping has still to be unloaded and put away. It is better they do it now rather than leave it until the morning. Cha feeds Charlie, who is hungry. Murray starts to unload the groceries. His job is to bring them in and place them on the worktop, the table, or anywhere that there is available space. Murray has just finished unloading the car, and Cha comes to the door, "hurray up slowcoach," he is amazed. He had not stopped. She grabs a bundle of tins, and Murray follows with as much as he can safely carry and dumps them on the worktop. He is not even attempting to put them away as apart from where the beer and the fizzies are kept. He has no idea where she puts anything. Murray continues transferring all the items into the house, and before they know it. It has all miraculously been stored away. The house cleaning products have been placed in plastic bags and are being stored outside.

Murray is sitting at the table when Cha appears with a couple of beers, they are not cold, but they are wet. They clink the bottles together and say a mutual "Kiss my arse" and have a slug or two. "I don't know about you, but I needed that," says Cha. She asks if he is hungry. Charlie barks at this, thinking that she was also invited. They smile at her, and she comes over for a clap. Murray is hungry, but he can wait, and there is no immediate hurry for Cha to rustle something up. He thinks they are both just relieved to be back home, and they just take some time to relax. Cha hands Murray some sketches and asks, "Can you make these?" He smokes and has another beer while Cha makes some noise and, fingers crossed, hopefully, some food.

The remains of the pheasant have been chopped up and mixed with tinned tomatoes, potatoes, and mixed vegetables. She has also added some spice to give it a bit of a bite. It is presented to the table in a large bowl, and they ladle a helping or two on their plates. Murray would like to do some of the cooking just to be doing his fair share, but the last time he asked, he was offered the possibility of a violent attack, so Murray swallows his pride and keeps his mouth firmly shut. He thinks that she can cook so much better than him, so he puts it down to a win-win.

In between mouthfuls of the stew, she asks if it is possible. Murray thinks yes, but there is about at least a week's work of fabrication there. While they are eating, he goes through the process. "I will have to cut the top off, then make some sort of flange and coat the joining faces with wax-coated rubber to connect it. In order to make a request for them to be directional, I will have to measure the thickness and crisscross the cylinder like a chessboard. The fuses you have described, I can make, but I think that an additional orifice will have to be added to do the final fill."

They go over this with the aid of sketches and modify the designs as they go through the complete process. As for loading them into position, it can be done with two ropes, and Murray does not think this will be a problem. He can see that she is deep in contemplation, and as Murray does not fully understand the chemical process, he leaves that side of the project to her. Murray is more than willing to help, but only if she allows it, and he knows she will only ask for help in this department if she really needs it. The food was gone; this was all that they had to eat all day. It is agreed that

Murray will only make a prototype, and if that is suitable, they will then step up and go for a full batch production.

Being too hyped up to sleep, they drink and smoke into the early hours. To ease their tension and maybe to get her back on him for falling asleep, Cha disappears and comes back dressed as the sexiest nurse on the planet. High heels, seamed stockings, suspenders, the works. Part of him is thinking that he should never have told her his fantasies one night when they were very, very drunk. Bobby is thinking of telling her more and telling her every day. She hands him a card; it reads: *Say nothing and do as you are told, or the nurse will be unhappy, xxx Cha.* Murray is led upstairs, and he thinks he has died and gone to heaven.

They are no visitors to their dreams tonight. Together, they fall asleep in an embrace, and that is how they wake up in the morning. His arms are still wrapped around her when she wakes up before him. Cha playfully bites his nose to let him know that it is time to wake up; his eyes open slowly. She is right in his face. "Baby, it is great that you are holding me like you never ever want to let me go, but I need to pee."

He mutters, "Hi Mrs B, love you too," and relaxes his grip. Murray turns over, and she skelps his arse as she hops out of bed. He follows her out and just can't help himself and joins her in the shower, "Honest, your honour. It was Bobby's idea."

Breakfast is light, nothing special it is tinned ravioli. Cha thinks it is one of the vilest things ever invented, earning a dual position at the top of the chart with tinned semolina, which she has previously told Murray that, given a choice between a dead dog's sperm and semolina, the dead dog's spent matter would win hands down. Murray is thinking about what she will make of tinned tapioca. He eats most of it and washes it down with tea and a couple of tins of last man on the planet.

In the big shed Cha today is going to be Murray's assistant. He shows her every step of the marking-out process. Then proceeds to cut the top of the cylinder off. Cha wants to check the inside to make sure that it is dry and damp-free. When she finishes her checks and is satisfied, they cover the top with a plastic bin liner. Murray then shows her how they are going to make the connecting flanges and the material that they have to connect them. At the same time, Murray sets about adding the additional hole in the top. To seal the additional hole, he has to invent something. For this, he uses a 25 mm diameter bolt and nut. It will be very ugly, but it should work. Murray screws the nut up the bolt as far as possible prior to chopping the extra. The nut is then seal welded onto the top of the cylinder.

Cha, in the meantime, has made a trial fit fuse assembly and is waiting for him to complete the flanges. Murray has cut them and is now in the process of batch-drilling the two sections to ensure a compact fit. He could do with a break, but horses on. A couple of hours later, all the drilling and welding are now complete. He glues on the rubber. They have a break while the glue is drying. Cha is in charge of the chemical department and has made the batch of glue. She reckons it will take about half an hour to set.

Chapter Fifteen

They go out of the shed and have a quick lunch break. Bobby has warned him to expect fish, and even though tuna is not on the like-to-eat list. Murray understands that refusing to eat is futile and scoffs it down. Cheeky chops tell him wryly that "Bobby will be pleased with the nutritional value." There is time for a smoke before the trial fit, but as Murray notices that Cha is getting impatient, he takes the smoke with him and smokes it while he works. There is no element of danger as all the chemicals have not been mixed and are at present in an inert state.

Going through the trial fit by the numbers, they establish a sequential order of assembly. If it goes wrong or they find an additional problem, they go back to the beginning and restart the process.

Cha loads up the main part of the cylinder with an imaginary medium. The sides are gently tapped to compact the fill. More imaginary medium is added to the brim, and the rubberised flanges are fitted. So far, all is good. Through the remaining orifice, the additional medium is added. Then sealed. This last section can be coated in the glue mixture to make it completely watertight. "Well, what do you think?" Murray asks. Cha looks at him seriously and tells him that she thinks he could make anything, and maybe the next time, they will discuss the industrial process for boiling methanol and thermal distillation. Murray takes that as a yes. She is happy with the process.

Murray has laid out the remaining cylinders; marked them up with identification numbers and cut lines. Cha has seen what has to be done, and rather than just sit and watch him, she and Charlie are going to look for something for the pot. "Okay, see you later." She, instead of kissing him, grabs Bobby playfully and whispers in a French accent, "Tell Bobby I will see him later," and he can see her grinning as she leaves; *what a woman*. Murray does not think that it was meant to be an inspirational speech, but for the record, it is the best thing that he has ever heard.

Later Cha returns with Charlie and tells him that dinner is just about ready if he would like to come home and eat. Murray switches off the generator and joins them. She looks at Murray and tells him that he will have to shower. Having not worked at this for a long time, he had forgotten about what a horrible manky job it actually is. They amble home, Cha is asked what is for dinner but refuses to divulge. On getting home, Murray is ordered to go and get clean; he dumps his clothes on the bathroom floor and immerses himself in the luxurious stream of hot water. The bathroom door opens, followed by Cha entering the shower. She tells him straight up that it was Bobby's idea.

She leaves before him; Murray shaves and goes down and joins her ten minutes later. He cannot be bothered getting dressed and just sticks on the dressing gown that is hanging on the door. Cha is dressed in some sort of loose-fitting robe, so he is happy that he is not overdressed. Cha tells him that dinner will be ready in ten minutes, and she hopes that he has an appetite and bless her soul; she has a tin of the last man on the planet and a small banger rolled for him ready on the table. Not wanting to offend, Murray sparks it up while she whizzes about in the kitchen.

Murray is told to close his eyes and not to peak. When he opens them, he is presented with a rack of ribs on the table. Murray does not ask where the lamb came from, but it looks and tastes delicious. The rack is sitting on a bed of rice, and even that looks fantastic. Cha cuts a portion off for him, and he tries to attack it with a fork and knife, but this is totally unsuccessful, and he reverts to eating it with his fingers. It has been a lifetime since he remembers sucking the juices from his fingers, and he savours every single morsel. Murray is not allowed to help her tidy up, and it is not negotiable. They have a beer to wash down the food and end up crashing out on the couch.

In the morning, Murray is, for once, up before her. He gives her a quick peck on the cheek before going to work. She arrives a few hours later, bright-eyed and bushy-tailed. He shows her the progress, and she is delighted. All that remains is a couple of hours' worth of welding. She disappears into the small office to make the fuses, and Murray sticks the bucket to his head and burns some rods.

They have lunch while the metal cools. Murray has been told to expect to be eating lamb for the next few days, and it will have to be eaten before it goes off. Charlie has aspirations of chewing the leg bones, but Murray is not too keen on her eating the sharp bone fragments and wrapping them up; he tosses them in the fire later. He does share some of the meat with her just to keep her happy.

Cha goes into the office to make and mix the glue concoction, and Murray lays out the parts in pairs. They have this down to a fine art; She brushes on the mixture, and he places and clamps down on the rubber in place. Murray gets to solder the stripped wires and connect them to the sockets. Cha prepares the bulbs which have, prior to modification, been tried and tested. The wires are fed backwards through the plastic stopper that has been glued to the bottom of the nozzle that previously housed the outlet valve. When there are in position, another helping of the glue mix is poured in the top to hold them in place.

The camping stove is heating up the remnants of the candles, which are slowly melting in the battered pot, which is dented and scared, giving it the appearance of being involved in a train crash. The six valve housings are filled first, and while cooling, a second batch is prepared for the gaskets. The top hats are inverted once the wax has cooled, and the gaskets are covered in the molten wax. The overspill is removed by a knife and put back in the pot. Cha, the resident chemist, has removed the dog from the premises; all electrical equipment has been isolated. They both have on-white disposable suits and air-filtered masks. The sheeting is laid out as smoothly as possible, and the chemical compound has been spread out evenly and sifted to remove any lumps. Cha signals him when she has completed the first soaking with the modified house cleaning agents, and Murray writes the time down on the wall. After the allotted time is over, the now dry medium is raked and sifted again, and the whole process is repeated eight times.

Cha moves up the row and pours the medium in slowly into the open gas bottles, and Murray follows behind her, gently tapping the sides of the bottles with a piece of broom shaft to compact the mixture. They continue the process until the bottles are full. A final check is carried out to check, and when satisfactory, the chemist nods for the caps to be fitted. Murray lines up the boltholes and places the caps into position. The chemist hands him the bolts, and his hand tightens; once secure, he applies the torque required to make them watertight. When all the cylinders are at this stage, they go back to the start, and Murray holds the funnel while the chemist pours in more medium to fill the remaining space. She nods when he is required to restart the compacting. When the fill is complete, she nods twice, and he carefully inserts the plastic bolt into the seal-welded nut. The chemist returns from the office with the last glue mix, and together they coat the plastic bolts, the edges of the flanges, the waxed fuse connections, and lastly, all the bolts.

The water and bleach mixture is sprinkled on the floor, and they brush the area clean, pushing the excess towards the doors. At this point, they open the double doors and sweep what remains outside onto the road. The double doors are closed, and they get white-suited up and put on disposable shoes. Walking over to the car, the petrol cans are removed. Murray makes his way over to the waste ground and soaks the items that have been placed there. The remaining petrol he pours on the ground. Cha is there to meet him when the can is empty, and she continues pouring. They light the petrol and watch as it slowly streaks across to the waste ground. On reaching the dumped items, it bursts into a ball of flame. There is lots of black smoke, but at this time of night, no one will notice.

On arrival back at the house, Charlie is let out immediately. With their new outfits, they could easily pass as escapee psychiatric patients, and the suits are removed before entering the house and deposited in one of the large bins outside. The shower is set at full pressure, and they stay under the spray, standing motionless, eyes closed, arms folded until the hot water runs out, returning back instantly to reality.

"Baby! Tea on the table," the voice from downstairs calls up. Dressed, he joins her at the table. The tea tastes different, the powdered milk still gives it the aftertaste of baby puke, but the tea has been changed. Cha gets up, goes over to the kitchen, and waves a box at him; these are a nice change. Murray asks her, on a scale of one to ten, "How dangerous was today?"

"Twenty-five!" She says but relaxes since that was the dangerous part. They still both have red indentations on their faces from the elastic that held the masks in place. Charlie is looking at both of them with those big eyes pleading to be fed, implying that she has been on a near-to-starvation diet for weeks, and if not fed soon, the RSPA will be at the door shortly to issue them with court orders and hopefully take her to somewhere nice where they will feed her on demand; Cha gives in and feeds her and Murray has some more tea and a well-deserved banger. He was not even allowed to have a lighter on his person. Lots of rules today, but totally understandably so.

Murray thinks that he is not hungry, that is, until he sees the lamb on skewers. Cha tells him that it is an old family Mediterranean recipe. The tinned chickpeas have been mashed and mixed with sultanas and raisins. The taste just hits him, and he will have to add this to his favourite list. The list has been growing exponentially, and the last time he checked, they were on the third edition. They go to sleep,

272

and there are no mucky footprints on the sheets in the morning.

Breakfast is quick, just some tea and leftovers from last night's meal, which tastes even better. They go over the plan for the loading of the cylinders. Murray talks, and Cha listens. Most of the plan she likes but lets him finish before adding a single word, "Static," Murray looks at her, totally confused.

"We will have to do the last part of the plan naked, as static could be the end of us."

"Okay, fair enough," the plan is revised, and a quick tidy, and they walk up. To be safe, Charlie is left at home; the back door has been left open, and the gate at the end of the overgrown garden has been locked.

The cylinders have been loaded, it is a nice day, and Bobby loves showing off. All he has on are his boots. He could make love to Cha right here, right now. Sensing the slight movement in Bobby. "Would you like a cold shower? Please remind me to add bromide to the medicinal shopping list!" Murray raises his hands in the air confessing that he is just a human after all.

Bobby goes back to sleep, and the telescopic handler moves slowly along the track. On reaching the appointed parking place, Murray unties the first cylinder. Cha holds the protruding wires, and Murray manhandles the bottle off the covered forks and stands it upright. Slowly they move as one. Murray moves the cylinder on its base, gently rolling it on its edge while Cha makes sure the wire is not damaged. The length of the wire is about thirty feet long, and the end is wrapped up in a plastic bag. If it gets damp at all, it is just going to be a waste of time. Slowly but surely, they reach the endpoint. Cha places the looped wire on the ground and holds the cylinder. Murray goes back across and collects the sling and the rope. He returns and attaches the sling. He sets the bite and wraps it to make it slip-free. Once satisfied, he secures the rope.

The rope is laid out on a loop behind him. Murray gently manoeuvres the cylinder over the edge, and Cha feeds the wire as the cylinder slowly enters the water. There seems to be no bottom, but after what seems like a lifetime, he feels the change on the rope and lets the rope gently slip through his gloved hand, and he lets the cylinder settle into the multiple layers of silt below.

A house brick is placed over the bag containing the end of the wire. The process is repeated for three of the cylinders, and then they have a break. The work is strenuous, and the short time allocated to have some liquid lunch is very much appreciated. The remaining cylinders are slowly and carefully put in place, the work was much harder than anticipated, and they have to stop. Cha goes and has now returned with some refreshments. They have some chunks of lamb, rice, and a couple of beers. Murray is allowed to smoke but only at a safe distance away. The lunch break is over, and they grab the tools required and go over the walkway and start to connect the gathered wires. All the ends are labelled and numbered.

The six double wires with the soldered ends are secured into the line of plastic connectors, and all the screws are tightened and checked. At the other end of the connecting blocks, the six double wires that have been crimped and inserted into a larger single connector are then connected to the vacant slots of the multiport connector. Into the single connector, the last wire is fed into the slot as Cha walks back to the safe zone. Murray feeds her the cable and secures it with rocks that are placed to hold it in position. The wire has been split at the end and attached to the battery connectors. The battery that they are connecting to is dead. They get dressed, and Murray pops open the bonnet, and the jump leads are connected.

"Shall we go for it?" Murray turns on the ignition, and the engine fires to life and nothing happens. He is about to go out and check the connections, but Cha tells him to rev the engine. Doing as he is told, Murray presses the pedal.

The ground shudders, and reminiscent of an action movie, an enormous plume of water and silt erupts with an almighty roar. A shredded cylinder is propelled through the air and crashes into the wall on their right, and ricochets into the rear passenger's door. At the same time, they see one emerging from the water like a Polaris missile and hear the crash as it smashes through the roof of the big shed.

It is over in seconds, and they cannot believe it. A meter this way or a meter that way is all that has separated them from death, the right-hand side passenger's door has been separated from the frame, and the projectile has pushed it through the cab jamming it against the left-hand side door. The backs of the front seats have been ripped, and they have been more than lucky. The engine is still running, switching it off. They go outside and survey the damage. It looks like it has been raining muck. Everything in front of the now damaged-beyond-repair car has been splattered by the silt. The water level is slowly going down.

Murray and Cha still cannot believe how lucky they have been to survive this totally unscathed. The light is starting to fade, and they agree to go back to the house. The car is abandoned where it sits, and they walk back.

Murray asks Cha if she really has had much experience with explosives, and she just looks at him. She explains that with most explosives, you can calculate the damage that will be produced, the affected area, and even the radius of the falling debris. Unfortunately, with the homemade variety, this has too many parameters to work it out accurately, and it is generally better to have a little extra, just in case. She adds that maybe he had just made the cylinders too good, and it is entirely his fault. She sticks her tongue out at him as if to say, Fuck off.

This clears the air, and they agree to no more explosions for a while. Upon entering the house, Charlie is over the moon that they have returned and barks at their arrival. Cha has a brandy to steady her nerves. Murray does not like spirits and just starts rolling some bangers and has some tins of last man on the planet. Cha has another couple of stiff brandies and is slowly coming back to normal. Murray smokes away and has no intentions of ever being normal and even has a beer to speed up his process of self-medication.

Cha gets up and comes back with a bottle of wine. She pours a large glass and helps herself to one of the ready rolls on the table. "The next time I say can you have a look at these drawings, just do us both a favour and say that it is not possible. We nearly got killed today, and for what? Free electricity?"

Murray assures her and tells her that it is okay and that they really had no choice. Sooner or later the petrol and diesel supplies will be depleted or unable to use and therefore they don't really have a choice. This makes her laugh, she does not believe a word of it, but it would be nice to get rid of some of the constant noise that the semi-permanent generators produce.

Murray asks her if there is anything he can get for her, "Another bottle of wine, some flowers, and some music would be nice."

He looks at her, "I can supply the first one if you tell me where it is hidden and if there is a specific type."

She points, "The fourth cupboard on the bottom and the one with the gold foil, and I will have two of them, please."

"On the second request, tomorrow I will set up not one but two generators, and we could wire up some lights and heaters in the greenhouse, and maybe we can get some flowers." She looks at him, expecting a mention of the special seeds. Murray does, but not in the way she expects. "I have about a kilo of the green stuff left, so we can give the flowers top priority."

She nods her head at this, and he gets the "Okay, you have a deal."

"On the third item, I do not have any music to play for you. As far as I can remember, you don't like my singing!"

She laughs at this, saying, "I remember. What was it? Oh yeah, something about only me and on this planet with the added Texas drawl, and by the way, I don't think 'the King' was from Texas," and more laughing. Murray feels better that she is relaxing, but he is a little miffed as Murray thinks that his Elvis impersonation was pretty good.

"On the number three item, there is a box in the wardrobe. It is easy to find as it is the only one there. If you go and get it, I think I can," She pauses to drink more wine and then, "How do I say it? Oh yeah, rattle something up, and seen as you have been an angel, I will let you play anything you want, but I get to select which genre." Murray agrees and goes right now while he can still see reasonably clearly and walk without colliding with the walls and furniture.

He returns just as she is opening another bottle, the bottle is pointed in his direction, and just as he comes into range, she shouts, "Incoming!" as the cork is released and flies into the picture above his head, a hiccup is followed by an "Oops." The box is deposited on the table, and she has a large gulp before she starts to rummage. Anything that she pulls out and is deemed unsuitable, she discards by tossing it over her shoulder; Charlie goes and takes some cover. Murray is really enjoying this, and she can make all the mess that she wants. He will not be clearing it up.

After some more frantic searching, she has found all that she thinks should work. All of this stuff has been in this box for as long as they have stayed in this house. Murray looks at the pile of batteries, various handmade looms, more batteries, battery-operated speakers, even more batteries, and his mobile phone. He looks at her in amazement. She remembers everything and forgets nothing. As per usual, she is correct. Everything that is here can be connected. How long the power will last is another matter. The phone is wired up, and as expected, there are no bars for signal coverage. The music library is still accessible.

She is telling Murray that it is getting hot, and maybe she is a little drunk, and warns him that she is going to remove her clothes. Does she really need to issue Bobby with an advance warning? In her best Scottish accent, she asks, "Who wakes up first in the morning, Bobby or me?" They laugh at this. Murray asks her if this is a special breakfast request, and in reply, she gives him the finger. What a girl.

They now have some power. Murray cannot see what percentage is available, the little lightning symbol is visible, but he is not able to read the number. He asks, "What will madam's first choice be? Any requests?" Murray has quite an eclectic taste, but apart from his favourite genres, the choice will be fairly limited.

Cha has a slug from the bottle. Murray offers to go and get her a glass, "Okay, but not a silly wine glass. Can I have one of those tumbler things, and the bigger, the better, please." He obliges and returns with a couple. Not to be outdone, she fills both and lights up a smoke. Exhaling the smoke, she asks for some soothing classical music. "Okay, Mr DJ, if you don't put on something soon, I will put on some Korean pop music; maestro, give me music!"

Murray announces that his first selection, it is a much loved classical piece. He presses the play button, and the stringed instruments fill the room and our ears with soothing harmonics and, in his opinion, pure unadulterated joy. Murray closes his eyes, and his soul drifts off, totally encapsulated by the music.

A little tap on the table and he is being asked, "What is this called again?" He tells her the title; she looks puzzled and asks, "Is this about an old guy several hundred years ago dreaming about the future of ladies' underwear?"

He tells her, "No, that is not what it is about, but it is a nice thought." This gets another finger; She lets it play out and requests more of the same. Murray searches frantically; she pretends that she has fallen asleep while waiting before the next classical piece in D minor comes on. It only started when she announced that she knew this one, and it reminds her of the time before she ran away from the orphanage after getting into trouble, being arrested by the police, and then sent to a special government facility.

She looks at him as he tells her that he has seen this movie and that maybe she could this once tell him a little about herself. She has another glass of wine, the smoke hanging from her lips. She opens another bottle. The music is set to random, and they let it play out. Murray does turn it down so that he can hear every single word. Filling her glasses, she lifts the bottle to her mouth and guzzles down the rest. Taking a draw and exhaling, she says, "Okay, just this once."

"I went to a private boarding school; I think I was there since I was about ten. It was nothing special, just a private school full of spoiled rich kids. I don't remember making many friends, and my favourite class was art. I loved the peace and quiet and just loved painting."

"After graduation, my marks guaranteed me a place at the most prestigious private university in Korea. I excelled at everything. I was not first in the class, but only because I did not want to be. This is where I first learned martial arts, and I gained my first black belt at an early age."

"The guys in the suits were going around the universities at the time, and we were all tested. My marks were exceptional, and I was selected for some more tests and interviews. These I all passed with flying colours. I was removed from the university and put into a special training academy. The dropout rate was pretty high, but before I knew I was posted to various places, most of the work I carried out was top secret, and before long, I was transferred to the security assigned to protect our diplomats and various trade delegations." A brief pause, a drink. "And then I met you."

They now had some deep blues playing; the guy's fingers were burning with his intense playing. Cha asks what it is he is playing. He is about to tell her what it is and what they are singing about, but she halts him in mid-sentence and tells him that it is fucking awful. "Have you any of that soul music?"

Murray is well and truly miffed, but you either hate blues or love them. There is no in-between. He submits and goes through the playlists till he finds the requested one and presses the play and repeat button. Murray also turns it up a little.

They are both pretty wasted, she has drunk him well and truly under the table, but he is not much of a drinker and learned at an early age that hangovers are a really unpleasant way to start the day. Cha announces to no one in particular that she would like to dance; it takes a while for her to say it. It takes Murray even longer to reply that he will dance if she can stand. They surrender and curl up on the sofa. The music is left on. Some dudes are belting it out, pleading for someone to hang on as they slide into a night of sleep.

Chapter Sixteen

They are in the field where the last pheasant was taken. The old woman with the hooded cloak is standing facing them. Her arms are outstretched reaching up to the sky. The crowd behind her also has robes on but are kneeling behind her. Some are ringing bells, others are chanting. The words are unrecognisable, but it goes on forever. The chanting stops, and all they hear are the soft chimes of the bells.

Charlie is barking to get out, Cha mutters something, and Murray mutters something back. Charlie is still barking. He is gently nudged in the ribs; Murray grunts and refuses to wake. Cha nudges him a little harder, and he grudgingly opens one eye, and he says something like he wishes that she had her own key. Slowly Murray starts to move. The table is overflowing with empty bottles, glasses, and cans. He mutters something about, did you leave the door open? Cha mutters something back about maybe Charlie does have her own key. Murray should have a major hangover, and he figures that Cha should be on life support.

Murray sits up and gently gives Cha a shake. She mutters something along the lines of telling Bobby mummy is tired, and he can play later. Murray's head is swimming, not about the missing hangover but the muddy footprints on the floor and the open door.

"Cha, wake up baby, we have to talk," and Murray gives her another shake.

"Okay baby, give me a minute," she sat up and looked about, rubbed her eyes, and she had no noticeable hangover.

"Hi, baby, what the matter? Can I have a shower before Bobby awakes?" She is slowly coming to her senses and is now noticing what he has seen.

Cha comes out of her coma; they take a closer look at the footsteps, and they do belong to them. Murray scratches his head, opens a can of last man on the planet, passes it to Cha, and opens another one for himself. Cha sips hers as she thinks it deserves the same popular rating as semolina on her list of things to avoid. He guzzles his in one go and opens another. Sparking up a ready roll, he asks her what she remembers, and together they go through the dream.

This time they don't get into the what's, whys, and what ifs and get dressed and head straight up to the big shed. The AWD is still as they had left it. Murray opens the hood and removes the battery; Cha has the shed doors open and has popped the hood on the red truck. The cylinder had smashed through the roof and had embedded itself in one of the industrial washing machines.

Murray connects the borrowed battery, and the engine starts on the first turn. Cha jumps in, and they drive up through the field and onto the road that leads them up to the field with the fallen tree. He pulls up, gets out, opens the gate, and they drive through the field. It looked no different than the last time they saw it.

They are starting to think about all sorts of things. Maybe it was the drink and some shock syndrome relating to their near-death experience. That is until they notice small bells laid out neatly on the fallen tree trunk. On examination, they are identical and full of symbols that are from no known language. Cha is the resident linguistic expert and is totally stumped. Murray is more than confused and smokes, hoping that it will produce an instant calming effect; deep down inside, he knows it won't.

They search the field, but there is nothing else to find. Sitting on the trunk, they wonder about what to do next; utterly confused, they get back in the truck and drive back and park outside the big shed. The weir has been well and truly breached, there is a large hole that has allowed the water level to drop, but the sludge and silt are still there. Sure, it is moving, but the viscosity is only allowing for minimum movement.

They walk around to the other side of the weir and notice the slow flow emanating from the breech. The level of the entire feed pond has reduced evenly, meaning that there is a slopped surface underneath. Murray is thinking to himself if they were to redirect the flow, the additional water could help reduce the viscosity and speed up the draining process. He gives Cha his expanded theory; before she can answer,

Charlie gets very unsettled and begins barking and growling like a dog possessed and then ran off. Charlie really does not like being up here.

They go over to the required diversion. Murray walks across the pile of boulders and removes several, and continues to work carefully, removing as many as possible without falling in. Cha has blocked off the overflow, and they watch as the water mixes with the residual sediment. Slowly the flow increases, and they watch. To double-check that it is working, they backtrack over to the other side of the weir, and by the time they get there, the flow has increased significantly.

It has started to rain. At first, it is just a light shower, but the sky darkens, and the heavens release a torrential downpour. They are not dressed for this and retreat back to the truck and go and look for Charlie. She is lying on the porch, sheltering from the downpour, and as always, has that 'where is my dinner?' attitude. Maybe all the barking was just to warn them about the oncoming rainstorm. They rush in to avoid getting soaked, and even at that, their short journey from the truck to the porch has Cha getting towels to dry their hair.

Charlie gets fed and has no intention of going for a walk. The rain shows no signs of abating, and the sky is full of dark rain clouds. There is nothing that requires them to go out in this weather, but they are still concerned about the dream.

Cha has a look at the table and looks at him; Murray shakes his head and tells her all the wine bottles are down to you and you alone. Murray adds that if it was he who had consumed them, she would be visiting him in the hospital. She asks if she was a little tipsy, and he tells her the truth and tells her she was steaming.

The contents of the box brought down from the wardrobe are next. She spots them and asks why are the contents of the box scattered all over the room. Murray tells her that during her selection of the bits and pieces required to play some music that, she had decided to decorate the room with them. "I wasn't violent. Honestly, you can tell me the truth." Murray makes up a story about an exotic sexual adventure. At this, she bursts out laughing, knowing that he is bluffing. "You wish," and at that, she starts to tidy up. Murray gives her a hand; while she collects the batteries and the assorted contents that have been scattered on the floor. He starts on the table.

The fire is on, and he empty's everything that will burn on the flames. The glasses he places on the worktop and the bottles go into a bag and are deposited in one of the bins outside. Cha asks if he is hungry, but he has no appetite, and he would love a cuppa. There are in for the day. It has been a while since they have had time to play a board game, and he knows she enjoys playing. She is not ultra-competitive and enjoys playing like him. It is not the winning that counts.

It is the playing and the banter that goes with it. They have quite a selection in the game's cupboard. Cha runs a bath while Murray has a look. He delivers her tea in the nice cup with the flowers and goes through the list of what they have.

They settle for a little competition, Chess, crib, and gin rummy. Before they even start to play, Murray suggests that to avoid any disappointments, disagreements, and gunplay that perhaps they should iron out the rules. She smiles, he knows that she will try and cheat, but it is all part of the playing, and he reaches over and kisses her. She breaks off the embrace, "Don't even think that that is going to make me soft. We play every game for real, and it is the best of the three. Even if you are getting whipped at everything, you still have to play to the end.' Murray laughs and leaves her to relax in the warm water and finish her tea in peace.

He potters about downstairs and sets out the chessboard. Murray is not sure if he remembers to play crib and will have to think of a different game. He gets the money out of a property game and separates it into two equal piles. He thinks that she will be a demon of a poker player, so that is out of the question, and they could play blackjack or brag. Again, they will have to iron out the rules.

Murray goes back upstairs and checks if she wants anything else to drink, "A small glass of wine, please," He knows that she has been planning something because when he went in, she was lying in the water smiling. Murray goes back downstairs, Charlie wants out, but this is her quickest pee ever; straight out and straight back in. Murray holds the door closed while she shakes the water from her coat. Once she comes back in, she deposits herself in front of the fire and promptly drifts back off to sleep.

Murray hears Cha get out of the bath; she asks if I would like a quick dip in the second-hand water. He is about to say 'no thanks,' and he notices Mrs B look and says, "Yes, I think I will. and don't forget to shave." He undresses as he heads into the bathroom, leaving a trail of clothes in his wake, just remembering to remove his socks before he enters the bath. Murray just gets comfy, and he is just about to close his eyes when she comes in with a pile of clothes. She is naked and tells him that for a wee change, he can put these on. Murray looks at the suit and shirt and instantly thinks, no fucking way, but rethinks and nods in agreement.

She does not ask him if he wants anything and arrives minutes later with a banger, a glass containing a mixture of wine and last man on the planet. "Take your time, baby, and I will see you downstairs." she is still not wearing anything.

Murray relaxes; the rain is still pouring it down outside; he can hear it battering against the windows. Cha must have added some more hot water. He relaxes some more and looks at the tie. It is awfully thin, and then it dawns on him that it is a bowtie, and he has no idea what he is meant to do with it. He washes all over, submerges his head several times, gets out of the water, and shaves. Amazingly the clothes fit him. Murray even finds a comb in one of the pockets. He has not combed his hair in years. One time is not going to kill him.

Murray is all dressed, he has attempted to fix the bowtie but surrenders, and all he has done is feed it through the button-down collar, and he has left it with the tails at each side. He goes downstairs, Cha is sitting at the table, and she gets up when he gets to the table. Her top is see-through, and her nipples are hidden behind the flowery design. The skirt is long and buttoned up the side, and she has loosened only enough to allow her to walk. The high heels have added several inches to her height. She is stunning, and already Bobby wishes that he had eaten lots of fish. She says nothing and comes over and fixes the bowtie, he gets a whiff of the perfume, and Murray thinks that he will just give in and surrender now. There is a glass waiting for him, the same mixture as before, and Murray will admit that he cannot taste the wine. She has a small banger in a long cigarette holder and leans over, asking if I have a light. She knows the contours of her cleavage are directly in his line of sight, and she asks, "What would you like to play first Murray?" she is just winding him up to get him all flustered. All this is just another performance to help her win.

They decide on cards, and it is agreed that it will be three cards brag with rotating floaters, working up from the ace to king. The Top hand is discussed and agreed upon. The

291

banker will be rotated on a five-deal shuffle, and the ante will be a hundred. The pack is cut to see who deals first. She wins the cut, deals the cards, arcs her back, and pushes her chest out slightly. It is enough for him to see her erect nipples. Bobby pleads with him to give in now.

Murray does not look at his cards and bets 200 blind. She looks at hers and places 400 in the pot. He continues for another couple of rounds. Murray looks at his hand and has 9 high. He surrenders his cards, and she removes the whole pot, sliding it over to her side of the table. It is then that he notices she is wearing long false black nails. Bobby is now shouting.

Cha deals the cards, Murray does not look and bets 200, and she covers with the 400. This time it goes for five rounds before he looks. He has 2 10's and a 2 giving him a pile of 10's. He just knows she has higher than this and surrenders his cards. Murray loses the next three hands and takes his turn at dealing. He deals out the hands. She does not look at hers and stands up to get more wine. She stops and pretends to adjust her stockings; Bobby now has a high-wattage megaphone. She looks at her cards and bets 500. He covers it with 250, again 500 hundred, and ups to 500. She looks at him and licks her lips, and places 1000 in the pot. Murray stands up to go and get a can of last man on the planet. Bobby, at this point, is dying to come out and say hello. He catches Cha looking but says nothing.

It is Murray's shout, and he places 1000. He has still not looked at his cards, 2000 to play, he tells her. Cha places the 2000 and calls. Murray turns over his cards. He has a 7, a jack, and a 2, jack high. She turns over 3 aces. The lady wins.

Murray does not have a lot of money left and offers a one-card turnover for all the cash; she agrees all the money is put in the pot. The cards are shuffled. Murray cuts first. He has the 10 of diamonds. Cha takes her card, and the ace of spades falls out of her sleeve. She says nothing, Murray looks at her. He asks her if she has any more cards hidden, and she does. He needs to search for her. Bobby wants to call Interpol. He gets up from the table, walks over to her, and stands her up. She takes his hands and places them on her breasts. They make love on the table, on the chair, and end up in the bedroom. A trail of discarded clothes and even more discarded high-domination playing cards leads from the table all the way up the stairs leading all the way to the bedroom.

Cha falls asleep in his arms, Murray lies there beside her and can't help thinking that she is just truly wonderful and he owes her so much. She does more than her fair share of everything, and at the end of the day, it is just not fair on her. Sleep does not come at all this night. He is not going to lie there and toss and turn. Cha is sound asleep, and he quietly slips out of bed. He goes to the bathroom. His normal everyday clothes are still here. He puts them on and goes downstairs. Murray sticks a pan of hot water on and tidy's up while waiting for the kettle to boil. He makes a pot of tea; it takes quite a while as he has to search for where she hides the tea bags. Eventually finding them, he sits at the table and is still in deep thought. He is not overly worried but can't help thinking that lately, the dreams have some meaning, and the strange thing about it is that he can't figure out exactly what it is. All his life, he has had these strange encounters, he is not gifted in any way with the spirit world, but he would say that he is sensitive. On more than many occasions, he has had premonitions, he senses cold places where the hairs on the back of his neck stand up, and he instinctually knows that something is wrong, something bad has happened in the past. He heard voices and later on found out that the person had died. Murray had never told anyone of these events, but something was not right here. He gets this overwhelming feeling that this place is for something good, and the general feeling of this is that this is a place full of happiness and so much well-being that even in the dead of winter, the place is full of light. Murray is content here and can't help but think he has been here before. He is so at home here.

Murray snaps out of his dilemma, rolls his first banger of the day, and starts to clean the place up. He conjures the fire back into life. He even washes all the floors. The trail of our card-playing clothes he has picked up and has even folded and left them in a neat pile on the sofa. It is still raining

294

heavily outside, and Charlie is going to go out, but only when she has to.

He is still not hungry and potters about. Murray finds some headphones in the box and plays around with the batteries till he gets his old phone working. He does not even look at the messages and doesn't even consider checking his mail or for missed calls. Murray plugs the cans in and selects some moody, slow three o'clock in-the-morning jazz and immerses himself in the music.

Murray gets comfy, slouching on one of the chairs; he drinks more tea and smokes. When the jazz has run through its full playlist, he gets up and replaces the nearly done candles with new ones. Opens a can of juice and has another smoke. This one, he loads up and disappears into some slow blues. For this genre, he needs a bit of oomph and takes the volume up a notch or two. Murray adjusts the EQ to make it sound grittier and relaxes as the Les Pauls scream and cry. The mix of the minor and major scales merge with the melodies creating harmonies that warm him to the bone. In the old world, he had always wanted to go and visit Chicago and visit the places where the legends created these sounds.

The band leader is introducing a song. Murray loves this tune. The slide guitar solo is in two parts. The first one is gentle and soothing, and the second one is dirty and is almost as good as sex. He turns the volume up full and absorbs every single note. It is mid-morning, and Cha has not stirred.

Quietly as possible, he goes up the stairs and looks in to check that she is okay. He had not seen her for a few hours, and he was already missing her. Murray goes to the bathroom and starts to run a bath for her. He even looks under the sink and rummages about for one of the bath bomb things. The label that describes the type of scent has long gone, and even though it is the last one, he places it in the water. Murray knows that this is one of her favourite things, just to spend time relaxing in the warm water, and why not? He knows that she will enjoy this.

Mr Black has had a look at the weather outside, and the sky is still dark and overcast. The rain is on for the day. He is back downstairs. The batteries are depleted, replacing them is important. The cans go back on, and the early American shock rock group and his original band blast out tunes about growing up, insecurity, and dead infants. Even though these are cheap headphones and even though it is very old, the production is almost perfect. When the current playlist is exhausted, all the stuff is returned to the box. He eventually finds the cup with the painted flowers and vines. Murray gently wakes up Cha, leaves the tea beside the now-ready bath, and lets her relax in the perfumed water.

Murray has the toxic cup in one hand and a banger in the other and relaxes into nothingness. With one thing or another, they had been busy for a while, and it would not do them any harm to relax and take it easy. It can rain all it wants.

Cha comes down later. Murray can smell her before he sees her. Putting her arms around him, she tells him that it was a lovely surprise to wake up to. Murray smiles and tells her that he loves her and holds her in his arms, gently touching her face and giving her several kisses. She notices that he has tidied up some but does not say anything. She does ask if he would like some breakfast. Murray says, "Sure," and Cha goes off into the kitchen.

The voice comes back, informing Murray that she is doing something with Tuna and asks if he would like some. Murray politely says no, "Can I have some semolina for a change?"

In the kitchen, Cha is mentally preparing herself to open the can of semolina. She pings the ring pull and, in one swift action, removes the lid. She holds her breath during the whole process and aborts the contents into a bowl. "Here you go, baby," and she places it in front of him. Murray can't understand why she does not like this, and Cha stays in the kitchen until he returns his now empty plate.

"That was fantastic," he tells her. Cha looks at Murray as if he has just landed from a faraway distant galaxy. He knows that she finds the whole process disgusting and asks her if he could have another one.

Cha looks at Murray and tells him to help himself, pointing to where she hides the tins. They are situated next to the cleaning fluids and the remaining cans of semolina and nestled in between the chemical spray that can do anything and the drain cleaner. Murray eats this straight out of the tin. He has a stodge craving. When it is just about finished, he asks where the creamed rice hides. Cha shouts back that he will never find it as they do not have any. Depositing the now empty can in the trash. Murray goes and joins her at the table. As usual, the smart-ass had guessed his next question and had the shopping list out. Murray adds his favourite stodge to the list.

It is still thumping down outside, and Murray still has the same attitude; that he has no intention of crossing the threshold. In the old world, it is a day for curling up on the sofa and watching movies. Strangely enough, they found no televisions in the house. Cha has decided to do some painting today, Murray gives her a hand to drag the stuff downstairs, and she sets it up in the room. He gives her some space to let her get on with it and goes in search of a book.

The room is as he remembers it, and Murray does not know where to start. There are books on the floor, books in boxes. He will start filling up the empty shelves, and he thinks that sooner or later, a title will jump out at him. Murray goes and fetches some of his refreshments from downstairs. Cha is engrossed in her picture. He says nothing as he grabs some stuff and quietly goes back upstairs. He scans the room; there is no alphabetical order by titles or authors. It is all has been laid out in random. On a more careful examination, Murray reads all the titles and starts to pick and mix, history over here, food over here. It takes forever.

Murray starts rearranging the food section; he browses through the pages as he places them on the shelves. The European ones have the same food as them, but the titles are sometimes way over the top, and upon closer inspection of the ingredient list and the added pictures, he is amused to find traditional Scottish recipes with an added sauce transforming a basic fare into some pretentious sounding meal. The Italian books are so arrogant, implying that they are the only ones who can cook and that every other style of cooking is barbaric and not fit for dogs. Murray thinks he will add these to the newly listed pile destined for the fire.

He does like the pictures displayed in the ones from the Middle East. It has a diagram of cooking with the aid of a pit. Murray has no idea where they can source a goat, but they could always use a substitute. The history section is huge and covers everything you can think of. Murray is sitting in the corner reading one on siege machines of the Middle Ages. It is a brutal description of the theoretical building methods to the alleged methods of defending against them. He puts the book back in its place and gets on with refilling the shelves from the piles that have been building up on the floor, sometimes just guessing as he cannot read the title or there is no title at all. All that is left is on the floor; are the Italian cooking books that he is looking forward to incinerating, a pile of loose papers, and some books that are damaged beyond repair.

He has the candles on. Seated in the corner, Murray smokes as he goes through the loose papers; some are junk, and he just adds to the pasta pile. Murray notices that the numbers are odd; they are nothing that he has ever seen before. They look more like symbols.

Murray looks closer at the pictures; some are too faded to make anything out of the near invisible lines. He sees pictures of men dressed as beasts, pictures of beasts dressed as men, and the only readable item they have in common is the symbols at the bottom of the pages. He goes through them several times; he finishes reading them and leaves them in a neat, tidy pile.

The books are a different matter; some are so fragile and delicate that they turn to powder as he opens the pages. These also have strange symbols at the bottom of the pages. In all the books, he only finds one picture. It shows a woman dressed in robes, arms stretched towards the sky with her congregation, heads bowed, kneeling behind her. Murray stares at it for a long while, transfixed by the title. The symbols on the standing woman's robe are mostly faded but are. He is sure the same style as the ones indicated on the loose pages stacked on the table.

Murray does not know how long he has been sitting here, but the candles are nearly depleted. The long uneven strands of wax having run down the holders, mixing with the previously deposited wax, have solidified into a tangled multi-coloured mess.

Cha interrupts the stillness, "Hi baby, have you fallen asleep?" As she opens the door, he gets up and greets her as if he has not seen her for a long, long time. She looks at him before she says anything. Murray tells her that he is okay and has just been reading too much in the bad light. Murray tells her, as he kills the remaining candles, that he will be down in a minute.

Her watercolour is complete, it is beautiful, and the details are breathtaking. Murray stares at it and asks her if it has a title. "I was thinking about calling it the welcoming." He looks at her and rushes back up the stairs. Returning, he sits at the table, sparks up a banger, and hands her a single piece of paper.

She looks at it, looks at her picture, and is now sitting at the table looking at Murray. Her picture, the single page from the book picture, depicts the same scene and the same title, and even more alarming is the fact that they were there, albeit it was in a shared dream, but never the less, they were there in body, mind, and soul.

Cha reaches over. He hands her the smoke. They sit there in near silence, which is only broken by Charlie's snoring and the sound of the rain. Rather than talk about it, Murray takes her upstairs and shows her the pile of pages, and points out the symbolic significance of the page identification. They gather all the pages along with the tattered books and take them downstairs. Together they double-check, and he has missed nothing. There are no clues hidden in the pages. Sleep evades them. They are too restless to go to bed and spend the night on the sofa. They must have managed to get in a couple of hours. They wake up together and check first for mucky footprints and mucky feet. The rain, at last, has stopped, although their collective feelings are more than a little apprehensive. There is no choice, and they have to return.

The place of the dreams has not changed, and there is nothing new to find. The little bells are where they left them. The pond is another matter. Charlie refuses to go anywhere near it. She does not bark. She does not growl. She just runs away.

The silt has just about been washed away. Only a few inches remain, and various objects that are protruding from the dark mess. There are many skeletons in every configuration imaginable. Some have separated and have scattered over the area. Others are nearly intact except for the missing heads or limbs. There are several suited in armour with projectiles protruding from the eye slits.

Chapter Seventeen

They are looking at the carnage from hundreds of years ago. It is impossible to count the exact number as some of the bits and pieces must have been moved down stream in the downpour. On examination at the breech in the weir, they notice white objects strewn over the downstream course of the water.

Checking the depth of the remaining sludge, they prod and investigate the human debris before them. There are many discarded weapons in all shapes and forms, some must be from the Middle Ages, but they also notice some early firearms.

It is only then that they notice the coffins; the final count is thirteen, and on closer inspection, the coffins have holes in them and have been weighted down. One coffin has a partially broken lid, which has scratch marks on the inside. These poor souls were entombed in the coffins alive and then submerged in the water.

Murray and Cha agree that they should be moved; even though they dispatched some bad guys recently to a watery grave, this is totally different. The coffins contain people that deserved better than this. Charlie has not returned, and this has been the reason that she had scarpered. They start to tidy the mess; armed with brushes, they sweep over, pushing the remaining silt mixed with the water in the direction of the breech.

The bones and skeletons are placed in one pile, the weapons in another. The coffins they do not touch. After several hours they have quite a collection of each. The weapon pile is immense. Some have been mass-produced. Others are more sophisticated and, after some cleaning, show all the signs of being made by a master craftsman. The symbols they noticed on the loose pages are also on these weapons. These are separated into two weapon piles as they search through, looking at the remaining pile for any unusual markings.

They have a break and discuss what to do with the coffins. After much deliberation, it is agreed that they should be interned where the bells were found. As this place has frequently been recurring, they feel that under these circumstances, this is the only decision that can be made. They also agree that they should do this as soon as possible, even if it involves working round the clock.

The opening in the temporary dam is rebuilt, and the overflow reopened. This will dry the area and allow them to move the coffins easier. There is an old military-type vehicle with an attached winch and a small crane it is located in one of the storage sheds. After a bit of swearing from Murray, it starts. Cha helps bleed and refill the hydraulics and most of the lever's work. The coffins are carefully moved as the winch drags them out of the pond, and they are stored on the bed of the vehicle. There is an overwhelming sadness while they do this, and they don't smoke, and work is done in sombre silence.

An area is marked out, and Murray starts digging the ground, which is relatively soft and free from rocks. Cha is over at the pond and has started to remove the old mass-produced weapons. She takes a bundle at a time and dumps them in the wooded area, and on the return journey, she carries some sticks and starts to build a funeral pyre. After several trips, the weapon pile and the bundle of bones have both been reduced.

Murray digs until he thinks that have enough depth and sufficient area to bury the thirteen, but he realises that he needs the mini digger to complete the task. Joining Cha, he helps her complete the task. All the weapons have been dumped, and he is dragging over more wood to add to the pile.

Daylight is now fading fast, and they bring the mini digger up and complete the mass grave, gently lowering the coffins into the ground. They should say something, but they can't think of anything that would be suitable. All thirteen have been placed in the ground, the ornate weapons they feel would be disrespectful if they were dumped. They are placed on and around the coffins, all except one, the dagger with the pommel identical to Cha's wedding ring that they keep.

Murray thinks that they have missed something, and they drive back to the house. Charlie is on the porch but does not want to play. She must sense something from their urgency and is happy just to goes and lies beside the fire. Murray gathers the papers and damaged books. Returning straight to the field, they share the items. Cha and Murray spread them evenly amongst the coffins along with the bells, except two of them. They turn and slowly ring the bells before placing them in the mass grave. Cha helps him cover the coffins, and several hours later, the mass grave has been filled. They walk over the surface to compact the soil and then add more of the soil.

Walking over to the pyre, Murray sprinkles it with petrol and ignites it from a distance. The pile bursts into flames. They sit and watch the pile slowly being consumed, and only then do they smoke. They feel quite at ease, leaving the wind to disperse the ashes.

Dawn appears, and so does the old woman in the hooded cloak. They hear her voice, and she implores them not to worry, assuring them that there is nothing to fear. She is between them now and reaches out and takes their hands.

They walk as she glides between them; she is in the process of giving reassurances to trust her. She leads them over to the weir. And stops at a slightly different-coloured section of the wall. Clapping her hands twice an opening appears. The wall crumbles, exposing a medium sized chest.

They are instructed to remove the chest and take it home. Reaching out, she places a hand on each of their heads *55558 14777*. Cha sees the first part of the ten-digit sequence. Murray sees the second.

At this, the old woman in the hooded cloak disappears, and they work in silence as the chest is removed from the recess in the wall. It is not heavy as they manhandle it out of the hole and carry it to their vehicle. On arrival at the house, they open the door, and Charlie runs off immediately.

The chest is dry and opens easily. The contents are wrapped in black material. It has symbols that they do not know nor what they signify, but they recognise them from the previous encounters to be identical to the symbols on the old woman's cloak. The contents are lifted out and placed on the table. After slowly unwrapping the material, a silver box with other symbols is revealed.

So far, Today has been quite an adventure; they could talk about the most recent events, but both of them are still in a state of shock. The old woman was totally convincing, and they just trusted her without question. She gave the impression that they had all met somewhere before.

Cha and Murray take turns examining the ornate box; there are no indications of how they are meant to open it. They both agree that forced entry is not a good idea. Murray suggests that perhaps some tea would help them both think. Cha thinks some food would be a good idea too. Murray's appetite is non-existent, but he submits and agrees to eat something. He rattles a monster together and smokes while he holds the box in his hands, rotating it this way, rotating it that way. Looking and searching for any visible signs of possible entry. Murray is perplexed, Cha re-joins him at the table with some tea, and after searching, she admits that she is also stumped.

Leaving it alone, they eat the Tuna something, Murray's stomach does not resist, nor does it send out the normal early warnings of the imminent unpleasantness. He drinks lots of tea, and as there is none left for Cha, she makes another pot. Surprisingly they are still hungry, and she rattles up another meal. Murray does not know the title of this, but it is a selection of vegetables and rice all mixed in together.

While sitting eating, Cha and Murray discuss what they are meant to do to open the box. Everything they have tried has produced no results. Every examination from every conceivable angle has shown no signs of seams, buttons or switches. They still agree that forcing it open is really not a good idea. Running through the previous events, they go over everything frame by frame for clues, but the only one that comes to mind is the ten-digit sequence. Several hours later, all they have been doing is reminiscent of the childhood party game of passing the parcel.

Murray is still totally perplexed and reaches over and takes Cha's hand. A mysterious click, followed by a subtle mechanical sound, emanates from the box. All that has been done differently is to hold hands and hold the box at the same time. They watch and listen. When the noises have abated, they examine the box again. There are two sets of wheels now visible on one side of the box. They are contained in a recess, and each contains a set of five exquisitely numbered wheels.

The only clue that has been issued, as far as they can recollect, is the ten-digit number. Somehow neither of them had envisaged that it was just a simple case of inputting the numbers. They share the box, looking at possible ways that it would work. This is all making Murray's head work overtime, and he needs some fresh air. Cha joins him, and they go outside. There is no sign of Charlie, and they hope that she is just out exploring. Murray is worried, but Cha reassures him that Charlie will be fine. Exhaling some smoke, Murray thinks out loud and says to no one in particular that as the box revealed the numbered wheels when all three items were connected, perhaps we repeated the process and selected the numbers. He asks Cha what she thinks, and she agrees that they should at least give it a try. Murray takes the final drag and flicks his smoke into the hearth.

Holding hands, the two sets of five-digit numbers are dialled, and nothing happens. The numbers are double-checked, and it is confirmed that the sequence is correct.

Again, they are stumped. Perhaps instead of holding hands, we should hold that box and dial the numbers at exactly the same time.

On the next attempt, the box is held on the table between them. Both of them hold an edge each, and they slowly, with their free hand, input the preselected numbers simultaneously. There is an audible click, and at exactly the same time, they are injected with a miniature needle. The box slowly opens, and they hear and see gas being omitted from the now-opening lid.

We came here a long time ago in an age when your species was very primitive. In the beginning, all we could do was survive, and over the coming centuries, we merged into your primitive civilisations. This was a time of great peace. Gradually we guided you towards various advancements, and through various innovations, your species advanced.

Unfortunately, greed and corruption advanced hand in hand with this. Our species was partly responsible for this, and it produced a huge rift in our previously agreed agenda.

One faction or another of our species has tried for centuries to wipe out the others. We separated totally from this and looked for an alternative way to survive. Our withdrawal from the opposing factions, in the beginning, was largely ignored, and as we were a minority, we were left alone.

This world was heading for disaster, and the planet would eventually be destroyed. Although we have witnessed the many positive aspects of your species, we saw the many negative ones. The opposing factions wanted total control, and unfortunately, many of your species were easily coerced into playing an active part.

Where necessary, we interfered in halting the advancement of the opposing groups, and over the years, we have lost many of our own. Sadly, we are now so few in numbers, and as a last-ditch effort, you have been awakened.

In the past, we have fought wars to change the results, carried out assassinations, and manipulated currencies, all to stop in their tracks the plans that were put in place by the others.

The others have continued fighting each other and have, over the centuries, severely depleted our numbers. A great evil is emerging and must be stopped.

All the descriptions are lived through vivid realms where they are fighting wars, surviving bombings, running from atomic blasts with their skin peeling off, fighting in jungles, fighting on horseback, being pursued through deserts and jungles, and being tortured in various prisons.

They were flying in planes attacking other planes, bombing cities, strafing enemy positions, in submarines ordering the firing of torpedoes, surviving arrows that looked like black rain, escaping through tunnels, being

hanged, being led to the guillotine, on trial, being given a
last request before facing the firing squad.

The list continued, and they were ashamedly part of our
preconceived history. Every single event that they
momentarily lived through was manipulated to achieve the
desired results, and the most disturbing fact was that
humanity embraced all of this, took an active part and all the
warring factions who proclaimed that they were righteous.

You think that you selected to stay here in this place. This
place selected you. You are the hope for a new beginning.
You are the hope for the future, and you are the hope to right
all the wrongs and set the course for our species' success.
You are the last of our kind.

The old woman in the hooded cloak is standing in front
of them, arms raised to the sun. As she glides backwards, she
disappears and fades from the picture.

They lay awake in bed; Cha is entwined in his arms.
They have no idea of how they got here, and the last that they
remember, they had been sitting at the table. Murray looks
at Cha and just loves her more than life itself.

A voice in Murray's head speaks, "I know you do, and
the feeling is mutual, but when it comes down to it, I think I
love you more than that." Murray does not see her lips move,
she has not stirred, and upon a closer inspection, her hair
looks longer, and although he can't be sure, she looks
younger.

Murray hears Cha's voice again. He looks at her and listens, "Well, I suppose that we should get up now. Again, her lips do not move.

Cha gets up, stretches and looks at Murray, "I think you need a shave?" He puts a hand to his face expecting to feel some stubble, but Murray is visibly shocked to have developed a fully formed beard. Murray had shaved a couple of days before; he remembers it was the same night that they had played cards. The couple goes down the stairs, not saying anything. Murray is worried. He looks in the mirror. Sure enough, he does have a full beard. He also notes that his hair is longer, and apart from that, he feels fine.

The table is empty; there is no sign of the box. He looks at Cha, and she looks at him. Murray is about to mention what you remember, and she replies again without moving her lips that she remembers sitting at the table trying to get the small box with the strange symbols opened.

Holding up his hands, he asks her directly if she can read his thoughts. She looks at him and speaks, telling him that she woke up to hear him say that he loved her more than life itself, adding that was one of the nicest things anyone has ever said to her.

Murray is visibly shaken; he has, since he met her, never ever had one negative about her. He needs a smoke; Cha retrieves a tin of the last man on the planet, brings it over, and goes and sticks a pan of water on to boil. Charlie is still absent; Murray forgets about rolling a banger and opens the door, and shouts for Charlie to return home. He shouts for ages, and he misses her dearly and hopes that she is okay. "I think that I should. We should be out looking for her." Cha tells him not to worry. Charlie will be fine and return when she is ready. Dogs sometimes have this thing where they have to off and explore.

Purposely he leaves the door open just in case, plonks himself back at the table and continues where he had left off. He has a cup of tea waiting on him. They go through what they can remember. Cha does most of the talking. Murray listens intently, and in-between draws of the smoke, she adds in bits of the remembered dream that he does not understand and requires some form of clarification.

Charlie has still not returned, and it has been at least a couple of hours since they got up. Murray runs the tap and checks to see if the water is hot. The facial hair has got to go. He goes to the door and tries shouting at Charlie again, but she does not return. Cha notices his distress and assures him that she will be fine. "Maybe she was just freaked out by the recent events. After all, she had sensed something was not quite right before us and was upset also."

The fire is set and ignited. Both of them are very hungry, and Cha in quick time magically rustles something up. For once, he knows what it is, but it is amazing what she can do with a tin of spam, and he washes it down with several cups of tea.

Murray goes and showers taking longer than usual, as he has to remove the excessive growth on his face. He emerges from the bathroom and examines the results in the nearest mirror, and surprisingly, he looks younger. Murray does not feel any different, and apart from Cha being able to hear his inner thoughts, all still seems to be the same. While he was hacking off the beard, he was thinking about how long it would actually take to grow, and he calculated that it would be about a month to grow. The big question running about in his brain is, to put it bluntly, where the fuck did that time go? He has no recollection of anything apart from opening the box.

Cha is at the table smoking, and Murray asks her again to go through the previous events at the end of her recollection. He explains the time it would take to grow a beard. For the record, she cannot explain the missing time. Murray does not even look at the clock. Cha informs him that she also has lots of questions. For instance, are they to set off on a completely different course of action? Are they destined to go and find trouble? Do they have to wait for trouble to come to them? Going on the information that is available, the list could be endless. If Murray thinks about it anymore, his brain has a more than fair chance of fucking imploding. He is hungry again and asks Cha if there is any food. Murray is really not up to going out and killing anything and will be more than happy with tinned food.

Rather than discuss the socio-economic and political ramifications of the shared dream. He suggests that starting tomorrow, they could get stuck into doing some work. Maybe, even finish off all the jobs that they had started but for various reasons had not completed. At least it would take his brain off of self-destruct mode.

Murray has no intention of starting anything today. For the moment, he is quite content to eat, get wasted, and, for once in his life, perhaps even an early night and go for a fresh start in the morning. Cha just looks at him, "I will make something in a minute or two, but if you think that you are missing all those days, then the truck will not start?" This is a reasonable question, and it requires an answer. They get up and go outside. The car starts on the first turn, and to prove that all is well, they take it for a spin. This has offered no further explanation, and the pair of them are totally stumped and no closer to the truth and have no specific timeframe relating to how long they were missing from normal day-to-day life.

As they are already in the vehicle, a drive around the estate is called for, stopping periodically and getting out and looking. By the end of the journey, with every track being covered, Murray is hoarse through shouting for Charlie. He is sad and cannot pretend Charlie is more than just a pet;

Charlie is more than a working dog. Charlie was family. There is no hiding Murray's severe disappointment at not finding her. He is positively certain that Cha misses her too, but on reflection, his dogs, throughout his years, have always thought that there was always this special bond and Charlie was his best friend.

Now seated back at the table, Cha ignores him, and he wallows in remorse. Murray knows that this cannot continue, as it will rip him apart, and he snaps out of it. He gets up and puts his arms around her, and tells her that he is okay now. Cha cooked, and they ate, making conversation about this and that, and they did not venture into; if these events really had happened and did they honestly think that was actually orchestrated.

It's now morning, and still, no Charlie. If he does not stop feeling like this, it will shut him down. Murray blocks the thoughts out, makes tea and starts to work out the jobs that need to be completed.

The largest is the reinstatement of the weir and the hopeful reintroduction of a decent electricity supply. There is no huge stockpile of gadgets lying in storage, waiting for juice, and it would be nice just to switch on the lights on, not to mention charging car batteries would be a whole lot easier. Murray reassures Cha that today he is okay and promises not to redevelop his genetic, natural Scottish trait and wallow in self-pity; putting their arms around each other, he smiles as he tells her this time, she does not need to administer a swift kick to his wedding tackle.

The weir reassemble job is surveyed, and they make a list of what is required need to get on with it. Between the layers of cement work drying out, they manage to have a good look at the workings. Another sealed-up channel is located that feeds the house wheel. This is great news and means that the housing supply should, when in operation would be ample enough for all their electrical requirements.

After a good all-around survey of the area, they found and located lots of items that had not been previously noticed, including another water wheel, which had been hidden behind a thick unkempt growth of natural vegetation. They were thinking about chopping down the growth that has been there for god knows how long. Until Cha points out the wheels are cast iron and why not torch the bushes? Murray agrees as he sees this as a hard task made easy. He can see another previously unseen opening in the wall, and Murray gets the task of cleaning it out. It has the making of a horrible smelly job, and Cha asks if she will need to contact a leading international health organisation. He just ignores her and gets on with the clearing. When he finishes, he is not allowed in the car and has to walk home. Murray is made to undress outside, and Cha points him in the direction of the waiting bath.

The pair of them really have been at work non-stop, and the days have rolled by extremely quickly. Never once have they dwelled on the past. There have been no adventures outside their realm of safety, nor have they had any uninvited visitors.

Cha does not know exactly how long they have been out working. They both know it has been weeks, but either way, all of the tasks are now complete. Everything has been done, even down to repairing the big shed roof and removing the scrap car and washing machine.

All that remains is to reinstate the water supply to the weir. The powdered residue from the cremation has all blown away, and all that remains is a scorch mark on the ground. It is possible that Cha could have manufactured another homemade explosive device, but both of them are really not keen on this, and it is agreed to do it by hand. Luckily the weather is warmer, and they will be able to go into the water and remove the obstacle by hand. Murray does not remember putting this amount of rubble into the water, but they start early in the morning. There is just no other way of doing it. What he is unable to hump out is gently rolled to the side, some are extremely stubborn, and these are manipulated by spades and crowbars.

At last, all the work is complete, it has turned out to be a lovely evening, and they stay out. It had been a long while since they had slept out under the stars. Cha takes great delight in pointing up and going through all the names of the constellations. Murray could listen to this forever and takes the opportunity and points to a rouge shooting star and asks what that one is called. She thinks for a moment before replying, "That one is named after you. It is known as smartass!"

On the break of morning, they walk back, hand in hand, strolling like loved-up teenagers to the house and low and behold, they have a decent electricity supply. The fridge freezers are making strange vibrating noises, and Murray thinks it is just in protest at the number of tinned goods, and they would like to transition back to their normal purpose.

Cha and Murray split up and go around trying every switch; they do not try every socket, as the only lamps they have are in the sitting room. After searching for replacement bulbs and fuses, all of them are now working. The find of the juice-guzzling storage heaters needs to be addressed. Every one of them is unplugged, and the connecting wires are removed, making them permanently disconnected. The fridge freezer alone is a luxury in itself, the lights an added bonus, but these types of heaters just eat electricity 24/7, and they do not have enough supply to keep them running.

Together they survey what they have. Cha asks if there is anything else that he would like added. He has spoken about this before, and although Murray is sure she will remember. He tells her that a Christmas tree all year round would be nice. She has remembered, and he recognises the look she gave him when he had initially mentioned it all that time ago.

She agrees, and it will be added to the list. Asking what size, Murray tells her it does not matter as long as it has sparkly lights that gently change patterns. Not only to be fair, but just in case, Murray asks her the same question. Cha would like a CD player adding that to have the luxury of playing music would be just wonderful. At breakfast and at dinner and just at any time, whenever they wanted. "We could get a huge selection of CDs and not just musical ones. You can get jungle soundtracks train journeys; the list is endless."

Strangely enough, none of them has mentioned a flat-screen television or a movie player. Murray has seen all the movies he can think of, and he gets the impression that Cha was never one to sit around watching soaps or fake reality programmes or a big fan of daytime TV.

This will also get added to the list. Murray remembers to chip in that it would be nice if they could, maybe, if we have room, get a decent pair of speakers. She looks at him, and he could spend a lifetime explaining the subtle nuances of decent pair speakers that enhance the whole listening experience, but Cha stops him mid-sentence and says, "Okay, we will add them to the list." In the morning, they mull over breakfast, and both of them are sick of eating tinned food. Today if the opportunity arises, they will get something for the pot.

They venture out to check all of the recently completed works. The big shed is fine and tidy, the scrap has been removed, and the increased water supply to the reigning industrial washing machines works with no problem. The clothes are seemly cleaner, and row upon row is hanging out in the improvised lines.

The Orangery is turning out to be very special; all that was planted is growing, some buds have formed, and Cha is very excited that soon she will have real flowers to smell and, most importantly, paint. The biggest surprise is the first sign of water in the little stream that feeds its way through the main section.

Chapter Eighteen

It is only at present an interment trickle, but he calls Cha over and shows it to her. The shared hope is that this will eventually fill the course and self-clean over time. They collectively imagine being in here surrounded by all the colours, all the smells, hearing the small waterfalls as the water trickles through the manmade course with the collection of small birds chattering in the background.

Everything that has been checked out is good, and at least for now, our collective job list is complete. The only task at hand is their appetite. They avoid the field; this is agreed to be a non-hunting zone on the grounds that it does not seem to be the correct or proper thing to do, and they look elsewhere for food. Murray thinks rabbit would be nice, but the quacking in the near distance changes his mind. Cha is on the trigger and bags several ducks. He gets the task of cleaning the meat while Cha concocts some spicy sauce and some accompanying vegetables. It smells out of this world. As per the normal rules, he is not allowed anywhere near the kitchen, and no quarter will be given if he is apprehended red-handed, performing a sneaky unauthorised taste. Murray is starving and could eat it all.

Under starters orders, he sets the table, eating by candlelight, and the meal is just fantastic. The sweet chilli has left a coating on the duck meat, and when eaten, it just activates taste buds that had been long forgotten about. Murray must add this to his favourite list. If he remembers correctly, they are now on the fourth revision. He offers to tidy up the plates, but there is no food remaining, and the recently reactivated fridge freezer will be very disappointed in attaining no additional visitors to the now-dead animals residing in the freezer compartment.

The only remaining job to do is give the collections of sprouting plants the once over and assign them to the allocated positions and configurations that Cha has envisaged. While she is living out her dreams in her private gardening world: Murray gets to work on a promise that he had made to her, almost like years ago. Second generator, he has managed to move from the main house area and has connected the two of them together and is now sorting out the various configurations of wiring looms to make a time-controlled system to control the heat input into the Orangery. The windows have all been cleaned again. Murray likes this job, and as part of the deal, one drunken night, he had told her about a window cleaner mate of his, who, when Murray bumped into him from time to time, would always tell him stories about his adventures with a lonely suburban stay at home housewives. It always amazed Murray that none of the husbands had ever found out and seriously assaulted him and also that even as he was backing away from him to escape in the car, he would relive his stories right up to the last minute.

When it came to the major task of the Orangey windows, Cha had promised in a drunken state to pretend that her husband was working offshore and she was needful of some much-missed love and attention. She was amazed when Murray admitted that he had never played away from home, and she was even more amazed that he would be more than happy with a smile. Cha had other ideas, and it was the examination nurse, the teacher and ones that he cannot remember ever telling her the job titles or the accents of the characters she portrayed, but as always, the lovemaking was just out of this world.

Murray has the looms ready, and he double-checks the circuits. The control panels have been modified and joined together, and hopefully, as one stops, the other will start. On entry, the greenhouses are full of blooms, and a few flowers are trying to escape the confines of the bulbs. The wires are connected to the various cables that have been used to heat the soil, and he connects the wires to the terminals in the homemade board.

She holds her hand out; Murray thinks she just wants to shake hands at the nearly completed task, but she looks at him and asks if he would like to donate any seeds to the project. He has not got them on him, and he can go and get them now or later. She tells Murray that he should go and get them now. He returns later, and she is busy working away, sleeves rolled up as she potters about in her much-preferred world.

Cha tells him that she has gone through all the switches, and everything is working. Murray hands over his treasure. He is about to go through the planting process, the separation of the males and females, and all the information that he had imprinted in his brain over the years from his brother. Cha just looks at him, looks at all the budding plants, and he gets the drift. Murray will let her get on with it and remembers that 75% pure alcohol will be needed to add to the list.

A halt is called several hours after daylight has faded. Murray is quite hungry and looks forward to her latest cooking experiment. He has resigned himself to the fact that Charlie has gone, and although he is tempted to go and look for her and physically has to restrain himself from calling out her name every time he opens the door. Murray misses her dearly and has a little secret cry when Cha is not looking. She pretends that she does not notice, but he knows that she misses nothing. He has never tried to hide anything from her, only the tears.

Murray has his first number of the day, the reasons being he is attempting to reduce his tolerance, as the green stuff is not affecting him as much as it should, and he is working with slowly dwindling supplies. If the greenhouse supply comes to fruition, he intends to make some super-duper solid, Murray has never made this before, and it is nearly as identical in the manufacturing process for the medical variety, but he has of yet no desire to make it.

Cha has informed him that he stinks to high heaven, and he is sent in the direction of the bathroom. On returning, Cha had the table all set out, with candles, wine, and the works. The meal was, as always, one of the best that he had ever tasted, and he had and for once, run out of compliments. Murray has a glass of wine but adds water to reduce the horrible taste and the even more horrible side effects that don't seem to happen in Cha's industrial digestive system. Once she had tried to tell him about one training session she was on and all the truly horrid things that she had to eat to survive and pass the test, he was throwing up less than halfway through her description and pleaded with her to talk about something else. Murray gives up on the water idea. It is not diluting the wine taste and the aftertaste at all, and he reverts to his old faithful. This, he notes, is down to the last four packs.

Murray is also informed that the tinned goods, amongst other things that they use, are also running low and sooner rather than later, they are going to have to adventure into the remains of the big world. They discuss the pro and cons, Murray does not want to, and as always, he has serious misgivings but takes into consideration the near experience of the thinly veiled warning given by the woman in the hooded cloak. He eventually gives in and agrees.

Cha drinks several bottles; the phones are dead; they will switch on, but none of the buttons works. She teases him so that she can sing. Murray enquires and asks if this could be a duet of the famous song, just me and you on this planet. She exposes her breasts and flashes, "Never in your wildest dreams!" and giggles at taking the rise out of him.

They continue to shoot the shit into the early hours, and they finish the evening making passionate love on the sofa. No French, Gypsy, KGB or any of the other night-time personas that Cha sometimes adopts, just her and that is always more than enough for him.

Positioned at their end of the bridge, the vehicles had been on standby for an hour, during which they had constantly scanned the other side through the binoculars and had noticed zero movements. They drive across as fast as they dare on reaching the other side, charge up the hill and pull into the first vacant layby available. This is a double one, and the abandoned vehicles on the roadside of the parking spot afford them some cover.

They wait it out, listening and scanning the horizon for movement, and none is spotted. The road is followed for as much as possible, only crossing to the central reservation when the way ahead is blocked, this manoeuvre had been carried out several times before, and the only time when they were unable to do this was when they had to couple up their vehicles and drag some obstacles out of the path. A normal two-hour journey had taken some six hours. Along the route, they observed some burnt-out cars and some with bullet holes.

The city now lies before them. The light will be fading soon. The plan is to wait, and when darkness is upon them, they will slowly edge into the large shopping centre on the outskirts of town.

They edge in, no lights, and the revs are kept at a minimum. Murray's truck is very unhappy about being in first and second gear, and the temperature gauge is coming out in sympathy. Cha in the newly acquired 4x4 from Sweden is experiencing no problems, and they park outside a national chain noted for selling lots of medical supplies. Stealthily making their way across the car park through the abandoned cars, Cha gently jemmies a door, and they slip inside, hopefully unnoticed, into the department store. The base camp is set up in the little office located in the dispensary. This has not been ransacked and remains intact.

At his eye level, Murray can't help but notice the packs of Viagra. Cha notices what he is looking at, and while she sets up the camp stove to boil some water tells him the story of one of her department co-workers who was found dead in the red-light district of Amsterdam. At first, his death was viewed as suspicious due to the fact of what he had done for occupation and what missions he had been active on. It was not until the autopsy was carried out that it was discovered he had overdone it on the blue tablets. Handing him the tea, she places her hand between his legs, giving Murray a quick peck on the cheek and assuring Bobby that he did not need them. Murray feels about fifty feet tall, and he thinks this is a very well-given and received compliment. He is thinking, okay, Bobby, and he thinks that they may have to support the accolade when their thoughts are replaced, and he is firmly brought back to reality by "I will take the first watch."

Murray chuckles when she goes, thinking back to when Viagra started hitting the streets. Boy, was it popular, and it carried all the special deals buy one for such a price and five for the special price. Murray remembers one nutter who used to take him with an ecstasy tablet. He showed him a tablet. It looked like a dog worming tablet. Perish the thought of wondering how he ended up.

Settling into the shared sleeping bag, he gets as comfy as he can and manages a few hours. The tea is ready when Murray goes to relieve Cha. She is all business handing over the watch details. He salutes her, "Smart-ass," as she disappears into our hideaway.

Murray takes over and seriously pays attention and watches every movement, crisp potato packets and several soft drinks and super strong lager cans. He thinks that he can hear some vehicles moving but only for a few seconds. It could have very well been, and it was far away or maybe just a possibility of his grey matter making things up because he is bored out of his skin. Murray follows the strict no-smoking rules along with all the other rules that are applicable on duty.

Murray's duty watch is over when; Cha is just about to tap him on the shoulder. Without speaking, he knew she was there, and he had heard her thinking about doing this when she was making breakfast. He turns around, and they greet each other with a huge cuddle and some kissing. Their number one rule that never will change is they really don't know when the last day will be, and what a terrible burden to carry about the thought of. I wish I had told you that I loved you.

He packs up after the morsels that Cha has left him are consumed. Murray meets her at the door. She covers him as Murray edges slowly over and sticks the bags, including the additional one that contains the much-needed medical supplies, in the back of her vehicle. They watch and listen, and now that it is getting light, they can view what shops are here to restock their supplies. The first one to catch Chas's interest is a wholesale garden and agricultural supplier. It is a little way up the lot, three doors up from Pat's specialist drink supplies. Murray had never heard of this one but will be visiting on the way back. He thinks that Pat maybe will supply the brand that he is after.

The shutter of the Agricultural store is firmly closed, and as quietly as possible, Murray persuades the lock to surrender; he is unable to stop the audible screech, and the thunder as the shutter rolls up violently and stops suddenly. The fronts of the other shops act like sails capturing the sounds that bounce to and from each other. They stay perfectly still. After seeing nil movement, he reaches in. The shutter has not come all the way up and stretches to breach the barrier of the door.

There have been no visitors here for a long time; the place has a huge collection of dust. As they had discussed this possibility, they donned the dust masks and tiptoed inside. It is Aladdin's cave, the selection is something else, and they are bowled over by the descriptions. Wilkinson's vacuum-packed potatoes are all varieties available, and Blackmore's Scandinavian vegetable selection is also available in vacuum packs. This place has the works, and they gather as much as they will need, plus a little extra just in case. Some of the items they had never heard of, but they take a fair selection and load it into the back of the Cha's 4X4. Taking their time to gently persuade the shutter back down so as to hide their entry and exit.

Cha is jubilant about this find, and they have taken more than enough. With careful planning and a good bit of luck, hopefully, they will get a good crop from this and hopefully figure out to store and get them all to seed for the following seasons. Even if they find nothing else on this trip, this find has made it all worthwhile. Watching and waiting again, and when nothing moves, they scan the shop signs above the entrances. The fashion shops do nothing for Murray, he has several outfits, and he needs no more clothes. There is a specialist ladies' underwear shop, and a woman with a cats-eyes mask decorates the sign with the added words we dare you. Cha looks at Murray and asks, "Are you complaining about what I sometimes wear?"

He tells her, "Never."

Several shopfronts are down. It's Danny's Hot Hi-Fi deals; this trip just gets better and better. It is not an absolute necessity, but Cha has rarely asked for anything, and Murray wants to get her one. He is sure that if Danny was here, he would agree.

Murray motions that they are going in, the shutter is not in place, and the door opens with a gentle kick. It is damp and dusty, and they assume the body on the floor is Danny or one of his customers. They search with the aid of the small torchlights and eventually find the unmissable special second-hand deals located at the back of the store. Surprisingly there is a huge selection of CDs, and it covers every imaginable taste that there is. It even has the lie back and relaxes to the sounds of the Amazon jungle section. Murray sticks a copy of stream trains of the old American West discreetly in his pocket; it may come in handy. They store the CD player with the speakers and his one little weakness, the gold-plated speaker cables, all ten packets at the front door. They would like to be out of here before sunset and find an empty box and stick as many CDs as possible without trying to pick too much crap. The neater they are stored, the more they can pack. Time is catching up, and they have to move it out.

In the remaining time left, they have the possibility of visiting two shops at maximum before the deadline approaches. Cha wants the big cash and carry, and Murray wants Pat's shop. The supermarket makes it a much closer prospect. They agree and hit the supermarket first. A rough estimate is that there is enough room for eight trolley fulls of canned goods that takes everything into consideration food, cigarettes, beer, wine, and cigarette papers. The first alarm is that the shutter has been broken and has been neatly placed back, as also is the door. They listen for anything out of the ordinary and, on hearing nothing, proceed forward. As always wary of possible violent disagreements, they have the guns ready to settle any disputes quickly.

All the family-size trolleys are still all interconnected. Removing the small bolt cutters from the backpack, Cha takes the guard pose and snips eight chains. The first stop is the tobacconist counter; experience has taught him that the boxes are secured in the office come store room. Cha picks the lock like a true professional. They swap places, and Murray goes in, and in five minutes flat, the first family trolley is partially filled and placed in pole position by the door.

The remaining trolleys are filled with various tinned goods, and all the selections, with the notable exception of semolina, ravioli and tapioca, all the goods are family-size. Now that the fridge is functional, they can store real food. All that remains is the herbs and spices stored in glass jars.

They are walking through the aisles adding items that complete the memorised list when they hear the stifles, at the same time as noticing the damp patches on the floor. The stifles are getting louder, and it is a woman; more stifles. They approach with caution. The man is standing above the woman, telling her to try and keep it down. She is looking at him, and the glare on her face looks like she could castrate him right now. He does not hear them approach. His wife or girlfriend is in childbirth. He notices Murray out the side of his eye and turns around, pointing his revolver at him. He has the trained marksman stance.

Cha tells Murray, without speaking, that it is okay and just put the gun down. Before the guy tells him to put it down, Murray tells him that he is going to lower his weapon. His companion groans louder. He does not know where to look. He looks at Murray, he looks at her, he looks again at Murray, and he has not noticed Cha, who is now right beside him with the gun at his head. Gently she asks him how far she is through the pregnancy; the woman answers about seven months. The guy still has the gun on Murray. Cha tells him on no uncertain terms to put the gun down, and there is a chance that they all can walk away from this! "You look like a sensible chap, and all you have to think about is if I was going to shoot, you would be dead." The woman's groans are louder still.

Midwife Cha takes charge. As per their instructions, they helped the woman up and moved her to the nearest office. Cha already has kicked open the door and cleared the desk in one swoop of her arm, "Place her on there, towels water, get the stove, some blankets and more towels." Looking at them because they have not gone, she is busy holding the woman's wrist and counting seconds on her watch.

The woman speaks, "Dean, don't be a prick. Just do as the doctor tells you!" They all look at her open-mouthed, even Cha. They do as instructed, hand over all the requested items to Cha, who informs them to keep out, and the door closes, blocking their view.

Dean looks at Murray, and he looks at Dean, and he gives him his gun back. Dean holds his hand out. It's okay. He tells him no need for any formalities here. Murray pulls out a ready roll and sparks up. The way Dean is looking at him, Murray knows he is a policeman. He does not wind him up and just smokes as normal. Murray tells him he should have a beer to relax, "A fucking good malt would be better." Murray laughs. The frost is gone; Dean disappears to return with a bottle of something Murray is not even going to attempt to pronounce, and he goes and returns with a four-pack of the last man on the planet. He even gives him a cup that he had swiped on the way around. He pours, and Murray pings a ring pull. Cheers.

They talk quietly. Dean talks about his woman and says this was an accident. Murray asks him if he forgot to come off at the cross. They laugh. Dean tells him about Emma. She grew up on a farm and ended up teaching at the Agricultural College, Dean asks about him, and Murray knows Dean is looking him over, running his face through various mug shot collections. Murray tells him that he spent his whole working life in a local workshop as a welder. He tells him Cha was a nurse who was on a painting holiday to Scotland and was unable to get home and ended up with him.

Murray's smoke is finished. He stubs it out and rips up the roach, and scatters it. Dean asks him if he wants to know what he has done for a living. Murray looks at him, cracks another tin open and sparks up and tells him, no, it is okay. Dean looks at him and asks if his stance gave it away. Murray nods and jokes that it is that and the size of his feet. Dean does not get the joke and wants to talk. Murray stops him and says if we are going to be sitting for some time, better if we get some seats. They go and rescue some multi-packs and pile them up on top of each other to make seats. Dean wants to talk, so he lets him. He married twice, divorced twice, and remarried for the third time, which he adds in the national police federation is an average statistic. Served time in traffic and later worked in the serious crime division.

Dean still wants to talk; he tells him it was a really shitty job. If working undercover, you have to be one hundred per cent someone else, and the hardest part of all is returning back to being your old self once the mission is over. He thinks that has a large part to play in the divorce rate, that and alcohol. Dean downs another malt as if to prove a point.

They get around to their present abodes; Emma and PC plod stay at the cinema, which is situated across the way, stuck in the corner. Murray tells him they have a little house in a hidden glade in the country. Murray does not think Dean has believed anything that he has told him, but to be honest, he could not care less.

The women have not shouted anything out yet, and apart from the occasional "Tell him that I fucking hate him!" and "If my brothers were still alive, they would be beating the shit out of you right fucking now!" Murray asks if she is always this charming. They do get the odd shout for some more towels and more pillows. "Personally, this is my first!" Dean does not get this joke, either. Murray is getting stiff legs and running out of things to say and tells him he has to go for a stretch and wants something to do. Murray grabs the last of the shopping trolleys and finds the herb and spice selection. He scans the little glass jars and proceeds to empty the lot into the trolley. He packs them all nicely and neatly. Murray knows he is watching behind him. Dean speaks up and asks if he does a bit of cooking, Murray can't help it, and he tells him that he is currently banned from the kitchen just the same as driving.

Dean understands and says sorry for all the observations that he has been doing on him, but as he can understand, they are not many nice people left, and they all have to be extra careful, but Dean also thanks Murray and Cha profusely as he does not know what to do, of course, he had been trained for various emergencies but delivering babies was way down the list.

Dean tells him that they are various gangs in the area. There was the blue team and the green team. They gradually got sick of killing each other, and the ones that remained eventually merged into the red team. They mainly stay around the town centre and, for some reason and have taken up residence in one of the main hotels. They have rarely ventured out this far, but they occasionally hear them shooting. Dean asks about the area where they are holed up. Murray tells him that, for now, it is pretty quiet, and they really don't get many visitors.

Oddly Dean asks if they have a dog. Murray tells him no, but he would love one, not a little dog but a reasonably sized one, one who is cheeky, clever and has their own sense of identity but, when the occasion is needed, will do what they are told. They are still talking hours later, exchanging doggie stories, when Cha returns, looking very serious. "Emma tells me to tell you that she loves you, and I have also to inform you that you are now the proud father of a baby girl. Nothing to worry about. The baby is all there and very healthy," the baby cries. Murray looks at him, "c'mon, Dean, go and see you, baby." Dean is crying. The tears are rolling down his face as he gets up to go and see her.

Cha looks at Murray, and he hands her a smoke, "It looks as if you have had quite a shift tonight." She replies as she exhales some smoke, "It has had its moments." They sit in silence, and he just looks at her in wonder. Cha sits up beside him, and they cuddle. She has her head on his shoulders. Murray knows what she is feeling, and he knows what she is thinking, but there is nothing that he can say. Murray gets up and pours her some of Dean's malt. She gulps it down and has another.

Cha tells him that Emma's exhausted, and if the full pregnancy term had run the course, none of them would have survived. You and Dean look as if you are getting on fine. Murray tells her how it was. She nods and tells him that the chances of them surviving the first winter as a trio are null and void. Murray asks, "Are you thinking about adopting them?"

She nods, "We can't live on our own forever, and they seem nice, but more than that, I think they deserve a chance." Murray pulls two ready mades of smoke from his pocket; she has another malt to match his last man on the planet. They smoke as they absorb the latest development.

Murray says, "Well, okay, if it does not work out, they could always leave."

Cha is delighted. "I knew you would agree, and I already told Emma that it would be okay, and she says that Dean will do as he is told." They burst into laughter. The guy obviously loves her very much. Murray asks her do they have a car, so she looks at him questionably, "Well, we will need more shopping, not just food, but new-borns need things too," putting her finger and thumb to her nose, they say the same word at the same time 'nappies.' They are in stitches when Dean arrives back. "They are both sleeping, and we are going to take you up on your generous offer. What do I need to do?"

They decide that another vehicle, something decent, is needed from memory. There is nothing suitable in the various parking lots outside. Dean speaks up about the garage where the police transport was repaired just across the road, and it was always full.

Murray drives Dean over just before the fist light. He is correct. They find a large unmarked four-door SUV type. They get it started in no time and return to the girls. Emma and the as-of-yet-unnamed baby are still sleeping. None of them knows what sizes to select in the baby section. They let Dean have the final choice. That way, if Emma says, "Who picked that?" they will just point at Dean. They do rip the piss out of him. By the time they have finished with all the stuff that they collectively think will be enough for the baby, and with the extra food and some malt for daddy, they have about ten trolleys worth.

All is now stored at the front door, and they will transfer the goods as quickly as possible. Their loads will go last as they are the easiest. Emma is now awake and feeding, they leave them to it, and Dean is in the loading gang. Their little convoy with the trolleys works a treat, and all have been emptied into the various vehicles, the empties returned to hide any evidence of their presence. They are loaded up and just waiting on Emma one and two getting ready. Murray has one more shop on the pre-agreed list to visit. Pat is not in the shop when he visits, and he is in luck; Murray's items are in stock. Anything over 151 proofs is selected. He is not greedy and takes a dozen cases. That is all the room they have left, and that also includes the front seat.

Chapter Nineteen

Murray gets the impression that Dean is in his previous job mode as they go over the route as much as possible with them prior to setting off, and it is agreed that they are going to drive all the way home without a stop. It is still pretty early, and they can do it if they don't have any unscheduled delays.

They drive in a convoy. Murray is in the front, the three newbies and followed by Cha in the back position, and all goes like clockwork, and they make it back before dark. Dean mentions that it is some little house. They show them a room upstairs where they think they will be fairly comfy in such times. The room has its own little bathroom suite attached, and it is clean. They let them get settled in, and they go downstairs. Murray and Cha know without discussing it that they will no longer, for the next foreseeable time, be able to smoke in the house. At this, they go out and smoke to get over the long drive.

The fridge is still working. When the courting couple is out of earshot, Murray tells Cha that he has a confession. They are like the nuns in the '60s musical confessing to the mother superiour. Murray produces a small teddy bear with the suitable for a new baby sticker. Cha bursts out laughing at him. At first, he thinks she is taking the piss till she produces the exact same one, with the exact same colour.

They go out and smoke before the unloading starts. There are a fair amount of goods to shift. The other vehicle can wait till Dean appears. They do it in a few hours; too tired to make something, they have some heated tinned food. It is too late to set up the CD, which is for now stored in the corner as is the high-proof alcohol. Murray notices another box, and it is a Christmas tree, one of them that comes with sparkly lights already attached. Cha has remembered. They curl up on the sofa, just too worn out to go up the stairs. Ending the day with a big hug and telling Cha that he was very proud of her today.

Murray wakes up in the morning, and Cha is on top of him; Bobby is instantly awake and ready for action. Cha is only rolling over him to escape from being crushed into the back of the sofa. Bobby is back sleeping before she is on her feet. Their guests have not stirred yet, and they will not disturb them.

Cha rustles something together in the kitchen. Murray goes outside and just drifts into the start of the day. He is thinking about just having an easy day and most definitely no driving. He hopes that Dean is not a football fanatic, a religious nutter or a political extremist. Apart from these exceptions, they can talk about anything else. Murray thinks he will eventually get his drift by the lack of response on these topics, and they will vanish from all conversations.

Cha is now beside him; as the morning is again brighter, they are eating outside. The mushroom and rice dish tastes delicious, and he asks for more. Murray knows that it has all been made from tinned goods, but it is that good; he honestly doesn't think his palette could differentiate between the minuscule subtle differences even if it compared to one that was made of fresh produce. Rather than just go out and leave them, which could be construed as being rude. Murray goes for a walk, and Cha mans the fort.

Murray walks up to the Orangery and looks everything over. Cha will be more than delighted with the mirage of plants. All the flowers have appeared, and the greenhouse especially is festooned in a multitude of colours, all shapes and sizes, and you can actually smell the various scents. He finds some of them overpowering, but that is only because they all are in a relatively confined space. He is thinking about watering them but then thinks again. Murray remembers that Cha has designed the water system, and it also has an added feeder, so he backs off. Imagining the amount of grief that he would receive for all eternity if any of them were to wither and die.

Somehow, he ends up at his dedicated plants. They are all poking out of the soil, and one or two little leaves are waving enthusiastically, truthfully, Murray is waving to them. He will wait until they have grown some more, and then he will start to cheat the light cycle. If his brother was here, Murray would put him in charge, and there would be a guaranteed bumper harvest. He thinks of the future, and although the seeds are meant to be one hundred per cent females only, one male would be a gift, and that would enable a seed supply for the next time.

Murray is really sick of smoking grass, and for a little change, he intends to make some solid. The chemical process, compared to what Cha had him assisting in it, is relatively harmless; sure, it could be dangerous, but controllable. Murray will run Cha through the process, and she will add and correct any errors that he is unaware of. Theoretically, he knows the process back to front. This was one of his brother's dream projects, but he was always too busy to actually start it. Murray has never made anything like it and has only seen a couple of homemade blogs on the Internet.

There is no sign of Cha; She will be putting out an APB, so he had better start back. Slowly Murray dawdles back to basecamp.

All of them are still awake; the baby is all bright-eyed and bushy-tailed. She does not speak or gurgle but scans the room, taking in everything almost like a secret inventory in which she knows what everything is and, more importantly, what all the items are used for. In-between viewing times, she is sucking on her mother's nipples and sleeping.

They sit about. Emma is clearly exhausted; Cha has made some food, nice and simple fare, sadly with none of the spices that they both prefer. The conversation is bouncing around what they are going to call the baby. They have been asked their names, and having a Cha and a Cha-Cha does not sound too appealing; after lots of deliberation, the happy couple decides on Martha after her granny, who by all accounts was feared by all her strappings sons and ruled with an iron fist. It sounds nice, and the baby's eyes light up even more when she hears it. For the next few hours, it is Martha this and Martha that.

Murray quietly slips outside and smokes, and Dean joins him. He casts no judgement on his chosen recreational activity, not that it would make any difference. Murray tells him there is a guided tour if he is up for it, and they set off. He shows him around. They end up at the filled pond. The water is only tickled by a gentle breeze; the sunlight occasionally hits one of the small ripples, momentarily dazzling them if they happen to be looking at the same spot.

Omitting the details of how they found out about this place or the tales of the previous occupants. Murray just gives him the tour and tells him as of yet, they have had no uninvited guests in the area, but he must always remember to carry a gun. He should have known better. The service revolver is exposed when Dean opens his jacket. Murray has a hunting rifle over his shoulder and has sofar not spotted anything to take a pot shot at. Dean asks who is the best shot; Murray tells him unashamedly that Cha is the best at everything. Dean tells him that Emma had tried to shoot him on the first day that they met, adding that it was only when he told her that the safety was still on that had probably saved him. He also confessed that when she discovered that she was in the club, she had many times looked at him and said maybe I should have shot you. Just a typical romantic couple as he sees it.

On his part, Murray tells him that apart from painting, Cha hates all and everything, including himself, and up until they had met, this was the most that he had ever heard her speak. Murray knows he does not believe a word, but he is not easy at this type of conversation.

Dean is introduced to the Orangery; this keeps him quiet for some time, and Murray's ears are grateful. He moves in and among the plants, running his hands through most of them and savouring the smells and scents. Murray thinks he has in the previous world had green fingers as he looks very relaxed and strangely at home. This is marked up as a plus sign, along with the non-attempted introduction of football, politics, and, God forbid, religion. Murray takes him round and shows him the electricity production system adding that it was truly awful until the feed dam outlet was improved. He says nothing and just listens to every word. Murray does not cross over to the walk that was Charlie's favourite place. It is still hitting a sore point, and maybe next time.

Dean has been observing him and his mannerisms since the moment that they met, and as they sit down to watch the wheel in motion, Dean tells Murray that the prison system is full of guys like him who made one mistake and have been incarcerated at her majesty's pleasure. He assures him that he does not think he is a bad guy, and if he had thought it for one second, they would not be here. Murray takes it that this is meant to be a compliment, and they head off looking for something for the pot. Moving through the small wooded area, Murray senses some movement in his peripheral vision range. On closer examination, after lots of squinting, they spot some roe deer. There are six of them. Through the scope, Murray inspects them at nearly the maximum range; with this rifle, it would be a waste of time, and the shot has to be closer. Murray motions to him, his intentions. Moving slowly back, they go around the opposite way. It takes longer as the animals are wary, and every time one of them looks in their direction, they instantly freeze. As luck would have it, the wind is going in the opposite direction, and they are somewhat a little dirty, as they sometimes have to hide, even if that involves lying on the ground. The range is now in their favour. Murray attaches the silencer and relaxes and selects one not too young, not too old and squeezes the trigger. It does not fall, and the herd moves off. "Oh well, beans on toast!" Murray jokes. He tells him that it would be the best meal ever, "Whoever thought that bread would be an issue."

Walking over to survey the area where the animal was shot, Murray does not think for one minute that he has missed and going over the tracks, Dean eventually finds the blood first. The animal has not dropped, and even though the wound is fatal, it takes a moment or two for the animal's brain to finally give in. They follow the tracks across a field and up through another wooded area to where the animal has fallen. Charlie would have led us here ages ago, but only if she had wanted too. The animal is graceful and majestic, and he has taken no pleasure in killing; it is only out of necessity. Murray does the thing that Cha has taught him and closes their eyes.

The gun is put on the ground. Dean picks it up, looks at him, hesitates and says that he is only holding it to keep it clean. He makes sure it is not loaded and puts on the safety. Murray just nods okay and removes the razor-sharp knife from his backpack, and starts gutting the animal. If Dean wants to make himself useful, he can dig a hole in the ground for the inners and skin. Murray mentions this to no one in particular. The quicker he does this, the better.

Cha has taught him correctly, and his hands are busy removing all the body parts that they do not eat. It is not heavy, and they take turns moving the carcass back to the house. Murray could have carried himself, or he could have let Dean carry it, but he just thought it would be a good idea to get him involved. He was going to be eating it, and he could help carry it. Murray does not like him, and all things being equal, he is sure that Dean is not too keen on him, but for everyone here, Murray will keep the peace. He is here just because of the circumstances, and they would never have connected in the real world. They are not only poles apart but more akin to being light-years apart.

The women are talking on the sofa, and Martha is asleep between them. The fire is on, and there is a little plastic bundle burning in the centre. They are noticing the meat. By the looks of the newbies, he thinks they have been eating out of cans for quite some considerable time, and it is quite possible that they would eat this raw. Emma wraps up the baby and goes and helps Cha chop up the meat. Being brought up on a farm, she has no problem with this. The other guy goes and gets washed and changed, and Murray quietly slips outside, drinks his juice and smokes continuously. It is not chain-smoking, but he has a fair blast. The meal is a simple fair; over the last while, Murray has grown accustomed to the exotic spices and flavours that Cha has assaulted his taste buds with and simple meat, potatoes and vegetables, no matter how nice it has been prepared and cooked, just does not cut it. Murray understands breastfeeding, and as ungrateful as it sounds, he does not have breasts, and no one is feeding them. Dinner lasts a lifetime, and Murray finds it really difficult, the only one who has noticed is Cha, and when he gets too quiet, she kicks him in the ankles under the table. Murray tries harder to keep the peace, but he really fucking hates it; he knows that they have to interconnect with people, but he hopes that it is at not every single moment of the day.

Cha will promise all sorts of inducements. Murray knows that it is he who is the problem, PC plod has bullshitted his whole working life, and this is perfectly normal for him. Murray gets on the programme and joins in, he does not laugh as much but volunteers to walk the baby up and down the room and pats her back after feeding, which is great; when he puts her back down, she screams blue murder. Already Martha and Murray are the best of friends. It is only when she is sound asleep that he hands her back over to her mother. Dean has mellowed out a little, and he has only had a can of beer, so Murray can't blame the booze, just himself.

Eventually, they fuck off to bed, and Murray thinks that he is going to get a good old earful, an earful that bad that he will wish to attain instantaneous deafness, but Cha tells him that as soon as they are out of earshot, "That was fucking difficult," and seeing the baby has made her feel funny and "How would I fancy some us time in the woods, in the Orangery just anywhere really but soon." Murray does not get the chance to reply, Bobby and she have made up their minds, and before he knows it, they are in the first available secluded space.

In the morning, they take them both on a guided tour, except they come across the holiday chalets that Murray had somehow missed off the itinerary yesterday. He thinks that they all had the same thought exactly at the same time, and the group saunter overs to have a look. Each one is in reasonable condition and has survived well with no occupants. A good clean out, all the dust and accumulated dirt, maybe even a wash from top to bottom, and yes, they could be habitable. Murray has a look at the electrics and being a small holiday home. It is only regulated for lights and a small fridge. The board is in a fairly clean condition, and at the most, he can only see light bulbs and fuses as a possible issues.

They cannot move them in there just yet, and they really have to be fair about this. They have lived on their wits for ages, and they will be nervous and apprehensive about just everything. They pose them no harm and bare them no ill will, but most of the time, everyone here is in the same boat, and they will all need to readjust. They talk about it, and it is not a forced conversation. Even Dean is talking about doing this but keeps asking if it is okay if he can do this, would you both mind if he could change this? Murray just tells him it now belongs to them for as long as they want, and if they need any help, all they have to do is ask.

Martha is hungry. He takes Dean to the big shed. Murray shows him everything that is available for their chalet. He imagines all the required items are here. It is just a case of locating where the previous occupants stored them.

The conversation that night is relatively easy, and even Martha feels it. Murray pretends to offer Martha a beer even Dean laughs. Today has been so much better than yesterday, so maybe, just maybe, there is hope after all. As soon as they go to bed, Cha demands attention from Bobby.

Breakfast; Murray is up first. Cha makes fun of him, pretending that she will have to drive somewhere and get him some Viagra, also adding that "Does it act on women?" and shaking her head, telling Murray that "You can even do it in your sleep." It is no surprise that Bobby is blowing a full fanfare ensemble when the breakfast consists of fish, fish and more fish.

Cha leaves a note for their house guests to do their own thing, informing them where they will be if they fancy coming down later, and they go out and give them some space. Emma knows more about the layout than they will ever know.

At the Orangery, Cha is in her own private orbit. All her plants have flowered. She has not lost a single one. Murray thinks he has heard her speaking to them in her indigenous language, and stoned as he is, he does not hear them reply. Cha has not smoked or drunk any alcohol for a couple of days now. Murray thinks that she may be in for something. He hopes it is not cold. Cha is in Plantsville and tells her he is going to the big shed; she hears him but is so engrossed in the plants she does not reply.

Murray arrives back several hours later and asks her what she thinks. He knew that he had seen a pram and had spent ages cleaning it. Not a modern trendy one, but it will be functional. She laughs, and he persuades her that he is hungry. As she unbuttons her trousers, she sings a little song. Murray does not quite make out the verses, but the chorus goes along the lines of I hope Bobby's hungry too. He is also fully aware that resistance is futile and removes his trousers. Once Bobby has done his duty, they skip down like they are still teenagers. Cha is more than pleased with the results, and all her worries have gone. The perambulator is handed over to the couple, who are pleased-ish, but either way, it is still better than carrying the little lump all day long. They place Martha inside, and she is happy, so they are all happy.

Lunch lasts longer than usual, and Emma has informed them that she is an expert at farming and that in return for their good fortune, she would like to help set up the land, adding that canned goods will not last forever. She asks some questions and elaborates at length on what could be done. They also put a plan together for making their proposed dwelling habitable. While Murray had been rummaging for the baby carriage, he had inadvertently come across numerous tins of paint, he adds that he has no idea what the colours were as the labels are not readable, but he had shaken them about, and even if they are lumped all they do is add some thinners.

The quests go out for a stroll taking turns to push the pram. They leave them to it. Murray tries to lock himself in the bathroom, and Cha threatens to remove the door with explosives unless he cooperates.

In around or about two weeks, they have them installed in their own little palace. It is spotless. Most of the time, the evening meals are at their house, and they are relatively easy events. Most of the conversation revolves around farming practices and Martha, who, to everyone's surprise, including his, has taken a shine to Murray. They showed Emma all the bits and pieces that they have and found some machinery that covers most of her list in the recently explored sheds, but unfortunately, they will have to go on an expedition for seeds to enable them to feed animals and, more importantly, to make bread, when it comes down to it that is the backbone of any civilisation.

Emma has made a list of what to look for and where to look, and they are just deliberating who is staying and who is going. Emma is a mother and is not going; this is a no-brainer; Emma says that the baby could come along. They all just say no exactly at the same time. It is just not going to happen. They decide that as Dean is the father that he is also staying. Dean would like to argue against this, letting us know that in the old world, he went on many dangerous operations.

Murray just looks at him straight and tells him he is staying and he could learn to plough the fields as he has the best teacher available. He is just telling them that if the shit hits the fan, at least they will still have each other. As far as he is concerned, the conversation is over. It has been decided. Cha goes over the maps with them. They have a good idea of the area, and as all they are going for is a seed, it should be a quick in and out. They work out a time frame, and Murray and Cha are going in the morning. They have an early night, and Cha tells him to knock it off and get some sleep.

The vehicles are loaded up; all they need is a check, rechecked and secured. Goodbyes are said. Martha has to be cuddled by Murray before she settles, and they head off. The bridge is the same as before, and just like the last time, they adhere to the same precautions. Pulling into the first stop over the other side, they wait, watch and listen. When they are satisfied, it's time to move on. Today they are venturing into uncharted territory, and they have no idea what to expect.

Heading past the signs for the city, they drive slowly. Continuously stopping and watching, all the observation methods that are employed yield no results; at last, with the city behind them, they were back on the open roads. On locating the sign that Emma had told them about, they turned off and headed inland. This was the town that had never really grown in any of the so-called booms and maintained its trade by bulk farming supplies. They had made a great time and entered the town slowly, driving following the directions laid out on the map. The warehouse was located, and although there had been signs of recent human activity on the way through the small-town, burned-out houses, broken windows and forced entry on various shops, the warehouse looked as if it had not been disturbed. This was the most boring time. All they had to was wait silently, watch and listen. Murray would always fall asleep. A no-smoking rule was even in place in the vehicle, and although he would love to go out and have a sneaky one, it was totally out of the question.

Cha was in charge of the operation, and when she thought that enough time had been spent watching, she gave Murray the signal, and they moved forward for a closer inspection. All around was quiet, no lights, no sounds, not a soul. They double-checked around the whole building and met back at the vehicles. Both of them reported that all was clear. The vehicles were restarted and slowly moved forward, the big double doors were persuaded to part, and they eased the transport inside. Before he could say anything, Cha told him that once they had checked and checked again, if there was an office, they could have a break before the loading started. As they had eaten very little since this morning, he was hungry, and if he got a smoke, that was fine, and if not, well, he would just have to wait till later. Cha was in the lead, and he followed her every move like her shadow. All clear, the office was located, which was totally devoid of any recent habitation.

As long as he only had one and opened the window to partially blow the smoke out, it was okay to smoke. It was not his favourite smoking environment, but it was all he was going to get. Once that was over, they set about searching for the items on Emma's list. Not only did they have to find them, but they also had to check them for things. Finding the items was the easy part. The testing took a while, and they were well into the night before they had any success. Murray and Cha were going to take turns loading the seed into bags and load it into the vehicles.

Cha had fallen asleep, and Murray just left her to it. It was not hard work, she had told him, as per the list, so many bags of this, so many bags of that and if there is any more space available, put in some bags of the other type. He was well into the task when Cha awakened before she got ripped into him for letting her sleep through; Murray just told her that she obviously needed it, and if she wasn't tired, she would not have slept soundly; there was no point in arguing about it. What is done is done. She was wide awake and was double-checking what he had bagged. Murray got the nod of approval. He had not noticed, but it was getting dusty, and they would have to put on the masks.

All done, it had taken longer than expected, but at least they could get out of here pronto. Cha opened the backs of the trucks, and he heaved the bags up onto the tailgate. Once so many were loaded, Murray jumped up and assisted her in getting them into a reasonable package that would not move around when in motion. An hour or so later, all was complete. Daylight would be here shortly, and they could get out of there.

Murray had to be honest; He thinks that it is great that they will eventually get bread. He does, however, imagine himself driving a tractor and ploughing the fields. He will manage to repair and modify all the machines by hook or by crook to get them all fully functional but the rest of it, no thanks, just not for him.

Chapter Twenty

The soon-to-be farmers head back the way they came as soon as the light has changed enough for them to see without headlights. The journey was totally uneventful until Cha had a flat tire; on exiting the number twenty-seven layby, Cha had to pull over. It had to be changed, and although they had forgotten to check, they were lucky enough to have one that was usable. Murray had to knock seven shades of shit out of them to get the wheel nuts moving; Murray is thinking of another item to add to the pre-journey checklist.

At first, it started as a faint noise in the distance, but it slowly started to get louder. One car turned into three cars, and the two cars were perusing the first car. It was not their problem, but they were blocking the road. Where they had decided to change the tyre, was the only passable space, so it looked like there was an incoming problem.

They are still too far away to make anything out, but as there is absolutely no chance of fixing it and moving on, leaving them to it. It looks like they will have an active part in whatever is going to happen. It would have been so much easier if they were not here. When he was younger, his dream present was an invisibility cloak. Murray always added this to his Santa list. He had done it faithfully every year, but it was never there for him in the morning. Murray thinks that a pair of them would really come in real handy, just about now.

Cha looks at them through the binoculars. The pursuers have green material tied to various parts of their vehicles, and the first car drives like it has been stolen. Murray gets that look from Cha, and the weapons are loaded and ready.

The front car notices them just in time and screeches to a halt. The occupants are undecided about what to do. They have behind them two cars that have been chasing them and very nearly caught up and an impassable obstacle in front of them. They are so close that they can hear the occupants of the front car screaming at each other as to what they are going to do. A door opens, and a teenage girl starts running from the car. She is nearly on top of Cha and only notices in time. She looks more than scared; "Please do not let them take us. Please, please." Cha tells her to move it and hurray! The girl quickly motions her friends to join her, likewise, they are all unarmed, they could all do with a good scrub.

They scamper over the obstacles and do as they are told and remain hidden; Murray has stayed quiet and has not moved. The cars with the green material tied onto various points draw to a halt. The four of them get out of the car like they own the highway. They walk across to where they have not, on purpose, blocked the road. The one with the silly hat, Murray thinks it could be a bowler, but it is that bashed. It is hard to tell, but the green feathers are rather fetching.

"Just come out. I know you are there! come out, and we can talk." The girls and now the two boys look at Cha, who puts a single finger up to her lips.

The one with the silly hat is stuck for words, but one of his chums, "I don't see the point in speaking to them. I just want to rape them!" Murray and Cha are at this stage, unsure if he just wants to rape the woman or, for all they know, he may want to rape them all. Murray is still Mr Invisible. One of the teenage boys has looked and seen the two vehicles but is at the same time looking at Cha, thinking out loud that she did not drive the two of them. Cha just looks him straight in the eye and again motions with her finger to her lip. He is not sure but kind of understands.

Eventually, the one with the silly hat has thought about what he to say, "I am going to give you another minute to think about it, and then we are coming to get you!" He looks very pleased with himself, and one of his erstwhile buddies even hi-fives him. Murray is thinking, fuck, these guys are good.

Just when they think that it cannot get any better, another three cars are approaching. Through his binoculars, Murray sees that they have no green material or any other material tied to parts of their cars. He really would like a smoke, but he knows that it is still not a viable option at present,

The four guys being led by the one in the silly hat don't know what to do. They all look at the leader for instructions, perhaps the feathers are magical, but he issues no commands. They are still standing there in the road when the other vehicles stop. The three cars empty out, and there is a face-off in progress. Murray, for the life of him, wishes it could be settled in a dance-off, not from the point of view of halting any life-threatening carnage just purely for entertainment.

Now we have the green feather gang, and opposite them, they now had ten bodies facing up to them. The guy in charge of the ten steps forward is about five feet tall, and by his build, he has either done lots of bodybuilding but only the top half, or he is not very good at taking steroids.

Murray nearly wets himself when he speaks, it is the worse Italian accent that he has ever heard, or maybe he is Italian, and his English is just shit. The more he continues to speak, Murray finds it harder to contain his laugh. He quietly reminds himself to add a camera to the shopping list.

Eventually, the green hat gang, after many stares of disbelief and several different variations of what the fuck he is saying, comes to the conclusion that he would like the girls back. He wants to punish the boys but is prepared to offer a compromise that they can keep the boys as long as he gets the girls, they will be left in peace, and they can live another day. The one with the green feathers says that they wanted some money as well. At this, there are incredulous looks of disbelief from all sides. The mutant top half is fuming and is so angry that the veins in his neck are viably bouncing. Being the brave leader that he is, walks back through his men and orders them to fire just as he ducks to safety.

The feather gang is wiped out, and the other suffers two fatalities and one wounded. Cha has clicked her gun into fully automatic and is emptying the box magazine into them. From his concealed position, he opens up the semi-automatic. They have both reloaded and are advancing. Any signs of life are promptly extinguished.

Frozen in terror, the youngsters are unsure what to do. The bravest among them asks, are they now our prisoners, to which Cha replies, "No, but we need to hear the story." Murray does not understand why she wants to hear it, but he will have to listen to it anyway.

The boys start, it works out that they are brothers, and at an early age, Cha stops then as if she has heard enough. She looks at the girls, "We are not related, but some people think," Cha stops them also. Murray has lit a smoke and does not pass it to Cha.

At this stage, he is just watching where this is going; "Can someone just give me the quick version without the family ties, school qualifications, how did you get here? And how did they manage to follow you?"

One of them piped up, "We were a bit down south of here; stole the car, stopped at the city a while back before the guy with the hat spotted us, and muscle man just appeared."

Cha thinks this is not good, "Did any more of the green gang see you?" They all shake their heads, "and what about the mutant Italian?"

"Oh, that's easy. It is one of his cars!"

This is what she wants to hear, "There must be a tracking device!" Look under the car, the boys search under the car, one of them finding a protruding wire from under the chassis. They open the boot and trace the wire to a clumpy box that is connected to the battery. On inspection of the other gangs' car, the crude receiver is found, they have to make decisions, and they have to make them quick.

"We have to dump all the cars in the water, it is the only way, and if we burn them, they will smell. If you roll them down the hill, they can be found."

"I know!" She looks at one of the boys, "That you think the gunshots could have been heard? The wind was carrying them in the opposite direction, and it was only for approximately two minutes. We may not be as lucky with the wind and the fires."

"So here is the way it is going to go the six cars and all the dead are going into the sea. They will have to go in from the middle of the bridge, which means we are going to have to dismantle and reassemble."

"I take that you all can drive?" They all nod. "Okay, take four cars down. Load three with as many bodies as possible."

They all nod; all then drive back in the one car, load up the remaining bodies, and then take the then cars down and wait." They all nod in unison and start loading up bodies while Murray continues to finish changing the flat tire.

Their vehicles are moved and parked to allow the transfer to take place. They don't have much time to discuss what has happened, but in the brief time that they get, Cha tells him that it is all going to be okay. After the last load, they check over the area. Most of the area is clean, the blood will slowly wash away with the wind and rain, the odd bullet case is chucked into the field, and they are satisfied that it is about as good as it is going to get it. They drive down to meet the young team.

Murray surveys the bridge to find the part that overlooks as far as they can see the deepest part of the firth running below them. The light is fading, and as soon as it gets dark, they are going to slowly and without lights put the vehicles over the edge.

After a search, they only have a limited supply of tools, but it should be enough to manage to make a big enough gap to send them over the edge. As the dark is just starting to appear, the gang goes over and follows the instructions and removes the selected items from the crash barrier. Murray has a smoke out of view from everyone in his truck, and when finished, he joins Cha to view the progress. It is just about complete, just some brute force and ignorance, and the final piece is removed. Slowly without any lights, the cars are brought over, one at a time. All the windows are opened, and they are sent on their final journey into the murky depths of the water.

The crash barrier components are replaced, and the now extended convoy heads on home. As per their instructions, they switch on and off their lights, and they reply with the main light confirming that all is okay. They meet us on the porch; Martha is fine, Dean has done some cleaning, and Emma is out for the count upstairs. They inform Dean that they have some more quests and there is nothing to worry about. He is welcome to sit up and hear the adventures, but he says he is deadbeat and will hear about it in the morning. They think he is just trying to be polite.

Cha asks if they are hungry and rustles them up food quickly, they all eat like this is the only food they have had in days. Murray goes outside and smokes. He is the only one who partakes. He comes in for tea; if there is any left, Cha has just brewed a fresh pot. Murray asks if they are all okay, and they nod.

They can only surmise what they have gone through, and at least tonight, they can be safe. Murray does not know what it was like where Cha grew up, but growing up here was hard enough, even when things were normal. Without trying to sound like overbearing parents or, worse, trying to sound cool when one is not. In a nice as possible way, they just say,

"The baby upstairs is quite scary and gets scarier when it is woken up early. You can all sleep down here tonight, and they will sort it out in the morning, and yes, I nearly forgot the bathroom is upstairs."

Vanishing upstairs to their bed, Murray is still smirking, and Cha fails to see the funny side, but he guesses that it is down to cultural differences. Either way, Murray goes to sleep with a grin on his face. He is not worried about the youngsters downstairs. Cha has told him that it is all going to be okay, and after all, Cha has been right up till now.

Everyone is still fast asleep. Murray walks down the stairs normally, reasoning that if anybody should wake up and see him creeping down the stairs or even just creeping about the kitchen, it would send out the totally wrong signals. He remembers where the cans are. He grabs a couple and goes outside and rolls a monster, cracks open a can and watches the day coming to life. Murray sometimes wonders if it is the other way about.

One of the boys comes outside. He says morning so as not to startle him; he has a can of soda. Murray has no intention of hiding what he is doing. He does not mention it, but he does thank him on behalf of all the others. He tells him that he was given this task by the others because he had more qualifications than them, and they felt that it was proper to give our appreciation but, at the same time, thought it was also important to put it across correctly.

Murray listens to what he says but tells him straight, "What were we really meant to do in a situation like that? We were, excuse the French, fucked if we did and fucked if we did not. We had no idea how it would end up, and all is in everyone's best interests that the good guys get to walk away."

He asks, "Why am I so sure that they are all the good guys?" Murray sparks up another and tells him, "Because all the bad guys are sleeping in the river." He thinks he is looking for a more philosophical explanation from him, but he does not have one. Murray breaks the ice and confesses that he was really hoping that it was going to be a dance-off.

Looking at him as if he is nuts but knows that he is only pretending to be nuts. "What happens when everyone gets up, and what I mean is that after breakfast? do we have to go in front of a committee and confess all our previous sins and take the oath to some organisation?" Murray's juice is finished, and so is his smoke. He rolls another, lights it up, and opens the new can. "I think that when everyone gets up, we will all have a nice breakfast. I don't know about you. I am quite partial to a curry for breakfast, and by the way, Cha makes a mean one; We will sit about and eat. The baby, her name is Martha, will look into the depths of your soul, and everybody will speak; you can say as much or as little as you wish, and as long as you are not a football, religious, or political psychopath, you will be welcome by one and all. As for you, are you going to be you, or are you going to be someone else, even holding a little back that is entirely up to you and yours?" Murray takes a puff, it is out, and he has to relight. He exhales, adding, "Everyone in there is guaranteed to be holding something back. This is somehow, by a twist of fate, a new chance for everyone, and it is entirely up to you what you wish to do with it. So, no committee and no saluting to any new-fangled flag or any new-fangled regime, but I tell the curry is very good." Just at that, Cha appears outside beside them. She says hi to the new guy and puts her arms around him, "Good morning Mr B followed by some kisses."

She asks the new guy if he and his friends eat breakfast, and he replies that they love curry; Murray thinks the new guy is going to fit in nicely, and if he is anything to go by, his friends will also work out just fine.

They are sitting at the table. There is room for everyone. They have even managed a rota for the shower, and they have all chipped in. Cha has produced fresh clothes from where Murray does not know, and the four new visitors, Cha and lastly Murray, all have showered by the time Emma, Dean, and Martha get up.

The curry is cooked by one of the boys, he is a wizard in the kitchen, and Cha is well impressed. She looks at Murray as she tells the newbie that he is banned from the kitchen for life.

Martha has a squeal when she sees Murray, and he reaches out to get her in his arms. She gives everyone a good look, missing nothing; she cuddles in while her mum makes her feed. Dean smells the curry and says, "That smells great! Sorry, M. But you know I can't resist."

M just says, "No problem, I have loads to choose from, and I am sure that handsome young man in the kitchen can make anything from the cooking world," they all hoot at this, even Martha.

Murray gives Martha back to M to feed, and he has time for another smoke. He is just outside, and Cha joins him, "You seem easier around people today. Are you okay?"

He just says that "Maybe I have grown up a little."

She looks at the joint burning in his hand, and Murray clarifies his previous statement, "But only a little at a time!" she smiles, kisses him, and "Breakfast in ten."

Martha has been fed and is squirming to escape into his arms; he takes her while M eats. He walks about till Martha burps; at this, she is sound asleep. Murray hands her back to M, who places her in the pram with her identical twin teddies.

They are all eating, and it's tea, water, and juice on the table. Everyone is just eating away, and it is good, not just the venison, but he thinks the rice is just as nice. Everyone compliments the food not because it is the polite thing to say but because it is excellent. "I suppose we should really introduce each other to each other!" It is Emma who is speaking out loud.

"My name is Emma, I am a farmer, and I like to be known as M."

She elbows the guy next to her, 'I am Dean, M's partner in crime. I was a postman, and now I just do what Martha and M tell me."

It is Cha's turn next, "I was on a painting holiday and ended up with this guy," pointing at Murray, who just happened to be passing when my car broke down."

Mr Black just introduces himself as "Murray, the emergency car repairman."

The newly arrived youngsters are slightly reticent. The one who was cooking this morning, "I am Frank, and in the old world, I worked in one of these fast-food places. If anyone asks for pizza, I will run away."

The girls; are on next. The one with dark hair is Linda, "I was a sales assistant in a large department store."

The smaller one is named Annette and insists with a please that no one calls her Netty and she had previously worked in a call centre. The last to go is the one who was outside having a chat with Murray earlier. He is called Al and was in-between jobs.

Martha is now awake and wants to be fed immediately, M unhooks the food supplies, and Dean delivers the baby to the source; no one bats an eyelid. Martha is still watching everything and everybody except when she feeds. Murray does not know why she wants to come to him all the time. Maybe he smells; Cha has told him many times that he stinks. He shoos her on his shoulder as they walk up and down the length of the room.

The aforementioned company sits and discusses who is doing what, and the conversation comes around to who is in charge. They all look at Murray, even Martha. All eyes are upon him, he wants to say fuck off, but he knows even as much as he would love to, they are looking at him for some form of guidance. Murray's head is already crunching. He thinks as he is saying it. "Do we really need to go into some of the things that were done in the past? Do we really need a leader; we are all here for one reason, and that is to escape the madness outside. Can we not just do it differently? Of course, we will all need to chip in and help where we can. We could have a job board and just stick the names up as to who wants to do what or, better still, who can do what. There are not that many of us here, so do we really need to go into all those in favour say aye and all the shit that goes with it?' There are questions about this and what about that. Cha gets up and goes out and reappears a short time later. The largest whiteboard that he has ever seen is nailed on the wall, and she provides everyone with a pen.

"It's easy!" Cha writes up Orangey, making somewhere nice to go and escape from the madness for a much-deserved place for regaining one's sanity.

M is on the board next, setting out the farm, fields, crops, and animals in block letters. Machinery has Murray's name on it in brackets.

Dean adds houses. He says, "Although it has been great staying in this house," seriously overdoing the fantastic host's speech, "But really, we have to spread out."

Everyone thinks that this is a good plan, and they all head over to the chalets. Dean proudly points to the one that he is going to be dwelling in with M and M. The youngsters look at each other. Al looks at Murray. "You can stay in one together; you can stay in one each. No one is going to tell you what to do it is your call."

M has laid out all the paint that she thinks she might like. The new arrivals have volunteered to help out with the painting as they think it is only fair that the couple with the baby should be the priority.

Annette and Linda have picked out houses next door to each other and want to wash them out and move in tonight. Murray takes them up to the big shed and shows them where to find the things that they will need.

376

Everyone is busy, and Murray goes in search of Cha. He has left the car at the big shed. He walks and can see them in the distance. His smoke is done by the time he meets them. The women are deep in conversation; every field can be used, with the exception of the one with the fallen tree, which is the topic that is going on when he arrives. He tells them that everyone is getting on with it, and he is at a loose end. Is there anything he can do to help? M has a list of machinery that she would like. He is handed the list and goes off and explores. This place has supplied them with everything, and he is sure that the unexplored sheds will produce the machines on M's want list. The last time he saw them, they were walking about with a large measuring tape, one of them reel types, and a notepad and pens.

Murray enters the shed that he had only previously just given a cursory glance, and yes, it has some farm machinery. He does not know what they are all called, but he knows someone who will. He has more luck in the next one, and Tractors'R'Us comes to mind.

Getting it started takes forever. It has been lying about for God knows how long and almost requires a complete strip-down. Murray is in the process of just completing the rebuild. It was at the top of the engine, he was under the engine, and he was just lying on his back, hoping that all the muscles would return back into place. Murray hears the car approach.

It is Al and Dean, "We just came looking for you to tell you that food is nearly ready." Murray must have been up here for hours. He tells Dean that the keys are in the dash, and as Murray thinks that he will be seriously involved in driving it, he can have the honours. Dean turns the key, and there is smoke everywhere, that much of it they have to escape out of the shed, even though the doors are open, it is still Smog-Ville. Through various hand signals and frantic arm movements, he gently eases it forward. It coughs, chugs, and hesitates, but he eventually manages to get it out the door. The fluid controlling the steering needs to be topped up and bled. Murray can see that Dean is desperate to go and tell his big boss M. He tells him that if he brings over the container with the squiggly blue writing, he can drive it home. Al gives him a hand with the hoses, and in no time at all, Dean is chugging down the road to deliver M the first item on the list.

Murray is cleaning his hands with some deleted down concoction, hoping that it will not remove the skin permanently from his hands in the process; he passes the rag over. "What's on your mind?"

Al looks at him, "I think Dean was anything but a postman, and if I had to guess, I would say that he was a copper, not a normal on-the-beat PC plod but maybe serious crime, don't get me wrong, he has been okay, not as laid back as you. But just something gives it away."

The now dead monster in his lips is reignited, and he speaks to Al, "Pizza parlour my arse, and in-between jobs, how can I put it, Al? You and your brother have survived on the streets long before the sickness, and sure, Dean maybe was not a postman, but I really don't want to know about any of your pasts. What we have is what we have, and I am sure we all possess some hidden talents that will someday, hopefully for the good of us all will, appear sooner or later."

Al says, "I want to come clean and tell you what I did!"

Murray tells him, "Nope, I really don't want to know, and if it's that serious, you would not be here. The food will be ready. We really should go."

Dean has delivered the tractor; M is over the moon and has already scored it out of her to-do, Murray's to-do list. Martha has taken to blowing raspberries and, even at this age, looks annoyed at him for abandoning her today and now has her hands up. How could he possibly refuse?

Chapter Twenty-One

The food is going out. The venison is now in a stew form and is pretty good, not in the same style as Chas but good all the same. Everyone discusses what they have done. Frank, Al, and the girls are moving out tonight. The girls had, on the first trip, secured enough items to move in. Several trips later, they have most of the stuff that they will need. Although they would be several more trips required, they had enough to get by with for now.

The most important topic that came up was uninvited guests. Cha informed them that all universities and college facilities in South Korea had a sort of military course that was compulsory to attend, and she would draw up a plan. They did not have enough guns or ammunition for everyone. The assembled cast was asked who could shoot; it was obvious that between all the tasks that had to be carried out, gun training would have to be added to the list. It is agreed that this issue should be addressed sooner rather than later. Unfortunately, this would involve heading past the direction of the blocked main road and into the territory that was a little upset the last time they had met. Nevertheless, it is required, and they will have to go. It agreed it would be a two-vehicle journey, guns, and ammunition shopping only. Every farmhouse and sporting goods shop in the area will be hit. Dean asks for some fishing equipment to be added and produces a list.

Cha and Annette are in one car, Al and Murray in the other. They set off after breakfast. Murray's passenger is pretty quiet, and there is no reprise of yesterday's conversation is forthcoming. As they head over the blockage on the road below, it is still noticeable that this is a scene of carnage and not a normal roadblock. Murray can feel Al looking at him rather than offending him by not answering the pending question that Murray feels is bursting to get out. He just tells Al that he has no idea what happened. Murray knows he does not believe a word of it, but they all have their secrets.

Cha pulls over up ahead. Annette gets out and pukes at the side of the road. As Murray draws up, she tells them that Frank's cooking has not agreed with her and she is okay, only a little tummy bug, and reassures Al that there is nothing to worry about.

Annette gets back into the car, and they continue the journey. In the car, Cha does not even look at her and asks her, "When are you going to tell him?"

"Is it that obvious?"

"how far are you gone?"

"I have missed two periods."

"I put it down at first to the shitty living conditions and all the crap we have had to go through and honestly felt a million times better since we arrived here."

381

There is no stopping her, and she just speaks. "Al will be great dad, the shit that he has gone through, him and his brother, was truly awful even before everyone got sick. The mother was the local bike; their father must have loved her an awful lot to put up with all the trouble that she brought home. She would run away with all the wages and only return once she had spent it all. The boys had to revert to stealing to survive; the father would always make excuses for the mother, telling them it would change; it would get better. Al was pretty smart at school, and he was awarded a bursary for going to one of the top universities. I think he had written a paper on the current, past, and future economic, political systems, and by all accounts, he had many offers. One night, he caught the mother and her current junky bastard companion going through his stuff for the bursary money and went apeshit. The boyfriend broke his neck on the way down the stairs. The mother just scarpered. Frank took the rap for Al telling him that he still has to go to Uni, it was a way out of this shit hole of an existence, and he would do well. The father died of a broken heart, and Frank ended up in a gladiator school over on the east coast, and every weekend possible, Al would make his way up to see his brother. It was on one of these journeys that the sickness appeared. The first thing Al had to do was to get to his brother; he just knew he was alive. He found his brother, and he was very weak, but he had survived. Al took ages to get the cell open and even now makes jokes. If you want to get out of jail, don't tell Al. When Frank was fit enough to travel, they headed back to where they grew up. It was along the road somewhere that they came into contact with the Italian and his gang." She tried to remember his name, but the nearest she could get to it sounded like one of the massively advertised chocolates that were popular at Christmas time. She describes the double barrel name as Ferro something or another, but does not quite remember the muscleman's nor the last name of the chocolate.

"At first, it was good, then the problems started, slowly at first, but it was evident after a while that he was nuts, not in a funny way; he was just a danger to be around, keeping out of his way was paramount in surviving another day. He had made it clear that me, Linda, and the entire group of women of and up to a certain age were his and his sole property alone, and unless he gave express permission, no one was allowed even to talk to them, let alone anything else, by that time we all had gotten to know each other and decided to escape."

"We thought that we were in the clear, and it was not until that we had entered into the city back there to steal fuel and find food that the guy with the silly hat had seen us and started the chase, the Italian guy showing up was just an added surprise. Al and Frank are good guys, and I really don't know what would have happened if you were on hand to save us." Cha hands her a packet of tissues and, before Annette asks, tells her not to worry. The secret will stay with her.

They have taken various small detours and have collected six shotguns and two hunting rifles. The gun cabinets were the best yields, as ammunition and cleaning kits. These are bundled in the car. The next stop is the sporting goods shop that Cha and Murray had visited a long time ago. It had not been entered since then, and they spent most of the day removing everything that could be of use, even adding a huge pile of fishing gear that Dean had requested. They had worked nonstop and were outside the shop debating where to go to have a break. They had not seen a living soul all morning. It was almost casual the way they were standing outside the shop, almost like two couples meeting on a normal Saturday afternoon shopping trip.

Cha noticed first; it was a woman with a white flag waving it to catch their attention. The woman is not armed and but even so, a defensive position is adopted. Scanning everywhere, Cha signals the woman to approach. The woman strides across. The white banner is just resting on her shoulder as she reaches them. My name is Ellie, and my mother has asked me to give you this. Murray is handed a note.

Hi son, I think you may remember me. I believe fatty and his now-gone friends described me as the rattily old lady. I did smile at your comment about the best tea you had tasted in ages. I have often wondered how you both are. The old regime is long gone, and we have changed things at the farmhouse for the better. I have a proposition for you, and if you wish, you can take my daughter hostage and come over and see me. Giving you my daughter in exchange for a conversation is not a bad deal in this day and age, and I hope this underlines my sincere, honest intentions for a little chinwag. The kettle is on, and I do hope you take up the offer.

Murray shows Cha the note, Ellie is relaxed and shows no sign of fear, and more importantly, she displays no inner signs of deviousness. Cha asks her, "What if we all show up? Would that be okay?"

She laughs. "That's what my mother said, adding okay, no problem. If it's okay with you, I will signal the other girls, and they will send word on for tea for four."

Cha looks at her and asks, "Girls! Oh, my mother forgot to add that the menfolk had a chance at being in charge, and you know as well as I know this did not work out very well for any of them!" During this time, Al and Annette are just looking and listening as to what the fuck is going on. Ellie looks at Cha. Cha nods that it is okay. The flag is waved four times as several well-hidden vehicles start-up drive into view.

All that comes out the window is various hands waving as they head off. "Oh, I was meant to be getting a lift with them. Would it be okay to travel with you?"

Cha tells her, "Okay, hop in." She jumps in with Cha and Annette.

They drive out to the farmhouse; the only surprise is the friendly waves they receive from various checkpoints along the away. The gates to the complex are fully opened on their approach. There is a chap about six feet tall, with short-cropped hair and no weapons, waiting to meet them as they disembark from their vehicles.

"Good afternoon. Ruby has asked me to come and greet you if you want to come in, your tea is waiting, and if you don't like the fillings, I can get the sandwiches changed out for something else. The vehicles will not be touched, and no one will even look at them, and you can take your weapons. I can't empathise enough that you will not need them, but please do hurray as the tea is getting cold; This way, please."

They are led through the door and up the stairs, no one looks at them, and all they can hear is laughing in the background, no shouting and Murray is pleased to note, no one marching about thinking that they are tough guys, some women pass them, "Hi Mark," and they all smile at him when they pass.

Ruby is up on her feet to welcome them; the last time Murray was here, it was far from as welcoming as this. Ruby looks at Mark. That will be fine for now, Mark. Thank you, and he is off.

They are invited to sit down. Ruby tells them to relax and help themselves to the food, and she pours the tea. Annette is scoffing at the homemade biscuits; Murray is worried about her fingers. Ruby and Cha exchange glances.

Milk and sugar are all added per their tastes, and they are silent while they sip the wondrous brew. It is out of this world. Ruby adds, "This is one of Mark's other jobs. As well as being a fantastic administrator, he has blended this mix. I call him twenty a day."

Cha looks at her, "Surprising, he does not smoke but likes a wee cuppa or two," this breaks the ice. She also adds that Mark has been very busy, and at least four of the newborns are his, "Possibly more, so don't be confused by the short blonde hair!"

They are all sitting relaxed. Ruby opens a drawer. Cha is ready in a second to blow her brains across the newly painted pink walls but relaxes when she is only holding a lighter and some cigarettes. 'You can smoke if you want,' as he is the only one, Murray sparks up a number.

Ruby speaks to Murray, "I have to admit that the last time we met, I had quite a chuckle when you said thanks for the tea. It took all my previous acting training to suppress the laughter. Fat boy and his chum were convinced that you would be crying by that time. Thanks, son, you made an old lady very happy that day, and I hope you like the changes that we have made."

The sandwiches are going down a treat, and the plates are clean. Ruby adds that "You can stay for dinner if you want, so I will not order anymore, but the tea pots are empty," and she presses a little bell.

The old lady has been replaced by Ellie, who just says "Hi," to everyone.

Ruby raises her eyes; "She likes working with Mark. Also, I know you are being very patient, but before we go on a guided tour, have some more tea, relax, and I will speak at length. If at any stage during the conversation, please feel free to interrupt, and I will answer any question that you may have."

Ruby lights up another cigarette, and Murray has his eyes closed, sipping yet another perfect brew. "After your last visit, it was several weeks before anyone would go to the front gate, never mind venture outside. They said there was a wild ninja woman who lived in the dark and was avenging her dead lover."

She looks at Cha, "The description they gave was nothing like what you actually look like, they said you were beautiful, I think that was accurate the rest we will never know."

"The old leadership was gone, the few that thought that they were going to walk straight into the vacant management positions were sadly mistaken, and unfortunately, they have gone also. It had to happen, and now we have quite a nice community, and before I forget, I apologise on behalf of my community for the way you were treated. They should never have attacked you in the first place."

Ruby has another cigarette, and Murray sparks up a number. "We have changed things for the better, our community is growing, and we hope all the garbage initially inherited from the old world and aided with greed and corruption from our previous leadership are well and truly gone. We have many discussions in this community, and we constantly worry about what is out there. We have had a few additional families arrive, and how they managed to make it here is truly amazing. The animals were everywhere, and we thought our leader was awful. They were nothing compared to the stories that we have heard, and this has given us great cause to worry."

Ellie opens the door and enters. Speaking openly to her mum, she reminds her that it is feeding time and maybe the guests would like to see it. Ruby says, "Relax, we feed the babies at the same time. It works out better this way. We tried other methods, but this, for some reason, worked. Would any of you like to see it?"

Annette looks at Al and says, "They would like to," Al does as he is told. The weapons are left on their seats, and they go off with Ellie.

When they are gone from the room, Ruby addresses Cha, "He does not know yet?" Murray looks at Cha. She just tells him that it was a woman thing. With them away on the guided baby tour, Ruby continues, "We have no one to repair our machinery, we did have, but I think they have gone to the big garage in the sky. We must have some items that you require, and we have many skills here, but that of a mechanic is not amongst them. I am led to believe that you may possess the skills that we are missing, and perhaps we could come to some sort of arrangement?"

They get down to the nitty-gritty of what they need, and Mark has supplied a very detailed list of the problems. Including make, model, problem, and, most importantly, a comprehensive spares list. Murray mulls over it.

More tea arrives, followed by "Are you hungry?" It is starting to get dark outside. They are not expected back till tomorrow, and why not. The meal arrives, and so do Al and Annette, Ruby and Cha know that she has told the young man the news, and as always, Murray is none the wiser.

They eat and talk about normal things; Ruby was on TV before, and he had never seen the programmes that she was on. Murray tells her a little about what he has done. Cha stuck to the painting story. Ruby said nothing but did not believe her. Al and Annette stuck to their stories. None of it mattered. None of it was a big deal. The diner plates are cleared away. They helped pile them up and thanked them all for the meal. Mark appears accompanied by Ellie with more replenished teapots.

Cha and Murray think that they will have to hammer out a deal, But Al sees something else, rather than a mere trade exchange and mutual co-operation where we do not just shoot each other on-site. He lets everyone continue.

Ruby has it all worked out, "In exchange, and a very fair exchange at that," she adds, and hands over a folder containing a comprehensive list of items available, complied previously by Mark to Cha. Murray knows that it is good by the reaction. It is just a minuscule movement with the muscles around her eyes but the movement never the less. "How many items are we allowed to select."

Ruby looks her straight in the eyes, "All of them are yours. I even have them packed and ready to transport. In addition to this, we can offer more in the future, and all we ask is that you can have our machines repaired and running. How you do this is up to you. Come over once a week, show some of our volunteers the basics, and maybe monitor them from time to time. I know that they will not learn it in a day. In addition to this, and I am sure that you will all agree at present, we are all living on the remnants of the old world, and basically, we are just parasites living off the dead.

391

Canned goods won't last forever, and we are going to have to produce them, and one day or another, someone is going to come and try and take them from us. You have some special skills, some that are very special, and all we ask is for friendship and a future for our children and us. We hope it does not come to wars, but you know there are people groups outside who have made no provisions for the future and will start advancing as they run out of food."

Ruby and Murray spark up at the same time. Ruby addresses Al, "Hey, kiddo! you like you want to say something." Al looks at Cha and him.

Murray holds up his hand, "Speak away."

"I understand what you are saying, all the implications of what is in store, and although I do see the logic in what you are saying, why don't you get to the point? That's really the important one, the one that you don't really know how to put across, the one that you have been saving till the end because this is the one that has worried you from the very start."

Ruby smiles, then blow out the smoke and nods okay. "Yes, he is right, bang on the button. What he is saying, what I am saying, what we all are saying is that without collective inter-community cooperation across all fronts,"

Al looks at her, "Okay, bottom line; on the current projections on the people we have, we do not have enough people to produce a future for our kind. Sure, we have lots of babies here, and I am sure that there are more on the way, but we have to think about the ones that come after that. If we breed among ourselves, it is doomed to failure."

"So, what exactly are you saying?"

"No, I am not suggesting a breeding programme, just saying that at present, we do not have an adequate number of people to maintain this much beyond the foreseeable future, and we will both have to expand and intermix."

Ruby looks at Al, and he puts in his ten-pence worth, "It boils down to genetics, and the rules are that you can't interbreed with your relations."

Murray smiles, "I do not have any relations," but he knows where he is coming from; lots of Royal families throughout the centuries have had various problems due to the ill-advised protectionism of their gene pool, and this happened not just in Europe but throughout the known world. Ruby adds, "We do not need to worry about this today, we do not need to worry about this tomorrow, but I am afraid we have to worry about it sometime in the future."

"I have got some rooms prepared for you if you wish you can stay, but after all this, if you want to walk away from all this, it is okay. I will understand, but rather than agree or disagree, have a think about all I have said and, more importantly, what Al has said. Mull it over, and we can talk about it in the morning, and lastly, breakfast anytime between 07:30 and 10:00 hours."

Ellie appears and shows them to their rooms; before she goes, "If you need anything, there is usually somebody about, and all you have to do is ask," and with that, she is off.

Cha and Murray share a bath. There was a selection of bath things, and Cha, much to his consternation, has him smelling of rose something. He asks her what she thinks, "Did you see the list of what she is offering, and all you have to do is fix things one day a week? I think we would be fools if we refused." They had noticed a bottle of vintage champers in a bucket of slowly melting ice.

Cha persuades him to get out of the bath and open it, Murray does not want any, but she tells him, "My bag is outside the room with the guns. Someone delivered it just before we got in the bath; no, they do not want trouble. They just want us to help them." Murray gets out of the bath to retrieve their things; he leaves the guns outside as a clear goodwill gesture and just brings the backpacks. Cha has poured the liquid, and he adds in some last man on the planet for, as Cha reminds him, is for his rather delicate palette. Unbeknown to Murray, Cha has sneaked some of her underwear and high heels, and as she is getting out of the bath, and tells him not to be too long, as the KGB woman has missed him. Don't you just love bath nights?

Breakfast was unbelievable, full of people chatting freely and laughing. Mark arrived and received lots of waves of "Hi

394

Mark" and "Spare seat over here, Mark!" He walked over to them and asked if it was okay to sit. No surprises. He just asked how breakfast was, and if there was something they would like that was not on the menu, all they had to do was ask. Mark tells them that the smoked fish is his favourite, and Murray bursts out laughing. Cha looks at him, and he just tells her that it is a man thing.

Mark is finishing up when Al and Annette arrive. Initially, Murray thinks that it is a charm offensive. Mark stands, greets them with a nice to meet you again, and shakes their hands. "I hope you enjoy the breakfast, and sorry, but I have to go to work, have a great day, and I hope you all enjoy yourself. Bye for now." Cha looks at Murray, and he just shrugs. Some people are just genuinely nice, and that is the way they are to everyone. He was totally wrong about the charm offensive, "But just Imagine if we were, all the same, adding it would be fucking terrible." Al's plate is big, but Annette's is bigger. Murray thinks they may be having an eating competition, but he thinks they may not have seen toast, scrambled eggs, and poached eggs for quite some time, also.

They are all full, Murray is heading out for a smoke, and he bumps into Ruby. "I did not see you at breakfast."

She says, "Good morning. I don't do breakfast; Ellie has given me grief for years. Smoke time, I presume?" Together they are heading to an area away from the door when Annette rushes out and pukes in the street.

Murray looks at Ruby, who says, "Poor girl," and hands her a handkerchief. They smoke and chat about nothing in particular, and Cha appears. Ruby asks straight out, "Do we have a deal?" Cha extends her hand, and they shake. When all is gang is assembled, Cha has the list and looks at all the assembled vehicles. All seems to be correct except the animals. Ruby is on the ball. "We have them ready for the next consignment when you have the enclosed area ready for the animals."

Between them, they agree that Murray will stay behind and some of the woman's all transport division will drive them over. Cha tells Annette that she can travel with Al. She is not thinking of them as a couple, just thinking about the smell of puke in the car. Cha and Murray cuddle and whisper, ending with, "I will see you in a couple of days."

They wave as they head out. Murray wants to get started and asks what they would like repaired first. He is taken to where they have assembled various vehicles and equipment that require some much-needed love and attention. Everything here is repairable. Murray is assigned, what they assure him, to be the finest student. The first thing that Murray notices is the number of cut fingers. He tells them that they all need to start wearing gloves, the industrial Kevlar type. Someone returns a few minutes later with an ample supply. He sets the students out in pairs; each group has its own problem set. Murray has all the reports in front of him. The car group is first as a collective they discuss the problem and go through the possibilities; the manuals are available they had not even read them. Murray teaches them that one should read and turn pages while the other does the work. The first pair get to work. This process is repeated as he puts each group to work. Then he returns back to the first group and goes over their problem. If Murray has to, he grabs a tool and shows them a little trick to solve the problem quicker, but only where necessary. Most of them will be okay. They just needed to know where to start.

They stop for lunch and arrive back on time. They get stuck in straight away, and all but one of the problems has been solved. They gather in a group and discuss what they have done, what they could still do, and what it could possibly be. Murray gets them to look underneath, and someone spots the frayed wire, "This, ladies and gentlemen, is one that even the professionals miss and is a perfect example that is often overlooked!"

The day is going in quicker than he thought. Mark appears just as first class is disbanding. Murray asks him where is the other stuff to be fixed. He tells him this is everything, and it is slowly building up, and eventually, they will have nothing left. Murray still has the original list and selects the most awkward item. He intends to stay up all night and strip it all down, clean and mark up what he thinks requires replacing. The empty vehicles arrive back he is given a note, "Hi baby, all is good here, the goods received are perfect, and M is on another planet just now. She has some serious ploughing and planting in mind for the future. I hope she is good in the tractor. No problems at this end. PS the chicken coup will be complete for tomorrow so the chickens can come over with you, Cha."

Well, that cheered him up. He is smoking. It says that no smoking is allowed, and Murray is the teacher, so he is exempt. He could do with another last man on the planet, but he has wiped out his supply. Ellie appears with a bag, "I was told that you may want these."

He asks. "Ruby?"

She says, "No, silly, Mark."

Murray thanks her and plods on. The major repair job is completely stripped and ready for the class in the morning. He is anything but sleepy and just picks one at random from the list. In an hour, it is repaired, and he puts the notes on the back of the report. Murray has wiped out another two by the time the students appear.

He says good morning and puts them to work. This time he rotates them from project to project, and just before lunch Murray pulls them in, explaining that true and accurate accounts are the only information that should be exchanged, no what's if, buts, or maybes. Lunchtime is already here. The last remaining trucks are about to head out, and Ruby appears, "What day do you want to return? You're done here for the day, and see you sometime next week. Any of the drivers will take you."

Murray is sleeping before they go out of the gate. He hears a chapping at the window, looks about, and remembers that he is in a truck; Cha is outside with her face at the window, she has pressed her nose fully against the window and is in the process of dragging her nostrils down the whole length.

Chapter Twenty-Two

As ordered, Murray goes for a much-needed bath while everyone else gets the unloading completed. They have material everywhere. It is stored in every available space. Cha comes and visits Murray and tells him that they are no problems and everyone is pulling together, and some additional storage space is required. M has even emptied one of the sheds, and most of the farming stuff is all in one place. Annette is sick most of the day, and apart from that, all is good, but the best part is that everybody has moved out of the house, and she has a special surprise for him.

Murray struggles to get out of the bath, and if he can manage it, he will stay in the water forever. He goes downstairs, and Cha has food on the table. It has candles, flowers, the works. She had poured him a glass of something and, bless her heart, she even made a small banger that for once did not look like she had just picked it up off the street. Cha arrives a wee while later and has a feathery thing on; high heels, the works, the whole kit, and caboodle. The CD player is even wired up. She struts, not walks, across and presses the play button. The can't remember his name and the band or somebody playing the same tune burst out of the speakers, and Cha set about teasing him, removing a little bit of clothing here, another small dance routine, another piece of clothing is casually dispensed with Bobby is screaming to escape the confines of his incarceration. If this is welcome that he receives every time he comes home, then he can't wait to go away again. Dinner is forgotten about, Murray carries her up the stairs, and they make love most of the night. It has only been two days, but it feels like a lifetime ago since she was in his arms.

Morning arrives, and no visitors, "We made a few changes, and everyone quite likes the idea of having breakfast at their place, and they will pop over later just to see who's doing what." The fish arrives shortly, and Bobby tells him to shut the fuck up and eat it.

M is here first, and Martha is over at Murray in a second. She is cooing and gurgling like mad. He is pleased that she remembers him and flattered by the attention. Murray has always had this thing with animals and babies.

Dean and the rest arrive shortly. They don't hang about, as they have things to do, and shortly after, Murray and Cha are out and about. M has stored all that needed storing; her list has been amended several times by the number of scores on the paper. Cha has started the weapons programme. Some can shoot, and some would like to be able to shoot, as guessed Dean requires no training, and Annette was exempt in her present condition; both Al and Frank passed, but only just.

The days roll in, and before they know it, Murray has to return over to the farmhouse. It is not that bad. The students attacked all the tasks that he had set for them. Some of the tasks had been passed with flying colours some were not so good; Murray organised a group session with both sets of issues and ironed out the little problems that occurred on each.

Today he announced he is going to slowly introduce the electrical systems and starts with the basics. Once the safety issues are signed, sealed, and delivered, he teaches the class how to work the multi-meter, pointing out that this will be their best friend for life, and if they take care of her, she will take care of them.

During lunch, Murray sets about looking at the tasks that the students have in front of them, he reads the initial notes and the additional ones that they have added, and today he is not going to move them about. They can finish the tasks that they had started. Again, Murray goes through the lists for the ones with the most problems. He starts stripping them down, and, in the time remaining, they can take turns to come over and see what he is doing. He is just about complete, and they have all done very well. He finishes just before dark, and it is too late to travel.

Although he wants to travel back immediately, they still do not travel at night, as it is just too dangerous, and as yet, they have no idea what attention this can attract. Murray saunters over to the canteen, and the only person he sees that he knows is Mark. Mark is sitting on his own; Murray asks him if he is okay. He says that he is fine. Murray notices that he has a little bottle of penicillin within view in his top pocket. He points to Mark's top pocket, letting him know discreetly that he can see them. Mark catches on straight away and says something along the lines of "Err mmmh, oh yeah, thanks," and they do not talk about it any further. As Murray can imagine, they will be no secrets in this place.

Murray is not tired and heads back to the maintenance department; he works a little and naps for a few hours. He finishes the tasks that he had been working on and goes home just at first light.

All is good when he arrives. Murray observes someone driving a tractor plume of dust coming off the back. He meets Cha, she sees him looking, and he asks, "Who is that?"

She tells him, "It is Linda. M reckons that she is a natural and she is that good she could have been a champion. This is only the second time she has been in one, the first one being a lesson."

The chickens have been busy, and even though Annette is still puking on the hour, she gathers all the eggs. "Martha has said her first word, and M had wagered with Dean that it was going to be mummy, and guess what?"

Murray tells her to get on with it. She is beaming as she tells him, "It was Murray." Oh, he will keep out of the way. No point in rubbing salt in the wounds. She tells him that it is okay. Everyone thinks it was funny, especially Dean.

They don't do the visiting thing, maybe the others do, but Murray is just not interested in it. He works with them all day, and come evening, Murray wants to spend it with Cha and Cha alone. It has slowly been getting lighter, and they work a little longer into the evening, but nothing silly. As a group, they are pretty well organised, and there is nothing that urgent that it has to get done immediately.

The weeks and the months just roll by. Murray's little group of fixers are doing great, and Ruby is more than impressed. The group can now fix most things, and now he has to only drive over in the morning, and unless they have some urgent breakdown or if they need help if he stays overnight, Cha joins him for a break, and she spends hours talking to Ruby.

Ruby is nuts but in the nicest possible way. She was telling Cha that Mark and Elle had a thing and eventually got officially paired up. Mark, at lunch, put it to Murray another way. He had been chasing her for ages, and all his charm had failed on her. She was not falling for it. He confessed over a shared smoke that he just knew that she was the one, and he was shitting himself, not about what Ruby thought, but all the other mothers of his kids but most of them had moved on and come the day of their exchanging rings they all had wished them well.

Murray's community was also doing well. Annette has passed the sickness thing and mostly helps out in the

Orangery. Cha tells him that she is good with the plants, and on the subject of plants, Murray's plants have been growing, and to put it mildly, they are fucking monsters. They also, against the faded 100% guarantee, had produced an additional male offspring, this guy and a mate were separated early on, and the seed that they are producing will be stored for next year. As to the quantity produced by the crop will last a year still remains to be seen. Murray had never done this before, but he had run it through Cha, and she thought that, in theory, it would be fine. They are going to attempt it one night before summer is gone. Slowly when Murray gets some spare time, he has been making all the pieces that will be required. The big pot with the handles took forever to find. Murray and the chemist are going to go for it tonight, and after dinner, they're setting off to the Orangery like they are still loved-up teenagers. The birds ignore them, and apart from the odd chirp and the rustling of feathers they are sleeping. Murray sets out their stall; the plants have been lifted, dipped in hot water, and dried completely. They have been shaken, and all the buds have been separated from the stocks and stems.

The first batch, all the buds are broken off and ground up. The rest of the plant material is chopped up and added to the high-content alcohol that could run a jet engine, never mind a car. It is stinking, and they have to put masks on. The small electrical stove is on full to heat the extra-large pot.

The contents are stirred and boiled for the amount of time that they have guessed should do the business. As the allocated time is reached, the mixture is poured into the trays.

The windows have been left open, but the smell of the alcohol is still overpowering. Murray hopes the fumes will dissipate overnight and the alcohol evaporates soon after that. Once that is done, he will slowly mix it all up with the good parts that he has put aside.

Fingers crossed, he will have something to smoke, and it will make a welcome change from the grass. Checking that the place is clean and tidy, they go down stairs, being extra careful to leave the doors open to allow the breeze to circulate throughout the building.

Walking back to the house, still, like teenagers, there is not a sound. It has just turned dark. The stars are few and far between, nowhere near as good as the display on a winter's night. They shower together for a change and make love in the cubicle. It was not planned; it just happened. Falling asleep in each other's arms, Murray is still knocked out by her super model smile even after all this time.

Murray and Cha are in the field with the fallen trunk, and the old woman with the hooded cloak is here with the gathering of the kneeled followers. There seem to be many more of them. The woman in the hood raises her hands in the air; the incantations start and end up in a drone that seems to hang in the air. A single small handbell rings just once, and when they open their eyes, there is another woman there beside them. Like Murray and Cha, she has no cloak on. The old woman speaks to her, and even though they are right beside her, they do not hear anything that is said. The new arrival looks like she had also met the old woman before but is as new to them as they are as new to her. The woman with wild red hair and piercing green eyes is standing facing them now.

The old woman with the hooded cloak introduces them to each other by name. They all hold out their right hand, and the old woman with the hooded cloak takes it in turns as she grasps their outstretched hand with both of hers. Before she departs, the old woman tells them that they will be good friends and all their children will be lifelong friends.

Morning comes, and Cha is sitting up, leaning on her elbows when he wakes. "Morning, handsome," initially, Murray thinks he has been naughty during sleep as it is not the first time they had woken up in the middle of the night hard at it, both of them swearing that this is how they had woken up.

"What do you remember about last night?"

"I was in the shower with you, and we washed," she is looking at him with that serious face. "Try harder."

Murray is slowly waking up, and he is also starting to remember. He is out the bed checking his feet. Even though the ground up by the fallen tree is dry, both their feet and the bed sheets are filthy.

Together they go through the steps of the collective dream. Everything matches. Cha mentions that this is not possible as a medical expert told her that she would never be able to give birth. In-between sobs and telling him this dream cannot possibly be true, and she is sorry for letting him down as she would never be able to give him any children, she tells Murray that she cries inside every time she sees him with Martha knowing that he is just a natural with children and she feels terrible that she has let him down and terribly ashamed for not telling him before.

He tells her that he loves her no matter what life has in store for them, and he would not dream of spending five Nano seconds on this plane of existence without her. Murray asks her if she can remember the woman's name, and she says, "Yes, it was Alicia."

Murray sits beside her and assures Cha that nothing has changed. They are going to be forever, they cuddle for a while, and when she is feeling her normal self, they go downstairs and think about breakfast. Murray needs a smoke; out of the ready rolled box, he helps himself to a monster and goes outside. Cha joins him with tea and is smoking also. Murray goes to the farmhouse later on and asks her to come with him. They could spend the day together and come home later or tomorrow morning. The group could survive without them, and it would do her good to escape for the day. At first, she says no, but he persists, and eventually, she agrees.

They are halfway through their quiet cuppa and just soaking up the morning bliss. The birds have been busy and are out in force. Their quiet morning is broken by the arrival of Al. He looks as if he has had a rough night. Murray asks if Annette is okay. He says she has not been sick for some time, but the baby was playing up last night, and both of them really did not get much sleep.

He adds, "I was speaking to Frank last night, and we thought that we had all been busy for a while. I mean, everything has been done from all the buildings, all the chalets, the big meetinghouse, even the first aid center. We thought that it would be a great idea that has a party night, not all drinking, singing, and dancing but a get-together with everyone. Call it a night off, we could have a big communal meal, and we all could chill out. We could even have along lie in the morning."

Cha says, "Yip, no problem, and tell everybody that it was your and Frank's idea."

Al says, "Bang on, everyone will love it."

Murray takes Chas's hand, and they go and see everyone and let them know that they are going over to the farmhouse and hopefully will be back tonight or tomorrow morning. Murray asks Al to check his chemistry experiment, and maybe it is not such a good idea for Annette to go up to the Orangery; she has been up most of the night, and he just asks her to take it easy. They meet up with Linda and Frank. Frank is delighted to be cooking for the get-together and asks if they could beg, borrow or steal some milk from the farmhouse. Linda has ants in her pants, and her chariot awaits.

They see M and Dean last. Martha is attempting to walk and is determined to do it, even though all the books say it is far too early. It is Martha who sees them first, and the arms are up straight away. Murray feels like shit about this, but outwardly he is just pretending to be normal. Martha makes it clear that she does not want him and is cuddling into Cha and has to be pulled off her when they say goodbye.

On the drive over, the journey is mostly spent in silence. Cha is happy to escape for the day and just tries to melt into the seat. Murray drives, and like her, he is also thinking about the dream. Murray informs her that the repair team is getting tested today, and it is possible that if they all pass, his visits could change to fortnightly. Murray tells her that was a suggestion from Ruby, not from him, as she has heard, "I will have to ask Murray, or Murray will have to fix it less and less."

Arriving at the farmhouse, Ruby is on her walkabout and greets Cha will her customary maternal cuddle. He just gets the usual, "Hi Murray, how are you."

410

He hunts down Mark, and Murray gets the "Hi Bud, how goes it," he tells him that he is fine. Murray asks Mark how is married life is; Mark tells him that it could not be better and assures Murray that the exam papers have all been sealed and have been kept under lock and key and as soon as he needs them, with a little chuckle, he will deliver them under armed guard.

Murray goes and plays at being a shepherd as he gathers his students, they look ever so serious, and he is concerned. "Look, this is only a test. Everything that will be presented to you is nothing that you have not all covered more than once, so please fucking chill out and relax."

Mark has arrived with the papers and no armed guard. Murray asks everybody to take a seat. He opens the box and puts the papers face down in front of all the students. He wishes them all the best of luck, and the two hours will start now. Mark has agreed to pop over and let Murray out for a smoke break. All he can hear is the pens and pencils and the occasional, "You sneaky bastard." Murray lets them get on with it. He has his fingers and toes crossed for each and every single one of them.

Cha is still with Ruby; they get on famously and are seen all over the compound. Everybody knows Cha as the scary lady who is really quite nice. Everybody knows her, and surprisingly she remembers all the names. They can be heard laughing from Ruby's office, and she is secretly called her other daughter. They are now in Ruby's office. Mark has just delivered tea, informing them that the exam is underway. They all laugh as Mark describes Murray as an expectant father pacing up and down, waiting on the imminent arrival of the baby. He makes his excuses and leaves them to it.

Looking at today's selection, "No cookies?"

Ruby asks her if she needs glasses, as there are cookies on the plate, "Oh, the pregnancy cookies?" At this, Cha bursts into tears and tells her that she would love a kid but has been told by experts that it is not possible. Ruby calms Cha down, saying that experts are not always correct and sometimes things just happen, and they can't always explain that also. "Hell, if I had listened to all the experts that had told me I had this, and it would develop into that, I would have been dead and buried years ago."

"I have a present for you. I meant to give it to you ages ago, but by the time I remembered, you had left. And come to think of it. I think that it has been too long since I have seen you, way, way too long."

Ruby rummages about in the drawer and pulls out a little box. Placing it on the desk. "This was my granny's and allegedly her grannies before that. I never got it valued as I was warned many times that I could never ever sell it. I was also told that I would know when to pass it on and how I would know, as I would be told."

Ruby looks at Cha, explaining, "She knows how strange it all sounds, but promises made to grannies are special. Anyway, I want you to have it, and I want you to make the same promise never to sell it, and well, the rest will come to you in time."

Cha objects, saying that it should go to her daughter, adding that she was sure that Ellie would love it. Ruby dismisses her argument, "My child Ellie has never seen it, and she has never had the dreams. Please put it on."

Cha wants to ask questions, but Ruby stops her, "No point in asking questions I would not know the answers to. I have only had two dreams, the first one and the one last night where I was shown my, well, it does not really matter. I was shown that you had to have this, and you really should wear it." Ruby says that she wished she knew more, but there was not anything else that she could tell her except her granny would have loved to have met you.

The tea has gone cold, and Ruby presses the buzzer, and a fresh pot arrives, "Sorry to be a pain, is there any of the other cookies? Oh good, could you please bring some for Cha, thanks?'

They wait in silence and only speak when the cookie lady has been and gone. Cha removed the necklace from the box, "You don't even have to look at it," Ruby said. "Put it on and have one of the preggy cookies. You will feel much better." Cha puts it on, has a cookie, and does feel better.

413

Ruby asks, "If she happens to have any of the special cigarettes that Murray smokes?" Cha pulls out one for each of them. They laugh away the afternoon.

The exam room is quiet, the ordeal is over, and all the finished papers have been passed to each other to mark up. All the names have been hidden, and nobody knows whose paper they are marking up.

Murray goes through every question and supplies the answer by the correct letter at the end of every one. In the end, they are allowed to enter the cubicle that he and Mark had devised at one of their secret smoking sessions. When the students enter the cubicle, they are allowed to reveal the identity of the owner of the paper and enter the result of the test. They then have to proceed back to their seat and are not allowed to say anything. When everyone is done, the cubicle is removed, and they all look at the board. Murray is delighted they have all passed. The examinees all want to go and have a beer to celebrate. Murray tells them that they can have the rest of the day off and is sorry he has to go and see Ruby. Unfortunately, he has to drive later but promises to have a drink with them the next time, adding that he knew that they would all pass.

Cha is still in Ruby's office; Murray knocks and enters. The woman looked very relaxed, "Hi, Mrs B" and cuddled Cha. "Well, Ruby, they all passed with full marks. You should be very proud of them. Ruby tells him they knew they

414

would pass due to them frequently running out of things to fix and pestering the life out of her for the initiation of a preventative maintenance programme."

More tea arrives; Murray remembers, "I have been asked if we could return with some milk. A couple of litres would be great. I promised the kids I would ask."

"No problem, If the bull ever decides to perform, maybe we could give you a calf. Till then, some spare milk it is." They chat till the tea is made, and not wanting to escape without the light, they bid their farewells. Cha promises to return soon and start the journey home.

Cha feels like driving and tells Murray that she is glad that she came over. She really likes Ruby, and they laugh more than they talk. Frank will be delighted that you remembered the milk. Murray has a monster, and they talk nonstop all the way home. Cheekily, Cha asks Murray when was the last time he had a proper medical examination. He thinks she was just saying this, too, stopping him from falling asleep in the car. Now Murray and Bobby are fully awake and count the meters till they are home. Cha adds Ruby says to make sure and tell you, "Seen as it is the summer, you do not need to come over for a couple of weeks."

Frank greets them as soon as they arrive, "Hi, and really sorry to be a prick. I just happened to be passing, and I had seen the car, but did you get the milk?"

"Of course," Murray asks him how much he actually needs. He tells him he needs about a pint. "we have about two litres, and if it is okay, we could freeze it till he needs it."

"Okay, but only one problem. I made the mistake of telling Linda, and she has been slavering over the idea of a milky coffee. Murray looks at him and ask if there is anything else?'

Frank is so fucking shy and blurts out, "Well, funny, you should mention it. Linda has spoken to everybody about it, and everyone is now slavering, even me." Cha looks at him and says to Frank, 'put aside what you need for your meal, and we can drink the rest with coffee. Just leave a little for Murray for his tea, and you have a deal. Say everybody comes over in about an hour,"

It just gives us a chance to clean up. "Deal. Yip, I will spread the word" He runs off. They just can't help but like him.

Hand in hand, they go into the house, "Do I have an appointment tonight?"

"I don't know, depends on the coffee?" Murray goes for a quick shower. He is going up to check his little pet project. Most, if not all, of the alcohol, has evaporated, it does not smell, and he mixes it all together. He still has quite a sticky mess. Murray scrapes a bit off and thinks that if he added some tobacco into it, then maybe it could work. He stores the

416

little bit of putty-like substance in a small round tin that Murray just happens to have in his pocket and just manages to get back down in time for the coffee. It is a really simple affair, but at one point, all you heard was, "Ahhh." The aroma wafting out of their cups, and the looks on their faces were priceless; they had several cups before all the milk was gone. Murray tells everyone that if the bull actually gets around to performing, they could get a calf and imagine coffee or tea every morning with fresh milk. M says, "When do you want me to go over? I could go now if you want."

They all laugh, and M says, "Why did you not ask me sooner? I think I was eight when my daddy showed me the secret of how to wake up the lazy bull!" They all laugh. M is not normally funny but is delighted that they all like her.

Murray wishes that every day was like this. Every one of them offers to clean up, but Cha tells them that it is okay. Her kitchen buddy, meaning Mr Black, will do it later, and for the first time ever, they all shake hands or cuddle before they leave. As a group, they really have crossed another barrier tonight, everyone is part of this little community, and that also includes Murray. When all our visitors have departed, he is shown a little jug of milk. Frank says, "As you actually remembered to ask, he kept this back for you, I have made you tea, and I need a shower and will see you in ten." Murray sips at the tea while he takes out the round tin and adds more tobacco till the mixture is workable. He rolls a couple and has only just lit it up when the nurse arrives.

He does not offer her one, she steals it and lights it up, and Murray knows that she is just teasing him. She is now over-selecting a CD and is pretending to have trouble finding one. Eventually, Cha finds one that she knows he will like.

It is a rock band that dominated the world in the 70s, the volume is dialled up a couple of notches, and she presses the play button. The guy who is belting it out big time is lovesick, and the woman he is with is driving him crazy. He belts it out more, and even in the quieter sections, every note that he reaches just tells you more and more that he is slowly going insane, not because the woman has a spell on him, just that without her, he would be totally lost. The guitar goes up and goes down with the wailing voice, not in perfect time, not in the perfect tones, but it is truly magical. The bass and the drums keep on an even keel as the song gets louder and more intense. They work it in and around the now-wailing screaming guitar and vocals. What is the most unbelievable thing about this song is that there are only four guys playing on it, and the most unbelievable is that this track was only a rehearsal at a sound check.

Murray notices the necklace that he has never seen before but does not mention it. Eventually, after what feels like an eternity, she struts over and informs him that his examination is long overdue; they end up making love in the kitchen that night. Cha thinks it must have been the milk.

Chapter Twenty-Three

For some reason, Murray is the first to venture up and into the kitchen, and out of the dregs of the milk, he just manages to get just enough for one cup. This he is holding like his most precious possession. Cha appears. Her hair is everywhere. She reaches out with, "Thanks, baby, I really could do with a cup," and takes the tea. She sits at the table and slowly puts her brain into wake-up mode.

Slipping outside, he opens a juice, smokes, and listens to the birdsong. They had done well this year; this was the most he had seen in a long time. Murray has even noticed a rare summer visitor jumping about pretending to be a blackbird, but the vivid white crest on the breast exposes him to be a distant cousin. Feeling quite chuffed at himself, he has never seen one of these before, and he is surprised at remembering its name. Cha joins him outside. She thanks Murray for the tea, he is just about to point out the visitor, and when he looks again, it is gone.

Murray is going to walk up to see M and her gang. If they need his help, he will gladly join in. Al has been helping Murray repair things and is now at the stage where he has stopped damaging his fingers. Annette is fucking huge and waddles, not walks; she entertains Martha during the day when M is planning the next farming activities. Murray joins them; M is in his face straight away, "Next time you are going to the farmhouse, I would like to come over with you and have a little chat with Mr Bull." Murray just nods. Al has his fingers all wrapped up; he says nothing. Dean, as always, looks like he is undercover ready to pounce on someone and read them the Miranda, whatever it is called. Murray really wishes that he would just relax a little. Dean does not drink much now, Murray had found a bottle of really old malt tucked away and gave it to him as a little present, and as far as he is aware, he has never opened it. Saying that he would keep it for a special occasion, Murray thinks that every day is a special occasion as he is still alive.

Cha appears, and the uneasy conversation breaks as easily as it had started. She flings her arms around Murray and kisses him. "If you are not needed here, I could do with some help." M nods that it is okay to pull him away. They head to the Orangery Cha pulls Murray into the first available greenhouse, and she tells him that she needs something and starts to remove her clothes and that she needs it straight away.

Frank has been busy and has put the word out that they are going to eat together tonight. He has told everyone at least twice. The meeting hall has never really been used before, but the brothers have been cleaning it out. It has not been painted; the wood panelling is still as it was when it was originally built. Most of the tables and chairs are stacked at the far end of the hall, but the ones that are going to be used have been pushed together to form a long table where they all could sit.

They arrived as requested. Cha and Murray are the last to arrive. He says sorry for being late, and they all laugh at him. They are all early. Al and Linda are on drink duty, and even Dean has a drink. Martha starts to squirm and is immediately handed over to Cha. Murray is not even given a passing glance these days.

Frank starts to bring out the food and insists that everyone helps themselves. It is mince and potatoes, and no one can remember the last time that they had real mashed potatoes, and to be honest, Murray would have been happy with that alone. Frank has made these and has added milk to them, Murray is noticed, closing his eyes and savouring every mouthful, and everyone laughs at him. Murray is fine with that and asks for more. Cha tonight looks different. Just something about her is different, he does not know what it is, but there is just that something. She has been through an awful lot, and Murray guesses it can't really be easy living with him all his little foibles.

The conversation flows, and toasts are cheered, and the most prevalent one is Cha and Murray. They are all happy to be here. Someone starts to say how grateful they are to Cha and Murray for taking them in. Murray stops them in their tracks and tells them how grateful they are to them for helping this place work, as without them, it would be nothing.

Dean surprises everyone and says he wants to make a speech. How could anyone possibly object? "At first, we were stuck in this supermarket. Martha was impatient, and these two appeared on the weekly shopping trip. I would like to thank M and all of you for putting up with all my shit, especially M for being woke up in the middle of the night with me shouting freeze mother fucker, pointing my gun at invisible bad guys, and most of all, for bringing in our beautiful daughter Martha into to this world, not forgetting the emergency midwife who appeared at our moment of need." Dean produces the very old bottle of malt and goes around the table, pouring everyone a generous measure as he speaks. "A very good friend of mine gave me this a while back, and I have been saving it for a special occasion. I think that tonight is that very special occasion, and I would like you to raise your glasses to all of us!"

What can he say? Dean has come around, and Murray thinks everyone likes him, himself even? They are all looking at Murray and Cha, and he thinks that they are expecting another speech. He elbows Cha, and she elbows him back, but there is nothing that they could possibly add to that, never the less Cha gets up and says, "Health, happiness and to us!" she looks at Murray and says, "I want to get drunk now," They all have a great evening, the drinks

423

and the conversation flows easily, no terse words, everyone is happy. Murray still wishes that it could be like this all the time, but deep down, he knows that there is a change coming.

Cha tells him in the morning that she thinks she is dying and does not want any food or drink ever again. Murray just says, "I love you too," and goes downstairs, finding his clothes along the way. He needs several cans of last man on the planet to enable him to open both eyes properly. His elusive friend, the Ring Ouzel, is posing on the piece of grass in front of the house.

Murray smokes away, thinking nothing, just quite happy to be here and glad that he only had one whiskey. There were only two sober people last night Annette and Martha. Murray told everyone multiple times, according to Cha, that today was an easy day and to make the most of it. As to what day it is, what month it is, and what year it is, he has no inkling.

As Murray does not know when he will get his next lazy day, and Cha is upstairs trying to figure out if she is an animal, mineral, or vegetable. Murray slicks on the CD machine and selects some long-forgotten favourites, these were from long before my time when he was not even a twinkle in his parents' eyes when these bands were popular, but he loves the genre.

The band form New York are blasting out, and the out-of-tune guitars fight to keep up with the stuttering vocalist who wants to escape from the insane modern world that he was part of. Cha enters the room, having decided that it is safe to attempt being a biped, "Hi baby," Murray gets a wave from the hair-covered face, and her hand is barely able to wave. She slowly manages to open a can of juice and sips at it. Really wishing that she could be hooked up to a life support machine with multiple intravenous drips.

Murray kills the sounds and says he is going for a walk. He does not get far and shares the morning at the pond and with the ducks.

Dean has wanted to get more involved, and he has completed the index of the armoury, a list of all the available accommodations, and has even sorted out the first aid room. This he has done in his spare time or when M lets him off for the odd day.

Dean is walking up to the Orangery and has been furnished with a list from M. Murray, volunteers to join him. Cha has everything labelled, and he goes about snipping off what he needs. He needs a large jar with a secure lid. Murray knows where to get one when he returns. He has chopped the entire ingredients up. "I have been told that I have to add some urine in the jar, and as you were the only one who did not consume too much whiskey, as mine is inflammable, could you do the honours?" Murray dually obliges and fills it up till the line that he has indicated. Murray tells him that's me done and hands him the jar with the lid firmly secured. Dean then sets about shaking it, "I have to do this every morning for two weeks, and then M informs me that it will be then ready for the lazy bull at the farmhouse."

The following two weeks pass quickly, and nothing out of the ordinary happens. Days pass by peacefully, and Murray has even invented jobs to keep busy. They are going over to the farmhouse, M is in the back of the car and has never left Martha for this long before, but it is only for the day, and they will be back tonight.

Ellie meets them when they arrive. She tells Cha that Ruby is not looking too good, she is pretending that she is okay, but neither she nor Mark believes her. M is introduced and heads over to meet the people in charge of the livestock. Murray walks over with Mark to see his trained fixers, they are doing well, and for once, there is nothing to fix. A couple of natural leaders have emerged from the group, and they work well with each other. Mark compliments Murray on the job done.

Cha is with Ruby; she has just coughed again and hides the blood-speckled handkerchief. She is not happy as Ellie keeps catching her with cigarettes and wants to confiscate them. Ruby lights one up. "I am going to appoint Mark as my successor. He has a good idea of how this place runs, and everybody likes him, so that should not be a problem. I have left Ellie a note on my desk leaving instructions where I want to be buried," Cha is sad, but Ruby tells her that it is okay. She has known for quite a while now that she is sick, and the long sleep comes to us all eventually, and she will be really angry at her if she cries. "Just remember the good times we spent together. Do not waste valuable time on mourning." Ruby tells her that she would like to be buried with her kin. Cha looks at her as if she is meant to know where this is. Ruby tells her, "Of course you do."

Cha thinks and says, "Up by the fallen tree behind the filled pond. I knew you would know," followed by more coughing.

The tea arrives, and they sit and chat. Cha fights the tears back; she is going to miss her best friend. Murray returns without M. She is engrossed in an animated conversation about animal care, she has found several kindred spirits, and after discussing the lazy bull syndrome, they have moved on and even have missed lunch.

Ruby has fallen asleep on her chair, and Cha indicates that they should go. They meet Ellie on the stairs, and the two of them cuddle and share tears. Cha tells her that she is so sorry and Ruby has been like a mother she never had. They cuddle again, and Ellie promises to keep her informed. M is summoned, and then she has to be reminded that she has a baby at home and says goodbye to her new-found friends, and they set off. Cha pretends to sleep. M speaks the entire way back, non-fucking stop.

They drop M off, and she skedaddles off to see Martha. Cha tells Murray the news about Ruby when they are alone.

She is crying and sobs on his shoulders, telling him that today was especially hard as both of them knew that this was the last day that they would ever see each other. Murray holds Cha closer and lets her cry it out.

Somebody comes to the door, but Murray waves him or her away, telling them that they can come back later. Cha wants to be alone and walks up the stairs. Murray does not disturb her and sits outside the front door for the rest day so that nobody can disturb her. It is late when she emerges from the bedroom, her eyes are red, and she looks like she has had a good bubble, "Can we go for a walk?" They head up to the fallen tree. Cha, for once, feels comfortable here, and the grief that she is feeling slowly subsides.

In less than a week later, when the cars arrive, Ruby had passed away, and Mark gives them the sad news. There was a large turnout for the funeral, and everyone at the farmhouse wanted to come. In the end, the only way to do it was to allocate numbers and get them to pick. He told them that he understood everyone wanted to go, but they had to leave some people.

They all gather in the field; Mark and Ellie lead the procession to the grave. Cha and Murray are invited to join Ruby's closet and help with the lowering of the coffin. Mark says some very nice words and a mother-in-law joke that breaks the ice. Even Ellie laughs. They let her people fill in the earth, and they stand solemnly till it is complete. The sun is splitting the sky trust Ruby to pick the warmest day of the year. Murray and Cha back off and leave Ellie and Mark to say their final farewells in private.

Frank appears, and although no one has asked him, he has managed to rustle up something for everyone. Our people usher their people to the room. The people eat Mark's comments that he may have to kidnap the cook; Frank takes this as a compliment. M is engaged in conversation. It looks like her family concoction is working, and the bull is humping anything that moves, and by the noises that are coming from the field at night, he is not sleeping much either. M is delighted to have helped.

They leave all the people to mingle and escape outside for a smoke. Murray smokes. Mark just says, "Well, bud, I wish we were meeting under better circumstances. She really was quite a girl, I told her I did not want to take over, but she gave me no choice." Murray can only imagine the conversation. He is watching the sky and will soon have to round up his flock, Murray tells him he can come over anytime, and they shake hands, watching as he and his gang set off.

Everyone, including Cha, helps Frank tidy up; Cha pulls him aside and thanks him for pulling out the stops. Frank just tells her what he is here for, adding that if there were going to be any weddings, he would prefer some advance notice.

Cha is gutted and slips out back to the house as soon as she thinks it is suitable. Murray finds her in the bath, which is heavily scented, "Ellie gave me these, they belonged to Ruby, and she thought I would like them." He looks at the necklace closely.

Cha says oh, that, "Ruby gave me that ages ago." The symbols look familiar, but Murray says nothing.

The summer is now nearly over, M is getting all the plans in place, and the biggest event will be the potato harvest, and they will be doing the first one by hand. There is a machine, but it needs spare parts. They have had a search, and even Mark does not have them. He has offered to let us borrow the machine, but M says that this is not a good idea.

Annette is feeling like shit, and after taking her to the bigger medical facility over at the farmhouse, Ellie has offered her to stay there till at least the baby is born. Al will go with her as he would be no good over here. They are shorthanded, picking the potatoes is hard work, and having M in charge is a real pain, but as much as he wants to escape for all the time it takes, Murray keeps quiet. Dean thanks him, telling him that he knows she breathes through her arse sometimes, but he loves her and puts up with it.

The gang has been at the spuds for nearly a week, and up until now, fingers crossed, they have been lucky, and the rain has only given them sporadic appearances. Cha and Murray look forward to getting in the bath at the end of the shift.

Murray cannot remember being this tired before, but no point in complaining. It has to be done. M has it all planned out.

Cha sometimes looks distant, and after several of these episodes, Murray asks her if something's wrong. She tells him no, and first, then, out of the blue, she tells him that her sister will be arriving soon. "What sister?" and then she explains the conversation that she had with Ruby. They had never held any secrets from each other, and at first, Murray is hurt because she did not tell him, but she explains and goes back to the last dream and the woman with the red hair and green eyes, Alicia, her name is. Murray thinks about the dream, it was quite a while ago, and Cha said at first, she thought that I could hear the voices also, but after a while, she realised that it was only her, and as she did not have any answers for him. That was the only reason that she left it out, as she thought that he would think that she was going nuts and would only worry about that. Also and with the funeral and being busy, it just was easier to keep it all in.

"Just now, they have crossed the channel and are heading up through the south to get here.' Murray is like, "The channel and they, how many?" He asks, "Not sure," replies Cha, "I think there are a few babies the same age as Martha, some young adults the same age as the brothers, and then Alicia, who is in charge."

Murray asks if she has anything else to tell him. She says that there is, and he waits. "I do love you. There is no point in getting angry about it, but 'how do you propose to tell the others? I was not going to tell them till nearer the time and only telling you because I could not hold it from you any longer or my head would implode."

It is a bit of a secret to keep, but as always, she is correct, they would only ask lots of questions, and Cha tells him that it will be fine and, after all, it is only still part of the dream and well, dreams don't always come true.

The spuds have all been gathered, and at last, the backbreaking work is over. Linda ploughs over the fields and churns everything up, returning it back to just a mucky field. The rest of them are going through the piles of potatoes and sorting them out as per M's instructions. Murray, for one, will be glad when this is all over and promises to get a part for the machine next time.

Cha has declared a break in all activities for a few days, and only if something is an emergency will they muster. Murray potters about and check everything he can think of. Linda is complaining that her pet tractor is making some noises, and it is pulled into the big shed for a severe going over. You would think that she is waiting for her baby to be born, and Murray eventually has to tell her to go away, "I will let her know as soon as I find anything." She is back shortly, "I have found the problem, and just to get rid of her, he says that she needs the following spare parts. We do not have them, But Mark's guys may be able to supply them." Murray also knows that it would be good for her to go and see Annette.

Cha and Murray, at last, have some time to themselves; lately, even though they had told everyone to take it easy, they still have been busy. Even getting Linda out of his face as he thinks it is well deserved, Frank was all for it as he had no communication with his brother for ages. It would do them and us good.

She has promised a burn your socks off, curry, and Murray is really looking forward to this. He has developed this spice thing, and as of yet, none of our neighbours have the acquired taste. So, they will receive no visitors tonight. Murray has even agreed to let Cha pick the music. He knows there will be no rock music and boo hoo, no flailing guitars, and no maxed-out 100 watt valve amps. He is hoping that he will enjoy it anyway. The tones of the Amazon jungle do take Murray by surprise; Cha tells Murray that it is mood music only to work in the background to enhance the atmosphere. Murray asks her if that is a tiger he can hear and she matter of fact, informs him that you don't get tigers in South America, adding that he is on the wrong continent and the cat is a jaguar. The food is radioactive hot, and Murray loves every single bite. They have eaten and are now in front of the fire, just relaxing. In the background, the Jaguar has been replaced by what Murray thinks are insect noises, but he dares not ask. It is good to see Cha relaxed. Murray can't remember the last time they had an evening like this, and he is enjoying every second.

Murray hears a scratching noise, and he thinks it is some other animal that is appearing on the CD, but the bark immediately makes him jump up from the sofa. Murray knows this bark, and he runs to the door. This is Charlie, another bark. Murray opens the door, and there she is. She is absolutely bedraggled. Her hair is all matted, and by the added scars on her face, it looks like she has had an argument or two.

She walks in and barks to let everyone know that she is home. Cha is crying, and Murray is in fucking bits; the tears are running down his face. He is inconsolable, this is one of his best friends, and all he can do is cry. Cha asks, "Are you hungry?" and the bark says it all.

Charlie eats everything that is put in front of her, and then she runs about the place, her propeller tail destroying everything that it comes in contact with. None of it matters. Cha looks at Murray, and the tears are still running. He knows that he is a grown man, but this is his dog. He grabs her, and she licks his face. This just makes him worse. She is stinking, and they will need to bathe her. The trio head up the stairs. They expect that they will have to wrestle to get her in the water, but they are wrong. Charlie goes in with no problem at all. They even get a woof, almost a sign of approval.

She is so dirty that they have to wash her several times to get all the crap from her coat. After the final wash, they run a dog comb through her coat and end up with a huge pile of matted hair. Some of it was that matted it had to be cut off. Woof, she wants out. Murray helps her out. She looks bigger, but he thinks, as he has not seen her in ages it is just his imagination. They do not get the towels over her in time as she shakes her coat dry. Murray also cries at this.

They have her downstairs, Charlie has now retaken her position in front of the fire, and Murray is just beside himself. Charlie is home. Murray really wants to go around all the doors, even Dean's, and tell them the great news about Charlie.

There is snoring coming from the direction of the fire. He leaves her with Cha and goes and cleans the debris in the bathroom. Murray just chucks it in plastic bags. The towels are wrecked, and no matter how many times they are washed, they will never clean. He is even singing as he tidies up.

Murray goes back downstairs and tells Cha that this is great, even saying that it is going to be a great year. Charlie is back, and they are complete. Murray hopes that she will get on with the new arrivals, but when it comes down to it, if they don't, well, it is as simple as this, Charlie was here before them all, and he is sorry, but they will have to leave, Charlie's home, Charlie's home.

Murray thinks Cha is having thoughts that he is seriously mentally unstable and maybe he will require a sedative as he has not even looked at his smoke since Charlie arrived. Murray tells her that there is a very straightforward explanation. Okay, she says, "Explain away."

Cha and Murray are back at the table; Charlie is still snoring away. "When I was young, I used to ask for a dog, not every single day, but nearly every day, and I never got one. When I did eventually get one, we were inseparable; everywhere I went, the dog came with me. I loved that dog more than anyone. I used to spend all my pocket money on it. If my friends did not like my dog, they were no longer my friends. We spent years together and never spent a night apart. When the dog died, I did not speak to anyone for weeks. I stopped eating I ended up being sick. So sorry for being overcome with emotion. It is only me, and it is a doggy thing, and sorry, I honestly just can't help it. Even now, even before Charlie, I am unable to watch animal movies, and if I can remember, since the age of three, I have not been able to watch them. I have thumped various people over the years if I caught them mistreating animals. The number of complaints that my parents had knocking at the door was unbelievable. Eventually, everybody would leave my dog and me alone. That first dog just looked and sounded exactly like Charlie.' Cha is crying, and Murray has not stopped crying since he opened the door. They go to bed, Murray had built up the fire, and it has taken longer than expected because Charlie was sleeping and did not move, but that was okay. He would do anything for their dog.

Cha is in bed before him, and there is that cheeky smile. She is trying hard to suppress it but is not being too successful at it. Murray has to say to her, "Okay, what have you been up to?"

She pulls back the covers and is completely naked, "Don't forget you have two girls to take care of." Murray thinks this has been the best day of his life.

Charlie barks. She is hungry and wants out to do doggy things. Murray thinks she wants the doggy things first and opens the door to let her out. M was on her way over, and Charlie just ignored her and ran off to do her doggy things, then ran back in for breakfast. M comes in anyway; Charlie is eating and pretending not to see her. "I thought I heard barking last night. I did not know you had a dog?" Cha tells her it is a long story. Murray is waiting on the what about Martha, but she pre-empts him and asks, "Is it okay to bring Martha over as it is always good policy to introduce children to dogs as soon as possible." They agree, might as well get it over with. Cha and Murray have not discussed it, but he thinks she will know whose side he will take if it comes to it.

Back they come, Martha is squirming to get out of her mums' arms, and Charlie just sits, looks at Cha, looks at Murray, and wags her tail. M puts Martha on the floor, and she crawls over to Charlie. Charlie lies on the floor, and Martha cuddles into her and promptly falls asleep. Murray tries not to cry, but just in the event of any tears escaping, he slips out on the pretence of going out for a much-needed smoke.

Chapter Twenty-Four

Cha and M talk nonstop. As he re-enters the room, they have news. Charlie is pregnant, and Murray does not stoop as low to call her a dirty little stop out. He is actually thinking about what to call all the puppies. Giving any of them away is not an option. Charlie and babies, the thought had never crossed his mind.

Dean eventually appears and is introduced to Charlie. Martha is still sleeping, so Charlie does not move. Dean reaches over and lets Charlie sniff his hand. A wag of the tail, Dean can stay too. Murray thinks it is ages since Dean and M have had any time for each other and offers to watch Martha, they can come and get her later, or they will bring her over. Dean is all for it. M is reticent at first but gives in, and they head off. They just sit and watch the two on the floor. Martha is now awake and now sitting, making baby noises to Charlie, one ear up, one ear down, head cocked to the side. Cha goes over and takes Martha in her arms. Martha wants to feed. Cha looks sad, but to keep Marta from screaming, she uncaps her boobie, and Martha latches on. Murray can't understand why Cha is crying, but Martha is actually feeding and presently is sucking teats for the international team.

Murray really does not know what to say, but he cries. Charlie wants to go out, and he leaves them to it and takes

Charlie to her favourite place. If she needs another bath, that's fine. Charlie does not run around with her normal madness and does not even want to splash through the water. She heads straight up to her observation point and howls to let the world know that she is home. When she has had enough, they walk back. The other two are fast asleep in bed. Murray does not know who looks the happiest Cha, Charlie, Martha, or himself. A woof from Charlie, and she darts downstairs, hungry and ready to let everyone know; Murray feeds her straight away, twice. He has just finished loading the fire, and Charlie is back sleeping in her usual position in seconds.

Cha and Martha are awake; they are on the sofa. 'Goo-goo' and 'gaga' are the only words Murray can make out, Martha is playing with Cha's hair with one hand, and the other is stroking her face. Cha looks sad. Murray asks her if she is okay. She tells him that she is fine, "Honestly, I am okay."

M and Dean are on their way over, they are going to be a little shy at coming out with it, but eventually, they will tell them that they are leaving in the morning. M was really excited over at the farmhouse, and the farming community needed a lead. Murray looks at her, about to ask her how she knows. She looks at Martha, "She has been telling me that it is okay, not to worry, it is okay." At this, she hands Martha to Murray to cuddle, and over the goo-goo and gaga, he gets the same message. They will both miss this little pumpkin, but it is not their decision to either make or alter it.

The door goes, and Cha says, "Just in time, Martha will be hungry" Charlie just ignores the visitors. It is M who does the talking, and Cha is right. They are leaving in the morning and feel it is the best decision for them, Dean is attempting to speak, and Cha stops him saying. "It's okay. I can understand you have a young family and the facilities over there are so much better than ours, not to mention they have loads of other children for Martha to play with, to grow up with, we truly can sympathise with your decision and tell Mark that we do understand and you have all our support." Dean does not know what to say. They could have one of these fake conversations where they say things like I will come and visit and please keep in touch. They just say bye, and they give Martha their farewell cuddle. They cuddle in close, and she has a hand on each of them. Cha closes the door behind them. Charlie gives a single woof.

Cha opens a bottle of wine and pours a large glass; Murray gets one of his cans, and she makes him a mix that he can drink without the horrible taste. She sticks on some soul and tweaks the volume. Charlie understands and drags herself up the stairs to her other long-forgotten spot. Murray has a few smokes ready, and Cha helps herself. She is deep in thought and tells Murray that it is okay, "They never really planned to stay, and they had survived here before when it was just the two of them, so honestly, it is no big deal."

In the morning, they all make it short and sweet; their car is all loaded, and both couples wish each other well and wave farewell. Mark will be worried, and they empathise that they must tell him, "That we know." Mark is a good guy and would never do anything behind our back, and if push comes to shove, he would be the first to offer help in any shape or form.

Today they go for a walk with Charlie. It is just like the old times, except Charlie does not go splashing through the water but still likes to sit up at her favourite watching place. Charlie decides when it is time to return, and they head back to the house, where she deposits herself in front of the fire and is dead to the world in seconds.

They hear a car arrive, and it is Frank. He is on his own, and he looks sheepish, but he lightens up when he enters and sees the water. "Looks like I arrived just in time," and hands over the milk. They don't need to talk; He tells them that he had passed M and them on the road, and he has more news. "Annette likes it over there, and no amount of persuading her will make her want to come back. Al is gutted but loves her." Me, oh, I am back. Linda is in love with a tractor over there, and to be honest with you, I will not miss her, so is that tea ready or what?"

Cha tells Frank that it is okay if he wants to go and be closer to his brother. He says, "No, he likes it here and is staying if that is okay?" Murray tells him that he can stay for long as he wants. Frank is going over to chuck out Linda's clothes and will see them later, adding, "Oh, any of that curry on the go?"

Charlie had slept through the entire conversation. Frank arrives back later and eats and tries to persuade Cha to give up the recipe. She promises to show him one day. Murray tells him that they intend to check out the grounds tomorrow, and he is more than welcome to come and join them any time after breakfast. If he wants to come over for scrambled eggs, he is more than welcome.

Murray gets him out, Franks heads over, and he goes to get the eggs. Charlie is up wagging her tail when Murray gets back; they have loads, so he breaks two into her bowl, and she makes them instantly disappear.

Cha is up first in the morning; Murray follows her down shortly; Charlie is looking for more eggs. "Do you think Frank will be okay?"

Murray tells her, "Some people need more space than others, and we don't know what his and Linda's relationship was like, so maybe it is for the better that they split now?"

Just at that, Frank arrives, "Oh, if I am too early, I could come back," they say to come in, and he has not met Charlie. Charlie comes over, wags her tail, and goes off to lie in front of the fire, dreaming of eggs and other food. The scrambled eggs are whisked to perfection, and Frank thinks that he will give up cooking as he does not think he can compete in the same league as Cha, who tells him to stop it. They are telling Frank how they met, trying to keep him from moping about, but he says that he knows what we are doing and he is okay. All Linda would do was talk about tractors, tractors, and more fucking tractors, and he knew it was not going anywhere ages ago. Just at that, they pass the tractor that is in the big shed.

They just ignore it and walk on, they have brought the rifles to do some hunting, but as Frank is shooting, they have nothing in the bag. He has missed everything. It looks as if they have beans on toast, and the bread is not like real bread but similar. They are just getting settled, and dinner is over. Frank and Murray eat every bite, and Cha thinks it is disgusting and feeds hers to Charlie.

Cha insists on tidying up, telling Frank that he does not need to go as soon as he eats. She even gives him a beer and tells him that he needs to relax. "There are plenty of women out there who would consider him a good catch." So, he should stop worrying. Maybe tomorrow, things could change.

They ask him what he would like to do tomorrow. Most of the work is up to date, and apart from the chicken eggs collection and a quick check, they could do anything that he

444

wanted; Charlie's barking interrupts us. Alicia is finely here, and she has just walked in the door. Cha goes up to her and greets her like a long-lost friend. "Hi, sis!"

Frank is speechless. He looks at Murray and says, "Sister?" Murray tells him that it is a long story. Alicia tells anyone who would listen that she is starving. Frank is up and offers to cook.

Alicia smiles. "There are a collection of lost souls outside."

He opens the door, "It looks like I will be busy after all!" They follow suit, and sure enough, there are cars, there are trucks, and a couple of minibusses.

All the people are milling about, Alicia shouts something in a language that Murray, Cha, and Frank don't understand, and they all turn and look. Speaking to Frank, "I have just told them that you can cook better than their mothers and if they all follow you, that you will cook till they can't eat anymore. I also told them that you will show them where to go if they follow you."

Frank is staring at her as if she is nuts, "But do any of them speak English? I only told them you would cook, nothing about speaking!"

"See you later," she waves goodbye to Frank and closes the door. Turning to Murray and Cha, she says, "A shower or a bath would be, at this present moment in time, would just be an absolute luxury," eying up what is in Murray's hand, she reaches out, and he surrenders it, her soul sister shows her where everything is. They will go and check on Frank later.

In the kitchen, Cha rustles up something for her to eat and puts more water on to boil. Murray starts to laugh. Cha asks why he is laughing. Murray tells her Frank was feeling sorry for himself, thinking that he would never meet anyone again and if he did, it could be in years, and in the next ten minutes, there was a coachload of people outside, and he had counted at least half a dozen girls in the same age group, maybe there is more and by all accounts, none of them speak English, the poor boy.

Cha tells him that he is cruel, and he should have at least had some sympathy for him; Murray tells her that Frank is going to have to learn to swim and learn pretty fast.

Alicia returns back downstairs. The first thing that Murray notices is that the necklace, it is exactly the same as Cha's, and the vibrant red hair has been tied up and not sticking out sideways. She still looks crazy, and her green eyes are piercing. She looks nothing like a sister that Cha would have.

"Make yourself at home," while she is eating, they go through the dream thing; all three of them had only appeared in a dream together once, the one where it ends with the old woman in the hooded cloak taking their hands in introducing them to each other in turn. Out of all the other dreams, this is the only one that they all had shared. Alicia is starving and eats while she is talking. She interrupts and laughs. She asks about Frank. They quickly tell her his story, and all she can say is that he is a poor boy. They don't understand why she is sorry for him; she is laughing again. Some of the girls over there, their menfolk don't even know where the kitchen is, and here, we have put a guy who is as good as a cook as you say. Right now, they will be staking their claim on who is going to get him. "We must go over and save him."

Murray does not understand and asks, "What is the problem?"

Both Cha and Alicia look at him, "You told him that they don't speak English?"

Alicia replied, "Who said that they have to talk?"

They all go over; Frank is behind the counter. Everyone is eating, but he is preparing more. There is a girl behind the counter with him chopping up onions. She is wrapped up, the headscarf covering most of her face. The knife is quick; the onions are sliced and chopped like a professional. As they walk in, another woman approaches the hatch at the counter. She lifts it and goes to move in to get behind the counter. The corkboard beside her head catches the knife as it sticks firmly into the wall. This happens as they just go in the door. Alicia informs us that they are too late one of the girls, Katerina, AKA the cat, has staked a claim, and the other girls will keep away as, putting it mildly, even the men are scared of her.

Cat waves over to them. Alicia looks at the knife on the wall. Cat just shrugs her shoulders and mouths sorry. They go over and see Frank. He is busy as ever; every heat source he can cook on is being utilised, and all you can hear is people eating. The Cat says something as she squeezes past. They look at Alicia, who is smiling, "It is nothing but mark my words. This girl plays for keeps."

Alicia goes through the crowd, and not one of them speaks enough English, maybe a word here, a word here and there, but she assures them that with the amount of shit, they all had to go through to get here, there is not one of them that she would not die for. At this, she said that there were more, but she either could not get to them in time or they were lost along the way.

They all look at Alicia with the utmost respect, and she knows every single one of them by name. None of them look frightened. They all look like they have been on the road for a long time. They are all hungry and dirty. They will need to show them where everything is. They can choose the rooms that they want, and if Dean had set up everything as he had said, there should be clean towels and all the things that they will need.

The Cat Returns, the scarf has been removed, and she has on a tight jumpsuit and a pair of tough-looking boots. Her hair hangs down to her waist, and she has on a little make-up and looks totally different. Frank has a gulp when he sees her. Obviously, he had not thrown out all of Linda's clothes quite yet. They watched the drama unfold, "I'm sorry these old things will have to do just now, hope you like?" all this is said in some deep Eastern European language, at this the Cat turns around to the rest of the single girls, none of them returns the look.

Alicia just smiles, "I forgot to tell you that you don't need to show Cat around. She is, as you have just witnessed is, more than capable of sorting herself out."

Alicia says something, and they chatter away. Several people get up and move, and they get up with them, go out, and show them the rooms. Dean had done a great job, and everything that he said he had done was the truth. He even had bundles of clothes in each room, and one room just contained a huge pile of clothes and nothing else. They show them around each of the rooms except for Franks. The Cat had left her old clothes outside, not because they were dirty and mostly threadbare, just as a warning to others that she was a resident here. Alicia could not help laughing.

They walk back to the meeting room, the people that they had shown to the rooms are chatting excitedly with the others, and they are asking questions and nodding in approval.

Cat is busy behind the counter showing Frank that she has been paying attention and she is preparing what he has asked her to do. No one goes anywhere near them. Cat, on seeing them return, speaks to Alicia, and she nods. Cat whistles, stand on a table, and shouts something out. They all listen and nod. Cat bows and jumps back down. Murray asks what that was all about, she has just told them that Frank is not doing the cleaning, and she expects to find it all clinically clean and ready to use in the morning.

They bid them all goodnight. Frank looks at them; Murray goes back and tells him discretely that "I don't think Cat has any interest in tractors!" Frank looks totally confused.

The trio retreats back to the house, Charlie is still asleep, but she has a wag of the tail when they go in. They have more tea and smoke, and they exchange stories. Alicia asks about Frank, and they tell her the story about Linda, "Cat does not like tractors, but she can be quite frightening; The first time I met her, she was being hunted by five guys. I went to go and help her. There was no need. She had killed them all before I got there, slit all their throats without blinking. We don't know where she is from, maybe Azerbaijan or somewhere out that way. If I were in a scrap, I would be glad that she was on my side. She has been in a couple of scrapes on the way over. It was not a good experience for the others. She is like a little sister everyone wishes they had."

Alicia was in Europe when the sickness started, and since then, she has been rounding up the crowd that is over in the galley eating. It had taken ages to find them all, the language barrier did not help much, and at times the dreams were really confusing, but as the frequency increased, it got easier.

"You should see Europe. They are various little gangs trying to gain control. Slowly these merge together and then fight it out with other gangs for control of a bigger area. Sometimes we had to lie low for days before moving on, we were ambushed a couple of times, and the way that worked out was that some of our people were careless and just did not take enough care. Cat was a big help then. She used to go out and scout the way ahead, sometimes gone for days, and we only moved when it was safe. She always brought back food. Some of the older ones called her mother for a while, but they eventually just called her Cat. To be perfectly honest, I don't think we would have made it without her. The others are a fair mix. No idea what their skills were, but the old woman with the hooded cloak showed me where to find them, and that's where I found them. I have lost count of the number of countries that we travelled through, and that's not even including the boat journey. You should have seen that. The ports are stinking, dead everywhere. I think we crossed from somewhere near the Belgium-Netherlands border and ended up on the East coast of England. I'm sure we heard planes one night and explosions going off in the distance. It was that far away and hard to tell for sure, but there were lots of fires everywhere. The gangs down there were much the same, no one offered to help us, and I hope it all has been worth it. These people have lost so much getting here, and I pray that it all works out as we really have nowhere else to go to."

They get onto the subject of the old woman with the hooded cloak, and the symbols that Murray is sure are on the necklaces, but as they don't have a reference, it is difficult to prove.

Cha goes first, "This was given to me by my friend Ruby. All she could tell me was that this was her granny's and her grannies before her. It had been in possession of her family for generations. She had had some dreams but nowhere near as many as us. I could not understand why it did not go to her daughter, but Ruby explained it is not the wearer who decides whom it is passed on to; it is the old woman. She told me her granny had told her she was never allowed to sell it. Lastly, adding that Ruby is buried up in the field, and she had told her that some of her ancestors are buried up there. That's all that Ruby had to tell me, I did ask her some questions, but she said that I would not understand, but I really think deep down that she was not allowed to disclose anymore."

Alicia refills the glasses and asks for a smoke; Murray just tells her to help herself. "My granny gave it to me before

452

she died. I was dragged to see her at an early age with all my brothers and sisters. I was the odd one out, the only one with red hair. All my aunts and uncles were shit scared of her, but we took to each other straight away, and it ended up that I used to go and visit her on my own. She was lovely and used to tell me these wonderful stories that would start in the afternoon and end in the early hours of the morning, and she would make me laugh. I remembered that we laughed more than anything else. We also used to read lots of books, and she would take great interest in my schoolwork, which was so much more than what my parents did. They never looked at them once. I was in the top three of the class at everything. I loved history, and this was solely down to my granny. She used to tell me stories that were not in the books at that time, and no matter how many times the historians had rewritten the story or what recent archaeological evidence was exhumed, they would never tell the truth of what she called the great age. When I got older, much to the consternation of my other siblings, she took me on holiday everywhere we went to America. Someone was to meet us at the airport, and when they did not turn up. My granny just about turned. She took me into the toilet, made me cut my long hair, and told me not to open the cubicle door until she came back, she dyed our hair, and we pretended to be other people for a few days while went drove south. In South America, we flew back to Europe, and for many weeks she took me everywhere, you name it! We were there; the most amazing holiday ever, and to think my Granny then stayed in a little flat tucked away in a grotty housing estate. I never ever asked her about the money, and she never discussed it. I got the impression that she thought it was vulgar. We spent several days at the Vatican, I don't know how she arranged it, but we had a personal tour at night when all the visitors had left. They spoke into the small hours and had to wait till the tourists had started to arrive before we could leave. I would not say that the man was scared, but he listened very carefully to every word that she said. From there, it was almost as if we went to every capital city in Europe, sometimes by car, sometimes by train, but never again by plane. In some cities, we only stayed a day or sometimes only a couple of hours, and we always left by a different form of transport than by the one we had arrived in. I had lots of hats and even remembered that my Granny made me pretend that I was wheelchair-bound to get to the front of some huge queue. She never looked flustered or scared and made me feel like it was just a special game for us. Eventually, we returned to England, and this time we had some people waiting to meet us; they looked scary, they did not speak, and they drove us everywhere. I got the distinct impression that my Granny was in charge, as they never once asked any questions, and she never ever paid them. We went to the huge big house in the country. I think it was the stately home of some lord and Lady. They had tours on where you pay and are showed round the gardens and some of the rooms, we were in this room looking at these paintings, and as the tour moved on, Granny took a seat and lit a cigarette. This I was shocked at because I had never seen her smoke. An attendant came through and was all flustered that she was smoking, my granny said just one word, and he ran off. Minutes later, we were escorted through to meet the Lady of the house, she was in the middle of something with all these seemly important people and had to leave whatever it was to come and speak to my granny, and I have never seen anyone looked so scared, I think she would even frighten Cat. Granny did all the talking, and the Lady just sat and rattled in her jewellery. Whatever was said to her made her appear several decades older. Granny never batted an eyelid as we left. She took me to Blackpool, and when I was there, my hair was turned back to normal, and we returned home by bus. My granny never ever discussed the holiday with anyone. All she told me to say when I returned back to school several months later was that I was on holiday with my Granny at Blackpool. We never saw much of each other after that. I was told to stick in at school and pass all my exams. I went to visit her from time to time, but she was never the same. My last visit was the strangest, she told me that I was not to go back home and was to travel somewhere, anywhere in Europe, but I had to get out of the UK and not tell anyone

I was leaving or where I was going. She gave me money to survive, I asked her what about my exams, my job at the university and she told me that it was no longer important and that's when she gave me the necklace. I had to give her a big cuddle and leave after dark, and that was the last I had ever heard of her. I think she knew the old lady with the hooded cloak in the dreams."

They all need another drink now, they have wine, and Murray has last man on the planet with a splash of red. Charlie wants out for a leak and looks at Murray. He gives her some food and piles the fire up. He thinks that they are going to be talking all night. Murray and Charlie go out for a walk and leave the sisters to it.

They go through their dreams to make sure that nothing has been omitted. They remember the bells and the chanting, and they are positive that they have missed nothing. Cha says in the last conversation with Ruby. She told her something that she just ignored at the time; she told her, "That you were coming, we would be great friends, but strangely she said our children would be the very best of friends. I am saying this is odd because I am barren. I have been told by experts that I will never have any children. But yet only the other day, my breasts had produced milk, and I had fed another child. This just was no ordinary child, way advanced for its years and just special. It was always watching, and I just felt that it knew what I was thinking. I know it sounds silly, but we both experienced it at the same time. There are other children in the community over the way, but nothing like Martha, nothing at all."

Chapter Twenty-Five

The bottle is empty when Murray returns, and he goes and gets them another. Alicia rolls and Murray is presently surprised. It is pretty good, almost like she attended the same training course. He fills up their glasses, and they talk some more. The trio smoke, and drink, taking all that has been said into consideration. Murray thinks they are missing something, and there is no one else to whom they can go and ask questions.

Alicia says a strange thing: she never got any of the bugs or diseases that all the other kids got. Murray laughs and recounts when the kids at his school called him a mutant, as he was the only one who never got measles, mumps, or even a common cold. Cha had no recollection of any of them, even the Asian variants; she never got any. She added that sometimes the places that they were sent to, the medical team got all the inoculations wrong, and many of the crew got seriously sick. But as far as she can remember, she had no health issues.

Alicia is off again. What about your parents? They are stumped at the question. She starts again, "I told you that I was the only one with red hair. I looked nothing like them. In fact, I do not even think that they liked me. I think that I was adopted and not through official channels."

Cha admits she has little memory of her parents and was basically shipped off at a young age and basically forgotten about them. Murray says, "Yeah, I had a brother. We did not look anything like each other, his parents were normal, and he, funnily enough, was the only one who never got sick."

Alicia scratches her head, "All the people over there, none of them have a solid parental story. Every single one of them is a stray. I know it is a wild one, but what if they were all adopted and adopted outside the legal system? I have spoken at lengths to all of them. The ones who have some recollections were also nothing like their siblings, and they have never had as much as a cold."

Murray wants to look at the necklaces. He thinks they may hold clues, but Cha and Alicia are immediately defensive and do not want to take them off. Murray tells them that he is not expecting them to remove them; all they have to do is take them out from under their shirts. Half-hearted, they do as he requests, the symbols are identical, both equally undecipherable, but every twist, every stone, even the chain, is the exact mirror image of the other.

They have been up all night; it is Charlie who lets them know by barking, wanting out, and feeding again. They call a halt to their discussions. Murray feeds Charlie and persuades her to come out for a walk; she does not want to go far and walks back to the house just before halfway.

Cha and Alicia have had a quick shower and have freshened up. They have been up all night, and Murray takes the hint. He showers and shaves while they chat in the kitchen. Murray comes down the stairs, and they are laughing. He asks, "What have I missed?" They are discussing if Frank has survived the night, and Murray wonders out loud if Cat is really that dangerous. Alicia says they should bring her over one night and let her tell her story; maybe this will remove any and all of his doubt.

The trio walks over to the meeting house. Frank looks tired but happy; Cat has changed her appearance. Her hair is now curly, and on some sort of big fluffy jumper, but she still looks dangerous, even in bright pink. The place is spotless. Frank has started making breakfast, and the place is filling out. He says that he has no problems, maybe some meat in the next couple of days, but apart from that, all is good.

Alicia speaks to her people, and they are all good. They are happy that there is no more traveling and ask a few questions about what they can do to help. Alicia translates, and Murray tells her that they can just relax as they have had a very long journey and should just take it easy for a few days; they speak again, and Murray is asked where they can wash their clothes. He can take them up after breakfast and show them the industrial washing machines after they finish eating.

Leaving them to it, he goes back to check on Charlie, who is still sleeping. Murray does not disturb her. He makes sure that she has water and that the fire is still going. Murray quickly darts up to the Orangery and collects some flowers. Returning to the house, he fills the vase that he had found during his rummaging about with the flowers and, adding a little sugar to the water, places it in their bedroom upstairs.

Murray had just settled in the chair when Cha and Alicia returned. They think visiting the farmhouse and reminding him that Frank needs meat in the next couple of days is a good idea. Murray thinks about whom he should take with him out shooting, and he knows who Alicia is going to suggest, but he is going to ask. Before he asks the question, he hears their voices in his head both at the same time, both with the same answer, Cat. They laugh; Murray should have known better.

Cha and Alicia get ready to go, and if they set off soon, they should be back before dark. Murray goes and finds Frank. He tells him that he will go and get some meat; if it is okay with him, he will ask Cat. Frank nods that it is okay with him. Murray motions to Cat and makes animal signs and shooting signs. She nods.

Murray takes her to get a gun, she just holds them upright, trying out the weight, and when she has to pick one that she has deemed suitable, all she says is, "Okay." Murray just nods. She breaks open the breach and has a look inside.

Happy with the inspection, she again replies, "Okay," and they head off. The bright pink fluffy jumper has been covered up by the looks of it, one of Frank's jackets. Murray gives her a bag of cartridges. She says, "Okay." They head into the woods, and she hears the pheasants before him. The birds make the mistake of flying too close to her, and she gets the two of them. Everything she aims at, she gets; Murray thinks the next time around, he will just give her the gun. In fact, Murray thinks she can just keep the gun and go out anytime she wants. Cat had bagged a dozen pheasants and several wood pigeons and said, "Okay." Murray nods. They make their way back. Frank should be sleeping.

Cha and Alicia have arrived at the farmhouse, Mark is pleased to see them; he is embarrassed but shouldn't be. Cha introduces Alicia. Mark leads them to his office and requests some tea and biscuits. In his office, he says that "The people asking to stay was a great shock to him, and at first, he was going to refuse as it was not very cool, after all, that you and Murray had done for us and your closeness to Ruby, I was going to send them all back. Only when they told us that you had both okayed it was I still very pissed off at them. I know I should not have done it, but I told them there are all on a probationary trial period to be reviewed in a couple of months. Well, pissed off, I was." This was the first time Cha had ever seen Mark angry. He asks, "How is Murray? I hope all is well. I hope I miss our conversations, and if he is not over soon, I will have to come and see him. He is a great friend, and we all need friends. His team of fixers is doing well, but not a patch on the master." The tea arrives. Alicia is introduced to the special biscuits, and like everyone who has tasted them, she loves them. Mark and Cha chuckle as he tells her their name of them.

"So, what brings you over?"

Cha tells him, "We have some new arrivals, and Alicia will have a starring role. I thought it would be good to introduce her before she turns up unexpectedly. Better to put a name to the face."

"I get that; excellent idea. I am going on my rounds, and by the way, the bull has had every cow here, and it looks like most of them are with a calf, so fingers crossed and you can have your own milk supply next year, on the subject of milk; I had one of my team stick some in your car, and told them to it without being asked the next time. Please! Tell Murray I am so embarrassed by all of this, really I am. They are so ungrateful." Just at this, we see M. She is in-depth with some farm people going over some agricultural thing with charts and a pointer. "Don't get me wrong, all she does is work, and even her partner wants to work, but I am not too sure what I can put him on yet, so to keep him busy, he is in the kitchen. The young guy is in the fixing team, and no problems."

"We are just about to feed the babies. Shall we go and see? The Annette one has still not had the baby yet, but the doctor reckons she will be in bed very soon."

The babies are all spotless and very healthy; Martha is in a creche, and Alicia spots her straight away or is it the other way around? She has her arms up, and Mark says, "Go on, then give her a cuddle," Martha is getting bigger and reaches over to touch Alicia as Cha picks her up.

Alicia takes her hand. "Hello to you too."

Cha puts her back before the nanny arrives, "Good move, I am even scared of the nanny," and they all laugh. His tour is over; they go back to his office. "You know, without me even saying it, that if there is anything we can do for you, all you have to do is ask."

"We know that, and we would do the same for you. I just came over to introduce a new face, and come over and see us soon, and don't forget Ellie. How is she? I forgot to tell you the good news she is pregnant and the doctor has ordered her to rest. She will be disappointed not to see you. You have to see her before you go, if not I will get grief so, please c'mon, we can go just now, even a quick hello. She is not too happy about being stuck in bed, and you might just cheer her up. Ellie, baby, look who I have to see you."

Mark says that he will leave them to it; Ellie is introduced to Alicia, and they chat, mostly about Linda, tractors, Frank, and the Cat. Ellie thanks them for coming to see her and promises to come and visit sometime soon.

They catch up with Mark just before they are about to leave. "Thanks for that, I heard Ellie laughing as I passed. Your visit was the best medicine ever. I promise that I will see you soon, Alicia. Nice to meet you." He is off to some meeting. Cha and Alicia travel back, and on the journey, they talk about Martha and wonder if Frank is still alive. Alicia mentions that although she gets the impression that Martha is way smarter than her years, she did not sense anything from her.

Murray is at the table; Cat has gone with the fare. Charlie has been fed again and is now back sleeping in front of the fire, and apart from an odd whimper and the occasional fart, she is fast asleep. Cha opens the front door; Murray gets up to greet her. They have another cuddle and still that smile; "I have milk, and Mark was mortified. I told him that he could come over anytime."

Alicia has delivered the milk over to the meetinghouse; Frank is alive and going through a list of items. Cat is cutting up the birds humming away to herself. A few people are there. The rest are out and about. Alicia speaks to a few of them. Washing clothes and just the freedom of being able to walk about without fear is what is discussed.

Cat has laid her claim on Frank; Alicia goes over and tells them that she has some milk for them. Alicia asks Frank if he is okay. He nods, "I am fine. A little surprised that she had moved in even before I had spoken to her, but yes, I am fine." Frank asks if she is hungry and rustles up a quick omelette. He puts some out for the three of them, and the remainder he takes over to the people who are sitting in the corner.

They are sitting at a table, and Alicia tells Frank that he will have to share the workload. As good as he is, it is just way too much. Alicia speaks directly to Cat, asking her to make up a list of all the people and their skills and bring it over to the house when it is complete.

Cha is upstairs getting dressed. She had told him when they were alone that she needed something, and Murray had just gathered up the clothes that had been scattered about in haste to get naked and put them away before Alicia had returned. He meets her in the bedroom. The tears are running down her face. Murray asks her what is wrong, and she informs him that no one has ever given her a bunch of flowers before, and she is crying because she is happy. Murray takes her in his arms and tells her she can have flowers every day.

***

The three of them are now sitting at the table. They sit in silence. The milk makes a huge difference to the tea, and for a few minutes, they just sit and drink, savouring the brew.

Alicia starts, "Cat will be over later with a list of who's is who and what they can do. You should really hear her story."

Cha thinks that even though it will be dangerous, at some time in the near future, they are going to have to go on a major shopping trip. Winter will be here soon, and it would be the last chance to stock up. As they now have many more mouths to feed, the crop that M had sewn will not be ready till the following year, and what they have in stock will be enough, but that does not allow for any extra. Also, the new people will need winter clothes, so they are going to have to organise this soon, say within the next two weeks at the latest.

Charlie barks and Cat appears. She has some packages with her, which she dumps on the table and goes over to Charlie. She lies on the floor and speaks to her. Charlie rolls over and lets Cat rub her underbelly, "I like dogs. They do not lie."

The packages are bread, some meat, and the list. Cat comes over and joins them at the table. The bread and meat are shared, and they go through the list. Alicia asks, "What are the marks at the side of the names. These people now work in the kitchen, okay" the trio shake their heads. There are 30 people, and most of the skillsets are covered, the biggest problem being the communication barrier. One way or another, they will just have to work a way around it.

Alicia lights a smoke, and Cat looks at her, so it ends up that they are all sitting smoking, and Cat is to speak. If and when they don't understand, Alicia will translate.

"My childhood was normal, well, sort of normal. My father was like a doctor, not a qualified doctor, but people used to come to him when they were sick, and he would make them concoctions with a little mortar and pedestal. My family mostly ignored me. I was always in trouble for one thing or another. I was moved from one school to another and would prefer to spend my time with animals rather than people. Animals were less of a problem. On the way home from school, I would often visit the old lady, everyone thought that she was a witch and stayed clear of her, but to me, she was nice. She would make cake for me when I finished school, and she would make me laugh. She was very kind. She would show me all these books, and she would tell these fantastic stories that would last for hours. My family would complain, but I would not listen. Every day I would go and see the old lady. One day when I came home from school there were many strange cars in the street they were in my family's house. I thought that my father had finally gotten into trouble for pretending to be a doctor. The old lady that day said I must listen to her. She gave me a bag, made me change, and told me I had to run, Just get away. She gave me money and told me I must go west to Europe and never come back. It was then that the shooting started. The old lady pushes me out the back door, and I have to go now. I run and run. Later I look back, and the village where I stay is burning. They had killed everyone. For a long time, I have traveled. I had no papers, and when the money ran out, I had to steal to survive. I am good at this and eventually get to Europe, but one day I get unlucky, and the police catch me. They put me in a cell, and I get my picture taken. My fingertips are made dirty, and they keep me in a cage. They do not speak to me; I do not speak their language. Some days pass, and a man who they all look scared of arrives. He shouts at them, I am searched, but they do not find anything. A lady searches me again; this time, she tells me she is a doctor and searches everywhere.

The man takes me away and asks many questions, not about my family but about the old lady, her stories, and did she give me any presents. I tell many lies; I just tell them that she has told me many fairy tales. I make them up as I go along. Many times he gets angry and shouts at me. I just pretend that I am a silly little scared girl, and when I cry like a baby, he marches out of the office. He comes back and has cakes for me and even one of the little books where you get the packet of pencils and colour in to make it look pretty. I make a big mess on every page. This goes on for weeks. Every day he comes to visit me and always asks the same questions. I keep to the same story. One day, he makes a big mistake and gets too close to me when I am making a big mess, and I stick the pencil in his eye. I escaped; I was only small then and too quick for the men to catch. It was like a game as I escaped through the legs of the man at the door. I go and get my things and keep running. I go from city to city, never staying for long. Sometimes I see the man with the patch over his eye. I do not think he believed my stories. I used to see the old lady, but only in my dreams would she be standing there with a yellow suitcase directing me in which direction I should travel. The old lady did give me a present, and I have kept it hidden since then. She told me that one day I would meet a lady who would help me, and after a long journey, she would take me home. This did not happen; I am here, and I will do no more running. The old lady told me many things. She told me when I found home, I would meet a Blackman who would be a nice man. I was to trust him; he would protect me to the very end, he would take care of me when I got sick, and above all else, he would treat me like a daughter that he never had."

The story is so sad that even Cha has a tear to shed, Charlie barks for attention, and Cat wants to feed her and take her out. Murray tells her that he will come with her if she wants, and they go out with Charlie. The walk is longer today; Charlie takes her time and even does some barking to let everyone and everything know that she is back. They end up at her favourite spot. Cat and Murray sit on the rocks and smoke, and she talks to Charlie. He has no idea what she is saying, but Charlie is lapping it up. When she stops, Charlie hits her with a paw, and her famous one ear up, one ear down looks, which makes Cat laugh out loud. Murray even laughs. It is just infectious. They talk for ages. He tells her stories from his past, even the stories about Charlie and the old woman that they have seen from time to time.

Cat holds out her hand to Katerina, Katerina Kalashnikova. He shakes her hand Murray, Murray Black. The dog walkers have been away for a while, and they should go back. Anyone watching them would think that it was just a father and his daughter out for a stroll with the family dog.

They continue to walk and talk, Cat is crying, and Murray has to ask her why, "I think I am home now, and I have never felt like this in a long, long time. You are like a father, a father I have never had, and she turns to face him, the tears running down both of their faces. Murray also feels the same way. She is like the daughter that he has never had. They cuddle as daddy and daughter do and dry their faces before they return back.

Murray enters the house, and Cat tells him she will be back in ten minutes. Charlie does not want to come in, and she decides to remain outside.

There is a meal on the go. The table is set, and Murray tells them that another place is required. He badly needs a smoke. Alicia has just finished rolling one, the roach has only been inserted inside, and he takes it, saying thanks, and sparks it up. Cha notices his change and asks if all is okay. She asks him if Cat is really that dangerous. Murray tells them both that she is anything but crazy and she is coming back over.

Charlie barks as she enters with Cat. The propeller tail has returned. Several things get caught in the whirlwind and are now languishing on the floor. Alicia asks about Frank, "Oh, he is busy." Someone gave him some apples and made kebabs on skewers, and everyone was happy. They have started calling him nephew. "I told him that I would see him later."

They sit to eat, as always, it is out fucking standing, they tell Cat the stories of the old woman, and they laugh at the dirty feet and sheet incidents. The plates are being tidied up. Cat offers to help, but she is told no problem. She has a can of juice, the others wine, and Murray just has the usual tin of the last man on the planet. The stories continue, and they laugh. Cha gives a brief outline of the next shopping trip, and it gets serious. This is going to be the most dangerous adventure yet, and although they are all seriously worried, it still has to happen.

Cat is digging in her pockets and produces a little yellow package. The leather pouch is very old; the leather is worn and bare in patches, "This is what the old lady gave me, and she told me that I would know when to open it." Placing it on the table, she unloosened the drawstring, and two necklaces came out. One Of them is identical to the ones that Cha and Alicia are wearing. The other has a different colour of stones and a slightly different design. The sizes of the chain are an exact mirror image. None of them really don't know what to say. Cha unearths hers from her shirt, closely followed by Alicia. Nothing is said. Charlie breaks the silence by barking, not an alarming bark, just a bark.

Cha says that they should put them on. Murray asks, "Why me?" Alicia says there is no one else here apart from you two who don't already have one. They don't deliberate about who should put on what one. Cha and Alicia are wearing identical ones, so it is a reasonable assumption that they should all be matching, and Cat should have the same type as the other one. They reckon that Murray should wear it. Murray is not sure and thinks they should take their time as once they go on, they go on forever, never to be removed unless directed otherwise by the dreams.

Cat makes the decision, and it is by rights, only hers to make. She is the one who has carried them all the way through Europe and sacrificed much more than they will ever know to keep them safe. She hands one to Murray and takes the other for herself. He looks at her, and she looks straight back at him. They all take a deep breath and put them on. Nothing happens, and they are relieved and maybe just a tad disappointed.

Now they are four. Whatever it is meant by the significance, they are still totally unaware. The conversation continues, and Cha has a plan in place for the gathering of provisions. They will start the preparatory work in the morning. Cat gives each of them a cuddle before she leaves. Murray lasts a little longer. After all, she is the daughter that he has never had.

Cat has gone, so they smoke more. The last couple of days have been unexpected, to say the least, but all seem to be gelling together insofar as they have had no problems. Murray asks about the uncle thing with Frank, and Alicia tells him that it is a term of endearment. She adds that they are also calling Cat the scary lady who is really quite nice, Both Cha and Murray are in fits of laughter at this, and through stops and starts, they explain where they had heard the expression before.

They give Alicia an abbreviated version of the greedy fat man with the pith hat. Alicia tells them that she has had enough to drink and it is going off to sleep. They all have a full card for tomorrow, and they are going to attempt an early start.

It's now just Cha and Murray; she fancies a bath, and he jumps at the chance of joining her. Murray is halfway up the stairs in front of her and has the water running before she enters the bathroom. They make love in the bath; it is the first time in days that they have managed to get some 'us' time. They dry each other and rest in each other's arms. Now snug and warm in bed and very nearly asleep, Cha asks him what he really thinks about Cat. Murray tells her he thinks that she is like a daughter that he never had, so much more than a daughter, almost like a double daughter.

They had both heard the tales, but more like, only the edited highlights of some of the stories. Cha and Murray also noticed how the people moved quickly out of their way. Alicia had told them some snippets of what she had personally witnessed on the journey and wholeheartedly confessed that without her, none of the group would have made it.

Chapter Twenty-Six

There is a full moon somewhere, way up there, the sky is overcast, but they know it is there. The ground has a thick mist rolling over it; it is impenetrable, and none of the invited guests can see anything below their thighs.

Murray is standing in a line together with Cha, Alicia, and Cat. The old lady with the hooded cloak is present, and her choir is barely visible. This time they are silent. Even the normally ever-present drone is inaudible.

Her arms are raised to the sky, a single bell chime is heard, and four hooded assistants emerge from the swirling mist. The smoking incense burners are placed at their faces, and they breathe in unison the odourless, tasteless fumes. Another single chime sounds, and they are gone.

In the morning, Cha nudges the sleeping monster awake, "Hi baby, are you still alive?" Murray wrestles slowly away from his subconscious state. One eye is open, and the other one is trying really hard. Eventually, it manages to open, and they form a functional pair. Murray submits a mumbled confession that he is alive. She does not ask him if he had cleaned his feet last night, as she remembers bath time with Murray. She just holds up the muck-engrained sheets.

They go downstairs. Alicia has been up for a while. The teapot is fairly hot, and Murray helps himself and pours two cups. He hands one over to Cha, they look under the table, and Alicia's feet are as dirty as theirs. They exchange what is remembered, which is still, even with the shared information, little or nothing to go on. Murray mentions that they should speak to Cat. She must have heard them. Charlie barks as she enters the house.

"I had this really strange dream last night, and when I looked at my feet this morning, they were," interrupting her at this point, they have got up from that table and have exposed their equally dirty feet. They go through the shared experience, and there is nothing to add, even with the additional input from Cat.

Rather than sitting about, worrying about what is and what may never be, they have agreed to get on with it, and they have several issues to sort out this morning.

Frank has fed them all and has all his allocated staff busy at work. The others are outside. Having been selected and placed in their groups, they are being led to the tasks at hand. Murray has the drivers, and once they have picked a vehicle on the list, they are being put through their paces. If any irregularities are noticed in their vehicles' performance, they will be noted and added to the to-do list.

Cha has been the allocated shooters and has them stripping and rebuilding. She makes them do it time and time again until they all get it right. Cat, even though she is desperate to get on the shooting team, has been allocated a crew to go and clean a shed, which has been allocated for the storage of all the tinned goods. Alicia is checking with everyone, starting with Frank. They sit and huddle and go through the pages and pages of food.

Some of Murray's drivers are bemused by getting a set of keys and looking at the keys and then the screwdrivers and other improvised devices that they much prefer. Murray goes to great lengths to explain that the keys are the way to go. A couple of problems have already been reported, and they are now on their way to the mechanics, who he has been told can fix anything. Murray will eventually work his way up to check the progress. Getting them not to rev the engines like fucking mad is going to drive Murray crazy. This will need to be corrected as the group's collective safety depends on it.

The shooters, having now progressed to the actual shooting, have been issued a set of targets. They have been set a series of distances and will be assessed on completion. Cat is getting on with it and, rather than be a sit-and-watch leader, has jumped into it, and if everyone works like her, they will be the first to finish.

Murray is going through the motions with one of the drivers, trying to explain that his clutch changes just a little too rough when Alicia approaches. They exchange hellos; she then asks, "All is well in Murray-Shire?" He laughs at her description; Mr Black informs her that he had thought there would be fucking insurmountable problems with the various fucking lingoes, but surprisingly there have been none. Alicia looks at him, rolls her eyes, and walks away.

Murray eventually works his way up to his mechanics and smokes while he observes. These guys are so much better than him. Most garages have these expensive units that engines are plugged into, and the analyser spits out readings and replacement parts and the required modifications required to improve them. These guys can do it by sound and feel. They are honestly that good.

Alicia is now with Cha, who is now going through the shooting results. All are good. Some of them just require a little more patience, but that is the only problem; otherwise, she is pleased with the results.

Cat has finished, and her crew is now in the process of storing the removed contents in other available spaces in various sheds throughout the property. All that remains is the moving in of the stacking and storage units, which are covered up outside and will be transferred and installed once the washed unit is dry.

Everyone has to assemble at the meetinghouse once the evening meal is over. The first thing that they notice is that the room looks brighter. Frank notices them and says that they added some of the plants from the Orangery, and for some reason, he did not think that Cha would mind. Cha tells him that the place looks all the better for it.

Tonight, there is going to be a self-defence class, and everyone is expected to take part, and that includes them. As expected, Cha is the lead instructor and wants to be an inspirational leader that everyone looks up to; Alicia and Murray have been allocated as practice targets. Cha sets about to demonstrate how to take out a guard when they are moving, and when they are stationary, she gets great rounds of applause as she puts Murray on the ground with various techniques, the head butting, elbow, and kick and knee in the balls receive the most adulation. Alicia receives a much gentler demonstration and only gets prodded with the wooden spoon, which is being used for a pointed weapon demonstration. Someone asks, "What if the guard pulls a knife? what do you do to attack and defend an opponent with a knife?" Cha thinks for a second and asks for a volunteer. Cha looks at the crowd. The crowd looks at each other.

A shadow appears in the centre of the room. Cat has stepped forward; Cha says, "A round of applause for the volunteer, please." They all clap. Cha tells Cat that in order to demonstrate properly, she has to go for it, and she really has to try. Cat almost smiles and tells her she promises to be gentle.

They stand in the centre of the room, facing each other. Cha feints a move reversing it at the last minute, and Cat effortlessly sidesteps it, nearly catching Cha off balance with a surprise counter. Cha is very impressed. They thrust, parry, attack, and counter-attack. The whole room space is being used as their stage. The crowd has had to part several times to allow them through, as they jump, slide at and away from each other at one point. Cat has cartwheeled out of a deadly counter-attack that would have incapacitated anyone else.

They have been going through various moves for quite a while, and still, no one has given way. Most of the space in the room has been used at one point or another, and they are back in the centre of the room. Cat issues a particularly vicious attack Cha defends with an equally vicious counter-attack. It ends with Cha having her wooden spoon at Cat's throat. Cat smiles and looks down at her spoon. It is at Cha's heart. They step back from each other; Cha asks if there are any other volunteers; surprisingly, there are no takers.

Both of them are laughing and complimenting each other on the unexpected moves and equally unexpected counter moves. This is a secret world, and they pity anyone that has to go up against any of them, and heaven helps all who ever have the misfortune to go up against the pair of them at the same time. They are still laughing. Murray passes some of our people having a conversation as they are moving back the tables for the breakfast settings word is out. They are being called the scary sisters, very nice but very, very scary.

They have left them to it, and apart from meeting up later for an overview of what they have achieved today, they have the house to themselves. Alicia has stayed behind, going over the list with Frank doubling, checking again, item by item. "Well, what do you think?" Murray looks confused, and Charlie barks. "I think that a cup of tea would be very nice."

Cha laughs. "You know that's not what I was asking."

Murray asks, 'why don't you just tell me what you are thinking."

"I think Cat is very good, some of it totally unconventional, a mix of various styles, and I think she had me many times but did not follow it through, meaning Murray that she played me." Mr Black asks her if she is serious, and she tells him, "She is the best that she has ever seen. How would you put it, Murray? Unfucking stoppable!"

They have what is left over from last night's meal and hope that Alicia has already eaten. Charlie barks as the two of them come through the door. They sit and go through what has been done, the list is scrutinised, and they add to it. If they happen to come across any additional items, a sub-list is added entitled see and steal.

That's about all they can cover for tonight, and Alicia and Murray head out with Charlie. They smoke as they walk. Inside, Cha and Cat talk, "So where did you learn all that?" Referring to her adept street fighting skills.

"In the back-street gutters of Istanbul, Milan, Naples., I learned lots in Marseille, as it was the toughest, and you had to learn quickly, and you?" Cat asks.

"In the top military academy taught by the top instructors in South Korea." They are laughing like schoolgirls by the time the dog walkers arrive back. Charlie barks and wants food. Cat volunteers and feeds her and bids them all goodnight. Charlie looks at the door when Cat is gone, wags her tail, and goes straight back to sleep. Charlie is now spending more time sleeping than she is awake.

They sit at the table, and Cha tells them straight out the Cat is just unbelievable, and she has never had to try so hard. She ends with Cat could have beat her anytime, and she was just playing, and the bit at the end was only her letting her look good in front of everyone, and even that was on her terms. Cha cracks open a bottle and pours a stiff drink. She is clearly shaken. Alicia has found a book and waves. She will see them in the morning. Cha is okay now, adding that she is glad that they are on the same side.

Morning comes, and the team is already back at it. Everyone has been told what they are doing and who is travelling with whom. Murray has the drivers going through the process of driving without making excessive noise, and in all truth, it is not going well. Murray could shout and scream, but it would not do any good. He is sitting with his head in his hands. He lights a smoke and is about to re-run the whole process from start to finish when one of the mechanics appears. It could be Boris or Mikael. Murray is shit at remembering names, so he just says, "Hi, what gives" he takes him over to the back of his car.

Murray looks at him, wondering what is going on; He asks for the worst driver. That's an easy one. Rebecca is summoned and gets in and starts it up, and Vladimir, as it turns out, has made a device that fits over the end of the exhaust. He has saved the whole project. Murray gives him a bear hug which is difficult as he is a fucking giant, he gives Murray a smile with all the gold teeth, and that says it all. He says, pointing to every one of the vehicles. Rebecca now thinks she is a star and struts around as if waiting for the paparazzi. Murray is delighted; he tells them all to drive up to the garage. Knowing they will be up there all day. Maybe someone will even take Rebecca's picture.

Mr Black's part of the training is just about ready; one final rehearsal and they are good to go. He wanders around aimlessly and comes across Cha, just to give her students some inspiration. She has given them an hour to try and conceal themselves in a defined area. She is just on the way back to try and find them. Murray asks her, "How will the trainees know if she has spotted them?"

"Oh, you will love this. Just wait." He stays with her, and they smoke. They are not allowed to turn around until the required time is over. They hear a car approaching.

484

Out jumps Cat. She goes to the boot, grabs a sack, blows a kiss to Frank, and walks up to Cha beaming, "I found them, it took a while, but I have all that you asked me to find." Murray looks at them as they load up the paintball guns.

Cha walks in from the direction that the trainees expect, while Cat has doubled back and is now approaching from the opposite direction. In five minutes, all the trainees were shot. There are gathered together and told in the world that they are in, there would be no second chances and not to worry; the paint will wash off and the bruises will be gone in a couple of days. Cat gives Cha the paint gun and is off to inspect the new storage shed, the group is attempting to make it rodent-proof, and Cat hopes it will be complete at the end of today.

The gang of four meet up later, Alicia has cooked, and it is fish. Bobby tells Murray to eat it, and he lets it slide down his throat. He thinks they are in the mood for a girly chat and starts to bring down the kit that has to be checked.

The 7.62s, Mr. 50 cal, some 47s, 106s, and loads of ammunition. They don't have many loads for the .50 Cal. but they are only to be used on very special occasions. Murray has not brought any of the small-bore hunting rifles as already, they have been allocated to their owners, whom Cha has told they must sleep with them like a lover. They all have some homemade form of silencers fitted. The ones with the scopes were given to the best shots.

Murray sits and watches Charlie, she is getting fat, and he thinks that she will be having lots of puppies. Murray goes through the names in his head as he cleans the guns. He knows that Cha will double-check, but he intends to have no rejects. Every time Murray finishes one, he double-checks the action and treble-checks that the chamber is empty. He sits up all night, and the girls have disappeared ages ago. Murray will have problems sleeping tomorrow and will feel better if he cheats on his sleep just now.

Morning comes quickly enough, and Charlie wants out and fed. He fills her bowl, and she consumes it rapidly and refuses to move unless she receives a free refill. She must be really hungry, and Murray swears to God that she is even bigger than the last time he looked.

Today is the dress rehearsal, Cha blows the whistle once, and all the drivers, followed by their seconds and the shooters, make for their allocated vehicles. Cha blows the whistle twice, and they all come back out eventually. Cha is angry and marches in between them all, saying that "We have no room for mistakes; all it takes is one, and one only is all it takes, and it could be the end of us all. I think before we start again, you should all go back into the meetinghouse and discuss amongst yourselves what you have got wrong, and if it is not right, we will do this all day and all night if necessary until everyone gets it right. So off you go, and in one hour, I will blow the whistle.'

486

Murray watches, as does Alicia and Cat. This is Cha's baby, and they will say nothing to highlight the mistakes. Cha waits half an hour and blows the whistle once. They come bursting out the doors. This time they have the guns.

So far, so good. Every vehicle is checked. Rebecca is caught putting on make-up, and the whistle goes twice. This is repeated until after lunch. Cha is exhausted. She gathers them all together and tells them to get some rest. They move out at first light.

Alicia has gone through everything, and the amended list is the final one. She has promised to feed and check on Charlie. Frank has prepared an early breakfast and has even supplied a pack of food with liquid for all who are involved, they never asked, but he did it, and they would never talk him down for this. Frank has been doing wonders, and they have told him that he can have some days off when this is over, and hell, he can even go and see his brother Al who will be pleased to see him. Mark will be okay about it, and he might even be an uncle. Cat can go with him also, and they are pretty sure that they will come back, but no one is a prisoner here, and even if they did not return, they would not hold it against them.

Murray is having a monster and some wine diluted with the last man on the planet. He will need something to knock him over. Cha is as always cool as a cucumber and rehearsed the team strictly, Murray thinks the entire crew will see and re-enact the whole process by the numbers when they are sleeping.

They leave Alicia at the table reading and, for once, go to bed early. They think they have been a little too noisy as they hear the CD player coming on and the music is blasting out, The CD must have been on earlier as it is at the part where the singer is telling everyone that he likes it, and as they continue making love, Murray finally realises that he is not talking about rock and roll. They nod off; the guitarist's famous double stops reverberate inside his brain, a perfect end to a perfect day.

The Larks are up sharp; Charlie knows something is happening as she gets lots of attention from Cha and Murray. They are eating breakfast with the entire ensemble this morning. Frank, as promised, has put on a fantastic spread, and everyone will be supplied a bag of provisions to take with them at the door.

The scheduled departure is an hour before dawn and goes as planned. They move slowly at first, as it is still dark, their side protected by a hill, they can have the sidelights on, and the drivers are signalled forward to the hold points. Gradually switching their lights and engines off at the first rally point. They have been here positioned at the friendly end of the bridge for about an hour, and Cha, Cat, and Murray have scanned the other side for movements through the high-powered binoculars and have noticed nothing to report.

Cha drives across first and heads straight up the hill to the large double layby. Reaching a position that is visible to Cat through the binoculars, she transmits the all-clear signal. Cat leads the way, and the convoy heads across the bridge as fast as possible, within the confines of keeping the engine noise down to a bare minimum. Murray is tail end Charlie, and last across, he meets up with them in the layby.

Cat and Cha dart ahead and scan as far as possible. The crew waits, engines running and ready to go as soon as the signal is received. Murray spots the signal, and the vehicles slowly move out. The convoy travels as steadily as possible all the shooters have been told that this is where they have to watch the road and the roadsides.

The road is exactly the same as it was before. They follow this side of the road as far as possible, only moving on to the other side of the dual carriageway when they encounter obstacles. All their vehicles are able to cross the central reservations with ease; it could be different on the way back.

It has taken them about four hours to reach this far. Daylight is just about fading. The city lies before them, Cha and Cat set off checking the coast ahead, and everyone waits for what seems like a lifetime before they give the signal to proceed.

All the vehicle's lights are off as the convoy edges into the large shopping centre on the outskirts. Stealthily they make their way into the car park. Cha is in position with the American sniper rifle, and Cat guides the vehicles to the positions as discussed in detail at the rehearsal stage. The doors open, the shooters disembark, run across and take up their positions, blending in as much as possible with what is around them, all of them reminded by the paintball experience that this time will not end in a bruise if anything goes wrong.

After the allocated time, the drivers are out, Cat opens the door, and they pour into the first building. With the search for unwelcome occupants complete, the collecting of the required goods begins. Where possible complete pallets will be taken, and when this is exhausted, the options are to move on to something else or empty the shelves of the multi-packs in all the other various available options. They have a large amount of goods ready to pack on the awaiting transportation. When the food list is complete, they form a human chain. Goods are loaded out past the parcel style. When the first vehicle is loaded, the second is started. This is ongoing until the food is all loaded and, most importantly, the trolleys and pallet loaders are returned to where they sleep. A quick check, and they move on to the next target.

The vehicles are moved as slowly and quietly as possible. Cat takes watch as Murray opens the doors; the drivers are ready and enter as per plan. On this part, the troop has a list of all the clothes, boots, and shoe sizes required. Most have been memorised, but a master list will have to be checked before loading. This haul will take them to the limit on every vehicle. The looting is going smoothly. One group works on the foot wear, the others on coats and jackets. When they are complete, they move on to shirts, jumpers, trousers, pants, and socks. The multi-packs are the easiest and left to last. Denims, heavy work-type trousers, and shirts are major on the list, but they all work together, and soon they mass a cast of caged trolleys at the doors ready. Murray thinks as the trolleys stack up, they are going to struggle to get it all loaded. The last to appear is the multi-packs of pants, socks, and bundles of T-shirts.

Cat pulls Murray aside and shows him an addition to the if you see steal list. It is in Cha's handwriting, "You have to promise not to look when Cat asks for ten unobserved minutes." Murray has no choice but to agree. He turns his back and pretends he does not know anything about it.

The shop is more or less next-door, and Cat can be in and out before the normal clothes are loaded. She is back in ten minutes flat with two holdalls complete with the small padlocks securing the zips in place to prevent any peaking at the contents. She chucks it onto the last cage trolley to be loaded. As she passes, she looks as if butter would not melt in her mouth, and as if to prove a point, she puts a lollipop in her mouth as she passes to take up her allocated position. At long last, the convoy is good to go. They are still under cover of darkness as they stealthily leave the outskirts of the city. Murray is relieved it has been a huge operation which much at stake and insofar as no issues to deal with.

The shooters are slowly withdrawn from their positions and climb into their allocated vehicles as they slowly pass; Cat and Cha squeeze into the front vehicle, and as they approach their transport, they alight and go ahead to the first crossing position on the dual carriageway. One at one side, the other on the opposite ready to push and pull any stubborn vehicles across the central reservation. Murray takes up the tail-end Charlie position.

He would love a smoke, but they have banned it from this operation. It was his suggestion, so he cannot really complain. Daylight is starting to try and break through the darkness, and they are leaving just in time. The journey is slow and steady, with no unexpected obstacles, no breakdowns, and no sudden excessive noise or smoke-emitting monsters that put a blotch of smog in a clear morning sky.

The first crossing causes a slight delay, the first few vehicles pass easily, but the ground is soft, and as the latter end of their convoy crosses, Cat and Cha have to push and pull the last three vehicles over. Cha vehicle has boards stored for this purpose, but they all had agreed that they would not be used on the first crossing unless absolutely necessary. The vehicles have to wait until the complete convoy has crossed; the shooters are out taking up defensive positions. At last, the final loaded vehicle is over. Murray signals the very nice but very deadly girls to go ahead. His 4x4 will cross easily.

Cha and Cat are in position. They have examined the crossing and have three further scheduled crossing points planned. Cat will guide the vehicles. Cha will be on standby, ready to push or pull. Murray is at the back, thinking a cigarette would be nice while he sits there just watching and waiting. All the vehicles cross. Only the last one needs a little TLC. They have only two more crossings left, and after that, they are home. The last one is over the girl's race ahead, and all fingers and toes are crossed. This time they don't even wait for him. The penultimate crossing is easy; this one is the reinforced type originally housing a double crash barrier, which had been removed by others. The others, being them, this was a stealth mission carried out in the middle of the night in what feels like a lifetime ago. The girls are like military police, pointing and signalling to the drivers, cajoling and asserting their authority to move it on out and move it, pronto. Any time they had lost in the previous crossings, they made up for here. The girls dash to the next one. Murray thinks that they make a great team.

Chapter Twenty-Seven

Pirate convoy number one is nearly on the home straight. After this one, it's down the hill and across the bridge. This crossing is a mess. Before they even start to pass, the central reservation is not quite a swamp, but the surface is damp and very soft. The boards are laid out immediately. They are subjected to constant heavy loading, and to get the maximum usage, they are immediately turned over to try and reverse the bending that has transpired with each crossing. The girls, previously looking like military policewomen, now look more like farm girls getting dirtier with each vehicle. Anytime that they had made up for is now well and truly lost.

The drivers are told when they reach the other side. They have to drive straight home. Several of the shooters are out now assisting with the boards, some of which have now split. They are just about halfway there, and in the distance, you can see that the vehicles have almost even spacing between each one as they drive on the home straight. Several hours later and only three vehicles were left. The first and second are good and only require a little extra pushing and pulling.

Last but not least, everyone has to join in to get the last vehicle over the final hurdle. Murray is signalled to cross. The girls had decided to keep the convoy moving no stopping; Cha, as a gentle reminder, bangs the bonnet and signals him to move it. In the distance, the first of the supply convoy has reached the other side of the bridge. Murray drives on as instructed.

Cat has suddenly stopped in her tracks and informed Cha that there was another vehicle, possibly more than one, and they were approaching very fast. Cat opens the back of her vehicle, and Cha helps her drag across the spike strip. They only have a few seconds to spare and conceal themselves before the oncoming vehicle has all its tires shredded, and with the driver unable to control the abrupt changes in driveability, it crashes into an abandoned tour operators' coach.

Only one of the occupants emerges from the crashed vehicle, he is pleading for help, claiming that his pregnant girlfriend is still in the back and he is sorry, but they were escaping from a very bad situation that had killed several of their group. Cat does not trust him and wants to shoot him there and then. Cha says that they will have to check; Cat is covering, and Cha moves forward to check; she has only moved a single step when they both hear the faint, almost silent telescopic mechanism of the sleeve gun. She jumps to take up the space between the would-be shooter and Cha. The bullet catches Cat in the stomach. Cha had her machine gun up immediately when she saw Cat change her movements. Before Cat hit the ground, the shooter had been sprayed and was dead; Cha went over to the vehicle and needing help or not, they all received a single shot to the head.

Cat is back on her feet; "It's only a graze." She is attempting to get into her vehicle. Cha tells her that there is no way she is driving, and gently but firmly, even though she does not want to cooperate, puts Cat in her car.

Murray is waiting on the dynamic duo at the other side of the bridge. They should have been here by now. A single vehicle approaches fast. It is Cha. She draws to a halt beside him, "Quick, help me with her; she has been shot!"

They take her to the small medical facility that they have. It is only an office that was converted into a first aid facility. If they ever have any serious medical issues to deal with, the survival rates just don't exist. They don't even have a doctor. Cat is placed on the bed. Cha produces an evil-looking knife and slits open her top. There is blood everywhere. She has been lucky. A huge bruise the size of a football is already starting to materialise, the black-purple stain working its way from her navel down to her groin and up to her breasts. The bullet has passed straight through just above her hip. Cha cleans the wound; Cat curses her with every touch. "She will need stitches, and better if we take her through to the farmhouse." Cat curses them both as they press on some dressings and wrap her up in bandages; the blood is slowly starting to seep through. Murray volunteers to take her and slips away. Cha goes and informs Frank; Alicia meets her on the way, and she brings her up to date on route to give Frank the news.

Everybody is busy. Alicia, on hearing the news shouts one of the guys over, and he drives off with a couple of shooters to bring back Cat's car and the spike strip. They eventually find Frank. He takes the news calmly and gets on with what he is doing. Alicia thinks that he is cold and she is going to get ripped into him. Cha pulls her quickly to one side and tells her that he had more than an adventure growing up, "You have no idea what he and his brother had to put up with. Leave him be and go and calm down and then go and see him later."

Murray drives Cat to the farmhouse; for the first time in as long as he can remember, the lights are on full beam, they make a point of not driving in the dark for this very reason, but this is an exception. Murray tries really hard to miss the potholes but does not manage to miss them all. He has lost count of the number of languages that she has used to curse him. Murray likes it when she does the Italian ones in which to say them correctly, she had to use her hands, and although this made her pain worse, in order to emphasise the true authenticity, she had to do it. Out of all the other ones, the Russian curses sounded the scariest, she delivered with a cold stare, but for entertainment, he awards her ten out of ten.

As he reaches the first checkpoint, he flashes his lights in the agreed emergency code and screeches to a halt. The woman on duty sees the blood-stained clothes through the windscreen and stops him mid-sentence, tells the man who is at the barrier to get it raised, and fucking hurry and waves him through.

Arriving at the main gate is a different story; Dean is on duty and makes Murray go through the whole formality of the forms. Mr Black would like to go and seriously beat the fucking shit out of him, but he thinks of his daughter and bites his tongue for now.

Mark comes and meets them at the medical facility. He has heard about Dean, and before Murray can say anything, Mark tells him that he has put him back in the kitchen cleaning dishes. The trainee vet/trainee doctor is examining Cat, who is presently hissing at him.

They leave them to it; Mark gives him a smoke. It is greatly received they sit and chat. The doctor sends word that he wants to see Murray. "She is very lucky another couple of millimetres, and there would be nothing I could do for her, but she has bruised or broken ribs, no puncture to the lungs as far as I can see, but to stop the bleeding, I am going to have to open her up. She will need quite a few stitches when I finish with her, and I am going to have to sedate her. For that, I need your help as she has promised to rip my heart out if I as much as look at her again. However, there could be a major problem, If I need to give her a blood transfusion and I don't have the equipment even to check for a compatible source."

Murray takes off his jacket and rolls up his sleeves; the doctor looks at him. Murray tells him that he is one of the seven percent and is sorry that he does not have his blood donor card. The doctor is still none of the wiser; Murray tells him that he is O Neg, one of the seven percent club, and he could probably give animals blood.

The doctor looks at Murray and confesses that he has only just started reading about how to do this, and before the sickness, he was in training to be a vet and had only done a couple of neutering operations, and even under supervision, one of the subjects had died. Murray tells him that it will be okay and hc just has to get on with it. Ellie arrives, sticks on a white coat, and asks the vet what he wants her to do. Murray lays back and closes his eyes.

Ellie and the trainee veterinarian sedate Cat. First, they try a local, but Cat resists it. Ellie tells Cat straight that if she does not cooperate, she will die. Ms Kalashnikova surrenders her arm, and the doctor gives the knockout shot. Murray briefly wakes up as he feels the needle go in. He fades into unconsciousness with the vet looking at him, Murray wants to bark just to wind him up, but all he manages is a smile.

The operation goes on until they manage to stop the bleeding and clean up the damage caused by the bullet. They work for hours, having nothing more to go on than an old medical journal. The failed animal healer calls a halt to the proceedings. They finish stitching her up. She will have a lump missing out of her just above the hip, and the scar will be for life.

A cannula is inserted into the artery at Murray's wrist, it is checked and double-checked, and the bunny doctor uses nearly a roll of medical tape to secure it to his wrist. Cat is out cold; she has the vein at her elbow checked and a cannula inserted easily into the exposed vein. The doctor comments that she has very healthy veins. Reading some pages, he goes and gets some material and assistants to elevate Murray's bed, shows Ellie some pictures, and they set about withdrawing blood from Murray and delivering it into Cat. The patients are hooked up to IV drips; Cat is given antibiotics via the drip and a tetanus injection, and all they can do now is wait.

Mark comes by the medical centre and speaks to Ellie and the doctor; Ellie tells him that he really should send word to Cha. Mark thinks for a second, "I know the very person we can send."

Cha has been busy; all the looted goods have been sorted out. The tined goods have been separated out and stored in the shed; the excess has been stored in temporary accommodation. All the clothes have been separated into piles and distributed to those who wanted them. The two zipped and locked holdalls are lying in Chas' room, and she has not even looked at them.

Alicia and Cha have gone over and over all the preceding events, and several changes have been implemented. They are going to set up an observation post to watch the bridge twenty-four-seven, and in addition to that, sentry points at the entrance to the community. Cha knows that Murray will not like this, but she thinks that they need to start taking precautions.

The sentry points were hastily set up and are already manned. Cha and Alicia are sitting and eating. There is a knock on the door. It's Rebecca, still plastered in makeup, still looking for a photographer. She has a letter and informs them that there is a man at the gate. The letter is from Mark.

Cha bursts out laughing. The first sentence states that if Dean has opened the letter, she has his permission to shoot him. He goes on to say that the patients are now sleeping, and all we can do is wait. He goes on to state that between them, they don't have any real trained medical personnel, and perhaps in the future, the two communities could pool all the recourses. The patients are being monitored overnight, and if Frank wants to come over tonight, Dean has been instructed to drive him over.

Cha gives Alicia the note to read, and Alicia goes to give Frank the news. Dean is his normal self, and even though he is now just a postman, he is still observing everything and everyone. Frank accepts the invitation and goes away into the darkness with Dean. Charlie has been very quiet; several times, she has wandered upstairs looking for Murray around midnight. She wants out, and she goes out howls at night. A long eerie howl pierces the silence, and Cha fears for the worst.

Cha has a sleepless night and spends hours watching Charlie, who is now sleeping soundly by the fire. Alicia is up and makes breakfast Cha is miles away and does not even know that she is up and about till she is presented with breakfast and tea. Cha has no appetite, but Alicia persuades her that she will have to eat. They sit and talk about what has to be done.

A vehicle draws up outside, and Alicia tells Cha that the car is for her. Cha is told that she is no good to anyone here and she should go and see Murray, adding, "Charlie will be fine with her, and she promised to feed her." Cha at first refuses and eventually gives in and agrees. Alicia has already packed her a small bag takes her to the car, puts her into the passenger seat.

At the Farmhouse, Frank has reunited with Al, and they play catch up. Cat is still asleep in the next bed to a sleeping Murray. Al tries to persuade Frank to come and have a tour around the place, but Frank says his place is here with Cat and wants to be here when she awakes. He has been here all night, and the doctor is looking very pleased with himself. Her colour has returned, and all the checks are good.

Murray is another matter. His colour has paled, and all the checks he has carried out just don't add up. Thinking that he or one of his assistants had messed up, he re-ran the checks himself, and the numbers were exactly the same.

Cha arrives at the farmhouse and is greeted by Mark. They end up in his office, Cha does not want anything, but Mark says she at least has to have some tea. He tells her everything that he knows and takes her down, bumping into Ellie on the way. Ellie does not say much but gives her a huge cuddle telling her that it will be okay.

Cat is now awake, and Frank sits while the doctor tells her that he has to check her wound, and if she wants out of there, she has to be nice; muttering some of her favourite Russian swearwords under her breath, she agrees to an examination. All her results are good. She will be sore for at least several months as she has to refrain from all physical activity and short walks at first and gradually slowly build them up. No lifting, stretching, nothing strenuous, and the longer she refrains from this, the quicker that she will heal. He is pleased with the stitches, and her colour is back to normal. He purposely does not tell her when the stitches will be removed, as he just knows she will remove them herself.

He leaves the couple to talk. Frank tells her that he has a wheelchair outside. He has spoken to Alicia and Cha, and he can take as much time off as he needs. Frank tells her that his brother Al is here and has asked him to stay, but he has told him straight that he is not interested and is happy at the Watermill. Cat tells him that as soon as she is able to walk that they are going home. They see the doctor arriving with Cha. They both look worried. She tells Frank to get the chair, The Doctor tries to stop Cat from getting out of bed, but the look on her face lets him know that to say anything will be a waste of time. Cha nods, knowing that she is only going out to give her and the doctor some privacy, and tells her she will see her later and that perhaps it would be a good idea to put on some clothes.

Now that they are alone, the doctor has a folder in his hands. Cha is looking at the pale Murray. The Doctor says that "He really does not know where to start." He tells her that his blood type was very rare before the sickness, and now it is extremely rare, but he still looks worried and asks Cha straight out, "How old is Murray?" Cha tells him that they have never once discussed this. She laughs and tells the Doctor that he had told her on many occasions that he is going to live forever and has no intentions of ever getting old.

The doctor is looking at all the numbers in the various test reports; "All this information tells me that Murray is at least in his sixties, but looking at him, he does not even look 30. His body has taken much wear and tear over the years, and I just don't know what else to tell you. All I have done is remove blood from him to give to the crazy young woman. She would not have survived without it, she had lost so much before we got her, and she must have been in considerable pain. I offered her painkillers; anyone else in her condition would have been begging for them. She just looked me straight in the eye and told me that she had never taken a painkiller in her life. She really is quite a remarkable young lady." The Doctor is getting up to leave and adds, "Sorry. I meant to ask, are they Daddy and Daughter?"

Cha looks at the Doctor, "What makes you ask that?" Before they both went under, the last words were to take care of my daddy and take care of my daughter."

The Doctor goes and leaves them alone, Cha sits on the edge of the bed, "Well, Murray, what am I going to do with you? Charlie is looking for you every morning, I have even caught her stealing your smelly socks, and last night she was howling like a wolf. I think even Alicia knew she was not howling at the moon but howling for you, and you should see the size of her. She is so fat that you would think she was carrying a whole pack of dogs inside her. If I had let her, I think she would have jumped in the car and barked all the way here to get me to drive quicker." Cha, by now, is crying, and the tears are running down her face. Mark and Ellie have popped in to see her, but on noticing the tears, Marks tells her that he will see her later and discreetly backs out with Ellie.

Frank and Cat return later, Cat is determined that she is leaving in the morning, and the only reason that she is staying the night is that it is getting dark and no one will give her a car and adding that she is not fit enough to steal one.

Frank disappears off to see his brother and his ever-impatient pregnant girlfriend, who is huge. Cha looks at Cat, and they talk; Murray has still not moved and is still as white as a sheet. Cha tells her that the Doctor has told her there is nothing else that he can do, and it is up to Murray. Cats tell her that he will be fine, and although she has heard it from everyone lately, she knows that all will be okay. Maybe if he is fit enough to travel, she should take him home. If he is sleeping here, why can't he sleep in his own bed?

Cha gets up and leaves her, heading up to Mark's office. Mark is busy with papers. As Cha enters, he puts them down and asks his assistant to leave them now, and if he could pass the message on for some tea and biscuits, that would be greatly appreciated, and thanks them before they leave.

They sit and talk about nothing in particular until the tea arrives, Ruby is still sadly missed, and Cha thinks she could do with her now. Mark tells her the young lady was looking for a car and had intentions of leaving tonight. Cha tells him that she told her all about it but would take her home tomorrow, also adding that as Murray is in a deep sleep, she was intent on taking him home tomorrow, and if he has some form of suitable transport that she could borrow that would be great, Mark slips out the office quietly and leaves her sleeping on the chair, He returns with some covers and put them on her. He stations someone outside the door and leaves instructions "When she wakes, just help her with whatever she wants." He goes to the fixing things department and will be asking them to work through the night if necessary.

Cha wakes in the morning still in the chair. She looks at the covers, and Mark is at his desk. "I did not have the heart to wake you." Walking over, he takes the folded covers from her and opens the door. A short while later, breakfast arrives, and Cha is starving and eats a lot. Mark asks her if she wants more. He goes through the arrangements and tells her that when he asked for volunteers to work through the night on the Murraymobile, they all stepped forward. He tells her as well that he has some items to send over, the farming projects have produced way too much, and M has supplied some turnips, swedes, and other things that can be planted and some even stored for next year.

"The Murraymobile is currently being tested, and there are that many people who want to drive him home that do it fair he had to organise a lottery, and what a guy. I know he will pull through it only in a matter of time. I wish I could do more. Let me know what you think about the medical proposal that the Doctor has suggested. He has put some information that you might need to reference in the folder but take your time. Let's get Murray back on his feet."

At this, Ellie enters and comes straight over and gives her an almost sisterly hug. She tells her that "There will be no argument. She and the Doctor will be accompanying them over to the Watermill, and there is nothing to discuss about it. It is what they have decided. So, get your things together, and once the lottery is done by you," she adds, "We will be off."

Everyone is in the canteen. Mark turns the crank, and the makeshift tombola turns, stops, and puts his hand in a selects the winner, "And the winner is number 3417. There is a momentary pause as the crowd looks about. It is one of the fixers that Murray has trained, he is congratulated by his mates, and he goes to get his stuff. Murray is carried out on a stretcher; he would be mortified if he had seen this even in his sleep. Cha reckons that if he could, he would still avoid the fuss like the plague and have run away before anyone had noticed.

Cat is exactly just like Murray would be. She has refused all, and everything offered to her and is in the vehicle with Frank. He has promised the Doctor to drive carefully and to keep the peace. He will travel behind the Murraymobile. Mark is down to say his goodbyes and is talking to Ellie. Al appears, and thinking that he has decided to come and say goodbye to his brother, he announces that Annette's water has broken and they need the Doctor. Ellie is going to stay and complete the journey, but Cha tells her it is okay and that she should go and help. They promise to meet sometime soon. Mark says he wants to be kept up to date, and they say their goodbyes.

The journey over is taking forever, Cha smokes in the Murraymobile, even thinking that the aroma from Murray's favourite homemade cigarettes might even help him wake up, but Murray sleeps the whole way and does not even as much as twitch an eyelid.

Arriving back at the Watermill, everyone has stopped working. They cheer as Frank gets out first, the stand-in cook has been accused of trying to poison them, and several of the women think that he has been putting love potions in their meals. Cat appears, and although the pain is excruciating, she grins and bears it for the appearance of being happy that everyone is pleased to see her. In reality, this is where she stays, and she is home.

Cha thanks everyone and Murray is led into the house. He is led straight upstairs. Charlie is going nuts and refuses to leave the room. Cha just lets her stay there, and now she has a very smelly sock that she keeps with her all the time. The volunteer who had driven them over is thanked by Alicia and is gone. Cha is sitting at her normal spot at the table, sparks up a number, and just sits and looks into nothing. Life without Murray is just unimaginable.

Alicia comes in and makes some tea. Frank had sent over some of the spare milk. And once he had settled Cat in. He had set about getting the dinner ready for all the people who reckoned that they might have died if the temporary cook had continued.

Cha smiles at the story. Alicia is worried about her friend. "We could stick the CD player upstairs and play him some music." Asking Cha what his favourite pieces were.

Cha says, "No, just let him sleep for now." Cha opens a bottle of wine and has a large glass, and drinks away, telling Alicia of how and where they met and of all the adventures that they had shared.

She breaks down in tears as she is just so disappointed in herself for not being able to produce any children, but even though Murray had said frequently that he would not want five seconds on this plane of existence without her, she knows that he would have loved kids and would have been a great father. They talk late into the night. Charlie breaks the silence by howling. Charlie is back down the stairs and wants to be fed, she is even bigger than the last time, and Cha thinks she is maybe the fattest dog that she has ever seen.

Cha falls asleep on the sofa, waking up in the small hours. She panics as Murray is not here beside her and remembers and goes up to see him. He is still asleep and still as white as a ghost. Murray has now been asleep for two weeks. She has changed his clothes and washed him daily, but nothing has changed with him. She thinks that this will not go on forever, and sooner or later, she is going to lose him. This place is them, and if he goes, she could not stay here.

Alicia has been trying to persuade her to come out of the house, but as of yet, she has not wanted to face anyone. Dean arrived with a letter with the sad news that Annette and the baby did not survive, and soon after Al had vanished, they had searched everywhere, but he had not been found. Cha has to go and tell Frank the bad news, she has known him longer than the rest, and it is not fair to just lay this on Alicia. Lately, she has been doing everything.

Cha goes out for the first time, and everyone is nice. They do not ask, as they know that there is no news. She finds Frank in the kitchen, he knows that she has something to tell him, they grab a quiet corner, and she tells him what she knows. He takes it calmly and tells her that it is okay. He and his brother said their goodbyes a while back. He goes through the conversation. The last one they ever had at the Farmhouse, Al had wanted him to come over. He said it was great and he would love it. He had told them that he wasn't coming and he was not happy. "All we have done is run away from everything, and my days of running are over. This is where I stay, and yeah, sure, sorry about Annette and the baby, but there is nothing I can do about that."

He tells Cha that Cat is slowly driving him nuts, and it would be great if she could go and visit her. Cat was always talking about going over to see you but really did not want to disturb you, "So, could you go and see her?" Cha listens to him and goes around and chaps the door. Cat is up on her feet and surprised to see her. The two of them talk for ages, and their laughing can be heard outside. Those who hear it take it as a good sign, A sign that things are going to improve.

Cha catches up with Alicia. She is up at the farming group things are great, and they have big plans for the future. Alicia shows her what they have been up to. The sheds are cleared and cleaned, and everything is all arranged. They even have a list of everything that they have and where it is kept. All the farm machinery is up and running, all stored together. For the first time, they even have stocks of fresh produce, and Alicia has a little pet project that she wants to show her. They walk over to the Orangery, and Cha is overcome with emotion. She and Murray had spent many days and nights up here; sometimes, they just forgot the time, and before they knew it, morning had come. Charlie even used to stay. She liked barking at the birds. Even at this time of year, the place is full of birdsong. As she is saying this, a few ducks pass by in the indoor stream that Murray had constructed, quacking away, "They stay here, and I think all the others have flown away, but I think that they just don't want to go."

Alicia takes Cha into the greenhouses. All are budding with plants and flowers, and she has even organised another crop for Murray, "We have lots of medicinals growing, and one of the girls knows a little, and she will only go and learn medicine if it is okay with you." Cha tells her that she can go and try it, and if she feels like it is not for her, she is always welcome to come back at any time she wishes.

One of the other women approaches. She is telling Alicia that there is a big thunderstorm coming she can smell it. Cha and Alicia walk back. Cha, out of curiosity, looks at the heavens; it is a clear blue day with not a cloud in the sky.

Tonight, Cha is definitely better. Getting out has done her a world of good, and for the first time in weeks, she is going to do some cooking. She has even thought about asking Cat over, thinking about giving Frank's ears a break. She runs it past Alicia, who says, "I will go and see her." Cha cooks anyway.

Cat does come over, and all three of them enjoy the simple fare and get drunk together. They play music and make so much noise that they don't hear the thunderstorm approaching.

They are woken in the early hours, the peals of thunder sound like they are directly overhead. Cha cannot make up her mind which is louder than the thunder or the howls coming from Charlie. Charlie is giving birth, and they cannot get to the vet. They are gathered around her Cat has taken charge and tells them that this is Charlie's first time and she will be scared. Charlie licks Cat's hand when she touches her; Cat tells them that they need some towels and Luke warm water to wash the puppies that will be out soon.

Charlie howls even louder this time. They all think it is her pain, but her tail is wagging. Murray has just appeared at the bottom of the stairs, wondering what all the noise is about. Cha bursts into tears and rushes to him. Her arms are all over him. Murray has no idea what the fuss is about. He has no idea how long he has been asleep. He tells Cha that he is glad she is awake as he is starving.

Charlie goes back to howling at the pain; Murray goes over and speaks to her. He touches her. The puppies are going to be big. He feels the shape as they move about. Charlie looks at him to take the pain away. Murray soothes her telling her that it won't be long, not long at all.

The thunder continues, and the rain is torrential. It is a constant, unrelenting downpour. Cha remembers the last time, and she has no intentions of playing board games. Cat is with Charlie and will shout when something is happening. Murray honestly has no memory of what happened. He remembers taking Cat to the farmhouse to see the vet, and that is about it. Cat is calming Charlie into the corner, talking to her non-stop for a while. She shudders with pain but does not cry.

Murray eats everything in front of him and wants a smoke. Cha asks him if he thinks that this is really a good idea, and Murray just looks her straight in the eye and asks why, I told you that I am going to live forever, Sparks one that Alicia has rolled and drinks a couple of tins of last man on the planet. This done, he says that he has to go and see Charlie and hugs and gives Cha lots of kisses, "Our girl is having babies." The tears are running down her face. Murray has no idea how sad Cha is about not having children but lets him go and do his thing with Charlie, watching Cat and him at the dog. They really are like father and daughter.

The thunder ceases when the first pup is born. It is a boy, and it is fucking huge. Murray has helped Charlie deliver it, and Cat is now cleaning it. Cha and Alicia come over and see him, and he is a monster. Cat gives it to Cha, and it whimpers. She places it back on the ground beside Charlie, and he suckles into her teat and sucks away. Two minutes later and Cha is helping Cat clean her up, it is another boy, and he is just as fucking big and just as hungry. Murray is beside himself. We have Three dogs now.

Murray reckons by his own admission that he is stinking and tells Cha that he is going up to run a bath, that little smile barely noticeable to anyone but her. She sneaks up the stairs behind him. They make love in the bath, out of the bath, and in the bedroom. Lying in bed, Cha wants to say many things, but Murray stops her. "I know you were upset downstairs, and I honestly did not mean to upset you; I have told you many times that I would not want to spend five seconds on this plane of existence without you. I am also sorry for the worry I put you through lately, and maybe I was just tired, and my batteries needed to be recharged. If we were in the normal world, I would whisk you away somewhere special, but that's not possible."

They cuddle up, and just as Cha is nodding off, he whispers in her ear that he had a dream, and the old lady with the hooded cloak told him that he was going to be a father and it just was not just two puppies. Cha just ignores him, thinking that he is full of shit, and goes to sleep. Murray is up first in the morning. The rain is still pissing it down. He goes and sees his dog. She is sleeping. The pups are asleep also, but all the ears follow him in unison about the room like an interconnected motion sensor.

Alicia and Cat are sharing the sofa, and one of them snores like the dead. Murray is still banned from the kitchen, so he just has his favourite breakfast, a tin of fizzy, and seen as he is celebrating, rolls a monster. Murray goes outside and sits on the porch, not a soul in sight.

He goes back in, and Cha is awake. Her hair reminds him of pineapple the way she has it tied up. She is making breakfast. Bobby warns him in advance that it is fish. He is letting it slide down his throat, it really is vile, but he eats it. Cha is ravenous and tells Murray that she had a strange dream, not about the old woman but about him. She remembers what he had said to her before she fell asleep as she had another plateful of breakfast.

Alicia and Cat stir. Cat goes straight over to see Charlie, and Alicia comes and joins them at the table. Cha tells everyone that she forgot to tell them that she won him at a raffle. Murray asks if he was the star prize. Cha looks straight at him. "Why would you get the first prize? Just give me one reason why?"

He calmly opens up a tin of the energy drink and turns the writing around so that Cha can read it clearly. Last Man on the planet.

9 781916 540798

Printed by BoD™in Norderstedt, Germany